PEOPLE OF FOREST

A NEAR-FUTURE SCIENCE FICTION ADVENTURE

MARCUS MARTIN

CHAPTER ONE

PABLA

I'm crouching in a thicket with my body pressed low. The man I'm tracking is alone, separated from the others. He's trying to scan the ground but he's twitchy; flinching at every buzzing mosquito. The agitation is only driving his core temperature even higher; he's puffing and panting, making himself a magnet for the little bloodsuckers. Rule number one of the jungle, amigues: just let the bugs win.

The guy's sweating buckets and cursing his scanner, slapping the screen anxiously. He's clearly got a lot riding on whatever he's searching for. Or maybe he's just itching to get out of here. Perhaps they already told him we dip our arrows in poison. Sure, he's got a gun, but we both know he'd be dead before it's out of the holster.

Not that I'm angling for a fight today, I'm only here as contingency. Dream scenario: he and the other two give up the search, return to the township, and I get to spend the rest of the afternoon hiding among the trees, reading the encyclopedia.

That probably doesn't sound rebellious to you, but in

my community technology is all but forbidden. The elders strictly control our use of the equipment we inherited, citing it as the root of all evils. To be fair to them, the pitfalls of technology are evidenced quite extensively in the encyclopedia itself. But paradoxically, a digital book proving their point would be blasphemous, and I would get punished. Better to keep my head down and read this thing in peace. They still think the solar charger broke, anyway.

"We found a seam," comes a call from the trees further ahead.

My heart sinks. So much for a quiet afternoon. This situation is about to get very ugly.

My target abandons his patch and hurries to join his colleagues. I follow at a distance, keeping myself hidden. Through the trees ahead, I can see my father, or *Papai*, as we call him. His face is grave with concentration, as he silently reaches for an arrow. As the three cartellers unite around a single scanner, celebrating their discovery, Papai gives a nod to someone on their other side. My older sister, Oriana. There's only three years between us, but she acts like it's thirty most of the time. Papai's little pet, that one.

"See? I told you we'd find it here," cheers the carteller in the middle of the huddle.

There are pros and cons to this situation. Pros: the cartellers have converged in a single spot for the first time. Cons: They outnumber us five to three.

"Wait, that's *it*? This is nothing! We can't go back to the boss with that," says the second man, snatching the scanner.

"Puta! It's plenty to be starting with. You guys remember the last seam we found? That was huge for us! They're still digging it now. I'm telling you, it started out with a reading like this one."

"You are so full of shit old man. You weren't anywhere *near* the last seam they found."

"Maybe there is something to it?" pipes up the guy I've been following. He's stammering, nervously. "The traces here mean there could totally be more nearby. We should fan out and keep looking. I really don't wanna go back empty-handed."

"Fucking new kid," mutters the second man.

"Agreed. Back to it, boys, you know the drill: set your scanner coordinates to ground zero here, and we each take a different direction. We'll cluster on whoever's picking up most signal."

A bird chirps sonorously. The five men don't bat an eyelid; to them it sounds like more forest noise. But I know that unique inflection like it's my own name.

I lock eyes with Papai, who is several dozen yards away from me. His arrow is loaded, and his jaw set firm. He whistles twice. I'm shaking my head at him, it's too soon, surely? They've only found traces of the signal, and it could vanish to nothing, meaning then the bastards would soon leave us in peace.

A second bird call, this time from my sister's side. Oriana's glaring at me, nodding her head towards the men with their scanners. She whistles twice and draws her bow. Cursing, I do the same, pulling the arrow tight to my cheek and picking my mark.

A bird call from Papai once again. He's counting down.

Three.

Two.

My target jerks around, slapping mosquitos from his neck.

In the same instant, he locks eyes with me and wails.

"Tribals!"

I fire but he dives to the side, dodging my arrow while his cries alert the others. Oriana and Papai shoot, each felling a carteller, but the two most experienced men take cover. It's not their first ambush.

Oriana's darting through the trees, closing in on one of the cowering men. But she stops suddenly, letting out a sharp whistle. I hit the deck instantly, covering my ears as the cartellers detonate a sonic grenade.

A deafening tone pierces the air. I'm clutching my skull like it's about to explode. A gunshot rings out but I can't tell from where; my vision is doing somersaults. I'm trying to stand and reach for my bow but it's like gravity is falling over.

Another gunshot. My brain is battling the sonic fog. My eyes are focusing on a figure ahead. It's my target – the new boy. He's stumbling sideways, firing at someone.

There's no time to load an arrow. I run at him, drawing my knife. Falling upon him, I thrust the blade at his heart, but my judgement is still impaired. I pierce his thigh instead. He howls in pain. I recoil as a bullet narrowly misses my cheek. I throw out an arm and grab his wrist, pressing the pistol away from me as I twist the knife in his leg.

He drops the gun in agony. I rip the blade out and thrust it back down, this time striking him in the chest. I leave the young carteller to drown in his own blood as I crawl over the mud towards the sonic grenade. The hideous device is still pulverizing the airwaves. With a grunt, I twist the two halves apart until it snaps in two.

Silence.

For a moment I can hear only my own panting breath.

My knife is yards away, sticking out of the young carteller's heart. My bow and arrow are even further back.

Footsteps. Someone's running this way.

It's one of the cartellers. He's bleeding from the arm, but clutching a gun in the other hand. His eyes fill with hatred as he sees me. With a cry, he aims the pistol at me.

As his finger moves to the trigger, an arrow bursts through his chest. The man sinks to his knees and falls face-down into the mud.

Oriana appears behind him, looming over the pair of us.

"You OK?" she breathes.

I nod; relieved, scared, and embarrassed that my older sister had to save me again.

"Where's Papai?" she asks.

I look at her blankly, still a little dazed from the sonic grenade.

Oriana lets out a distinctive bird call, but there's no reply. She tries again. Only the usual rainforest racket of insects and gibbons answers.

"Stay here," she urges, drawing her bow.

With that, she sprints off into the forest.

Movement nearby catches my eye. The young carteller is twitching, reaching for something. I stagger over to him. His pistol is too far out of reach. Instead, he's trying to call someone. I kneel down, straddling his midriff, and pull the blade out of his chest. He gurgles as blood seeps out of the cavity, before falling still.

I take the phone from his hand and wipe his blood off the screen. I've seen phones before, but I've never held one – not one that works, anyway. They're forbidden in my tribe, remember?

But this one's unlocked. And charged.

I glance around the bloody clearing. There's no one watching. If I'm caught with this, it will mean severe punishment. When we kill cartellers, we're obliged to destroy their equipment. Elder Tanok says their ways bring nothing but ruin.

Yet I can't take my eyes off the screen. It's a photo taken inside a city; up against a grand building made of old, decorated stone, and polished towering panels of glass. It must be outdated, because we all know the cities fell when the old country imploded.

The photo starts to move. My head's spinning as the video pans around a bustling market street. People are sitting in chairs and tables overflowing with food. Musicians are playing nearby while a crowd cheers them on. A group of armed men watch on, smoking. The camera spins around to show the person filming – it's the young carteller himself, grinning. Wait, he was *there*, in that city? Which would mean this footage is recent? Which means...

The elders are wrong. The cities are *alive!*

A cry snatches my attention away. No bird song this time, Oriana's calling out my name.

"Pabla! *Pablaaa!*"

I stow the dead man's phone in my hunting satchel, grab my knife, and run towards her voice.

Through the trees ahead, I see her kneeling. My father's legs are stretched beside her, splattered in blood.

"What is it?" I cry.

"A bullet got him," says Oriana. "He needs the healer, grab his legs, we have to carry him. Quickly!"

It takes us hours to reach the village, carrying father. Oriana stopped the bleeding with vine and moss bindings, but he's growing weaker by the minute. As we arrive he's barely strong enough to breathe.

His body is swept away by dozens of hands, as people rush out to help us. Word quickly spreads around the two hundred souls left in our community that my father is hurt. While to Oriana and me, Papai is simply our father, he holds great significance for the rest of the tribe. He is one of a kind; not just a hardy warrior, but he embodies the very essence of our people.

He is the Inkmaster.

As I look at him now, bloodstained and clammy, my mind refuses to accept what it's seeing. My eyes trace across the tapestry of forest art tattooed on father's skin. I'm racing from one pattern to another, just as I used to do when he would put me to bed as a child. I was always fascinated by how he crammed so much detail on one body. My fascination turned to admiration as I grew up, receiving tattoos of my own with each year that passed. His skill with the needle is incredible, as is his intuition.

On our twelfth birthdays, each member of our tribe receives a tattoo across their forehead, denoting their spirit. You don't get to choose – the Inkmaster sees it within you, and paints it for the world to know.

My ceremony was eight years ago now but I still remember it vividly. All the tribe were gathered around, watching the mighty Inkmaster at work, while I chewed the special leaves that block all pain. After several hours, I was given a blessing, and shown my spirit tattoo for the first time. I had been worried I might get a newt or a rodent or something embarrassing, but when I saw my reflection I whooped for joy. Papai had drawn on me a harpy eagle.

Tears form in my eyes as I stare at his weak body now. Flecks of red are dappled across his forehead, covering the mighty inked tree that sprouts from the bridge of his nose out across his whole face, stretching down to his neck and shoulders, and all across his body like the forest itself is flowing through his veins.

Within minutes of father being laid to recover, Elder Tanok arrives. He is a crinkly man two generations above me, and one of the founders of our community. Wise, moral, and strategic, he has steered our people since before I was born. He may be wrong about the cities, but there will be time for that later. In this moment of crisis his presence brings me hope. He has healed many people before, I have faith he can do it again.

People stand aside as Tanok shuffles to the front. He creaks down onto a stool and opens the rusty metal box he's brought, revealing our tribe's health scanner. The screen has always been cracked, so reading the display is difficult.

He switches the device on and sweeps it over my father's chest, making several passes over the bullet wounds in his abdomen. The machine bleeps and something flashes on the screen.

"He needs fluids to elevate his heartrate," says Tanok. "Maria, fetch water. Tuvo, bring salt, we need to disinfect the wound. The rest of you: pray to our ancestors that he may recover."

Oriana pushes her way through the crowd and disappears outside. I hurry after her, finding her leaning against a nearby hut stifling her sobs. She's our tribe's bravest and most skilled warrior, and I have *never* seen her show emotion like this before. Father's situation is more dire than I thought.

I place my arm around her and she leans in.

"Papai is not going to make it," she whimpers.

"Hush, sister, have faith. The ancestors will heal him," I soothe.

"The ancestors can't stop fate, little sister. His injuries

are too severe, even for them. You saw elder Tanok – he's got nothing. Water? Salt? They're not going to save our father."

"Then we need to do something else."

"What?"

"Get him to a hospital," I whisper.

Oriana breaks away from my embrace and stares at me, baffled.

"Is this one of your sick jokes, little sister? Why would you taunt me like this? You know there are no hospitals left!"

"But what if there *are*?" I counter. "What if even just one city survived the great collapse, maybe there are people there who can save him?"

"You're delirious, sister, if you think anything survived the war. The elders witnessed it for themselves."

"But-"

"It is not our place to seek fairytales and ruins! Father needs us here, where we can protect him."

"But, Oriana-"

"Enough! If you need me, Pabla, I'll be by Papai's side, praying to our ancestors. If you love him, you will do the same."

My hand moves to my satchel. I can feel the carteller's phone inside. As Pabla walks away, a knot is forming in my stomach. It is a truth I cannot ignore. If I am to save Papai, I must do the unthinkable.

CHAPTER TWO

LUKE

It's raining, I'm in the mountains, and I'm staring at a donkey.

"Is this strictly necessary?" I ask, unimpressed.

My guide shrugs at me. "You don't like it? Walk."

Normally I hope for a little more fluff around the edges when I hire a guide, but this ain't your regular tourist trail we're doing. Alfonso is a straight-talker. He's got a thick handlebar moustache, long black hair parted at the center, and a purple-and-green poncho. Oh, and a huge scar across his cheek that I'm not allowed to ask about otherwise he makes this deep growling noise and it gets awkward for several minutes. Not that I tried a bunch of times or anything...

"Come on, Alfonso, what was wrong with the van? I love your van, we were having a great time! Sorry for what I said about the playlist, I didn't mean it. Your wife has a beautiful voice and I'm sure she'll be a real hit."

"My wife sings like a banshee," shrugs the guide. "It is a fact. Just like the border. You can only get across on a mule.

"Non comprende, brosef. What?"

"I am saying you must embrace the things in life that you cannot change."

"You used *that* philosophy to get hitched? No wonder you spend all day escaping your country."

"Are you married, Señor Remini?"

"Twice divorced, actually."

"This is not a surprise to me. Perhaps you should embrace more of what you cannot change? Get on the donkey."

Ugh. This is what I get for trying to smuggle myself into a failed state: some guy in a poncho telling me that my marriage failed because of donkeys. Why didn't I just fly into the country direct, I hear you ask? Great freakin' question. You think I didn't think of that already?

I gotta make the crossing without my government tracking me. Hence, the unconventional route. The Northern Bloc has a habit of branding you a terrorist or just revoking your passport if you go to places on their "naughty list". So I flew into a neighboring country on the "nice list". They're doing pretty good for themselves, enjoying a new trading relationship with the Northern Bloc and its lovely tariffs which are totally balanced and not at all designed to perpetuate the status quo. Ahem. Meanwhile, their neighboring state, the gigantic former country of Mazonil, is closed to practically all international trade and is quietly reverting to the Stone Age. But hey, civil wars tend to do that if they go on for too long.

I'm not a war correspondent, by the way, let's just be clear about that. I'm here because the war in Mazonil is over. Technically. My plan is to pick my way through the ruins of their civilization, tactfully stepping over the ashes of their culture and dreams, as I try to get to the bottom of the biggest mystery on Earth: who screwed up the sky?

OK, I'm still working on the headline. Right now, I'm just focused on getting *into* this dystopian Disneyland and back out before it bites me in the ass. See, I'm on the hunt for something rare and exquisite. More endangered and elusive than the snow tiger.

I'm gonna get me a rainforest.

"Hola! Oy, señor, are you getting on the mule or what?"

"Oh, sorry Alfonso, I was savoring the moment. And kinda hoping a nice concierge car might appear if we waited a little longer."

"No more waiting, señor, I must return the mule to my cousin by midnight, it is a rental."

Rented mules? I could *totally* make an app for that? Remind me to cash in on that idea when I'm home.

"You see? Look here, señor, my phone. I already down to three stars on *Mulio* app."

Dammit.

"Every time a customer like you makes me late, my cousin gives me a bad review. Price goes up, my reputation goes down. Lose-lose. Time is money. So get on the donkey, señor, because we are going right now."

I can't argue with economics. They usually trump sentiment, anyhow. Excuse me while I climb aboard this noble beast. First impressions of riding a mule: stinky. Second impressions: stinky *and* uncomfortable. I feel like my gooch is being pulped.

"How far till we're over the border, Alfonso?" I grunt.

"Six hours, señor."

"You expect me to sit on this thing for *six hours*? I'll turn up sterile!"

"Were you planning on fathering children in Mazonil?"

"Absolutely not. But I reserve the right to keep that as an option!"

"Relax, señor. I can get you new balls for a good price. You want to see my ball app?"

"No, Alfonso, no I do not."

Bearing in mind the courage it's taken for me to even get on this donkey, the fear I'm about to experience might push me over the edge. As we round the side of the mountain, a deep ravine presents itself. What one might call: a vertical drop; sudden death; or *a really fucking stupid route*. Oh, and what's that across it? The world's creakiest, scraggiest, most haunted-looking rope bridge. As I watch its broken, rotten slats jiggling in the ferocious winds, I get a sense for why this country is on the banned list.

"Alfonso, you gotta be fucking kidding me!"

"Is fine, all fine," he says, confidently striding onwards, and pulling my donkey with him.

"There's no way this bridge strong enough for all of us!" I cry.

He waves his hand dismissively and says something back but I can't hear him over the howling wind.

The donkey's foot slips and a hunk of wood breaks away, freefalling for an age before smashing into the river below. There's nothing worse than watching something tumble to its fate, and hearing the impact several seconds after you saw it.

The guide draws us on until we're halfway over the ravine. The bridge is bowing under our weight, and the ropes on either side creak loudly as they sway. The hand rail is somewhere by my ankles, while the rest of me towers freely above certain death on either side.

As we near the half-way point, I'm clinging to the mule like a koala on shrooms, when Alfonso stops the donkey and turns to face me.

"OK señor, now we talk."

"Here? Are you crazy?"

"It is the best time."

"For what?"

"To renegotiate our fee."

"Your fee? You're seriously doing this now?"

"Of course, señor. Maximum leverage."

"Do you do this with all your clients?"

"Of course."

"But you have five stars on the app!"

"I give excellent service, señor."

"This isn't service, this is exploitation! Blackmail!"

"You are welcome to cancel the gig and make your own way back, señor, but I do not recommend it. It is very hard to turn a donkey on this bridge. Many would fall in the attempt. It is much easier give your dear guide Alfonso a handsome tip."

"Motherfucker. How much?"

"Just add two zeroes to the original gig."

"Two z- that's my whole budget for the trip!"

"Good thing I'm not asking for three then, isn't it?"

"This is daylight robbery!"

"Not at all, señor. I am merely providing a service to a client at the prevailing market rate. The value of my service is correlated to the danger faced by the client, and my ability to provide a solution to that danger. It is basic market forces, nothing unusual."

The bridge creaks loudly and the mule shuffles, whining. I think it hates this part of the trip as much as I do. I take out my phone and open the app, adding a ludicrously generous tip to Alfonso's fee.

"There, are you happy now? I'm broke."

"Excellent. One more thing before we continue señor. Kindly leave me a quick review?"

One thing to note: when someone in this part of the world tells you there's another six hours to go on the journey, what they really mean is twelve hours and no lunch break. Alright that's not *strictly* true; Alfonso has lunch. He brought snacks, because he knew it would be a crazy long mountainous hike with zero stores on the way.

As we finally reach the first township of Mazonil, my hopes of a restorative meal vanish. At a glance, the ratio of nutrients to grease here is on a par with the old fast food outlets of the twentieth century. Minus the free toys. And judging by the stares I'm getting from the locals, if the food doesn't kill me, they will. I stick out like a penguin in the Serengeti.

The township is a weird settlement, like a cross between an old spaghetti western and a haulage center. The town is made up of dirt tracks, street food, decaying buildings, exposed wires, and the sense that there might be a twenty-way shoot out any moment.

The buildings, if you can call them that, are arranged in two straight lines on either side of a crumbling road. It looks like someone built two strip malls outta junk then pitted them against each other in a fight.

A horn blares and Alfonso hastily pulls us over. We take shelter between two shacks in the nick of time. A convoy of juggernauts hurtles through the town. The trucks span the entire width of the street, practically grazing the sides of the buildings. The procession lasts a full minute until the last truck disappears into the dust and the street stops trembling.

The local townspeople step out from between stalls and alleys, resuming their business as if nothing happened.

Meanwhile I'm sweating like a guy who just dodged a fifty-ton bikini wax.

Alfonso helps me off the donkey and leans me against the wall like I'm a mop.

"You wait here, señor. I go find my friend," he says, taking the reins.

"Woah, woah, you can't just leave me here!"

"I find friend. They take you further into Mazonil."

"What if you don't come back?"

"I'm coming back, señor. I always take care my customers."

"Like you did on that bridge? No way. I'm keeping your donkey as my insurance."

"It is not my donkey, it is a rental."

"OK, then I'm keeping your *cousin's* rental donkey until you're back."

Alfonso mutters something that my universal translator doesn't quite recognize, but which the AI approximates as "cousin-mother-donkey-lover."

I think I get the gist. Though the rhyme scheme is a curious bonus.

Alfonso disappears and I'm suddenly I'm just some guy in someone else's town holding someone else's donkey. I'm winning at something, but I don't think it's life.

"Screw this," I say, tying up the donkey.

If there's one thing I'm good at, it's tying knots. I got two badges when I was in the young explorers' club at high school. Both of them were for attendance, but I swear I was within a hair's breadth of the big prize.

With the donkey secure, it's high time I get on with what I do best. Or at least, what I do regularly. And this is: investigating things. Starting with that greasy diner across the road.

"Hola! Say, amigue, can I trouble you for a burger?"

"Si! Naturalmente," replies the rotund woman. "Beef? Goat? Ham? Fish?"

There's a muttered call from out back. "I told you, we're out of fish!"

The woman yells something aggressive over her shoulder, way too fast for my translator to pick up, then returns to me, all sweetness and rainbows.

"Sorry señor, no fish."

Some shifting of crates and another muttered call from out back. "Wait! I found something that could be fish."

The woman swears at the man some more, then returns her gaze to me, all smiles again.

"We have fish after all, señor. How would you like it cooked? I can poach it in milk?"

"Uh, not so much." I reply, not quite in the mood for a "fish" burger, let alone one which requires cow's milk. What an unholy meat-mermaid that would be. "Do you have anything plant-based?"

The woman checks with her partner out back, then replies: "Bread burger?"

Ugh, just call it what it is: a sandwich-wich. Still, beggars can't be choosers. I'm starving, so I confirm that I'll take it.

"Five minutes," says the woman.

Five minutes to stick half a bun inside another bun? Oh god, are they frying the middle bun? I can feel my arteries clogging just by the smell of this place.

"Is twenty four."

"Huh?"

"You pay now, yes? Twenty four."

"Oh, uh, my guide has my money. I'll pay on collection, thanks," I say.

The woman's smile vanishes, and she shouts something out back that sounds a lot like "cancel the bread burger."

"Woah, let's not be hasty there, I'm sure we can come to some sort of an arrangement," I say, as my stomach rumbles loudly.

I'm rifling through my backpack for something non-essential that I can barter with. That's the trouble with being such a minimalist packer: when you make every pound count, it's hard to shed them. I told my ex-wife much the same thing when she tried hiring me a personal trainer. My hand lands on something L-shaped and metallic. My hex key. Perfect.

"Here. Would this buy me a bread burger?" I say, handing it over.

The random tools we Northern Blockers take for granted are hard to come by in places like this, you see.

"No," says the woman.

"No?"

"No. Is bad deal. Insulting."

"Oh. My apologies. Can I have the hex key back, if you're not going to-"

"It's mine now. You want a bread burger too? It's gonna cost you double."

What is it with the people here hiking the price? Anyway, double makes no difference to a guy with zero currency left.

"One moment, Ma'am," I assure her. "I'll be right back."

A quick hop and a skip later, I am the proud owner of one apocalyptically oily bread burger, and she is the delighted owner of someone's cousin's donkey. As I polish off the last of my gourmet dinner, which, I'll be honest, is growing on me by the mouthful, a familiar figure wends their way down the road. Only this time he's hitching a ride on a hoverbike. Upgrade!

We're about to exchange pleasantries when another convoy of juggernauts blares its way through the township. We both press ourselves flat into the nearest cubby, then emerge once the coast is clear.

"Where's my donkey?" says Alfonso, concerned.

"*Your* donkey? I thought it was a rental."

"You tell me now or I will beating you!"

"Cool it. It's a little early to take a bruising, even by my standards. I parked your donkey with some friends for safekeeping until your return. Come on, I'll show you."

I lead Alfonso and his driver to my favorite local restaurant down the road.

"Whaddup, amigue! I'm back with some more loyal customers. Delicious sandwich-wich, by the way, my compliments to the chef."

"Bem-vinda, welcome," replies the woman, all sweetness again. "What can I get for you all? We have beef, goat, ham, fish, and a very exciting new dish just in-"

"Oh crap. Uh, gentlemen, perhaps coming here was a mistake, shall we head on?" I interject.

I'm trying to lead Alfonso away but the woman's on a roll.

"The bread burger!" she declares, proudly.

Phew.

"Served with fresh donkey meat."

Ah fuck.

"*Donkey?* You mean-" stammers Alfonso.

"Look, brosef, don't be mad, I can explain-" I begin.

Thwack.

OK, maybe I deserved that. But it still hurt.

"Ouch! Alfonso, be reasonable, let's talk about this!

Besides, I thought we agreed it was a little early for me to take a pounding? In case you're wondering, that's *also* something I told my ex-wife. Am I right?"

Thwack.

"You owe me a donkey, señor."

"Technically, I owe your *cousin* a donkey. But given that you charged me a hundred times the usual fee for this little trip, I'm sure you can cover the difference."

"Donkeys are expensive!"

"More expensive than your friend's hoverbike here?"

"Yes!"

"Wait, seriously?"

"Hoverbikes are cheap. Everyone has a hoverbike. Mazonil used to manufacturer them for the whole world, before the great collapse. When all trade stopped, hoverbikes were just left sitting in warehouses, going nowhere. So the people helped themselves."

"Then why the hell do you need a donkey?"

"It's a good excuse to get you on the creepy footbridge," shrugs Alfonso.

"You know what, *brosef*, where I come from, we've got a word for people like you."

"Asshole?"

"Genius."

"Though asshole is better, no? It is a play on words – because of the donkey."

Alfonso's driver friend paces back towards the hoverbike and flicks the motor on, revving the fans impatiently. I guess that's my cue to leave.

"I'm gonna miss you, Alfonso. I trust your driver friend here is also planning to extort me? Please explain you've already drained my account. I can offer him precisely one hex key. That's it."

"It is no problem, señor. Driver understands the situation. I have paid him already. You just hitch a ride now."

"Then I bid you farewell, Alfonso. I hope your driver friend proves to be as erudite and conversational as you, dear fellow."

"He is a grumpy mute."

"Oh. Well, uh, at least he can't smell worse than the donkey."

"He does. Enjoy your trip."

Alfonso waltzes off back towards the diner and starts haggling with the woman at the counter. I wave nervously to my new driver, who's about to take me into the heart of this broken country, and quite possibly the most remote habitat left on earth. I hope Alfonso was kidding about this guy being mute, because I'm on the hunt for answers, and I'm banking on the driver having at least some. There's something seriously wrong going on in this country, and I don't just mean the civil war. If my hunch is right, the ramifications are gonna be felt way beyond old Mazonil's borders.

CHAPTER THREE

PABLA

Oriana has returned to Papai's bedside, where she and the others are praying for his recovery. I should be in there, but I can't take it. Not again, not after mother.

She always said it was our duty to protect the forest. Mother called us the "custodians". Then twelve years ago, she started coughing up blood. Within a matter of weeks she had gone from being one of our most vibrant leaders to yet another body for the forest to reclaim.

I had prayed then, as hard as I could, to every ancestor in this forest, to every tree, to every spirit floating through the branches and leaves all around us.

And they did nothing.

Just as I could see my mother fading away from me, day by day, so could she see my faith dying with her. I think that hurt her most of all.

You must understand this about my people: we are not stupid. We're resourceful, independent, and our entire lives are built around working with the forest, not against it. But with that comes a passionate aversion to anything that is *not* "of the forest". Be it people, equipment, or ideas.

So a phone, with a video of a dead carteller, and evidence of thriving modern cities within range of us, well, that's pretty much all three strikes, isn't it? Not that anyone else in my tribe would get that reference. I don't think they read the encyclopedia entry on baseball.

The timing of all this couldn't be worse. My community is becoming more conservative by the hour, as they pray with bated breath for their precious Inkmaster to be saved. While at the same time, I'm hiding among the trees, out of sight, out of faith, and harboring contraband that embodies everything we were told to resist.

I shouldn't be on this thing.

And yet I can't put it down. I can't shake the grating anger that's ringing in my ears: the elders *lied* to us. They've sworn, time and again, that the last cities fell decades ago, and that the only people left are scavengers seeking to steal the forest from us.

But the people in the video don't all look like scavengers. Some of them look happy, they're even dancing. Others look better fed than anyone I've seen in my life.

Back when my mother was dying, we used that broken health scanner. The same ancient device that told us Papai needs fluids and salt right now. Or at least, that's what Tanok chose to share from the diagnosis. He's the only one who reads what it says, the rest of us must simply take his word for it, as we always have done. When mother was ill, they used the machine every day to monitor her condition, doing everything it advised save for one, crucial thing: *find a hospital.*

The diagnostic machine gave that warning every day, and each day they ignored it. Whenever Oriana and I asked what it meant, they told us it was an error; that hospitals don't exist anymore.

I can't let the same thing happen to father. He's all I have left. If the elders lied to us about the cities, I can only assume they did so believing it was in our best interests. Which is why I hope – I *pray* – they understand and forgive me for what I'm about to do.

The phone is intuitive to use. I used to play with an old disconnected one as a child, until we lost it fleeing cartel fighting. Or did we lose the solar charger with it? I can't remember which we lost first, but the point is, I've used one of these before. Kind of.

OK this one's way more advanced. Like, *way* more. It's asking me questions and responding to my facial expressions. I'm telling it to hush, and it's producing a wiry tentacle that fits in my ear!

"Call the hospital," I whisper.

The nearest hospital to you is Bragotti City. Estimated journey time by foot is nine days, seven hours and-

"My father is sick. Is there anyone nearer who can help?"

There is a robotic medical unit interface in Township Fueva. Estimated journey time by foot is two days, eleven hours and-

"Pabla? Sister, where are you?"

Crap, that's Oriana! I rip the ear cable out and shove the phone into my satchel.

"What are you doing all the way out here?" she says, approaching.

"Uh... I needed some space."

"I get it. It's a lot to process."

She takes a muddy perch beside me and places an arm round my shoulder. For a moment I lean back against the thick, scarred bark of the broad tree and accept my older sister's love. It's rare for her to show affection like this; Papai must be deteriorating. While I have a harpy eagle on my forehead, Papai gave Oriana something fiercer still: a black caiman. It suits her perfectly: stealthy, calculating, territorial, and deadly. It makes her an ideal guardian of our tribe. But our Papai, the Inkmaster, sees people in their entirety. He knew that beneath that fierce jaw and tough armor lies a soft, vulnerable side, and for once she's letting me see it.

Oriana's clutching a small orangey-pink sea shell that makes my heart skip a beat with disbelief; it's an heirloom I thought we'd lost long ago. The grooves on the top side have been smoothed away by years of us rubbing it for good luck. The shell was a gift from our mother; something her own mother had passed down to her from travels to our country's distant coast. Oriana must have been keeping it safe all this time. As I see her nervously rubbing it once more, praying for our father to heal, I yearn for our childhood; for the time before mother passed away, before we knew of the people trying to steal the forest from us.

"I'm sorry I was harsh earlier," says Oriana, squeezing my shoulder.

"Don't worry about it. Sorry I bungled the attack."

"It wasn't your fault he turned around, it was just bad luck. You did fine."

"That's kind of you to say, but we both know you saved my ass – for the tenth time."

"Tenth? Try hundredth," she chuckles.

"Oriana, I need to ask you a favor and you're not going to like it. It's about Papai... I think we should get him to a hospital."

"This again! Are you insane? That's the *last* thing he would want us to do!"

"That doesn't mean it's wrong!"

"Uh, I'm pretty sure that's exactly what it means. Besides, where would we even take him? All the hospitals are gone."

"There's one in Bragotti City. It's nine days' hike, but maybe we could find a quicker route if we used the river?"

"How do you know that?" says Oriana, her eyes narrowing.

"One of the elders mentioned back when mother was sick," I lie.

"No way," she retorts. "We're not going. Papai's in no state to survive that kind of trek. Besides, you must have misunderstood the elders. There's nothing there; the city will be in ruins."

"You don't *know* that," I insist.

"What do you think we would find, hmm? A warm welcome and people rushing out to help us save Papai? The people in places like Bragotti are dogs, and they won't rest until they've killed every last one of us," she spits.

"What people? What are you talking about?"

Her eyes widen. They've moved past my face to my satchel, and they're lingering on the stray phone cable that's hanging from the side. Teeth clenched and nostrils flared, she balls up her fists, trying to control her rage as she asks, "What. Is. *That?*"

"Oriana, I can explain..."

She seizes my arm and pulls me closer, snatching the bag from my waist and ripping the phone out.

"How *could* you?" she gasps.

She drops the device to the floor like it's burned her hand and she steps back, staring at it, aghast.

"Listen to me, sister, don't freak out. I found it on a carteller I killed earlier and it's still working. This could be a gift from our ancestors, we mustn't ignore it – we can use it to get father to the hospital and save him!"

"Do you have *any* idea how dangerous it is bringing that thing into our home? Get rid of it at once!"

"No way. It's Papai's only hope."

"Do it now, Pabla, or I'll do it for you," she growls.

"I can't let that happen, sister. Not again. As a child I stayed quiet and trusted in the elders as mother lay dying. I'm not making the same mistake again."

"These devices, this technology, it's not our way, little sister."

"Then maybe our way is the wrong way! Maybe the cartels have it right?"

Oriana looks at me astonished; she's never heard such a crazy thought. I press my advantage. Her mind is open for a rare moment, and I might be able to convince her the same way I was convinced.

"Look," I say, grabbing the phone again. "See the video? The city is alive! People are there, smiling, happy, in buildings with restaurants and music, and so many other things we thought were gone! All these years, the elders have been telling us a lie."

"Maybe there was a reason!" she snaps.

I wasn't expecting this. I step back, blinking, as my mind processes her tone and posture.

"You... you *knew* they were lying?" I stammer.

"It's not as simple as truth or lies, little sister. You have to believe me when I say they're trying to protect us."

"By pretending the old world doesn't exist? So they can let father die in a hut? Is that protection?"

"The elders carry a heavy burden, Pabla. They must

think beyond individual lives to safeguard the whole tribe, and the species that depend on our protection. If we fall, the forest falls. And how do we fall? By letting our hearts become poisoned by the evils of the old world."

"But they can *save* Papai!" I insist.

Oriana shakes her head sadly, like she's our mother and I'm still an eight-year-old. I *hate* it when she does that.

A cry rings out from the village. Our heads snap in the direction of the call. More voices are resonating through the forest. Smoke is rising into the sky.

"Fire!"

The trees encircling our village are ablaze. The forest is filling with the roaring crackle, the rush of the wind, the cries of animals. Thick black smoke is everywhere as the fire consumes the first row of huts. People are fleeing past us, carrying whatever possessions they could snatch from the flames.

Somewhere through the smog, a whistle sounds. Fire scouts are signaling an escape path. People are running in family pods, helping their elders and infants to keep moving. But if they don't speed up, they'll never reach the river in time.

We're battling the evacuation flow as we push further into the burning village. Through the smoke, our hut emerges. All the people keeping vigil by our father's bedside have fled, save for one neighbor who is desperately trying to rouse him.

"Papai!" cries Oriana, rushing forwards.

"He won't wake up," stammers our neighbor.

"Marcela, we have to go!" comes an urgent call.

Her husband's arrived behind us. He's clutching their crying baby in one arm and a laden bag in the other. Marcela rises to her feet and darts from the hut.

"I'm so sorry, we will pray for him!" she cries, abandoning us to deal with father alone.

"Grab his legs!" says Oriana.

Having carried Papai for miles already, I know what to expect. We haul him off the bed and shuffle to the doorway. Oriana is framed against the threshold. An inferno of orange and black swirls behind her. My eyes are wide with fear as the fiery devastation closes in.

"Let's go!" yells Oriana.

Snapping out of my trance, I heave. We drag father into the village square. We're the last people here. Everyone is too busy saving their own families to help us. We're carrying him as fast as we can but the ground is uneven and his weight sways between us like a fleshy hammock. Oriana's facing away from me, clutching father's heavy arms behind her and she leads us through the haze.

My foot catches on a tree root and I stumble, landing hard on my knees. Father's eyes don't even flicker. His head just lolls to the side, with that fixed, pained expression he's worn since the cartel shot him.

"Papai, wake up!" I cry.

"We don't have time for this, come on," yells Oriana.

An expression of dread sweeps across her face. Her jaw slackens and she ducks, just in time. A drone skims past her head. Now I see how the fire is spreading so fast; the cartel are behind it, and they're are using pyro drones against us. The *cowards*!

The flaming drone speeds through the trees like a burning boomerang. Every leaf or branch it touches ignites into a ferocious blaze. It arcs upwards each time; soaring high above the canopy before swooping back down to engulf its prey in fire.

Another drone rushes by, skimming the roofs of three huts and leaving a streak of orange across them all. The flames take hold with abnormal zeal, swiftly cleaving the thatched roofs in two and spreading to the walls.

Seizing Papai's legs once again I haul him from the ground. Oriana and I stumble forwards, trying to follow our people through the smoke, listening for whistle blasts amidst the cries of terror.

The fire is burning at all levels, from smoldering mulch to raging flames above our heads. Two walls of orange separate us from our fleeing kin, whose silhouettes are growing fainter. The boomerang drones swoop again, scorching the ground beside us.

"This way!" yells Oriana, pulling forwards.

There's a gap in the flames but it's growing narrower by the second. My feet are moving as fast as they can but father's body is slowing us. Hot embers are scorching my soles. The heat of the blaze is prickling all over my skin. The two orange curtains are drawing together, just moments from sealing us inside the ring of fire.

Father's body twitches and Oriana stops suddenly; he's clutching her arm. His eyes flutter open.

"Go... both of you... Leave me and *go!*" he croaks.

"Never," says Oriana. "Pabla, come on!"

We redouble our grip and run forwards, only to tumble over in a heap. I lock eyes with my father, among the smoldering mud and leaves. He's trying to speak again but he's too weak. His expression is urgent, his face contorted with pain, his eyes bulging. I know what he's saying.

Grabbing Oriana's hand I pull her away with all my strength. She resists, suddenly realizing what's happening, but it's too late; I have the momentum. Flames scorch my shoulders as we race towards the closing curtains of fire. I spin Oriana around and hurl her through the gap, diving straight after her. Oriana scrambles to her feet but the passage has vanished. A pure wall of fire glows in its place.

"Papai!" screams Oriana.

Father's body is a shadow through the flames. As the pyro drones shriek overhead, scorching the trees around us, I grab my sister's hand and run.

CHAPTER FOUR

LUKE

I always dreamed of owning a motorbike. If years of marketing has taught me anything, it's that babes love motorbikes and that marketing never lies. As one of my old professors used to say: capitalism is a science, but *marketing* is an art, and correlation means condensation, and conversation means constipation. Or something like that. Looking back, "professor" might have been a rap name. But the dude had a cool motorbike and a hot girlfriend, and I think we can all agree that as a fat, bald white man who recently got robbed on a donkey, I deserve both.

My woman would cling to my ripped body as we lean into corners, chasing the coastline. Her hair would blow in the breeze, but it would be a holographic projection from her helmet because she's a safety-conscious sex icon and I dig that. She'd caress the contours of my abs, which came free with the bike.

That, at least, is how I always pictured my first motorbike ride. Technically this thing's a hoverbike, so I guess I haven't totally annihilated that dream. I'm not the one driving right now, by the way. That would be Katova.

He's the new smuggler handling my five star retreat into the heart of this ailing country. Katova has knee pads, elbow pads, a thick helmet, and he's clutching the controls like he's riding a bull.

That's because the road beneath us is terrible. It's forty percent potholes, sixty percent ditches, and a bonus hundred percent lethal. I thought the whole point of a hover bike was to *hover* over this shit, but the bike seems to mimic every last defect in the tarmac.

I, of course, have neither helmet nor pads, and am friggin' terrified. I'm clinging to Katova's waist like he's a life raft off the damned Titanic. At least *he's* got a six pack. All I got is a middle-aged muffin top and semi that I'd prefer not to discuss.

"So, uh, Katova, were you born here?" I say, casually, like I'm more than just a human anal bead.

"No, señor, I came here for the health service and job prospects," replies Katova.

"Really?"

"Sure. It is a famously abundant country. Overflowing with opportunity. Everyone here feels safe and very happy."

"Uh-huh... Say, Katova, would you describe yourself as a sarcastic person?"

"No."

"OK good. Because sometimes with these universal translators it can be hard to... Wait, when you say 'no', was *that* sarcasm?"

"*No*, señor."

"I feel like this is one of those tests, where there's a good angel and a bad angel, and I should be asking what the other angel would say you would say?"

"The other angel is an asshole. Ignore him."

"Wait, is that you speaking or you speaking *as* the other angel?"

"Si."

"Christ, I wish I'd never asked."

"How about some music, señor? Alfonso's wife recently recorded-"

"Uh, no that won't be necessary! Besides, I need to learn more about your country. Do you ever miss the old Mazonil? You know, before the government failed in the great collapse? What was it, ten years ago now?"

"The collapse was ten years ago, si, but the government was failing a long time before that," says Katova. His tone shifts, and for the first time I can tell he's being real with me. "A country does not fall apart overnight. This nightmare was eighty years in the making. The great collapse was merely the final act in our suffering. But I am confused. Why would you want to come to my country? Why are you paying for me to take you deep into the forest? You know there's nothing there, right?"

"There's always something, Katova. Nothing's ever truly nothing."

"Quote of the day."

"Thank you!"

"No, I mean, I read that once. My old office had a 'quote of the day' calendar."

"And of all the quotes, that one stuck with you?"

"They all stuck – eventually. We used the same calendar for eleven years. You just have to change three hundred and sixty five weekdays by hand, and it's as good as new."

"That sounds awful."

"Not my problem. It was the job of the calendar mechanic to fix it."

"Wait, your office had a person whose sole job was to go around manually changing the days on old paper calendars?"

"Of course. All government offices had a calendar mechanic."

"Yikes. How many offices did your government have?"

"Thousands. But the real question, señor, is how many calendars were in each one?"

"OK I'm getting a sense of why this country failed."

"And yet you have come here for a picnic?"

"I'm not *actually* here on holiday. I'm investigating. I got a hunch there's a cover up going on and the story could be huge. I'm journalist of the year, you know?"

"Ugh. Great, now I owe Alfonso five credits. He bet me you'd say that twice before we got half way."

"Alfonso knows too? Man, my reputation proceeds me."

"What is your big hunch?"

"Mazonil has the last mature rainforest on Earth, right?"

"Right."

"Which basically makes you a giant air-conditioning unit for the planet."

"Sounds important. Does that pay well?"

"Not a dime, but it's a real honor."

"In Mazonil, we tend to honor people with payment. Otherwise they kill us."

"Or hold you hostage on a creaky bridge?"

"Exactly."

"I hope that's not a hint, Katova. I told you already, your boy Alfonso cleaned me out. Which doubly-sucks for me cos I'm doing this job on spec. My editor refused to give me an advance. Something about blah blah this trip is illegal blah blah auditors blah blah federal investigation. She says 'blah' a lot, by the way. She used to be a lawyer. So I'm doing this all off my own steam, like a hero. Let the record reflect that, Katova. I'm a hero. Fixing the world, one planet-sized AC unit at a time."

"Like a mechanic?"

"Yeah, but one who repairs the *truth*, am I right? Ooh, I like that. Luke Remini: Truth mechanic."

"Truth is in the eye of the beholder, señor."

"Huh?"

"That was a quote from February dinner-time calendar."

"Wait, you had a different calendar for each *meal* of the day? Was your government just burning money?"

"The people burned money towards the end. The paper from the notes became cheaper than the fuel. So the government moved everything to crypto. Much harder to burn a digital currency. Though many people tried."

I sneeze and something red splatters across Katova's ponytail. God dammit, my nose is bleeding.

"Yo, Katova, pull over," I mumble.

"Why do you sound like train station announcer?" says Katova.

He cranes his neck and sees me pinching the bridge of my nose. Twigging the situation, he brings us to a halt by the empty roadside.

"You get nose bleeds often, señor?"

"No, it's a new thing."

"You think it's the stress of your job? My uncle had a stressful job. Many nosebleeds."

"What did he do?"

"Calendar mechanic."

Katova passes me some tissues and I stuff my nostrils. In the Northern Bloc, I could've hailed an AI medic like a cab, and it would've done micro surgery on my nose by now. But

I chose to leave all that behind. Which in hindsight may have been impulsive.

I thought I had a couple of weeks' before the symptoms would start. God dammit I *hate* it when doctors are right. They told me not to interrupt the treatment, but guess which genius thought they knew better after five minutes of internet searching while watching TV in a bar. Ugh, whatever. I never claimed to be *doctor* of the year. I better figure out what's going on in Mazonil pronto, otherwise I'm gonna be needing a whole lot more than just tissues.

As we speed away on the hoverbike, my eyes drift across the greenery on either side. The ancient forest is reaching out to us with open arms; endless rows of crops are finally giving away to clusters of trees, which are growing thicker by the minute.

Which has got me stumped. The forest seems to be in rude health; it's dense and green, kind of what I'd expect a forest to look like. So what in hell's name is causing these insane readings?

CO_2 has spiked worldwide, but everyone's too distracted by the cold war to be investigating the cause. Everyone but me. These levels are almost like the start of the century, back when we were burning hydrocarbons like it was going out of fashion. Which it was, because we had all realized we could just cut out the middle man and burn hydrogen instead. For anyone who skipped high school science, the waste product when you burn hydrogen is... drumroll please... water! Yup. Well done, class. Have a cookie, and go ask your grandparents what the hell they were thinking.

It's not just CO_2 that's the problem. While that's been rising precipitously, humidity has been *falling*, uh, precipitatiously...? As in, the air over Mazonil's rainforest is drying out, indicating that the forest is no longer feeding the global rain cycle. Which means the rains are *failing* in countries thousands of miles away.

But like I said, everyone's too busy notice, what with the cold war, the ocean scandal, the moon thing. Ugh, it's a lot, I get it. But at some point they're gonna have to stop relying on my award-winning journalism saving the day.

"Incident ahead," says Katova.

"What's the problem, sugar?"

Did I just call him "sugar?" Ah crap. I think this bike is breeding an unprofessional level of familiarity between us. Damn that six pack of his.

"Everything should be fine, señor," he replies. "Keep holding tight and don't worry about death."

Before I can object to him priming me with death thoughts, we rocket forwards. Blocking the road ahead is a fallen tree and an upturned truck. People are standing around on either side, waving to us frantically.

"Katova, we need to stop and help them!" I yell.

"Help my ass!" replies Katova.

We're less than a hundred yards from the crash site, and we're moving at breakneck speed. A safety belt fastens itself across my legs. That can't be good. Fifty yards. Thirty. Ten. My eyes are bowling balls as we're about to plough head first into the carnage.

"Here we go!" yells Katova.

He jacks a lever. The front of the hoverbike dips down sharply, throwing the rear end upwards. The whole bike vertically vaults over the crash site. Katova twists the handlebars as we fly through the air, spinning us around so that the bike lands the right way up. Though now we're facing the way we came, and the other side of the "crash" is a whole different story.

A gang of four shabbily dressed men are crouched behind the overturned truck clutching weapons. Their faces fall in astonishment, then rage, as they witness our circus trick. The foremost man leaps up from his hiding place and takes aim.

"Freeze!" he yells.

Katova flicks a button on his bike, firing a stun blast into the man's chest. The man collapses, twitching, but the other three are loading their archaic rifles. Katova spins us around and slams the accelerator.

Bullets whizz past as we speed away. I glance over my shoulder but to my horror they're giving chase. Take back what I said about archaic gear, these guys have got two shiny hoverbikes plus a turbo-charged quad bike on the ground.

The forest has formed a green wall on either side of the road; there's no way our bike can escape into it without us wiping out against a trunk or a branch. Our only hope is to try and outpace the raiders by road, but they're closing in.

"What do they want from us?" I yell.

"Your organs for harvest, your flesh for food, and your skin for leather," says Katova.

"Are you serious right now?"

"Welcome to Mazonil."

"This isn't what I signed up for! God dammit, Katova, I've got awards but I'm not a war correspondent, I used to write sports! God damn, that bullet nearly hit me!"

"Relax. Shooting is a sport. It's in the Olympics."

"Get us out of here already!"

"Gladly. But first we should renegotiate my fee."

One of the raiders pulls up beside us and draws a pistol. Katova slams us against him and hits a button. Blades shoot out from our hull and pierce the guy's air cushion, sending his bike spiraling into a tree.

"I know that guy - he used to be an accountant!" cheers Katova. "So crazy that we both ended up here. Small world, huh? Duck!"

Katova leans around and balances a pistol on my shoulder, firing at the quad bike below. We swerve dangerously close to the tree line, zig-zagging as Katova tries to shoot the slaloming quad bike.

"Maybe I should take the gun!" I yell.

"It's tied to my handprint, it won't work for you!" he replies.

"Then maybe I should drive?"

"Have you ever driven a hoverbike before?"

"No, but I won't be doing it for long – you need to get those people off our asses now!"

"This will be tricky, señor. Take the handles!" he yells.

The bike swerves again as he relinquishes his grip. I lunge forwards with a yelp and grab hold of the bars, reaching around Katova's torso. I'm leaning to the side, trying to see past him so I can steer straight, but Katova's using me as a climbing frame.

"Surely this thing has an autopilot!" I cry.

"Don't move, keep steady!"

Katova twists around. With a jolt, he lands on my lap, straddling me. Clutching my back, he fires at the raiders.

"Are all your rides this intimate?" I yell.

"What do you mean?" he yells back.

"I mean I'm riding the bike, you're riding me, and there's a lot of bouncing going on here!"

"So?" he yells, firing several rounds.

He elbows my arm, forcing us to swerve from a hail of bullets.

"I'm just saying, I would've appreciated a little notice before this became explicitly sexual!" I yell.

"Man sex looks different to this, señor. It was sexual when you were behind me, now it's purely pragmatic."

He pulls me tight and lets off a round at the raiders.

"Seriously, brosef, I feel like we're docking!"

"Señor, death is upon us, it's not the time to worry about such things!"

"It wasn't on my bucket list, that's all!"

"Why would you write a list on a bucket?"

"Wait, if you don't know that idiom, there's no way we're talking about the same kinda docking."

"It's when the foreskin-"

"OK! Definitely on the same page."

We swerve again, dodging a fresh volley of bullets.

"Dammit Katova, stay still! If this escape involves any more rubbing, there's no *way* the newspaper's reimbursing me for the ride."

Something latches onto the hull of the bike with a thud. Suddenly the quad bike and hoverbike drop back.

"What was that?"

"Oh crap!" cries Katova. "Hold onto the-"

His words are cut short as an electrical charge bursts across the bike. The seconds that follow seem to unfold in slow motion. The bike's controls flicker then black out entirely. My belt buckle detaches. We lose our six feet of altitude and plunge to the ground, hitting it hard and bouncing like a pebble. Katova and I are both thrown from the bike, landing on opposite sides of the road.

I stagger to my feet, gasping in pain. The raiders are racing towards us. As the quad bike driver takes aim at my sorry ass, there's only one thing for it. I throw myself from the road and sprint into the trees.

I'm tripping over roots, tangling myself in vines and webs, and getting bitten and stung by the whole damned forest. I'm seriously regretting getting my travel vaccines in a clearance sale.

One of the raiders has jumped from the quad bike and is chasing me on foot. There's some shooting going on by the road, so I can only assume Katova's putting up a fight.

Woah, suddenly I'm sliding, slipping, tumbling down an embankment. Where the hell did all the trees go? This whole hillside's been cleared. I'm speeding down it like human bob sleigh! Wait, is that...?

Splash.

I'm in a huge, murky brown river, and it's sweeping me away. Success, I'm saved! Spluttering, I float onto my back and give the raider a one-finger salute, celebrating my maverick escape. The guy's staring at me with a sense of... wait, is that mirth?

I spin around to see downstream. The current's getting faster. There's no way I can reach the sides. Holy crap, why does the river disappear into the horizon? That huge plume of mist and cloud has all the hallmarks of a waterfall. And I'm headed right at it.

CHAPTER FIVE

PABLA

After a day and a half of trekking, crossing rivers, valleys, and dense jungle, we are finally stopping for rest. All two hundred people from my village have made it this far, save for Papai. Our father was the only casualty of the blaze. Oriana hasn't spoken to me since I forced her away from him.

Exhausted, I set up my make-shift camp among the trees, between two other families. The whole tribe's energy is depleted, and everyone has the same priority: sunlight. We all find a patch to bask in, where shafts of gold reach through the leafy canopy. My skin tingles ecstatically. The rays rejuvenate me like nothing else; more than food, even. The tattoos across my body pulsate, caressing my whole being.

All too soon the nourishment is over. The entire village is summoned to the head of the caravan. The three elders are standing before a small, dead-looking tree. Its leaves are bare, and its stature diminutive compared to the soaring trunks all around it. Its barren branches are curious; all radiating out to form the same flat disc like a mushroom.

There's something familiar about this dead old lump, but I can't place it. As I squeeze through the crowd to perch nearer the front, I see a faint tiger pattern on the tree's bark and it hits me.

Papai's spirit tattoo – it's an unmistakable match. The only difference is that the ink version across father's face was rich with leaves and vines, whereas this specimen is a husk that has been long dead.

Quiet falls across the village as the elders call for our attention. Elder Shanarani places her hand against the dead tree and whispers, then steps back. The crowd gasps, myself included, as a residual imprint of Shanarani's hand glows yellow on the bark. A hatch opens in the trunk and a mechanical arm extends out, clutching a glass vial which Shanarani takes. As the tree seals itself, Shanarani raises the vial up over us all like an offering.

I need to emphasize how insane this is. Our village has barely had contact with the outside world. Technology from the old days of Mazonil has always been taboo, and the few ageing devices we share are regarded with suspicion. Our inventory amounts to a decrepit medical scanner, a digital encyclopedia that's three decades out of date, and a radio, used only to track cartels movements.

Even talk of technology is forbidden, and we all understand why: the old ways led to the great collapse; both economic and ecological. To protect the forest, its people must be pure of heart and mind, which can only come if a society is free from the evils of damaging devices.

So to now watch elder Shanarani, one of those crusty old technophobic zealots, lead us to an artificial tree in the middle of nowhere, open it with a palm sensor, and extract some sort of organic specimen from a vault is nothing short of mind blowing. Throw in the fact that as a child father had this very tree tattooed on his forehead by the *previous* Inkmaster, and I'm in a total head spin.

"It is time," croaks elder Tanok, addressing the village, "That you all learned the full truth about our past."

As murmurs sweep through the crowd, I lean into Oriana beside me. I ask if she knows what is going on, but I only get silence back. She's still mad. *I* know I saved both our lives, but in her eyes, all I did was condemn our father to die alone.

Elder Tanok clears his throat once more.

"As people, we are of the forest, and have been for millennia. For a time our ancestors turned their back on this sacred connection. But we vowed to once again be the custodians of this green temple. The fate of this forest..."

"Is the fate of its people!" we all cry in unison.

That call and response is our tribe's mantra; something all us Centada people learn from their earliest days. Every person here believes it for one simple reason: it is self-evidently the truth. But, as I am starting to see, it is not the *whole* truth...

"As your leaders," continues elder Tanok, "we have had to make difficult choices about what is best for our people, and for our forest. For this reason, there have been things we have not told you.

"Your, beautiful, pure souls, are of the forest. It is where you were all born, it is where you live, and one day it is where your spirits will rest. It is not, however, where I, myself, or the elders standing beside me, were born."

A ripple of shock spreads around the village at this implausible notion. Some of the youngsters laugh, thinking it's a joke. Their parents look puzzled. Their grandparents look angry. Oriana looks numb.

"We elders were born in the cities of the country

formerly known as Mazonil, which falsely laid claims to these lands," continues Tanok. "Growing up, we watched corrupt politicians and industries run the whole nation into the ground. We saw the great collapse coming and we chose to look beyond it. We knew the government would fail, and that a protracted civil war would follow. But we knew something bigger was at stake. The fate of a forest upon which a whole planet depends.

"Eighty years ago we came to this forest to save it. We formed an allegiance of like minds and vowed to protect what little wilderness remained. We vowed to undo the sins of our forefathers, and to once again become people of this sacred place.

"But to live in synergy with such a fragile ecosystem required us to adapt. The vial you see elder Shanarani holding contains the secret that has allowed our tribe to prosper. We call it: black forest algae.

"Working with elders from three other tribes, we engineered the algae in our final city years, collaborating across laboratories. Taking inspiration from what some marine creatures achieved eons ago, we sought a symbiotic relationship with the algae. It photosynthesizes on our behalf, generating energy when food is scarce. It is magnitudes more efficient than the chlorophyll you see in the green leaves around you. We still require plant-based foods, but we need not kill our fellow forest creatures for their flesh. This was a vital precondition to our stewardship of the forest. The damage Mazonil had inflicted meant we could only come with one core aim: to do no harm. The black forest algae is how we transcended our primal past."

"Elder, are you saying that black stuff's in my blood?" says a boy at the front, eyeballing the vial.

"It is in your skin, young one," interjects Shanarani.

"Tattoos have been part of forest tradition for tens of thousands of years. Perhaps this was no coincidence - they were the best way to inject the algae permanently. Our hope was that it would become a heritable trait across our tribe within a few generations, but this is taking longer than we expected. You are each born with two or more identical rings of black freckles on different parts of your body. These are algae you have inherited at birth. But they are not enough on their own.

"And so we created the position of Inkmaster; one person who would be trusted with the vital duty of imbuing each member of the Centada with the right amount of black forest algae. The Inmkaster gives us all new tattoos each year that we age, steadily increasing the amount of algae in our bodies, while ensuring youngsters like you do not develop an auto-immune allergy. It is vital that our bodies tolerate their new energy source, and through beautiful patterns and diligence, turning your algal freckles into constellations, the Inkmaster shows them the way."

My head is spinning. Did Shanarani just say my father *knew* about the algae? Surely he would have told us, his own children? No. There's no way he could have known. He *must* have thought he was just doing a religious duty like the rest of us were raised to believe. Before I can gather my thoughts, elder Tanok continues his address.

"Yesterday our village, our peaceful home of eighty years, was burned to the ground by cartellers; an enemy that has risen from the ashes of Mazonil to plunder what remains of the forest. For decades, we have repelled them, fighting to reverse their damage, but they have grown bolder and more numerous. Since the great collapse ten years ago, they have turned from a group of hapless rebels into an organized gang with sophisticated weapons.

"My people, with agony in my heart, I must tell you we are beyond the point of fighting them. We must find our fellow tribes in the North. I pray that together we can defend what is left. All forest peoples are being forced into ever-shrinking territories, and the risk of an indigenous war over resources is great. It is what the cartels dream of.

"But with the black forest algae, we can induct more tribes into our ways. By using our skin to feed from the sun, this land can support everyone. That is my prayer, and I commend it to the tribe."

No sooner has elder Tanok finished than consternation erupts across the assembly. A tsunami of questions and accusations clashes in the air.

"One at a time!" croaks Tanok, sifting through the waving hands. "You, Anam."

Anam, one of my father's friends, rises to her feet with her fists balled.

"The cartel have destroyed our home. If we run again, they will only come for us later. Maybe weeks, maybe years from now, but they will come. We must turn and fight them *now*, and reclaim what they have stolen. Tanok, you raised us to be custodians of the forest, and for that I am grateful. But because of that, I must refuse what you are asking of us now. The forest needs us. We cannot abandon it!"

What the hell? Why is she talking about fighting the cartels? Did she miss everything Tanok just said? He and the others have been deceiving us for decades! We shouldn't be fighting cartellers, we should be handing this snake over to them ourselves. The *hypocrite!*

My blood's boiling at the scale of the elders' lies. They deprived us of technology all our lives, claiming it was sinful and corrupting, and yet our very *skin* is a product of genetic engineering techniques they themselves pioneered!

We're not people of the forest. We're people of a laboratory. And yet we've just spent almost two days fleeing through the mud because our wooden huts were burned down by a cartel drone. Our whole tribe was conceived at the cutting edge of science, then raised in ignorance.

My mother, my father, both of them would still be alive if we had been told the truth about the outside world. As I stare at the frail, elderly Tanok now, I no longer see a kindly man of wisdom and morality. I see a liar. A traitor. A *murderer*.

I'm quivering with rage, but before I can speak, Kabil takes the floor. He's from two generations above me, the one between my father and the elders. I seriously hope he's about to speak some sense into them all.

"Anam is right, we cannot run from the cartellers," he declares. "Fleeing would betray our forest, and condemn the souls of our ancestors living in these trees. Our only choice is to stand up and fight. We may not have technology like our enemy, but we know the land. We must embrace guerilla war."

Half of my village is howling in support. I can't believe what I'm hearing. How are they all still so blind? I leap to my feet, spitting with rage at the insanity around me.

"You *idiots*!" I cry. "Can't you see what's going on here? The elders have conditioned us to think technology is our enemy; that it is the same thing as the cartellers and the failures of Mazonil. But Tanok has just admitted that we only exist because they used technology to alter us!"

"Our skin is the only exception," insists Tanok. "A single evil to facilitate so much good. Technology is a slippery slope. It seduced the minds of Mazonil's politicians and people, perpetuating a throw-away culture of economic growth at all costs. Because of technology they presided over *genocide* in this forest, eradicating millions of years of ancient habitat and species and for what?"

"Their sins do not change yours, Tanok. You *lied* to us," I yell.

"To protect you all from making the same mistakes!"

"The only mistake we can make now is to keep listening to you. Hear me, everyone! To survive, we must embrace the thing that makes our enemies strong. All this talk of guerilla war and tree spirits has brought us nothing but ruin. Our whole village was destroyed with a single drone! Wake up, people! We shouldn't be fighting the cartellers. If we want to survive, we should *join* them!"

"You don't mean that, Pabla," says elder Shanarani, aghast.

"They have technology that you denied us. Technology that could have saved my parents! You condemned Papai to die from his injuries, even though that broken old scanner *knew* a hospital could save him!"

"There are no more hospitals, Pabla. They were lost in the civil war, you know that," chimes the younger woman, Anam.

"Until moments ago, Anam, I thought the tattoos on my skin were a mark of our culture. Now we find they are the scars of genetic experiments forced on us all. So I ask you, when you tell me there are no more hospitals, how can you be sure?"

Anam can say nothing to this. Mutterings of disapproval float all around me.

"Enough," interrupts Tanok. "The cartellers will be on our trail. We must vote now: either we stand and fight, or we seek refuge in the North."

"Wait, Tanok," interjects Shanarani, "Before the tribe votes, we must ensure the black forest algae is preserved.

We are one of only three tribes on the planet to possess this strain. It must yet save *all* forest people. We need a champion to get our vial to the Northern stronghold, alone. I call upon the Inkmaster to answer the call."

"The Inkmaster's dead, you fucking idiot!" I scream. "You watched him burn! You *let* him burn!"

"Your father is dead, and I am sorry for your loss, Pabla. But the spirit of the Inkmaster lives on. He will have appointed a successor. I ask that person to come forward now. Reveal your identity. To whom did the former Inkmaster choose to pass on the craft of life?"

Silence falls over the village as everyone looks around for the Inkmaster's successor. As a grim-faced figure rises to their feet, my jaw drops.

"He chose me," says Oriana.

"*You?*" I cry.

"Yes, sister, *me.*"

"Hypocrite!" I yell, shoving Oriana backwards.

She shrugs off my assault like it was nothing and glares at me, silently reminding everyone around that she's the most skilled warrior of us all. If she wanted me dead, I would be dead. Instead, her eyes move to my satchel and she clenches her teeth.

"All these high and mighty speeches you're making, Pabla. Do you want to tell them, or shall I?"

I'm staring at her with wide eyes. Is she seriously about to do what I think?

"If any of you are wondering why Papai chose me and not Pabla to be his successor, it is because he knew her. Like he knew all of us. The Inkmaster saw each of us for who we truly are, and he looked to my sister and knew that for all the love in the world, when it mattered the most, she could not be trusted. Pabla stole a phone from the cartel and brought it to our village. *That* is the reason they finally found us. *That* is what sparked the attack."

My face falls. Is this her revenge, for me making her abandon Papai? All eyes are glaring at me. The villagers are hissing, demanding immediate punishment. Oriana continues her address.

"Pabla's disobedience of our tribe's most fundamental rules is what killed my father, our Inkmaster. It is what destroyed our homes. But I will not make those same mistakes. I swear before you all, as the new Inkmaster, I will guard the vial with my life. I will deliver it to safety, and ensure the future of all tribes. You have my word. The fate of the forest?"

"Is the fate of its people!" cries the crowd.

Elder Shanarani hands the vial to Oriana with a solemn bow. Tanok steps past them and limps through the crowd until his ancient frame is yards from mine. He stares me directly in the eye, with a look of immense hurt and anger across his face.

"Pabla... What Oriana says... The phone... Tell me this isn't true?" he asks.

"I... I didn't think they could-"

Tanok silences me by raising his hand. He's so angry he's choking back the tears, his mouth quivering as he tries to control his tone.

"There is a reason technology is prohibited in our society. Yet you saw fit to circumvent that sacred rule, and look at the result, Pabla. We are all here because of you."

"Elder Tanok, waste no more breath on the traitor," interjects Shanarani. "We must move to the vote: do we stay and fight, or flee to the forest in the North?"

"Neither!" I yell. "For as long as we're living here we'll be persecuted. We should go to the city – I know it exists,

I've seen *recent* footage. They have electricity, hot water, baths, and foods like you've never imagined!"

"How easily you have been seduced," says Shanarani, shaking her head.

"Please, everyone, I'm sorry for the phone, I am, but we need to survive, and the city could be the best way for all of us!" I plead.

"And you are welcome to it," says Tanok.

"What?"

"Go, Pabla, go to the city. It is yours to endure. But from this moment on, know this: you may never return to this tribe. For your crimes, and what you have inflicted on this community, on your own kin, you are henceforth exiled from the Centada."

I'm staring around the assembly in disbelief, waiting for someone to counter the old man. I've spent my life with these people, working alongside them, tending the forest, subsisting and suffering through the elders' lies together, and yet now each of them is so consumed by anger that they're throwing me out? I turn my eyes to my sister; my last source of refuge. I know she's angry for all that's happened, but I'm her only family. And she's my only hope.

"Sister?" I whisper.

Oriana glares at me, clenched jaw, then spits at my feet.

"I have no sister. Get out of here, Pabla, before I make you."

CHAPTER SIX

LUKE

'm trying to back paddle against this river but the current's way too strong for me. Plus my waterlogged clothes are weighing me down, so just keeping my head above the surface is a hell of a battle. Sweet mercy, a log! With a few heroic strokes I intercept the floating driftwood and throw myself across it. Risk of imminent drowning: solved. As for problem two: bone-crushing mega-waterfall? That's officially top of my inbox.

There comes a point in life when you just gotta lean into a situation. Normally I pride myself on my undercover prowess; my steely reserve, my discreet manner. Now is not the time to be incognito.

"Heeeeeeeeeelllllllppppppppp!" I wail, at the top of my lungs. "Somebody help me!"

The raiders are nowhere to be seen, presumably busy stripping Katova for parts back up by the road.

"Yo! Cartel dudes, help me!" I'm yelling, "I'll give you a kidney if you do! You've got a hoverbike for Christ's sake, don't be assholes about this!"

Ugh. Gangs are *such* sore losers. We kill *one* of their goons and they take it personally.

"Don't be petty, guys, we can work this out!"

The waterfall's getting louder by the second. I swear, for every decibel, that's gotta be another ten feet I'll be falling. Oh god. This is why there are laws against swimming near waterfalls – it's a death wish! The *last* thing I have is a death wish. I love my life! OK, not my *life* per se, but I'm very attached to myself, and I'd be truly heartbroken if anything were to happen to me.

Something's tingling at my feet. Are there piranhas in Mazonil? Ah well, might as well let them have a nibble. The buffet cart's about to disappear forever, so get what you can now folks.

"Hang on, we're coming!" cries a voice from the opposite bank.

Holy crap, people! A young skinny man is running down the bank trying to keep pace. He's got a telescopic rod in his hand, which he's holding out to me like a posh person doing litter-picking.

"Grab hold of the rod!" he calls.

Clinging to my log-raft I kick hard. If I can just get far enough to the side, the river will bring me to the rod in the next... few... seconds! Got it! Oh my god, I actually did it! Wait, isn't he supposed to keep hold of the other end?

The skinny man's staring at his empty hands in dismay as he realizes he has the grip strength of a lettuce leaf.

"Heeeelp!" I cry again.

I'm trying to waggle the rod in his direction but the river's pulling me away. I'm out of his range, and it's too deep for him to wade in further.

Out of nowhere, a rope lands beside me. Another man has appeared on the shore, a little further downstream. He's yelling at me to put the lasso end over my shoulders, but the only way I can do that is by abandoning the log. Oh god, the waterfall's getting louder and louder. Here's to nothing!

I fling myself from the log and drag the rope around my waist. As soon as it's in place it tightens, spinning me around. This second man has enough strength for both of them; he's hauling me in with his own brute force.

But he's battling the current, which is pulling me downstream. I'm facing the edge of the waterfall, where the gushing river becomes sky and mist. The man's grunting with effort as his strength keeps me static; the two rival forces on my body held in brief equilibrium. I'm no stranger to fights over my body, but this is the first time one of the feuding lovers has been an immense hydrological phenomenon. Unless you count my first wife, of course.

He's doing it! Inch by inch the tide is turning; the man's strength is prevailing and he's reeling me in. Three cheers for my new hero: guy with a rope! My heel bashes something soft and clay-like. I've made it to the embankment, I can stand up again!

"Noble sir, you have saved me!" I proclaim.

I throw myself onto the muddy bank, exhausted, and stare at my rescuer with open adoration. But he's still clutching the rope. As he looms over me, something about his expression tells me he's not happy. I'm about to ask what his problem is when his boot lands against my chest and he hauls the lasso tight again.

"Which cartel are you from?" he growls.

He's got wrinkled eyes set in a fierce permanent hawk-like glare. Coffee-bean colored skin and pitted cheeks, set against a thick head of silvery hair, a wild bushy beard, and a forest of white chest hairs bursting through his military-green shirt.

"I'm... not... cartel!" I rasp.

My eyes are bulging as the rope squeezes my organs like a toy. The man flicks open a knife and holds it to my arm, then cuts my sleeve open. His face falls, as whatever he's expecting to see fails to materialize.

At that moment the skinny man arrives, presumably looking for his missing rod. He's got olive skin, big green eyes, bushy eyebrows, tousled brown hair, patchy stubble, and looks around twenty. On his left cheek there's an unusual circle of freckles, which is repeated almost identically on his right calf muscle. It doesn't *look* like a fashion statement, but it's definitely too neat to be natural, surely?

"Tell us who you are!" yells the strong man.

I'm still being strangled around the waist so I'm not sure how he's expecting me to respond here. Moreover, something's nibbling at my foot again. No, make that my leg. It feels like the piranhas are chomping at me, yet we're out of the water. The nibbling's getting more intense by the second. It's more of a burning sensation really. And it's hurting more than the waist-noose.

"Not... cartel!" I rasp, again.

"Liar," spits the strong man. "Tell me which cartel, or I will put you back in the river."

"Maybe he's foreign, like me?" frowns the skinny man. He gazes at my writhing legs, then the penny drops. "The water! He's been exposed, we need to treat him!"

"Fine. You treat, I interrogate," grunts the strong man, tightening his grip.

The skinny man opens his backpack and pulls out a first aid kit. With a pair of scissors he cuts lengthways along my cargo pants, from my ankle to my hip. He peels back the sodden fabric and reveals my leg, which is red raw and blistering. It looks more like microwaved cheese than skin.

I'm moaning and writhing like a kid at the dentist. The skinny man grabs something from his kit bag and sprays it across my skin. The effect is instantaneous, and glorious, like ice cold milk after chili.

"Ease up, Ramone, he's not cartel – you can see he hasn't been branded!" urges the skinny man.

As if disappointed, the strong man relinquishes the lasoo. Like a surly teenager, he tosses the rope onto my gasping chest and slouches off to smoke against a tree.

"Apologies for Ramone," says the young guy. "He can be a little sensitive when it comes to the cartel. Not that you're cartel."

"What... the hell... was that?" I pant, gesturing to my pockmarked leg.

"That's what we're trying to figure out. Something toxic. I'm Pietro by the way," adds the skinny guy.

"We need to keep moving," grunts Ramone.

The older man checks an ancient GPS device and scours the misty horizon, then flips it shut with a grunt.

"Damn," says Pietro. "Looks like we're way off course. Hey, I'm glad things worked out with the river, sorry about the pole earlier. Take it easy."

Pietro extends a hand for me to shake. I stare at him incredulously.

"Wait, you guys can't just leave!"

Ramone is already making his way towards the cliff edge, with Pietro shrugging apologetically then hurrying after him. I'm not having this – you can't save someone from certain death then just abandon them in the jungle!

I scramble after them with my pant legs flapping in the breeze. It's doing a wonderful job of soothing my river burns, and I've always been a fan of upper groin ventilation.

I skid to a halt beside them, sending a handful of pebbles tumbling over the cliff edge. Standing here, next to the immense lip of the waterfall, you get a true sense of the awesome power of nature. Oh Christ, I sound like my high school geography teacher. Just bear with me a second and I promise I won't talk about rock types.

The noise is tremendous. It's like someone's filling a bathtub with the taps on full, recording it, then playing it through the sound system at a stadium, then recording *that*, playing *that* through a colossal amplifier set up in a concert hall, then taking the final recording in a vintage vinyl sleeve, scaling a mountain, hurling it off the top, then just listening directly to the thunderous rush of the waterfall itself. OK not the best description but in my defense, my high school geography teacher sucked ass. I think he got fired for it, in fact. Not in a discriminatory sense, just in the NSFW sense.

Aside from the noise, there's a thin mist rising from the splash pool, reaching above the feeder river where I'm standing. I'd say it's a refreshing spritz but the mist is making my skin itch, just like the river. I'm gonna be needing more of that sweet, sweet ointment very soon indeed. Oh yeah, *that's* why they fired him! You just can't walk around a school saying shit like that.

Noise. Mist. What else? Oh yeah, the view's pretty dope. If you're into *desolation*, am I right? It sucks. Firstly, this waterfall is insanely high and I am *not* one for heights. Secondly, the view confirms all my worst fears.

I reckon the drop to the bottom is around three thousand feet down. Which means as I look outwards, the horizon is a good sixty miles away. So I should be seeing millions of acres of rainforest.

Should be.

What I'm seeing is a patchwork of scorched ground, mechanized clearance, and logging.

"We're too late," says Pietro, deflated.

"It's never too late to fight back," growls Ramone.

He opens his backpack and retrieves a harness, which he affixes to himself. He then hammers a peg into the rock, ties one end of the harness to it, gives Pietro a nod, and disappears over the edge.

The skinny man's looking at me sheepishly, clearly hesitant to unload his own harness.

"I suppose you'll be on your way, then?" he says, brightly.

"Oh yeah, I've been meaning to catch up with the cartel that threw me in the river. We're gonna get donuts and play bridge."

Pietro's face falters as he processes my sarcasm. I'm worried I may have a limited working relationship with this guy if that's his standard digestion speed for quips. I'm like a quip machine, you know? He's more like a quip pestle and mortar.

"So you're *not* going back into the jungle?" says Pietro.

"Er, *no.* I'm coming with you, pal."

"I'm not sure that's a good idea. Ramone's a lone wolf. He barely tolerates me, so I don't think he's going to be happy if you follow us."

"Yeah but he's halfway down the cliff already, so he's not here to argue. It's just you and me, kid, and I'm fucked if I get abandoned again."

"Again?"

"Oh, I have some childhood attachment issues. That's for another time."

Pietro's got a breathless disposition and licks his lips a

lot. If you picture a lizard with glasses, that's this guy. It's definitely weird that people like him still choose to wear glasses, but I guess he didn't want nanobots squirted into his eyeballs or whatever. Or maybe he's just insecure about his reading abilities and wants to look bookish. Either way, it's a moot point, because he looks like a freakin' lizard, and everyone knows lizards can't read for shit.

"I don't think this harness can hold both of us," stammers Pietro.

"No problem, I'll go down first, then throw it back up to you."

"Impossible; we're thirty-three hundred feet above the splash pool."

"For real? That's so cool, because I guessed three thousand!"

The kid looks at me blankly like that's *not* impressive, when really we all know if this was a pop quiz situation, everyone at my table would be slapping me on the back as I go up to collect the jackpot. Ugh, I miss bars. Remind me why I'm in the jungle again? Oh, yeah. Conscience.

"I'm sorry, I can't help you further, my work is extremely important," says Pietro.

He's edging away from me now, frantically unpacking his harness.

"Now let's be reasonable here, kid…"

I'm shuffling towards him. He's trying to back away but it's hard to concentrate on the loose rocks around us while strapping his shoulders in. He's got one arm through. If he gets the second one in, he's outta here, and I'm just some loser on top of a cliff. Journalist of the year deserves more than that for a farewell.

"Gimme that!" I yell, lunging at him.

The kid yelps and dives to the side. He's scrambling to

get his other arm in but I've grabbed it and I'm pulling him towards me. With his spare hand he throws the end cable around Ramone's peg, which has so far held rock-steady.

"Let... me... share!" I grunt.

He's moaning much the same, but with a different spin on the situation. Quite selfish, if you ask me.

"Don't... be... so... pig... headed!" I yell.

Pietro squeals as I force my arm through the spare shoulder strap. He's trying to get away, but we're half-bound together now. As he elbows and kicks, trying to force me out, we're rolling towards the cliff edge.

"Kid, be reasonable!"

"Get-off-me!" he cries.

My back presses against something firm; a spinal structure to the harness, caught between us. As it flaps in and out of my vision as we tussle, jerking it around, I spot a red button on the side. Pressing it can't be any worse than this, right?

The kid follows my gaze and his eyes widen. I'm reaching for this thing but he's fighting back, pushing my arm as hard as he can. Amazing how one minute some people can't even hold a rod properly, but when you try to throw them off a cliff with you, they suddenly become gym heroes.

"Stop... being... so... difficult!" I grunt, straining for the button.

"You don't know what you're doing!" he gasps.

"Age before beauty, kiddo!"

I overpower him and mash the red button.

"Aha!" I cry, triumphantly.

Instant regret.

Ribs shoot out of the harness spine and wrap around us. Lizard kid and I are slammed together like two halves of a sandwich. We're rolling uncontrollably towards the edge of the cliff. I think the peg cable might even be spinning us, I have no idea how this thing works but whoever designed it was a sadist. All I can see is a blur of ground-sky-lizard-face on repeat as we tumble. Both of us are yelping for help with the frenzied, stabbing cries of two people who are about to let out one very, very long scream.

"It's not designed for two!" squeals lizard boy. "It's only meant for-"

And with that, we drop.

It's a full five minutes before either of us are able to speak. As Pietro and I lie on the river bank, a small robot is busily sculpting wet clay beside us. The descent was, I'll be honest, traumatic, and we ended up in the splash pool, which apparently wasn't supposed to happen. Luckily the rope held, and Ramone stepped in to save our asses. Now we're lying on the bank like we've just been birthed. We're sheltering behind a tarpaulin screen Ramone's put up to shield us from the toxic waterfall mist. As he spritzes us with more of the cooling solution from lizard boy's bag, the 3D printing machine bleeps, signaling completion of its task.

Ramone disappears for a moment then returns, clutching an oar made of freshly-baked clay-fiber. He tosses it onto my belly.

"If you wanna come with us, gringo, you must paddle," he says.

This time I don't wait about. When that dude says he's off, he means it. I hurry to the river's edge, with my legs still shaking from half a mile of mechanized abseiling.

Ramone's packing away the tarpaulin and the 3D printer, and loading both into the end product: a generously-sized canoe, forged from riverbank clay, which the machine somehow managed to bake and seal in the blink of an eye. Man, if I get out of here, I'm getting me one of them.

Pietro pushes past me and takes a seat in the middle of the raft, while Ramone goes at the back. Guess I'm riding shotgun, then. I really hope neither of them clubs me over the head and throws me in the river. That would be a serious betrayal of a beautiful, blossoming friendship. Those two don't know it yet, but we're gonna be tight, us three. Adversity bonds people.

Me and lizard boy were *literally* bonded for a time, so really it's just Ramone I gotta connect with now. You know, invest in him, emotionally speaking. As we leave the waterfall behind us, I use my charm to soften him up.

"So, Ramone, is it?"

"Keep paddling, coño," he snaps.

"Woah, what's your problem amigue?"

"I am not your amigue, white man. Nor am I answerable to you."

"Roger that. I'm just trying to make friends, that's all."

"I don't need friends like you. Your kind are the reason my country is the way it is."

"That's a bit of an oversimplification," chimes Pietro.

"Thank you! See? My friend lizard boy gets it," I cheer.

"Don't call me that, and I'm not you're friend. You nearly killed us both on that cliff. I'm only speaking up to defend the record."

"Here we go..." sighs Ramone.

"Uh, what 'record' is that?" I ask.

"The academic record. It's all he ever talks about. He is

too thinky. We have enough thinky people already. What we need is action," grumbles Ramone.

"Huh, I see. So Pietro's a dork and you're a...?"

"Ranger."

"Like, a forest ranger? But who's employing you? The last government of Mazonil ended ten years ago."

"I employ myself," says Ramone. "The forest needs rangers, government or not. Hey, you need to alternate sides when you paddle. You keep dragging us left, gringo."

"This is my first time in a canoe, can you believe that? And it's a clay one too, so cute! I feel like I'm experiencing a lot of culture on this trip."

"Is this some kind of *game* to you, white man?" snaps Ramone.

His oar clatters as he leaps up, rocking the boat. His shoulders are heaving and his fists are balled, like he's ready to tear my head off.

"Woah, take a seat, big guy. I'm here for the same reason as you two – to find out what the hell's happening to the forest, and put an end to it."

Ramone says nothing. With a slosh he sits down and resumes paddling, staring across the river, seething.

"He's not really angry at you," says Pietro, after a moment's silence. "I am, but he's not."

"Uh, thanks for clarifying?"

"I'm merely correcting the record. Ramone's dealing with a lot. We all are."

"Who's 'we'?" I ask.

"Anyone living in the forest," says Pietro.

"You two live here?"

"Sort of. Ramone's nomadic. He's fighting the cartels, and tracking their incursions into indigenous territories," says Pietro, wistfully.

"Dang, Ramone, now I get it. That's a lot of emotional baggage for one person, no wonder you got the whole surly tough guy thing going on. Though in future you should tell your own backstory – it would be a lot more epic in your voice. No offence, kid, but you're more suited to playing someone with scales – uh, I mean spectacles. OK those two sound nothing alike. You look like a lizard, let's just all make our peace with that."

"For the record... I cannot deny this. But you're a turd for stating it," says Pietro, huffily.

"Pietro has been through a lot to make it here," says Ramone. "You should show him more respect, gringo."

"Oh, OK, I see, are you gonna do his story now? Is that how this dynamic works? If so, that's kinda cute. And very on-brand for the elderly married couple vibe I was going for earlier, but whatever, I'm not fussed about who gets credit for-"

"It was six years ago," interrupts Ramone, gazing across the river, "that Pietro was working as a conservation researcher in his state university. He volunteered to take part in another department's genetic study. It found that he was a first-generation Mazonilian immigrant, contrary to what his adoptive parents had told him."

"So he's here to trace his family? That's so moving!"

"No! Stop interrupting," snaps Ramone. "OK yes, that's actually correct. But you kind of ruined my delivery."

"Sorry bro, next time. OK, so how did you two meet?"

"A chain of contacts – friends-of-friends – led me to a township in this region," says Pietro, taking over. "When I arrived I thought it would be easy to track my ancestors down, but the cartels have proven very hostile to my kind."

"Bastardos," mutters Ramone.

"So I went back to my friends-of-friends chain, and they

eventually put me in touch with Ramone, who happened to be visiting another township and, unusually, on-grid. Or at least, to those who know him. We arranged a meet up, and here we are."

"Wait, Ramone, what do you get out of helping lizard boy?"

"My enemy's enemy is my friend," shrugs Ramone. "Pietro wishes to strengthen his tribe with technology and techniques from the developed world."

"While Ramone wishes to help those still living in these parts to fight back," says Pietro.

"Our goals are aligned," nods Ramone.

"Oh my god, you guys, *samesies!*" I gush. "We could totally be like the three Musketeers! No? Uh, how about the three amigues? Witches? Ugly sisters?"

"In my culture, five is the best grouping for comedy. We would say, we are like the five pangolins," says Ramone.

Ramone laughs heartily at his own "joke", which seems to crack Pietro up too. Normally I'd laugh along out of politeness, but this is fucking bullshit. There are clearly only three of us, and we're *definitely* more aligned to musketeers in the nature of our goals than a bunch of scaly ant eaters.

As I survey the patchy, barren land on either side, a question lingers in my mind.

"Why aren't the cartel using the river to transport the logs?" I ask.

The laughter from the back peters out. Both of their faces sour at this mention of the enemy.

"Elsewhere, they do," says Ramone. "This particular river flows in the wrong direction for their exporters. But that's not stopped them cutting everything they can, and shifting it by truck."

Something from the rear of the boat bleeps, and Ramone stops paddling. He removes a small cylinder from his backpack and inserts three clay blades into serrated slots. He then attaches the whole unit to the end of his oar and hangs it off the rear of the canoe like a rudder.

The boat surges forwards, and the water behind us forms a slick wash.

"The motor is charged?" says Pietro.

"Ya think?" I snort.

"We will take turns on the tiller," says Ramone. "I will go first, you two should sleep."

When I awaken, our surroundings have changed dramatically. We're in a narrow river now, just a few yards wide, gliding between mangroves. Pietro is on the tiller, looking sour-faced as he surveys the trees.

The leaves are wilting and covered in a layer of slime. The water lapping at the roots of the trees is foaming, and filled with fluorescent chemicals. Water stains are etched into all of the trunks, showing previous flood lines. Only, these ones look more like scorch marks.

"Ramone, wake up," says Pietro, using his heel to rouse the sleeping man. "Over there, look."

Ramone and I follow Pietro's gaze to a slither of sandy shoreline amidst the dying mangrove. Through the branches, just about visible, is a group of huts. Ramone slaps his cheeks, waking himself briskly and rifles through his backpack, while Pietro steers us closer.

We cut the motor and pull up. It's a secluded patch; whoever lived here clearly chose to keep access to the shore hidden. Ramone jumps out, clutching the hilt of his knife.

Pietro wedges the canoe between two roots, then he and I follow after Ramone, into the silent village.

The huts are traditional, made of long dried leaves forming domes like thatched igloos. Ramone calls out, first in his native language, then in a series of mock bird calls. No reply. And no surprise; the allotments are barren, the soil is parchment-dry and stained with the same blotches of color as the mangrove bark.

"Now you see the scale of the water problem?" says Pietro.

"You've really got no idea what's behind it?" I reply.

"Ramone, any indication which tribe used to live here?" calls Pietro, ignoring me.

"Unclear. But by the looks of it, it's been abandoned for some months now."

A deep, guttural grunt of pain emanates from the trees further inland. Ramone draws his knife in a flash.

"Uh... what the hell was that?" I ask, nervously.

The silver-haired ranger glares at me with a finger across his lips, then tip toes forwards, silently weaving between the huts. More deep grunts; a call of sorts. Ramone vanishes from sight. I'm holding my breath, while Pietro cranes his neck to see what's going on. Then a cry from the trees.

"Come quickly!" yells Ramone. "I need help!"

CHAPTER SEVEN

PABLA

Where do you go when your home has been burned to a crisp and your people cast you into exile? I'm weeping, sniveling, throwing rocks and branches at the trees in anger, cursing my ancestors, insulting their fictitious spirits, crying out with rage to the dead elders who kept the truth from us for so long.

I never asked for any of this. All I've ever tried to do is look after my community and our forest home. I held up my end of the bargain, and for what? To be lied to? Kept in the dark for twenty years? What else are they keeping from us? Are there more cities out there? More hospitals? Did the rest of the world survive the cold war?

I slump against a fruit tree, exhausted from hours of walking and crying. The phone bulges in my satchel, pressing into my ribs. I dig it out and hurl the damned thing at the ground, where it skids through the mulch. Drawing my knees to my chest, I sob uncontrollably, not knowing who I'm angrier at: my people or myself. If it hadn't been for my curiosity with the phone, the cartel would never have found our village. The blaze wouldn't have happened, and Papai would still be alive. No wonder they exiled me. If I was an elder, I would have done the same.

My tears abate and I sit for a time, surrendering to the numbness engulfing me. My tribe's predicament is still playing on my mind. Fight or flight? Surely there are better options than that? What about striking a deal? Or collaborating? Maybe the hospital could help us store the algal culture, if I could just persuade the elders to let us make contact?

My eyes flit to the phone. Dragging myself up, I slouch through the carpet of dead leaves and retrieve it from the dirt, brushing the muck from the screen. I turned the device off as we fled the fire, not daring to let the cartel know which way we were fleeing. But now I need it: I want to know what's out there; who can help us, and what else the elders have hidden from us.

As the device powers up, I marvel at the boot screen animation; a mesmerizing holographic display that seems to hover above the screen then vanish back into it. Whoever owned the device didn't care enough about security to put any sort of lock on it, so I'm in right away. But I have no idea how to use the thing. Instead, I'm just staring at the background once again, and that looping clip of the phone's previous owner in a city somewhere, looking happy and well fed.

Suddenly, the phone's playing a tune at me and a face appears on the screen. I have no idea what's happening, and I'm so startled that I drop it to the ground. I must've hit a button or something because the tune vanishes.

Hello? Who's there?

A man's head is floating above the screen in a 3D

hologram. He's got a Mohawk, two hoop earrings on one side, bright red lipstick, and a thick handlebar moustache.

Hellooo?

I lean over the phone, open-mouthed, and a tiny reflection of my face appears in the top corner of the screen. I fall backwards, majorly spooked out.

Hey, come back! I wanna talk! cries the man. *I don't bite, I promise.*

Inch by inch I crawl back towards the phone and peer over the screen.

Aha! Hey! Good! OK, don't move, stay there, I wanna talk. What's your name?

"Me?" I ask, perplexed.

Maybe the man can see a floating picture of my head on his end? I sort of know from the encyclopedia how phones work, but this thing's real, and I'm talking to a carteller. I'm freaked out!

Yeah, you, what's your name?

"Pabla. What's yours?"

The man laughs. Some people appear to be laughing near him, but I can't see them. For some reason, me not knowing his name is amusing to them.

I'm Stax. But most people call me Sarge.

"You're in the army?"

Not the army, though I guess you could say I'm in an army. To you people we're probably an army, aren't we?

More laughter from his end.

So, Pabla, you've got my guy's phone, which tells me you probably killed him?

"He was trespassing on our land!"

'Your' land, is it? I see. And what gives you people more right to the land than my people?

"We're on it, coño. *That's* our right. Unlike you, we don't destroy everything on it, we *care* for our land."

Hey, we care for your land too, you know. Or at least, what it's got to offer.

"Yesterday you bastards killed my father. If I ever find you, I will restore his honor."

Woah, easy tigress, let's not go bandying threats around for no reason. Your father's death is on him.

"Your men shot him!"

They didn't have to. We offered to buy the land from your people months ago but he said no.

"What?"

He didn't tell you?

It's one thing knowing the elders lied to us all, but each time I hear that my father lied to me too, it cuts even deeper.

Look, chava, don't be hard on yourself. These things happen. Your father made bad choices, and they ended in a bad outcome for him.

"Go to hell. He was a good, honest man. He was a man of love and peace and you killed him out of greed!"

The words sound hollow in my ears. I'm defending my father out of instinct, and love, yet it suddenly feels like I barely knew him at all.

All I'm saying is, hopefully you'll make better choices than he did.

"What do you mean?"

I'm offering you a way out. Your tribe has moved into new territory. We are willing to buy it from them.

"What about the old territory?"

It's ours now, chava. We're not gonna pay you for something we already own, that would be dumb. Look, we can put all this nasty business behind us. I'm offering a simple transaction here: we get the land, you people get more money than you can imagine, and everyone lives happily ever after. Am I on speaker, yeah? What do the others say?

"There are no others. I am alone."

Weird, I thought your kind stuck together like glue. I don't think I've ever seen one of you people alone. Always in twos and threes.

"Yeah, well, not me."

Loner by nature?

"I have been exiled."

The words stick in my throat, the very act of vocalizing them hammering home my dire isolation.

Did you do something bad? It's OK, you can tell me.

This Stax man is speaking to me like I'm a fucking child, like this is some kind of game to him.

"They blame me for the fact that *your* drones burned our village to the ground. The same drones that burned my father, the Inkmaster, alive."

I'm quivering with rage now, fighting the urge to smash the screen with a rock.

I'm sorry for your father. It is always regrettable when we are forced to kill, and we prefer to do it cleanly, so I'm sorry he got shot and burned. That's not how we normally do business. How come the rest of the tribe blamed you, though?

"Because I brought your man's phone into our village. I led you right to us."

Nonsense. We were already on our way. Sure, the signal helped the drones zero in, but we already knew where you people lived. Tribal villages are kinda easy to spot when you just fly a bunch of bird drones overhead. You folk probably didn't even notice we'd been tracking you for months – ever since your daddy turned us down. So there: I hope that sets your little conscience free. Your village was gonna burn today regardless of whether you took my guy's phone. But for what it's worth, I'm glad you did. Because now we are acquainted, and we get to have this little chat.

"I... I'm not to blame?"

Chava, all you have done is explore the natural curiosities of youth. If they're saying that's wrong, then that's the arrogance of the older generations. Hell, on my side we encourage ambition. We must all dream of a better life, surely?

"But your people are evil... You destroyed Mazonil..."

This place was broken long before I got squirted into it. I'm just making the best of a bad situation. Which is more than can be said for the Centada.

"What do you mean?"

Your way of life. It's so backward.

"It's traditional. We look after the forest. It's been this way for... for millennia."

I avert my gaze, worried he'll see into my doubt as I try to defend my people.

All right then, answer me this. If your way of life is the better one, then how come my people sleep on real beds, with full bellies, electricity and air conditioning, and all the modern comforts we desire, while you folk root around in the dirt, building houses out of mud and leaves, and letting each other die from simple injuries like bullet wounds?

His last words bring my eyes back to his hologram like lightening. It's like he's *trying* to anger me. But I can't think of anything to counter his claims. The video I saw is undeniable. A city, with dancing, and food, and lights. While my people have nothing.

The people running your tribe have lied to you, haven't they? I can see it in you. Your curiosity has been punished because they're scared of the truth getting out: that there's a better life on the other side. That once people discover it, they won't come back. So they've kept you all in ignorance, forcing your tribe to regress to the squalid ways of our ancestors. For a freethinking mind like yours, that must be pure torture. Am I right?

"It's been... hard," I admit.

No doubt. You have been oppressed; kept under the thumb by the generations above you. And now they've kicked you out for daring to question their hypocrisy. I tell you what, stranger. I'm going to make you an offer, the kind I've never made before. I believe we could use someone like you.

"You want me to join you?"

I do indeed.

"After all your side has done to my people?"

And after all your people have done to you? Chava, if your side had been honest from the start, there would be no beef between us now. We would be colleagues, living the same free lives as anyone else.

To think, I proposed this very allegiance to my people just hours ago and they threw me out. Yet now, faced with the choice for real, I'm recoiling as if being confronted by a snake. Am I walking the same path my father walked months ago? Did he have this very conversation?

"Joining you would be the ultimate betrayal of my kind," I reply.

Stop saying 'my people', 'my kind', and wake up already. You. Have. No. People. They kicked you out! And as far as I am concerned, good riddance to them. Your mind was wasted on them. I am offering you a way out, and a new people to join. A group where you will be respected. You say you want to get out of the forest and see what the world is really like? Then come and work for me. I'll get you to the city of your dreams, if that is what you wish.

"Is that the city I saw on this man's phone?" I say, unable to control the sudden leap in my voice.

What? That place? No way, that's just the shitty port town of Aquerba! I'm talking about the real deal: Paradise City.

"I have never heard of it."

That is because it was built after your great-grandparents decided to go play in the mud. It's a truly modern island state, hundreds of miles off-shore, where the trillionaires live.

"What does it look like?"

Here, I'll show you.

His fingers appear in the hologram as he taps something in front of his face. The screen refreshes with a video of a stunning, magical empire; the camera footage is soaring over the city, through its streets, between glistening glass buildings, fancy restaurants, and crystal blue waters filled with white yachts.

Pretty neat, huh?

"I have never seen anything like it," I whisper.

Of course, if you would rather spend the rest of your life in exile, in a shrinking forest, avoiding both your own people and mine, I understand.

"No," I blurt, taking both of us by surprise with the force. "That is not what I want."

Then let us work together. I can get you there, if you help me get your tribe's remaining land.

"I can't do that – they'll never go for any kind of deal. Some of them are already preparing to fight you to the death. I know these people and they will never back down. They would sooner lose their own lives than let you destroy the forest without resistance."

Stax sighs, wearily.

I think there are some serious misconceptions about what it is we cartels do. We have one interest, OK? Making money. Our goal is not to kill people. Killing people costs money. We want to make money.

"But I just told you: my people will fight to the death. You won't have a choice but to kill them."

Ah, but that is where you come in. You can save them from their own stupidity.

"How? They won't listen to me."

I'm not expecting you to persuade them to change plans. You just need to deliver something to them.

"Another fire drone?" I snap.

Not if you play your part right. You need to go back to them with a peace offering. Some fruit or vegetables or grass or whatever it is you people eat. Something they'll welcome. Say you are sorry, make them believe you, so that they are receptive to your peace token. Then you are going to lace it with a sleeping agent.

"You want me to drug my tribe?"

They are not your tribe anymore, remember? They kicked you out. Besides, either you do this or I send more pyro drones in. It is up to you.

"What will you do to them when they're unconscious?"

My men will relocate your old tribe to an indigenous reserve in the North. They will be well compensated for the land, too, so they will be arriving there as rich citizens in a habitat they know and understand. But for once they will have the ability to trade with outsiders too, should they wish.

"And if I do this for you, you will take me to Paradise City, to live with the trillionaires?"

Stax laughs, warmly, his red lipstick creasing into his moustache.

You will have to do more than one job if you want to live

there, chava. But the sooner you start earning, the sooner you can buy your ticket out of here. My cartel pays its people well. You will not regret joining us. Do we have a deal?

My heart is pounding as the words leave my mouth.

"Si. We have a deal. But wait, how am I going to administer the sleeping agent?"

I am dispatching a courier drone to your location which will have everything you need. Sit tight, it will be with you within the hour. I shall await word from you once the Centada are unconscious. My men will start getting into position now, and will be on standby for your signal.

"How do I message you? I do not know how to use this thing."

Oh, yeah, erm... What model did my guy have again? I think it's the G500 series... Hold down the central button, then scroll down a bunch of times, tap the screen twice, then compose the message. Then for contacts, let's see... Uh... You know what? After this call, just say to the phone 'silent mode', then keep the phone turned on. When you're ready, just say 'redial' out loud and the phone will dial me back, you won't need to press anything.

"Got it."

Good. As soon as we get your call, my men will make their move.

It takes me several stomach-churning hours to retrace my steps to the tribe. Only thirty adults remain; the warriors who chose to stay and fight. My approach must be careful and submissive. It is dusk, and the last thing I want is for them think I am an ambush. As I get closer, my nerves rocket. These people could strike me down upon sight.

My back is sore and scratched from carrying thirty pounds of durian all this way; nature's spikiest fruit. Either Stax was being vindictive, knowing it would be painful for me, or tactical, knowing the warriors would welcome this huge calorie yield. The prerecorded message on his drone had said the fruit was already laced with sedative. Meaning I just need to share it out.

"Halt!" comes a cry from the camp. "Who goes there?"

I freeze in my tracks, my ears pricked to the sounds of multiple bows being pulled taut.

"It is me, Pabla. I am sorry for everything... I have brought food..."

Anam steps forwards with a look of disgust.

"You have been exiled, Pabla. There is no coming back."

"I was exiled by elder Tanok. Is he still here?"

"He has retreated North with the others."

"Then I am looking at the bravest of my tribe. And I wish to offer my skills as a warrior to help you defeat the cartel."

"She is not one of us!" cries Kabil, lurking in the shadows.

"Quiet! Let's hear her out," snaps Anam. "Truly, why are you here, Pabla? Oriana said she'd kill you if you came back."

"I know. And I hope that proves to you the depth of my remorse; that I am risking my life, to offer myself to you all for the fight against our enemies."

"You brought the enemy to our door," hisses Kabil.

"She didn't *know* that's what she was doing," replies Anam. "She only made that mistake because your generation lied to the rest of us!"

Kabil mutters to himself by the fire, while Anam surveys my offering.

"You carried these here?"

"Si. You can't fight on an empty stomach."

Anam considers, then calls out to the group.

"Pabla has brought sustenance and seeks our forgiveness. She wants to fight with us, and I say we need all the warriors we can get. I say we allow her to demonstrate her repentance, in joining us in this sacred fight. Does anyone disagree?"

"Just take the food," says Kabil.

"Don't be an asshole, Kabil" snaps Anam.

There's a tense silence, while Anam casts her eyes around the assembly.

"Very well. Welcome home, Pabla."

The taut bows in the shadows around me slacken, and the archers return to their campfires. The word "home" rings in my ears as I follow Anam to the field kitchen; a simple log with a machete resting in it.

"Thank you, Anam. I swear I am here to do what is best for the tribe," I quake.

"Good. You can start by serving up your peace offering. Everyone is ravenous."

She slopes off to talk tactics with some of the others, while I chop the durian fruits into half portions. It doesn't take long, and I am soon offering this pungent fruit around the tribe, with repeated words of contrition. Each time someone offers their forgiveness, I feel another pang of guilt. I can only hope, when they all wake up in the Northern reserve some time from now, that they thank me for what I am doing to save their lives.

The last thing I want is to see my people go on a pointless suicide mission. After years of living in the technological dark ages, we have fallen so far behind the supposed enemy that death is the only outcome for those who choose to fight. We must evolve our outlook, embrace and discover the world beyond our territories, and stick together to survive. Fighting losing battles benefits no one. Earning riches in exchange for land we cannot defend? It is the only sensible thing to do.

"What's going on here?" comes a sharp voice.

Oriana is standing across the fire from me, with a full quiver of freshly carved arrows over her shoulder. The whittling blade is still in her hand. Strapped to the center of her chest is the precious vial of black forest algae.

"Sister... I have come for forgiveness," I say.

My eyes are welling up. Partly from the guilt of having to deceive them all just to protect them, and partly because those words are true. With our parents dead, and having been dispossessed by the tribe, my sister is the one thing I have left in this world to care about. Her forgiveness is what I crave most. I need to know she doesn't blame me for our father's death.

In a flash, she drops the quiver of arrows to the ground and loads one into her bow. The fire is glowing in her eyes as she hold the tension, her aim poised at my heart. The black caiman tattoo glistens across her forehead.

"How can I forgive you for what you did?"

"Because I am asking you to, sister, and you are all I have left."

Her lip quivers as she glares at me. She drops the bow, turns her back on me, and retreats to a group in the shadows. I finish handing out the remaining portions, then take the last piece to her.

"My peace offering, sister. I know it is not much, but it is a start. I have pledged myself to protecting our people no matter what. I hope you can believe that."

Oriana contemplates my words with a vice-like jaw, icily snatching the fruit from my hands.

"I thought you were going north with the others? Taking the vial to the stronghold?" I ask, tentatively.

"The elders agreed that I stand a better chance of reaching the North alone. After all, one person can react and hide more nimbly than an entire village of refugees. So I am staying one night with the warriors, before we part ways at dawn. They will go to what is left of our village and kill the cartel men working there. I will go north and get the algae to safety."

A splutter from across the camp interrupts our conversation. Kabil is choking on his fruit. I am astonished the old fool is even here. I am not sure what threat he poses as a warrior if he cannot even swallow his own dinner.

Another splutter, this time from the opposite side. Anam is choking too. Her eyes are bulging as she falls to her knees, clasping her throat. Oriana drops her fruit and rushes to Anam's aid.

All around us, sounds of choking erupt across the camp. The warriors fall to the ground, frothing at the mouth, their bloodshot eyes staring wildly, screaming silently for help as their lungs drown in their own fluid.

Oriana turns to me, aghast.

"What have you done?" she cries.

"It wasn't supposed to go like this!"

Before I can answer, the sound of rotor blades fills the air. Drones are speeding towards the camp, their spotlights intensifying as they close in. The forest crackles with the sound of people rushing through the foliage.

Stax's voice echoes from the drones overhead.

You are surrounded, amigues. If you are not yet dead, do yourself a favor and surrender now.

"They... they said it was a sedative!" I cry.

Oriana is shaking her head in disbelief. She is scanning the forest around us, watching for movement, choosing her direction of escape.

"Please, sister, stay. You cannot outrun them! Come with me, I beg you. There is a new future ahead that we can share together. Forget the algae! Forget the lies we were raised on!"

Tears are streaming down my cheeks as I beg Oriana to stay, but she stares at me like I am a ghost. As the drones' spotlights close in, she sprints for the forest, vanishing into the darkness. I drop to my knees with my hands raised above my head, while the dying warriors take their final, rattling breaths around me.

CHAPTER EIGHT

LUKE

Tufts of deep orange fur are scattered across the ground. I'm glancing over my shoulder as we go, kinda creeped out by the empty tribal huts surrounding us. Ramone's kneeling down with his back to us. There's a soft moaning coming from his direction.

"Are they...?" begins Pietro.

Ramone nods.

"I thought they were extinct? This is a miracle!"

"They're in a bad way," says Ramone.

I'm speechless. It's one thing to see an orangutan on old nature documentaries. It's another thing being within touching distance of two living ones.

"Mother and child," says Ramone, softly.

"Which means there must be a father somewhere in the forest, too!" says Pietro.

"Assuming he's not dead. Whatever has got these two might have already gotten him."

The mother's fur has fallen out in clumps, leaving bare patches of raw skin across her body. Her fingernails have fallen off and her eyelids are blistered. Frankly, this poor creature looks like she was mugged then doused in bleach.

She's barely conscious, trying feebly to swat us away from the infant clinging to her chest. The baby orangutan shrinks into its mother's patchy fur, gripping her tightly with all four limbs and hiding its face from us. Even for an infant, its arms look spindly and emaciated.

"Are they gonna make it?" I ask.

"Make it where?" grunts Ramone. "This is their home. If they cannot live here, what is there for them? A cage in a zoo? A cage in a laboratory?"

"He's got a point, Ramone, we need to get them out of here if we're gonna treat them. This looks like severe river poisoning, it's way beyond what we can handle. We need to call someone," says Pietro.

"You two gringos are still thinking like you're back home. Mazonil is a failed state. We are in the middle of the jungle. Cartels are active in all directions around us, and poachers too. If we make a call, we are broadcasting our location to every bandit in a two hundred mile radius. We might as well send up a flare."

"But we cannot simply leave them to die like this – they could be the last two orangutans in existence!" cries Pietro.

"Dammit I know!" snaps Ramone. "I need to think."

While Ramone gets up and paces I take his place, kneeling down beside the drowsy, sickly pair. I reach a tentative hand out and stroke the infant's delicate fur. The creature whimpers and presses itself closer to its mother's chest. She stirs, her blistered eyelids fluttering once more before she falls still.

"How long do they have?" I whisper.

"Hours, unless we can do something fast," says Pietro.

Ramone's voice sounds from behind some huts. He's

talking to someone. A few moments later, he paces back, clutching a phone. I'm curious as to what else he's got stashed in that backpack of his, but now's not the time to ask.

"I have spoken to a contact. They know how important this is, and they are sending a specialist drone to collect both animals. But we have to move from here."

"But this spot is secluded, no?" says Pietro. "The river gives us an escape option if cartel people come by land, and vice versa."

"The drone is flying to a secure landing place," replies Ramone.

"How? You said it yourself: this is a failed state, there *are* no secure landing spaces," says Pietro.

"There's an old military outpost twelve miles from here. It is still protected by a vertical air corridor."

"Er, mind filling me in on that one?" I interject.

"It is a standard feature across Mazonilian military bases. A signal jammer blocks all vertical signals up to cruising altitude. It was developed during the civil war; a way for the old government to resupply bases without cartels intercepting their drones."

"And you're sure these signal jammers are still active, a decade after the government lost?"

"They run on radioactive isotopes."

"Woah. Your government was digging in for the long haul. Wait, are we gonna get cancer if we go to this base? That would be a real bad choice for me right now. I didn't tell you guys but I kinda got a personal health situation going on that's-"

"-That is not our concern, gringo," interrupts Ramone.

"Roger that, big guy."

"Do not worry, the fuel cells are encased," whispers Pietro.

For once, I'm glad that lizard boy's around.

"How are we gonna get the orangutans to the old military base?" he continues, addressing Ramone.

"The base is by the river, we can use the canoe but we need to move fast. The cartels will already be triangulating our signal. They'll be coming for our organs, but when they see we are harboring two orangutans, it will be game over for all of us. Get ready to lift, and be as gentle as you can. You two weaklings take a leg each, I will take the mother's arms. Let's go."

Ramone cuts the outboard motor and lets the canoe nudge into the silty shore. The journey's taken us over an hour, and the mother orangutan has become unresponsive.

At a glance, there's nothing to distinguish this patch of beach from any other forest river bank for miles around. But on closer inspection, small horizontal slits are protruding from the earth. The lower portions are covered by mud, but the upper sections are unmistakably rectangular. There, hiding beneath ten years of soil and leaves, is our bunker.

Ramone stows his GPS tracker away and hops into the shallows, ready to lift. Pietro and I follow, and the three of us drag the animals up the shore as carefully as possible. The infant is distressed by our presence, clinging to its mother, wondering why she won't answer its cries.

"How do we get into this thing?" I ask.

"I don't know but we need to do it fast. The cartels will have been following our GPS signal. We need to get out of sight at once."

We place the orangutans on the ground and split up, all searching for a way into the bunker. I'm kicking dirt off the roof, looking for a hatch, but I can't see anything, just solid concrete. I hastily replace the disrupted matter, so it blends with the rest.

"This way!" calls Pietro.

Ramone and I join him by a row of trees further up the shore. He's found a hatch in between two ancient trunks. It's unlocked, which would make sense for a building abandoned by an army that gave up after it stopped receiving pay checks.

The flap is made of rotting slats of wood, and creaks as Pietro lifts it up. The underside reveals a teeming metropolis of bugs, causing Pietro to leap back in disgust. The hatch slams shut, spraying all of us in dirt and insects.

"Useless city boys, the pair of you," mutters Ramone.

Without flinching, he pops the hatch open and shines a torch inside the dusty subterranean cabin.

"We need to find the drone pad," he says, craning his neck.

"Won't it be above ground?" muses Pietro.

"There will be a hatch down there that they used for launches."

"How will we know what it looks like?" I ask.

"Look for the thing that looks like a hatch with a big radioactive signal jammer underneath it, gringo."

OK, I deserved that. We retrieve the sickly animals and lower them into the bunker, then seal ourselves in. I've not spent time in a disused jungle war bunker before, but I can safely say I've never hated anything more in my entire life.

There's like a bazillion creepy crawlies down here and it's dark as fuck. Ramone rigs up some light cubes from his bag, which reveal the extent of the bunker. It is *way* bigger than I expected. This is clearly the limousine version of bunkers. I wonder if they used to do bachelorette parties down here?

If anything, the lighting's making things worse. Now I can see every tiny wriggling bloodsucker crawling across the walls.

"Relax, they're herbivores," says Pietro, reading my mind. "Mostly."

He splits off from Ramone and heads off with a flashlight, exploring the opposite direction of the bunker. I'm rooted to the spot, trying not to scream.

You ever have that feeling as a kid when you were goofing around with a friend or relative and getting tickled, then they would playfully torture you by waggling their fingers just above your skin? I swear to God, that was worse than the actual tickling, just *horrible*. That's how I'm feeling right now. Like this whole freakin' room is waggling its insecty legs at me, waiting to strike at any moment.

"This could be something?" calls Pietro.

Stifling my bug inhibitions, I move through the concrete doorway to join him. He's dusting down a circular pad with a large, military-font "D" printed on top. Presumably, it stands for "Drone." Either that or the former army was a depressingly non-inclusive workplace. With a weird performative angle. Actually, I guess that would make this some kinda dick podium? Which one might consider inclusive, but to a different demographic, and probably not in the healthiest of ways.

"We need to get the hatch open," says Ramone, joining us.

He climbs onto the dick podium – I mean drone platform – and feels the ceiling for joints. In the old world, I would've put a dollar bill in his waist and asked him to dance. Ramone seems like the kind of guy who would've dragged me outside and drowned me in the bleach river, but it would've been worth it for the look on his face.

Pietro's trying a lever on the wall but it's defunct.

"I think we have to open it manually," he says.

"Gringo, get up here and help me push," snaps Ramone.

"My name's Luke. You do know that, right?"

"Never asked, never cared. Hurry up."

I clamber up beside him and stoop down so as not to scalp myself against the ceiling.

"My surname is Remini, by the way. Not that you care," I groan, straining to press the hatch upwards.

"I do not," grunts Ramone.

"It's a portmanteau. Remandaro from my mother's side, and Mincusa from my father."

Ramone ignores me and groans with effort, forcing the stiff hatch open. Pietro climbs up beside me and helps me push my half, which is probably twice the weight of Ramone's side.

"Aren't you gonna ask about the 'i'?" I pant.

"What?" grunts Ramone, straining over the final inches.

"Where does the 'i' in Remini come from?"

"Genetic donor?" interjects Pietro.

"Yes! How did you know?"

"Deduction. You lack the emotional versatility of someone raised in a polyamorous family, so a chromosomal donor makes more sense. May I guess, mitochondrial transfer?"

"Ah dammit, I just remembered you're an academic. OK, I'm revoking your quiz points. Now you're just killing my buzz."

"You two, hurry up!" says Ramone.

He reaches over the pair of us and shoves the flap fully open.

Sunlight and fresh air flood the drone pad, while bits of mulch and dead leaves blow in from the sides.

"We could totally make money on this stage, boys."

"What?"

"Your biceps, his ass, my charm. I'm just saying, there's a market for that."

A whirring sounds overhead, cutting my pitch short.

"Get off the pad!" yells Ramone.

"OK, we'll discuss it later-"

He drags me out of the way just in time. A huge transport quadcopter plummets from the sky in a vertical line like a base jumper. Its rotors kick in at the last second, filling the bunker with wind and noise, before it lands on the pad with a delicate thud.

A compartment on top of the quadcopter opens and a tiny camera rises to hover at eye level. Accompanying it is a larger floating cube with a medical cross printed on the side. A woman's face appears projected above it. She's of similar age and complexion to Ramone, and looks deeply concerned.

Ramone, is that you?

"Cynthia! Thank you for doing this!" says Ramone.

Where are the animals?

"Through here – follow me."

You'll need to do exactly as I say, Ramone, and move quickly. The cartels will be tracking this broadcast, and if they clocked the drone arriving, they're gonna move even faster to intercept.

"Understood," says Ramone.

While Pietro re-seals the sky hatch, Ramone leads the way through the bunker. We reach the two orangutans, neither of whom have moved since we laid them down. In fact, the infant's feeble whimpers have fallen silent.

The camera hovers above the two bodies, while the medical cube swoops down low and scans them from all sides.

Oh God, Ramone, this is serious.

"I know, that's why I called you."

No, I mean, neither the mother or child will last the flight back unless we act now.

"What do you mean 'act now'?"

We're going to have to improvise. It's the only shot they have. Oh Christ.

"Cynthia, what are you saying?"

Ramone, we have to do this right now, in situ. We have to operate.

CHAPTER NINE

PABLA

My head is spinning. I am surrounded by the bodies of every last warrior in my tribe. Cartellers are emerging from the trees with guns and backpacks, delighted to see that their enemy has already been wiped out. And who did their dirty work for them?

A drone floats toward me bearing a hologram. I recognize Sergeant Stax at once; his red lips are parted into an insidious grin.

Great job, Pabla, you really delivered.

"You lied to me, you bastard! You said they would be safe!"

I am so filled by shock I cannot shout, but my voice trembles with rage. Stax looks amused, pointedly looking away from the camera to groom his Mohawk.

Around me the cartellers are putting up huge white discs, flooding the forest with light as strong as day. Others are dragging the bodies into a pile. Stack's hologram rotates as he takes in the site, admiring his work.

I did not lie, chava, I just skipped to the inevitable

conclusion for your people. You told me they would fight to the death. So I sped things up.

Around me, a modular factory line is being assembled. As more machines are added, chainsaws roar into action behind them. Trees crash to the ground. Birds squawk in distress as their nests fall beneath them.

The trunks are fed straight into the factory line where the first unit shreds them into woodchip. The chip is then mixed with some granules which seem to extract all the moisture, releasing plumes of steam. The dry tinder is then burned in a speed furnace, where the ash is filtered and refined into black powder. This feeds into a separate machine, which appears to be printing long, ultra-thin beams and hexagonal structures. I think it is building more machines.

There's a commotion across the camp, followed by gunshots and cheers. A carteller drags a bloodied deer into the clearing. The men take selfies beside it, laughing and patting each other on the back, then toss the carcass into the wood chipper.

"How can you do that?" I cry.

My men do not eat bush meat, Pabla, they're not savages, laughs Stax.

The operation is expanding with terrifying efficiency. It's as if each time I blink, the forest retreats further away. Newly-printed machines take the place of trees, fueling the exponential rate of destruction.

"Sarge!" cries a carteller, running over.

What? says Stax, his hologram pivoting to face the newcomer.

"The drones have detected a survivor. They're in the forest, not far from here, but they're running away. They appear to be carrying some kind of organic matter that isn't on the database, but we think it could be pluridium causing a reading error."

My heart freezes. They've found Oriana.

Holy crap, that would be the catch of the year! But why would a native have pluridium? Pabla, do your people know about the rare earth minerals here?

"We're not interested in what's below the ground," I reply. "Our lives are above it."

Hmm. I don't buy it. I think they know exactly what they're carrying, and they wanna sell it to another cartel. Soldier, find that native and bring them in.

"We can't, Sarge, they shot the drone down."

So they're a warrior? Interesting.

Stax's drone turns to face me.

What's a lone warrior doing in the forest running away with something mysterious, when all the others were camped out here, sharpening their little arrows?

"They're probably trying to outrun you, you piece of shit," I snap.

Ha! I love your spirit, Pabla. Is that the right phrase? You people are all about spirits and hoodoowhatsit, aren't you? Or at least you were.

I'm glaring at Stax, resisting the urge to grab a branch and beat the crap out of his floating drone like a piñata. I know it wouldn't cause the man any bodily damage, wherever he is in real life, but it would satiate my rage.

What are they carrying?

"How should I know? Nothing valuable. We're simple forest people, after all. All about the hoodoowhatsit, isn't that right?"

We shall see.

Stax swivels around to face the carteller.

Take a comrade and go find the native. Bring me

whatever they're carrying. Oh, and keep them alive – we only get a good price if the organs are fresh.

"But Sarge, how am I gonna find them without the drone?"

Take another drone? Night vision goggles? I don't care how you do it, just get it done. Screw it, take Pabla with you.

"Me?"

"Her?"

Yes, and yes. She knows her people. She'll know how to track them.

The fact that my people do not track at night is moot. This is my only chance to save my sister, and I have to take it.

I expect you two and the captive back here within the hour. Any longer than that and I'll be docking your pay. Pabla, you want to escape this godforsaken country? Then move fast.

We have reached the drone's last location and now it's over to me. Using the cartel's night vision goggles, I search for footprints and signs of disturbance in the ground. I hold my hand out behind me, signaling for the carteller to halt, but the idiot keeps moving.

"Stop!" I hiss.

He frowns at me. "Uh... OK... Why?"

I point to the ground below us. We are on a ledge overlooking an embankment. There is stream fed by a tiny waterfall which is barely taller or wider than me. A set of foot prints descend the earthy embankment then double back on themselves, vanishing from sight beneath us. The fact that they do not reappear on the other side suggests to me that Oriana is sheltering directly below us. What state she is in I have no idea; I do not know what that last drone was equipped with. We have not seen any blood yet, but she may still be hurt; the cartel has so many ways to inflict pain and not all of them break the flesh.

"I think the native is below us," I whisper, gesturing clearly to the carteller.

The man peers over the edge, but there is no way of seeing underneath the rocky overhang. Lying down flat, he prepares his gun.

"You go down there and flush them out. Get them onto the other side of the stream, it will put them in range. Then I can get them with the stun gun," he says.

The fact he's lying down to whisper this plan is surely broadcasting our position to my sister below. But I cannot see a way to disagree with him without it looking suspicious, so I give him a nod.

If Oriana thinks a carteller is approaching, she will lay in wait with an arrow ready. I need to warn her it is me approaching. I am really counting on her *not* wanting me dead right now, despite everything she said before.

As I descend the muddy slope, I let out a bird call. It is the call we devised as children, to mean 'danger coming'. Back then, 'danger' meant one of our parents was angry because we had strayed too far from the village. I am praying she understands me now.

I make another chirp, taking care to project the whistles towards a tree so the carteller can't pinpoint the source. I reach the base of the embankment, where the footsteps turn back. There's a rock between my current position and the overhang by the stream, where the carteller is perched. He gestures at me to hurry up.

Skirting behind the rock, I duck down to plan my

approach. The next few seconds are critical. I have to show my face to Oriana, try to warn her about the guy directly above her who is trying to shoot her, while hoping she is not so enraged with me that she tries to kill me on sight. With another quick bird call and a deep breath, I peer out above the rock.

"Oriana? We need to tal-"

I hit the deck, narrowly dodging an arrow aimed right at my head. I think we can agree she is still pissed.

"Oriana! Quit it, I'm trying to help!" I hiss.

"What you say?" calls the carteller.

As I lean out from behind the rock another arrow pins me back.

"Big sister, cut it out! I'm trying to talk to you right now!" I cry.

"You have no right to call me that! Not after everything you've done," she retorts.

She sounds angry. The sort of boiling anger that would make most people shake too much to shoot cleanly. Not Oriana. She has always been ruthlessly effective. And tirelessly principled. It is suddenly a lethal combination for me.

I make a bird call again, trying to remind her of the danger overhead, but she is not interested.

"Whistle all you like, Pabla, but our childhood died with Papai. Trying to manipulate my emotions so that I let my guard down will achieve nothing."

"Idiota, I am trying to warn you of the guy above your head waiting to shoot you!" I reply.

"What? This was *not* the deal," yells the carteller.

"Cry me a river, asshole. Your cartel just poisoned my entire tribe!" I yell.

"Only because *you* betrayed us," interjects Oriana.

"*Thank* you," says the carteller, vindicated.

"Go fuck yourself, cartel pig!" Oriana yells.

"You people are a *lot* ruder in real life than in the folk tales."

"You like folk tales, huh?" snaps Oriana. "Have you heard the one about the youngest daughter who betrayed her entire family?"

"OK, that is *really* immature, Oriana," I retort. "You are being all passive aggressive from your little warrior cave over there."

"That's rich coming from the traitor hiding behind a rock!"

"I'm *above* the rock," says the carteller, puzzled.

"No-one's talking about you!" Oriana and I yell, in sync.

"Aww, see? You are still my big sis, Oriana. Please can we just talk this whole thing over?"

"I always knew you were a psychopath," she yells.

"Oh, so wanting a better life and thinking technology could actually *help* us makes me a psychopath does it?"

"I watched a soap once that said it would make you a sociopath," muses the carteller.

"Shut *up!*" we yell, again in sync.

"I told dad a bunch of times that there was something wrong in your head, but he never believed me. Now because of you he is dead!"

"You know it's not as simple as that!"

"Mew-*mew*-mew-mew-"

"Oh, *real* mature, Oriana."

"You want mature, little sister? How is this for mature?"

There's a *thunk*, then a whistling, first getting distant, then closer by the second. Out of nowhere, an arrow drops vertically from the sky and implants itself deep into the ground beside me, just inches from my thigh.

"Hey, *not cool*! That nearly hit me!"

"Which way did I miss?" she calls. "Actually, never mind, I can figure it out from your screams."

Another arrow plunges into the ground, this time practically shaving my opposite leg. The next one's gonna skew me like a kebab. There's nothing for it. I have to charge. With a cry of anger, I leap over the rock, ripping off my night vision goggles. I shine my flashlight directly in Oriana's eyes, blinding her and knocking her third shot off-target.

She tries to reload but I am on her in a heartbeat, tackling her to the ground. The light gets knocked from my hand as we roll through the dirt, grunting and screaming as we beat the hell out of each other.

"You... traitor!" she grunts, kneeing me hard in the groin, fully against the rules of our childhood scraps.

"Ouch, dead leg! You piece of shit, you know that is not allowed!" I yelp.

"Everyone is gone because of you!"

"I was trying to help them! That's what I have been trying to tell you all along! I made a deal to guarantee our safety but the cartel double-crossed me."

"Of course they did you fucking moron, they are a *cartel*!"

"Don't... call... me... a... moron!"

As she tries to strangle me, I pull on her hair. She grabs mine in retaliation. I punch her in the stomach. She elbows me in the eye. Oh crap, she is reaching for an arrow. That *puta* is gonna stab me! I throw myself on her leg but she kicks me in the collar bone, winding me. Rising onto her knees with a cry, she lifts the arrow with both hands, preparing to pierce my belly.

A burst of blue fills the rocky underpass and Oriana freezes, rigid.

"*Guau*. And I thought *my* family had issues," says the carteller.

He chuckles at his own joke as Oriana groans, saliva dribbling from her open mouth.

"Better take that thing away just in case the stun wears off – safety first," says the carteller.

He plucks the arrow from Oriana's hands and pushes her over. She lands on her side, rigid, with her arms raised above her raging head. My eyes fall on the object behind her; the vial of algae. *Mierda*, the carteller sees it too.

"Hiding in plain sight! I guess we don't need her alive after all," he cheers.

He flicks the stun gun and the sight turns from blue to red. As he takes aim at Oriana I throw myself forward, knocking him to the ground. The gun discharges, scorching the rock above her head.

"That's... my... sister!" I yell.

We are struggling in the mud. He is stronger than me, and no stranger to messy fist fights. I smash his hand against a rock, forcing him to drop the gun. He punches me hard in the jaw, throwing me backward. He lunges for the gun again but I kick it into the water, where the current takes it. With a yell, he throws himself at me. I grab Oriana's discarded arrow and thrust upwards. The tip pierces the man's stomach and tears inwards, moving up to his lungs.

The carteller's eyes bulge and blood splutters from his mouth. His weight slumps across me, limp. With a good deal of effort, I wriggle out from under him and kick his body over, rolling him twice until he falls into the stream.

I watch his body float away face-down in the moonlit waters. My body aches like hell but I am still in one piece. I wash the blood from my face then return to the rocky underpass, where I prop the discarded flashlight up in the corner, giving it an almost cozy ambience. I move Oriana's hunting equipment out of reach, just in case, then tenderly pull her up into a seated position.

The stun gun is wearing off, making her limbs malleable. I lean her back against the rock and sit beside her, taking the opportunity to catch my breath, while she waits for her brain to recover. Several minutes pass before she grunts a single word at me: "Talk."

"I am sorry, big sister, for everything that was my fault. I was naïve, twice, and it could have cost the lives of people I love. From father, to our tribe's warriors."

"Could have?" she splutters, indignantly.

"The truth is, the cartel were tracking us long before I took the phone into our village. Sergeant Stax, their commander, said they were going to burn us either way."

Oriana stares out to the river, not indicating whether this is good news or if she even believes it.

"You did more than just look at the phone, though, didn't you, Pabla? You spoke to them. Admit it." she says.

"Si. I spoke to them."

"Why?"

"Because you left me no choice! You had me exiled!"

"Because I thought you caused father's death! *And* the destruction of our home."

"So that is how you treat people in such a situation, sister?"

"Er, *yes*. It is literally the law."

"Then the law is *estúpida*. In fact, everything we have ever been told is either stupid, or a lie, or both," I say.

"You are still angry about the cities?" says Oriana.

"And you are not? We could have been living there!" I reply.

"Why? They are places of depravity and greed. Our way of life is pure, we bring balance to nature. They destroy it."

"How can you say such things when you have never seen one!"

Oriana avoids my gaze for a moment.

"Oriana? Is there something you're not telling me?" I ask.

She shifts uncomfortably. "Father took me to the city eight months ago."

My mouth is gaping but no words come. My father, the Inkmaster, devout upholder of our customs and ways, went to a city? *With* Oriana? And all the while they both pretended they did not know about cities, or hospitals, or the genetically engineered algae inside us. No, instead they upheld the elders' lies. Piously insisting that technology caused all the cities to crumble and Mazonilian society to collapse.

"You fucking hypocrites!" I splutter.

"We were only trying to do the same thing as you claim you were with the phone, Pabla. We were protecting the tribe."

"By going to a place you told us all did not exist?"

"Father had the elders' blessing."

"Of course he did! Those old bastards never said a word of truth in their lives, did they?"

"This was a one-off, Pabla. We met with the cartel to discuss a deal after other tribes in our area sold their land. The cartel offered us a large sum of money, or at least what they claimed was a large sum, and we agreed to the deal."

My head is doing cartwheels right now. This is too much. They *agreed* to a deal with the cartel?

"We sold fifty percent of our ancestral land to the cartel. In return, they promised to protect us from other cartels, and not to encroach any further on our remaining territory. At the time, it was the best way to protect the forest and the tribe."

"Yet here we are, eight months later, sister, and they just burned down the entire village!"

"That was a different cartel," says Oriana, shaking her head. "The group we allied with got into a turf war with Stax and his men. Our allies lost. We retreated into the forest and the elders vowed to make no more deals. Why do you think father took up patrolling as a warrior again? He felt personally responsible, like he had to undo his mistake and protect us all."

"He could have protected us by letting us move to a city!"

"Cities are nothing like the video you saw, Pabla! They are terrible places, filled with violence and pollution."

"Maybe, but they also have *hospitals*. All this time you have been blaming me for Papai's death. Yet *I* was the one who said we should take him to a hospital, and you shouted me down!"

"He wouldn't have needed a hospital if you had shot that carteller properly the first time!" snaps Oriana.

"Did you even want him to survive? Or did you want to take over as Inkmaster already?" I fume.

"How *dare* you!" gasps Oriana.

"You kept so many secrets from me, big sister. You and Papai knew about the algae and the cities. Maybe this was all just another secret deal you two struck?"

"Take that back!" cries Oriana.

"What about mother, hey? She's dead too because of your lies!"

"Mother knew."

"What?"

"Papai told her the truth, and she refused to go to a hospital. She believed it was her time."

From her pocket, Oriana pulls out the pinkish-orange sea shell mother gave us as children.

"Mother never wanted to be hooked up to some machine. She wanted her spirit to return to nature," continues Oriana. "That is what this shell means, sister. Maybe you can think about it next time you betray us all."

She throws the shell at me in anger. I flinch and it misses, striking the rock behind me. I pick it up from the wall and run my thumb over the chipped edge, where a chunk has broken off.

"Mother is dead because you two trapped her in the same sick web of lies you trapped me in. Now I am done with you. The Centada deserved to die. They lied to their own kind and hid from the truth. You people got what you deserved."

"Say that again," growls Oriana.

"Or what?"

"*Puta*, those warriors died because of your idiocy, and now you disrespect them like this! I will kill you myself and avenge their spirits. It will be all *you* deserve!"

She tries to stand but her limbs are still weak from the stun gun and she collapses to the ground.

"Goodbye forever, Oriana. The last warrior, the last Inkmaster, the last daughter of a failed tribe. What a legacy you leave behind you," I say, derisively.

As I walk away, she spits sand from her mouth and splutters with hatred, "Next time I see you, Pabla, I will end you! I will avenge the warriors you betrayed, and I will restore our tribe's honor!"

I do not reply. She can think that all she likes, but she will never see me again. That miserable, deluded soul cannot escape this cage of greenery; she cannot follow me where I am going. No matter what it takes, I am getting myself to the city.

I return to camp as dawn breaks. It has changed radically overnight, courtesy of the cartel and their machines. I almost don't recognize it, save for one detail: the pile of dead Centada warriors in the middle.

Men with chainsaws work ceaselessly to feed the machines, which continue building themselves out of the ashes of the chipped and burned wood. Opposite them, other machines are printing more of the long, slender blades. To what end, I do not know.

A dozen cartellers are surveying the cleared land on foot, each with a scanning device.

You're late.

Stax's hologram appears in front of me, his drone hovering uncomfortably close to my face.

Where's the other one?

"You don't even know his name?"

There are many faces in my division. He was new, and I was testing him out. You made it back, as I expected. But not within the hour we agreed. I'll have to dock your wages.

"I was required to do more than tracking, because of your man's inadequacies. If anything, you should be paying me double."

So you are still interested in getting paid, huh?

"Yes. And paid well, at that."

Where is the pluridium I sent you both to retrieve?

"False alarm."

I see. And what exactly happened to the other guy?

"The river took him. Nothing I could do."

Was that before or after you stabbed him and threw him in it?

Stax plays me an audio recording from the dead man's phone.

"If you know what happened, then why have you not killed me already?"

Because you proved your worth, Pabla.

"By killing one of your guys?"

You proved that you can track better than my men, and are more reliable than my drones. I am an ambitious soul, Pabla, and I plan on controlling the entire South one day. To do that, I need to flush out the last of the forest people. There are still thousands of your kind scattered around and I have only a hundred men. I need someone who can speed things along. Someone who gets it.

"You want me to betray more forest people for you?"

Call it betrayal if you want. I prefer to think of it as liberation. After all, there's a whole world out there just waiting to be seized by those who dare. You strike me as one of those people, Pabla. A pragmatist.

"You burned down my home and made me poison our warriors, what makes you think I want to join you?"

You came back. Because it is this, or living alone in the jungle forever. So do we have a deal or not?

An explosion rocks through the clearing as a green fireball swells from the ground, climbing several yards into the air before vanishing as instantly as it appeared. A portable scanning device falls to the ground with a thud. Two severed hands are stuck clinging to the side grips.

A lone carteller is rolling across the mud screaming in agony, while blood gushes from his wrist stumps.

That's more like it! cheers Stax.

His drone speeds towards the man and I follow, perplexed. Stax hovers by the fallen scanner and reads the display, whooping and hollering to himself, while the injured carteller writhes in pain.

Two more cartellers rush to their fallen peer with a medical kit. One of them splits off and grabs the toasted scanner, prizing the severed hands from the device. The heat of the explosion has melted the man's skin to the metal. The carteller rips each hand off with a gooey squelch.

The other newcomer has unpacked the medical kit and is letting it tend to his fallen comrade. The kit looks a damned sight newer and shinier than the rusty piece of crap we used back in the village to try and save Papai.

A periscope rises from the kit box and examines the patient, who is still bawling and rocking in agony. A strip emerges from the side and the carteller tears it off, sticking it to his colleague's neck. The injured man stops screaming at once and a soft, fuzzy smile spreads across his face. He sits up and looks at his bleeding stumps and giggles like he is drunk, then tries to stroke his comrade's cheeks with them, finding the whole game hilarious, while he continues to hemorrhage blood.

His friend humors him, keeping him distracted as six robotic tentacles emerge from the medical kit. In less than a minute, the surgical tentacles have reattached the man's hands and the kit has packed itself away. The healed carteller stares at his pristine hands in amazement, now enjoying the medication as a bonus.

My eyes drift to the pile of warrior bodies behind him, where another carteller is soaking them with cans of gasoline. Anger swells inside me. If those proud, pious idiots had only opened their minds a little, our whole community could have embraced technology like this! My father would have been saved in an instant. Maybe even my mother too, and god knows who else. But instead we watched them die because of our elders' lies and their selfish ideals. Looking at that pile of wasted life, of people I knew and loved, I feel sick to the core. But whatever blame is to be apportioned for their premature deaths, I refuse to take it anymore. Their choices were their own.

Stax's drone finishes examining the site of the blast then rises up into the center of the clearing. His voice becomes amplified, as he summons all the workers to gather before him.

Brothers, all your hard work is about to pay off. We have hit the jackpot. We have our first full seam of pluridium!

This is met by wild cheers and whoops of joy from the cartellers. Chainsaws rev and bullets fly in celebration.

As our esteemed colleague just demonstrated, this metal is as dangerous as it is precious. It is highly unstable, and explodes on contact with oxygen. But here's the good news. The world needs superconductors, and one seam of this stuff will fetch a hell of a price. Enough, in fact, for all you assholes to retire rich this very year.

More cheers from the men.

But to extract this seam, we need a highly specialized piece of equipment. That is kit we do not have, and cannot make, boys.

"Won't the CEO send it?" yells a guy from the crowd. "He always sends the big kit!"

He might, but it would take weeks to come. In that time,

if another cartel flies a recon drone this way, we will find ourselves in a turf war with every other motherfucker in Mazonil. However, there is an alternative solution, which I put to you now. There is a cartel a few days' ride from here who have such a drill in their possession. I humbly propose we alleviate them of that particular burden, and take what is rightfully ours from this here ground. What do you say?

A roar of cheers greets Stack's grinning hologram. He nods, sagely.

For this to work, boys, we will be risking our lives. And you know what they say: those who take the risk should get the reward, right? Which is why I am saying we do this one off the books. The CEO doesn't need to know. As far as he's concerned, we are still chopping down trees and drinking moonshine. By the time he gets wind, we'll all be outta this damned country, and you will all be on whatever rich asshole island you want. Who is with me?

The men cheer emphatically. A few of them toss pebbles into the fractured ground, prompting more blasts of green fire and laughter from the crowd.

Hey, enough of that! What bit about another cartel robbing us did you not hear? We need to keep this site secret, which means no goofing around with the green fire. People tend to notice green fire, even from far away! I need to know I can trust you all. If you are ready to be part of this, you must swear your loyalty to me. Take a knee, or take a hike.

One by one, the cartellers drop to their knees and bow their heads, until I am the last person left standing. Stax's drone turns towards me, a calm, indifferent look across his face.

What's it gonna be, Pabla?

My jaw tightens. I turn on my heel and make a beeline for the campfire. Snatching a burning branch from the edge,

I approach the pile of dead warriors. The bloodied foam has dried around their mouths. Many of their eyes are still open, glazed by death. As I stare at their dead bodies, I'm filled with anger. That they did this to themselves; but to all of us. I will not be like them. I will *not* make their mistakes. No more hiding. My fate is mine to choose.

I toss the burning branch at the base of the pyre. Flames erupt upwards, enveloping the bodies in a roaring blaze. I watch, feeling the intense heat burning my skin. Stepping back, I turn to face Stax. Fixing him with a long stare, I bow my head and take a knee.

CHAPTER TEN

LUKE

"Operate *now?*" splutters Pietro.

The skinny academic looks queasy at the very idea, while Ramone looks even more sultry than usual.

We don't have a choice. The mother is in a critical condition, if we don't act now, she'll die within the hour, says the vet, her hologram floating above the two orangutans.

"But it's not sterile down here," protests Pietro. "There's not even a table, we would be doing it on the ground!"

If she gets a secondary infection we can deal with it later. The critical priority is emergency surgery. I need one of you to remove the infant so we can open the mother up.

Ramone tenderly plucks the infant from its mother's chest. The baby whimpers drowsily as the ranger sweeps it into his shoulder, cradling it like a toddler.

Cynthia flies lower and inspects the adult orangutan's abdomen. A red laser dot appears on its body, projected by the drone.

I'm highlighting where to make the first incision, she says.

"This is madness!" shrieks Pietro. "None of us three are surgeons, and the cartel could arrive at any moment. If we open her up now, we won't be able to evacuate her until the surgery's complete. We could lose the opportunity to get her out of her at all," insists Pietro.

Either you do exactly as I say and stop second-guessing me, or you load those two into the drone as they are, and one hour from now I take delivery of two dead orangutans. It's your choice, says Cynthia.

"Could we evacuate the infant first, while the mother has the surgery?" I suggest.

If the cartel arrive that's exactly what you must do. But these are the last two of their kind anywhere on the planet; we're not splitting them up unless all else fails. The infant should be in a better state – the mother's organs will have filtered most of the toxins out before breast feeding. , But low levels are still dangerous to an infant so he also needs urgent attention. Somebody give him fluids from the medikit – the nanobots will begin detoxifying his blood. The other two of you: scrub up.

"With what?" I ask.

There's sanitizer in the box. Roll your sleeves up to your elbows and rub the gel over your hands and arms.

"I can't do this, I'm not good around blood," says Pietro.

I don't doubt him; the guy's swaying just at the mention of it. Ramone places the infant orangutan into Pietro's arms, then nudges the dizzy academic towards the medikit.

"Hydrate the child in the next room so he does not see what's going on in here," says Ramone.

Pietro nods, nervously. Holding the infant seems to be bringing him some comfort. Like a therapy animal. Which is definitely the wrong way round here.

"Roll your sleeves up, gringo" says Ramone.

"Me?"

Oh crap. I just became surgeon number two.

Ramone, I presume you still carry a knife?

"Si."

Sterilize it now. Other guy – Luke, is it? – take the blue pack from the box. Snap it open and inject the pointed end into the side of the orangutan's neck, wherever the fur is thinnest.

I tear the package open and retrieve a tiny syringe, then approach the comatose mother. I kneel beside her. She's lost so much fur there's ample access to raw skin. I inject the anesthetic as instructed.

OK, that should block the pain. Ramone, are you ready to make the first incision?

Ramone kneels on the opposite side and holds the blade above the mother's torso, angling the tip just below her sternum, where Cynthia is shining the laser dot.

Luke, what are you doing sitting down? Bring the medikit closer!

"OK, I appreciate this is a stressful situation for everyone, but it would be great if we could remember some of us are doing monkey surgery for the first time here."

It's not a monkey, it's an ape. Ugh, never mind. Just get the box!

"Can't you fly it closer?"

I'm focusing on the patient right now. Ramone, make the first cut. Luke, I need you to place the green patches across her chest.

"What are they?" I ask.

"How far do I cut?" says Ramone, at the same time.

Luke, the green patches from the box will restart her heart if she goes into cardiac arrest. They need to be parallel to each other. Ramone, cut down to the belly button, where

I'm pointing the dot now. You only want to cut an inch deep, so you're piercing the skin and muscle, not the organs below. Luke, grab four clamps from the box, and the blood filter.

"Uh, which look like...?"

Four clothes pegs and Aladdin's lamp, Christ!

"Got it!"

The clamps are like clothes pegs but with circular forceps. The gold-colored "lamp" has a tapered spout and transparent handle. My triumph vanishes as my attention returns to the ape, where Ramone has cut a full skin flap. It resembles the hatch we climbed through into this bunker. Blood is seeping across the ape's torso.

Luke, I need you to clamp the blood vessels before Ramone cuts away the damaged liver tissue. From my scanners it looks like one of the kidneys has become sceptic so we'll have to remove that completely. This is worse than I thought. Luke, I'm showing you where to clamp now, follow the laser dot.

I reach into the ape's exposed guts and place a clamp around each artery or vein that Cynthia highlights. Each blood vessel becomes fattened like water a balloon.

Good. Now I need you to hold the spout against the left side, between the pancreas and the large intestine. Ugh, between the thing that looks like a leaf, and the squiggly tube.

"Squiggly tube? Come on that's just patronizing. I do have some scientific training, you know?"

In veterinary science?

"No..."

Then nobody down here cares. Hurry up and get the filter in place, up against the first artery you clamped.

The spout is forked like a snake's tongue. As soon as it touches the organ, one of the forks latches onto the artery like a magnet. Blood flows through one half of the spout, disappearing through the golden central body of the "lamp", then streaming through the clear handle and back inside the "lamp".

"Uh, is that supposed to happen?"

Yes. Now, without pulling too hard, move the lamp to the corresponding vein. You're bypassing the organ. Follow the dot I'm shining. See it? Good. Hold the spout closer.

This is super weird. The first end of the spout has stayed embedded in the artery like a crocodile clip, and has revealed an extendable hose-like tube behind it, which is continuing to deliver blood into the "lamp".

I nudge the remaining spout tip against the vein and it latches on. Blood flows through it, this time leaving the lamp and flowing back into the ape's body.

"So just to be clear, your drone's medikit had all this crazy stuff in it, but not a scalpel?"

We can't put dangerous sharps in the cargo drones, just in case an animal wakes up mid-transit and injures themselves in attempts to break out. Besides, these kits aren't intended for full field surgery, they're normally for taking research samples.

"OK, well that might be something to feedback to your organization."

Oh my god are you always like this? Don't answer that. Ramone, are you ready to remove the infected tissue?

"Si. Tell me where to cut."

OK, follow the pattern of discoloration along the bottom half of the liver. The darker half is dead and needs to come out before it starts poisoning her body like those kidneys. Cut diagonally away from the top, like you're slicing it away in layers. There might be healthy tissue below that we can preserve. Luke, put that first blood filter on the ground where it's steady, and grab the orange and yellow packet from the box.

The pack contains a mini canister with a child-lock on top, and a trigger below.

Remove the safety lock and get ready to follow Ramone's knife. OK Ramone, it looks like the entire bottom half is a goner. Cut through to the rear and remove the dead portion. Luke, point that device at the surviving tissue and squeeze the trigger.

Ramone and I do as instructed. With the surviving half of the liver exposed, I lower the device towards it and squeeze. Ice-cold gas rushes out of the cylinder, coating the exposed organ in a kind of frost. I can feel the cold numbing my fingertips, as the metal cylinder itself ices over.

OK, the first organ is cauterized. We need to move on and repeat the procedure for each kidney.

Ramone shoves a clamp into my hand. He seals off one kidney while I do the other. Ugh, my nose is tingling something awful down here. Oh crap, I think I might be allergic to orangutan fur...

"Atchoo!"

What was that?

"Nothing. Distortion on the line," I say, hastily.

"Coño!" yells Ramone, "He just sneezed on the ape!"

"Technically, I think I just sneezed *in* it."

Christ, are you trying to ruin this creature's survival chances or what?

"No! Clearly I have some kind of undiagnosed ape fur allergy."

Why didn't you say so before the surgery!

"What part of *undiagnosed* did you not hear, Cynthia?"

When I said we can handle secondary infections later, I didn't mean go out of your way to cause one!

"Hey, I would appreciate a little less judgement and a little more sympathy, thank you. I've just discovered I have an underlying health condition that could potentially be very debilitating."

"An ape allergy?"

"I'll have you know, thousands of people are forced to take days off work each year because of seasonal allergies, and this orange fur ball is like hay fever with legs. A little more compassion would be – *atchoo!* – Oh crap, now I got another nose bleed. Oops, I think I might have sprinkled the monkey. Is no one gonna say *gesundheit?*"

Get out of the OR! Ramone, you need to finish this yourself, then we should start a course of antivirals immediately.

As I try to stop my nosebleed with tissue from the medikit, a cry echoes out from the tunnel.

"We've got company!" yells Pietro.

He's peering through the window slits overlooking the beach. Ramone abandons the ape for a moment and leaps to the edge of the bunker to see what's coming.

What's going on out there?

"With any luck, a delivery of cetirizine," I sniff.

Ugh, my throat and eyes are really starting to itch too. This is worse than the time my neighbor bought an entire litter of rescue kittens, then died and left me to raise them. Some people are just inconsiderate.

"Cynthia, the cartel have found us. There's a boat coming this way. We have to launch the drone!" cries Ramone.

You can't launch the mother like this, we need to finish operating and close up.

"We don't have a choice, you said this was the only option!"

We're not there yet, dammit. Buy us some time!

"Pietro, can you cause a diversion?" calls Ramone.

"Me?" says Pietro, horrified. "But I'm looking after the baby!"

"Give it to Luke," snaps Ramone.

"Oh, no, I can't take that thing, I'm allergic," I sniff.

"Fine, then Pietro, get your ass in here and help me close up. Luke, get your ass *out* there, and slow those bastards down."

"You expect me to just magic up a diversion out of nothing?" I splutter.

"Check the base, it must have some form of defense!"

Luke, we need five minutes to close or this has all been for nothing.

"What happened to just launching the infant?" says Pietro.

"No one was ever on board with that plan, Pietro. Get over here and make this one work," snaps Ramone.

"Yeah, *Pietro*," I add, smugly. "Atchoo! Ah crap. OK, I'm going."

I climb up from the operating floor, swaying a little from headrush, and stagger to the viewing slit. A speedboat's racing across the river towards us, just visible through the mangroves separating our two channels. They must be tracking Cynthia's signal, because they're making a beeline for us.

Think, Luke, think. If you were a former military bunker designer, what features would you have installed sixty-something years ago with a dwindling budget and limited technology?

Mines!

Hmm... But the cartel's scanners would surely pick them up. Besides, we crossed the water and beach with no problem, so that kinda rules them out. They might have booby-trapped the beach, though, to defend against landers? Seems a long-shot for a water channel. Gah, there's gotta be something lying around this place? Please don't tell me we've sealed ourselves in a concrete tomb...

I'm scrambling through the tunnel, past where Pietro got to. Ramone's lighting runs out here, and Pietro clearly didn't feel like exploring alone in the dark. Me neither. I grab one of Ramone's floor lights and hold it out like a lantern as I hurry through the corridor.

Aha! Seek and you shall find! This is the mother of all good news. It's a god damned bazooka! Or grenade launcher. Or some kind of anti-aircraft gun? OK I have no idea what it is exactly other than a big assed tube mounted on a turret, with a dusty crate next to it that looks *extremely* promising.

The cartel are rounding the mangrove and approaching our shore. I have to act fast. Hauling the lid off the box, I shake bugs and dead insect skins off my hands – ew, ew, ew – and lift out one magnificent, rusty old missile. Time to kick some serious ass, Luke Remini style.

I straighten up and place the pointy end of the rocket into the tube and... thunk. It doesn't fit. What the hell? What kind of army stocks the wrong-sized ammunition for its guns? Mother *fucker*!

In the back of my head, that irritating voice of reason sagely mutters, *the sort of army that loses a civil war.*

Dammit to hell! The cartel are about to land on the shore and I've got no way of launching these things!

I cast the light around, desperately looking for something, *anything*, that doesn't involve me popping up above ground like some whack-a-mole asshole, throwing these things by hand like a militant gofer.

Oh you've gotta be *kidding* me.

Standing in the next compartment, beside an identical dusty crate of shells, is another turret. But this time they've sawn the gun barrel lengthways, turning it into a half-pipe, behind which is – I shit you not – a catapult.

This isn't your average kid's catapult, this is more like the kind of stuff they used to destroy castles and whatnot, just with a weird funnel contraption to guide the outgoing missile. For the record, I have *major* reservations about this tactic. But the cartellers are climbing out of their boat. If this thing doesn't kill us, they sure will.

I shove the rocket on top of the half pipe, pull back the bungee cord, and, I'll be honest, close my eyes.

Twang.

The missile clears the bunker slit cleanly and soars across the air. Direct hit!

Wait, wasn't there supposed to be a huge explosion at this point?

I cast my eyes down at the box and see the ancient expiry date printed on the side. Son of a bitch! What kind of military buys rockets that expire the year *before* their war started?

OK don't answer that question.

The cartellers are looking at the water, puzzled, as the defunct missile bounces off their boat and plops into the water. Cocking their rifles, they leap into the shallows and storm the beach. Praying one of these things finds a magic spark, I load another missile and pull the elastic back harder this time.

Twang.

It whizzes away, this time hitting one of the cartel guys in the face! He's out cold! But the others have figured out where I am now and are firing right at me. They're lousy shooters when they're running, and the bullets are all hitting the concrete casing around us. I fire again, and again, forcing the cartel to the side, until they're out of sight.

Oh crap. Now they're going to flank us. Or whatever the vertical version of that is. Footsteps sound overhead. Think, think, if I was a carteller on top of a bunker, trying to subdue those inside, what would I do? Oh crap, they're gonna use a stun grenade! They won't risk a lethal one because they have no idea what the bounty is in here, but a stun one would buy them more than enough time to break in and own our asses.

"Seal the slits!" I cry.

I'm yelling to the others, running through the bunker, slamming up rickety panels to cover over the hatches.

"What are you doing?" yells Ramone.

"The cartel are above us! I tried repelling them but the missiles wouldn't explode."

"What missiles?"

I show Ramone the first crate. With a moment's hesitation, he snatches up a rocket, prizes the casing apart with his knife, and smacks a pressure sensor inside. He counts to four then opens the viewing panel and hurls it up onto the roof.

In the same motion, he slams the panel shut and hits the deck. The ground above us shudders as the missile explodes. There's shouting from the beach. Three voices. We must have killed a couple of the cartel, but not all of them. The three survivors above us are growing fainter, like they're beating a retreat. But it's not to their boat; they're running further inland to regroup before trying again.

"We need to get the apes out of here before they come back!" yells Ramone.

The three of us carry the unconscious mother to the

cargo drone. Her torso looks like a badly repaired sack. Various patches and devices are taped to her body, stabilizing her and the infant as best they can.

With a heave, we get the mother and her drowsy baby into the drone.

As soon as the drone launches, I'll cut communications and you'll be on your own. I'm sorry I can't help further, but it's vital no one tracks its flight path. Have you taken everything you can from the medikit?

"Yes, thank you for your generosity, Cynthia. Take care of our patients."

We will. God speed, Ramone.

Cynthia's hologram vanishes. The drone seals itself and the rotor blades fire up. The three of us force the hatch doors open then retreat behind a blast wall as the rocket powers up. Yup, there was me thinking this was just your average quadcopter, on a regular old D-pad. But I forgot this D-pad is nuclear powered, and is giving the drone some kind of launch electromagnetic charge.

With a boom, the drone explodes upwards like a missile, instantly disappearing among the clouds. We did it, we got the apes to safety! But before we can celebrate, there's an almighty crash from the bunker entrance as three cartellers burst in. They're armed, they're pissed, and they're running right at us.

CHAPTER ELEVEN

PABLA

It is a new day, and dusk is falling. We are lying face-down in the mud overlooking an enemy camp as the rain soaks us through. The enemy in question is a rival cartel that Sergeant Stax wants to target. Our mission? Get in, steal some drilling equipment, and get out before they know who did it.

Apparently we have long-standing beef with this cartel, yet Stax does not want his name on the raid. He cannot risk his own boss hearing about it. This mission is off the books, you see, because Sergeant Stax is striking out on his own.

Of course, he is following rule number one of being a kingpin: always get other people to do your dirty work. Especially if it involves lying down in wet mud.

I'm with Axl, who is Stax's right hand man. He seems like a salt-of-the-earth type. Reliable, hard-working, and a little bit dim. Stax can clearly count on him, without ever fearing being overthrown by him. Axl has a faint scar from cleft lip surgery, one eye much smaller than the other, and a zig-zag pattern shaved into his super short black hair.

We're on the top of a hill, all wearing cartel-issue

camouflage. The lapels on my arm have the insignis of an old Mazonilian army unit. Best not to dwell on how many owners this uniform has had.

The enemy are operating a mine. They have cleared several hectares of trees in the middle of otherwise undisturbed jungle, apparently in a bid to keep the location hidden from other gangs like ours.

The mine itself is under construction. Picture a giant bicycle wheel laid flat on the ground. But the spokes are lined with metal teeth, forming an excavation conveyor belt that scrapes earth and rock from the ground, pulling it into a cavity inside the spoke, where it is taken into the center of the wheel. From there, the rubble is carried away to a riddling machine, where it is separated into different metals. All the conveyor belts are encased in an oxygen-controlled atmosphere. That is what I am assuming, based on the gas canisters and pipping.

The spokes are V-shaped, by the way, in case you are wondering how they burrow. I think the whole thing is supposed to twist like a corkscrew. I am having to guess, though, because right now it is out of action. Ah, *now* I understand; the idiots chopped all the trees down, then burrowed into the center of a mound. No wonder there was a landslip as soon as the rain got heavy.

People are standing in between each of the spokes, manually digging the machine out of its own mess with shovels. Apparently the mining wheel loves earth and rock, but only on its own terms. Not when they smother all of its joints.

I think the people digging are slaves. Some cartellers are standing around supervising them, smoking cigarettes and cracking whips. On the opposite side of the pit, a tractor drone is working autonomously. It has a shunt on its grill, and is trying to push what remains of the slipped mound back away from the pit, and level it out in the surrounding grass.

"See that red pipe sticking out of the ground – beyond the tractor? That's a secondary pluridium drill. That's our target," says Axl.

"Why do they need two drills?"

"They're prospecting, seeing which way the seam runs."

"So that area's gonna end up like another pit?"

"If they find more pluridium, yeah."

"And if they don't?"

"They'll keep looking till they do."

"What if there is nothing in this whole clearing?"

"Then they'll clear some more and look there."

"They would clear it just to *look*?"

"They might get a few credits for the timber," shrugs Axl.

"How do we reach the red pipe undetected? It is in the open and there are guards on watch."

"That's down to you, forester," chuckles Axl.

"Me?"

He places a metallic pebble in my hand.

"You're gonna create a diversion. Go stick this on the side of the tractor then hide; the device will do the rest. When the diversion kicks in, meet me at the red pipe."

I stay close to the mud, crawling like a bear as I descend the mound. The two cartellers smoking nearest me are distracted; one is showing the other a video of people having sex. Beneath them, the slaves in the pit are shoveling mud with exhausted, glazed eyes. Many of them have the same complexion as me. I recognize the hair styles and tattoos of tribes we used to visit as children. I have not seen them in years, and now I know why.

For a split-second, guilt claws at me, but I shake it off. If anything, seeing those miserable wretches only increases my resolve. They let themselves be bottom of the pecking order. I am damned if that is how my life ends. The past can die in a pit for all I care; I will choose my own future.

A carteller cracks their whip, prompting howls of pain from one of the slaves. The others dip their heads and shovel harder. With everyone distracted, I take my chance and sprint for the tractor.

This is an insane gamble. I have to cover two hundred yards of open ground without being spotted by anyone. As I run, I catch a slave's gaze. She stares at me, open-mouthed, but says nothing as I go by.

I slam the pebble against the side of the tractor and it grips the hull magnetically. I do not stop for a second and keep sprinting until I skid in between two abandoned piles of earth. Panting, I roll onto my front and press myself flat to the mud, keeping my head up and scanning the perimeter of the pit. None of the cartellers spotted me. I made it!

Movement from the tractor catches my eye. Its electric motor allows it to change direction almost silently. It has driven behind one of the earthen piles and is shifting its great mass towards the pit. None of the cartellers realize what's happening until the slaves scream.

The tractor thrusts a wall of earth into the pit, crushing those working in the segment below. The other slaves scramble out, fearing for their lives. In the panic, the cartellers fear a revolt is underway and whip the slaves more, forcing the slaves to *actually* revolt. Meanwhile, the tractor is continuing out of control, garnering a second wall of mud and driving it towards the pit.

My eyes flit to the mound. Axl has reached the bottom and is sprinting towards the red pipe. I spring from my hiding place and rush to intercept him, arriving at the same time.

"How do we get the drill bit?" I pant.

"Watch and learn," he grunts, also out of breath.

He punches the controls on the side of the pipe. The screen comes to life, showing a schematic of current drilling depth, and the results from the soil analysis. Axl taps several more times until the screen refreshes. The drill is reversing direction.

"Come on, come on," he mutters, drumming his fingers across the steel column.

I'm looking around, praying no one has eyes on us. I thought this would be a quick snatch-and-grab. I never signed on to stand unarmed in the middle of an enemy field, wearing some dead soldier uniform.

Metallic creaks ring out from the pipe. The screen shows it's near.

"That's it, come on *cariña*, you got it," says Axl.

A gunshot rings out. One of the cartellers has killed a slave. Another slave tackles him and they wrestle across the ground. Other cartellers are trying and failing to control the haywire tractor, which is continuing to bury the primary mine.

Something clangs against the inside of the pipe. Axl spins the release wheel and wrenches the lid open.

"Forester, gimme a hand with this!"

We each grab a handle and pull. The tube is unbelievably heavy.

"God... damn... manual... override...!" grunts Axl.

With a groan, we drag the corkscrew drill upwards. Its sharp metal layers are filled with mud and rock. Finally, a razor-sharp drill tip emerges from the lip of the pipe. Axl hauls it to the side and we let it fall flat against the mud.

"We'll never get this to the hover bike, it's way too heavy!" I pant.

"Be cool, we only need the tip," says Axl, kneeling beside it.

Grabbing a wrench from his belt, Axl undoes the rivets, where the turquoise-colored drill tip meets the gray body. I'm crouching beside him, keeping lookout on the mayhem beyond us.

My eyes land on a hut next to the riddling unit. Something through the window catches my eye. A glint, with a tint of multi-color I've never seen before – glistening from red, green, amber, purple, seemingly every color there is.

"What is that?" I ask, pointing at the hut.

"Unless it's gonna shoot us, I'm not interested right now, kiddo," says Axl, moving onto the last rivet.

"I think they've got a diamond in there!" I whisper.

Axl's head snaps up.

"Diamond?"

"I think so!"

He twists, following my gaze.

"Holy crap. There's only one thing that can make that kind of color. These *hijos de puta* have got themselves a quantum crystal."

"What's that?"

"It's a slap in the face for us! We're pissing around risking our necks in the mud, trying to be millionaires, when there's a trillionaire's fortune inside that damned hut!"

He jerks down on the wrench in anger, and the turquoise drill head pops out.

"Then we should get it."

"Are you crazy? They haven't killed us yet, forester, but if we go in there it's guaranteed."

"If we get that thing then we become magnitudes richer. Forget escaping Mazonil within a year. If we get that crystal, I bet we can be out this *week*."

"Impossible, look, there's someone in there. Oh shit, it's their boss!"

"He does not seem to care what is happening to his mine right now?"

"He's a cartel boss! He would never dirty himself with this level of problem. It's for his deputies to fix, or they lose their heads. If he comes outside now, he looks weak in front of his men. A cartel boss can never look weak or scared."

"I am going in."

"What? It's a suicide mission!"

"Create a diversion for me and I will split the money with you later. Deal?"

"God *dammit*!" curses Axl.

He spits on the ground, succumbing to his own dreams of riches and fortunes, knowing it is a decision he will probably regret. Axl pockets the drill tip, which looks to be insanely light compared to the rest. With gritted teeth he gives me a nod and I sprint for the hut.

As I weave through the refinery equipment, closing in on the boss's hut, someone emerges from the trees opposite. I dart between some pipes and hide as they approach. It's an indigenous woman. She's unsupervised but has an electronic tag strapped to her ankle.

She has an attractive face, but it's hidden beneath layers of grime and the squalid state of her clothes. Balanced on her head is a basket of forest fruits, which she's carrying towards the boss's door. Sorry amigue, but this isn't gonna be your day.

Oriana and I spent our entire childhoods practicing creeping up on each other and the other trainee-warriors in our tribe, mastering the art of moving quickly and silently across the forest floor. With the muddy carpet beneath me, and the cries of the pit chaos to distract her, it's an easy job to knock her out.

It's less easy to steal the woman's clothes, but I manage it in less than a minute. Placing the fruit basket on my head, I take a wobbly step towards the door. This isn't something my tribe would ever do by the way, we're bag people, so this is clearly some cartel fetish.

The door is unlocked. Presumably locks would suggest weakness on behalf of the kingpin. Besides, who needs them when you have such reliable guards as the men outside, who are currently being whipped by their former slaves. Well, briefly whipped. The cartel guys do still have most of the guns, so I do not see a big underdog victory happening here. Then again, I also don't care. Like I said, the past can die in the pit.

As I enter the building, the first thing that strikes me is the scent. Sweet-smelling incense sticks are burning in the corner, and candles are dotted everywhere.

My eyes fall on the pairs of shoes lined up neatly by the door mat. Identical sets of boots in six different shades of orange. Sensing no alternative, I slip off the slave-woman's sandals and proceed onto the carpet barefoot. I try to play it cool as I cross the office floor towards the crystal, but this is the first time I have ever walked on carpet and it is *incredible*. Thick, fluffy, luxuriously soft, it is like my soles are getting a massage with every step. Hell, I think I am actually walking slower because of it, trying to eke out the experience. When I get my share of the crystal money, I am buying many carpets.

The glistening stone is mounted on the wall opposite me. It is levitating, presumably in a magnetic field. As it rotates, it flashes through each of its mesmerizing colors. I place the fruit basket down on the floor and make a beeline for it.

"Ah-ah," comes a voice from the far side. "Fruit goes on the dining table. *Then* you do the cushions."

The boss man has not even bothered to look up. He is busy swiping through a tablet, with his feet resting on a desk. He is wearing a cowboy hat, denim jeans studded with gemstones, and a weirdly shiny white skin complexion that at first glance looks Caucasian, but on closer inspection has a Mazonilian bronze color where he hasn't quite rubbed the cream properly.

I pick the basket of fruit up again and move towards the oval table in the center of the room, wondering how the hell I can steal the guy's crystal when he is in the room and I am armed with nothing but berries.

Another cry of help from outside, as the cartellers battle the insurrection and the haywire tractor. The man sighs wearily, like a father patiently waiting for his children to grow up and stop messing around. This guy is truly sure of himself. Could anything dislodge that veneer of control?

A huge boom echoes from outside. The office windows shatter and the walls shake. I drop the basket, instinctively curling into a ball and shielding my face. A huge billow of green fire is roaring out of the mining pit, raging unstoppably. The boss leaps to his feet in alarm.

"Coños!" he cries, grabbing his pistol and rushing from the room.

OK, so it turns out blowing up his entire site does the

trick. Way to go, Axl. Now I need to deliver my end of the bargain. I sprint across the room, dodging shards of glass among the carpet, and grab the crystal from its levitating trophy case. As soon as my fingers touch the stone, a klaxon rings out in the room.

A kitchen cabinet on the opposite wall opens up to reveal an autonomous machine gun. It scans the room, immediately locking onto my position and opening fire. I hit the deck, throwing over a coffee table for shelter. Now I get why he did not have a lock on the door.

Unauthorized access detected.

La hostia! The gun talks. I suppose I should not be surprised. Even the old technology in our village was interactive. Though none of it could blast my brains out.

Identify.

"Who, me?"

Identify.

"Er... housekeeping?"

Housekeeping. Processing. Facial identification required.

"You want to see my face?"

Affirmative.

"Do you promise you will not shoot me if I stand up?"

Affirmative. Asterisk.

"Asterisk?"

Terms apply.

"Please can you specify these terms?"

Truce valid for thirty seconds. May not be redeemed with any other truces. Offer applies to one human adult only. Truce may not be exchanged for cash value or use in other negotiations. Thank you for shopping with Property Patrol LLC. If you have been satisfied with this gun's service, please direct feedback to your Mall's concierge.

Mall? So the gun is stolen. I guess that makes sense.

Do you wish to proceed with the truce?

"What is the alternative?"

You will be treated as a hostile entity. Lethal force will be used to protect mall property.

"I accept the truce."

Facial identification required.

With limited options, I stand up from behind the coffee table, raising my hands. At least the klaxon has stopped ringing. I only hope the mayhem outside was loud enough for no one to hear.

Scanning. Confirmed. Housekeeping recognized. Security threat neutralized.

The gun folds itself away and disappears inside the cabinet. For a moment I am left wondering what just happened, but then I get it. The gun is *racist.*

Well, not the gun per se. More like the facial algorithm behind it. Or rather, the programmers behind *that.* OK, maybe they were not the cross-burning *proactively* racist types I used to read about, but they should have embraced a more diverse hiring policy.

You are probably wondering how I know so much about coding, as someone who grew up in a technophobic forest tribe? Remember, the only things we had to read growing up were digital text books and an encyclopedia, so my tribe were big time nerds.

"Why did you not use your knowledge to build solar panels or whatever?" I hear you thinking. The answer is simple: why would we? The forest gave us everything we needed. Why take more? Did I ever dream of seeing all the contraptions I read about in real life? Of course. But you must understand, such thoughts were taboo in our culture. We were taught freely about the old world, but all through the lens of its failings. We were given knowledge of what to *avoid*. Like building racist gun robots to defend shopping malls. Although in this instance, I will grant you, the racist cards have fallen in my favor.

The chaos is continuing outside, as the cartel try to control the blaze and save their precious pluridium. With the big boss distracted, and slaves absconding, I slip out the way I came and rush to the mound. Axl is there, hiding among the trees.

"I was getting close to leaving you, let's go!" he says.

As gunshots ring out from the camp, and jets of green fire shoot up into the air, we sprint back towards the road. The hover bike is hidden beneath a camo blanket; a low-tech net of fake leaves and scrub as old as Axl's uniform. But it is surprisingly effective. It retracts into the frame with the click of a button and we hop on.

"You get the crystal?" he asks, flicking up the kickstand.

"Si."

"Unbelievable! Boss is gonna *looove* us," cheers Axl.

Curious. Axl seems to think we are still going to share this with Stax. Maybe we will, initially. But he should be warned: terms apply.

CHAPTER TWELVE

LUKE

Pros of the situation: I'm no longer carrying a super heavy orangutan. Cons of the situation: the cartel have got their guns out and kicked their way into our bunker. Ramone flicks a control button on his backpack and the tunnel's lights go out, plunging us into darkness and buying us some time.

It transpires that the cartellers have an ingenious solution to this situation called a "gun candle". In other words, they're shooting in our general direction, and briefly illuminating the tunnel with bursts of light. Pietro and I are scrambling over each other, trying to get behind Ramone, who's leading the retreat further into the tunnel. It's like a being in a mosh pit with the strobe lights on.

The cartellers are yelling something. A pin drops to the ground, followed by a skidding sound. A tiny LED light is flashing on the side of a metal puck. Ramone yanks me backwards and boots the puck back at them.

Halfway between both groups, the stun grenade explodes. Blinding light fills the bunker, scorching our eyes.

At the same time, a sonic pulse pulverizes our auditory canals, triggering a deafening internal ringing in the ears.

I'm on the ground, clutching my head in pain. The others' muffled cries echo around me. Blurry cartel figures are on the ground opposite us, tripping over each other. Another gunshot rings out in the darkness and someone screams.

I'm being dragged backwards by the scruff of my neck. Now I'm propped against a wall, and there's a rumbling sound. As I clamber to my feet, still seeing blinding spots of light, a softer glow illuminates our space. A streak of daylight from the bunker's window slit; too small for us to crawl through, but a welcome source of air and light. Ramone's got a flashlight on, too, and is exploring the tunnel behind us. Pietro's wiping slobber from his mouth, and trying not to be sick.

The doorway we came through has been sealed off by rubble; Ramone pulled some kind of booby-trap defense lever that caused the former section to cave in. Whoever built these tunnels had one hell of a bloody mindset. They were clearly expecting their soldiers to fight to the bitter end. Me? I was ready to surrender the moment those guys burst in. There's zero shame in knowing when you're beat. The shame comes when you sneakily then renege on your surrender terms and make a cunning escape later. There's a portion of society that will judge you negatively for such behavior, which is why I gravitate towards the subset that rewards it. They're all assholes, but they get me.

Behind the curtain of rubble, I can hear the cartel arguing among themselves. Disappointingly, they weren't crushed in the escape. Although it sounds like they accidentally shot one of their own dudes, so that's a win. I think there are four of them left, and they're making their way back to the surface, looking for ways to trap us.

I feel like telling them the apes are gone, you know, so that maybe they leave us alone? But I'm pretty sure they're just as motivated by revenge at this point. Maybe I shouldn't have catapulted those rockets at them earlier. It probably got us off on the wrong foot.

A scratching noise sounds from the tunnel behind us. I turn around, expecting to see Ramone probing the walls or devising some clever escape route, but instead he's frozen, back to us, legs wide, hand raised to say "stop".

Ramone's flashlight is poised on a far corner of the tunnel that we've not yet explored. There's movement, flecks of dirt flying a few inches above the ground. Something's digging. I squint more closely. Something flat and metallic glints, flicking the soil behind it. Or is that two metal things, moving in alternation?

The scratching stops. The metal levers are frozen mid-air. They drop to the ground and paddle backwards. They're hinged at the top, kinda like the outline of a pointy house roof or... a pair of legs....

The flashlight vanishes.

"Nobody move," whispers Ramone.

My ears are filtering out the cartel's yelling above ground. Somehow my brain is focused on one thing only: the tip-tapping of spiny metal limbs across the dusty ground.

I'm blinking to adjust to the gloom. Our portion of the tunnel is well-lit, but the patch ahead doesn't have the same window slits. That is to say, we're on display, but whatever's down that tunnel is not.

The tip-tapping stops. The limbs shuffle to the side for a

moment, then retrace their steps into the shadow. The scratching resumes, and flecks of dirt fly through the air.

"What is that thing?" whispers Pietro.

"The machine that built this place. It could be the last one," says Ramone.

"Is it friendly?" I whisper.

"So long as it can't see you, yes. But it responds to movement, so if it looks at you, freeze."

"Why would it look at us? Let's just leave it to dig."

"Not an option, gringo. We must go past it. That is the only way out."

"Then why the hell did you cave the tunnel in?" I cry.

"I didn't know there was a *spider* in here!" hisses Ramone. "Would you rather we were on the other side of that rubble, getting shot by the cartel?"

"Oh fuck that, what a bullshit dichotomy. That's like when someone asks you if you'd rather sleep with your grandmother or eat your own toes. No sane person would choose either of those options, so it's a dumb question."

"What have your grandmother's toes got to do with this situation?" hisses Ramone.

"They were *my* toes. OK you've clearly not understand the options at all."

"You want us to eat your toes?" says Pietro, aghast.

"No, that's not what I'm suggesting!"

"I think I would rather face the spider," says Ramone.

"It's not a real option, guys, I was just using it as an example!"

"OK, but I'm still saying no."

"I'm *not* offering you my toes."

"I know, I just want everyone to be clear that if you *were* offering your toes, I would say no."

"Agreed. I would sleep with his grandma," adds Pietro.

"Dude, it wouldn't be *my* grandmother, it would be yours," I explain.

"Ew! That's disgusting. Why can't I have yours?"

"That's not how it works!"

"How what works?"

"The rules, OK?"

"I don't accept those rules."

"Me neither. I also want your grandmother," says Ramone.

"My grandma's not on the menu for either of you!" I protest.

"OK, then I want to see the menu."

"There is no menu! Why are you so obsessed with my grandmother now?"

"I do not want to eat your gringo toes," says Ramone.

"They wouldn't be *my-* God, have either of you understood this *at all*?"

"Family dynamics are clearly different in your culture. Let the record reflect that I do not want it for myself," says Pietro.

"This is *not* my culture!"

"Then why are you offering us grandmothers and toes?" says Ramone.

"It was an example! All I was doing was trying to elucidate the fact that blowing up the tunnel wasn't a choice I would have made!"

"Ah, like an analogy?" says Pietro.

"Exactly!"

"Why didn't you use the train dilemma?"

"What?"

"It is a famous psychology experiment – where they simulate people having to divert a train from one rail to the other to save five lives at the expense of one."

"What's that got to do with this fucking tunnel?"

"It's an example of only having two crappy choices on the table," shrugs Pietro.

"Why would there be a table in a tunnel?" says Ramone.

"Yeah, and why would my grandmother be on a train?" I add. "She *hates* trains. Everyone knows that. If you wanna get with her, you're gonna have to up your game, lizard boy, she don't put out for just anyone you know. Gotta take an interest in a gal."

"I think you are being patriarchal and presumptuous," mutters Pietro.

"You're saying you *shouldn't* get to know my gran before sleeping with her?" I retort.

"I'm saying she should be the one to set those parameters. It is not your place to assume on her behalf."

"I think I'm making a reasonable assumption in this instance, the woman's like a hundred," I reply.

"That is ageist *and* sexist, gringo," interjects Ramone. "Maybe all she wishes for in her twilight years is an animalistic pounding with an exotic stranger?" he says, flexing his biceps.

"*So* gross! Christ, this is like being trapped with Sartre and Freud. And before you say it, no that reference is *not* a former sportswriter trying too hard, it's journalist of the mother fucking year telling you two to leave his god damned nana alone!"

"L'enfer, c'est les autres, non?" says Pietro.

"Sorry bro but my translator doesn't speak asshole."

"You mean it doesn't *translate* asshole. I can assure you it *speaks* asshole perfectly well."

"You jumped up little-"

"Look, Mr. Remini, I'm just saying, I think you have a

regressive attitude towards female sexuality, and that those kinds of 'chivalrous' projections can actually disempower women in broader social contexts," says Pietro.

"Thanks for the life lesson, lizard boy. Remind me, you're like, what, twelve?"

"I told you he was ageist," mutters Ramone.

"Luke, please don't be offended. I am merely saying Ramone and I would be honored to satisfy your grandmother's natural sexual appetite as part of a sex act between consenting adults."

"What, so now it's a threesome? You guys are fucking gross! Stop talking about my grandmother's sex life already!"

"You're the one who brought it up, gringo."

"As an example of the worst imaginable dilemma!"

"Which, as discussed already, is ageist and insulting," says Pietro. "My university holds webinars on unconscious bias and I think you'd really benefit from attending one."

"What I'd benefit from is getting the fuck outta this tunnel so I don't have to stare at your lizard boy face!"

"Hey, I saved you from a river! A little courtesy and gratitude might be nice."

"Actually, Ramone saved me, because you have the tensile strength of a three-year-old."

"That's it. When we get out of here, we're settling this like men."

"Oh, you wanna go, lizard boy? Why wait till we're above ground? Let's go right here!"

"Uh, OK then. Here goes: Luke, I'm feeling hurt by your words, and would like to calmly discuss where all this anger is coming from."

"What the fuck? Punch me already!"

"Why would I punch you?"

"We're settling this like men!"

"You have a truly depressing grasp of gender norms, Luke. I would urge you to raise that with your therapist."

"In your dreams, Pietro. The only thing I'll be raising is what an asshole you are."

"Indeed. So your background is in sports journalism?"

"Mother-"

"Enough, you two!" interjects Ramone. "Are you quite finished?"

"Yeah. We're done because I won the fight," I say, puffing my chest.

"But you lost the-"

"Oh fuck off, Pietro, no one likes your quotes, all right? God, you're really making my dick itch."

"That's just the bunker roaches," says Ramone.

"Christ, get us out of here, man!"

"Si, I was trying that before you started on about grandmother's toes. To escape the bunker we must get past the spider."

"What spider?" I ask.

"The mechanical spider that we've been staring at this whole time."

"Holy crap, that thing's still there?"

"It lives down here, gringo. Good thing it only responds to movement and not sound. You would have had us killed a hundred times over by now."

"Huh. That *did* come up with my therapist..."

"OK, here we go," says Ramone. "If I say stop, you stop. Understood? Stay close. We need to get to the emergency escape hatch."

"What about the flashlight? I can't see shit through there!"

"I will use it to open the hatch, but not before. If we disturb the spider, it's game over," says Ramone.

He edges forwards. The spider's flinging muck backwards, seemingly unware of our presence. In the gloomy light of the tunnel, I can vaguely make out a hatch on the side of the wall. But there's a dark shadow next to it, which tells me the tunnel goes a heck of a lot further than we thought.

Ramone goes first, edging behind the spider, one step at a time. The machine keeps shoveling dirt, its body obscured by shadow. Pietro goes next, creeping forwards to join Ramone. He beckons me to join him. But Ramone has stalled. He's tracing his hands across the doorway.

"This isn't a hatch," he mutters. "It's an internal door."

I'm creeping to join them, feeling flecks of dirt land between my hiking shoes and my feet. That's definitely gonna rub later. As I reach Pietro, I realize how cramped the space in front of the doorway is. It's like we're squeezing into a metro at rush hour.

"Ramone, does that thing open or not?" whispers Pietro.

"I'm working on it!"

"The spider's getting dirt in my shoe," I moan.

"Shut your mouth, Luke," snaps Ramone.

"Hey, you used my name! We're totally bonding!"

Something twinges in my nostrils. A familiar, unstoppable tingling feeling. It's spreading up my nose.

"Oh God..."

"What?" says Pietro.

"Lizard boy, I think there's still orangutan fur on your swea..."

"Luke, no!"

"Swea..."

"Luke, keep it together!"

"Sweaaa*aaatchooo*!"

The force of my sneeze throws my whole body forwards, propelling my forehead into Pietro's chin. The skinny academic falls into Ramone, who in turn, stumbles sideways. Everyone freezes, panting.

The scratching sound has halted.

Eight mechanical limbs tip-tap their way around the dirt, as the spider rotates on the spot, revealing two, glowing red eyes.

"Nobody move," hisses Ramone.

I'm trying. Really, I am. But in my defense, I asked for an allergy tablet like thirty minutes ago, so I can't be held solely responsible.

The spider shuffles, scanning our corner for motion. Its gaze shifts from Ramone, through Pietro, to me.

"Ramone, get the door open!" I hiss, also keeping my jaw rigid.

"I'm trying, gringo!"

Ramone stealthily raises a hand and forces the handle. It lets out a rusty shriek, barely moving an inch.

"Dude, we need to h... hurr... *hatchoo!*"

I'm bent over, with the crook of my elbow covering my nose, staring down at the dirt. From the darkness, staring back me, are two glowing red eyes, accompanied by the sound of eight, razor-sharp blades being unsheathed.

CHAPTER THIRTEEN

PABLA

Change of plans. Meet in township. Rusty's Bar. Will explain later.

Stax's message was short, but Axl said that's just his style.

"Things often change quickly with Stax," he explains, cheerfully. "The guy's a man of ambition."

"Weird that he hangs out with you then."

"Ha! Agreed. Join me in this next shot?"

"No, I'm good."

"Come on, we're celebrating!"

"I don't drink that stuff."

"Was it illegal in your tribe or something? They're not here to make dumb rules anymore."

"Don't I know it."

"Here, just a measure to keep my company."

"I'll pass. You do you."

"Suit yourself, forester."

Axl gulps down both shots in quick succession, slamming them on the bar with a *whooee*! He's in high spirits after our raid on the other cartel. In his pocket is an essential drill bit for the pluridium extraction. In my pocket is the priceless quantum crystal.

We've been here for half an hour with no sign of Stax. Axl is unconcerned; saying the boss runs to his own timetable, not ours. He's embraced the opportunity to get drunk. I refuse; it would be foolish to make myself vulnerable around strangers in a new town.

The handful of other patrons are mostly keeping to themselves, huddled in groups of two and three, playing cards or talking in quiet conspiratorial tones, with hunched shoulders and furtive looks.

The bar is filthy. Rusty counters, seats made of wooden pallets, and a floor that's sprinkled with sawdust whenever it gets too muddy or wet from piss. Maybe Oriana was right, perhaps the cities are pure squalor. This shithole town had better not be representative of what else is out there.

I know it's my first time here but something doesn't feel right. People are giving us suspicious glances. They're probably not used to indigenous people like me frequenting the bar. But then again, Axl's not doing us any favors.

"Let me see the crystal," he hisses.

He has the worst stage whisper in the history of mankind, and his breath reeks as he leans in, pawing my arm.

"Later, when we're with Stax," I reply.

"Naw, don't be a spoil sport. Just a quick peek!" he whines.

"Axl, this doesn't feel right. Why haven't we heard from your boss?"

"Quit worrying, *chava*. Ain't no signal in the township. It's a black zone. We're off-grid, see? Only way to keep the peace. Otherwise everyone would be getting all up in everyone else's business, causing fights and raids and whatnot."

A door opens from a back room of the bar and two cartellers approach us. One has a tattoo of a hypersexualized female robot with enormous breasts on his upper arm. The style is very different to forest tattoos; his is multi-colored and looks like a photograph, whereas ours are plain black and hand-drawn. The carteller beside him is wearing a long sleeved shirt, but has a pockmarked face where acne once flourished. So in a sense, they are both decorated. Axl gives the men a cheery wave.

"What's happening amigues! Can I buy you two fine gentlemen a drink?"

"You're in an awfully good mood today, Axl. Had some good news, have we?" says the robot tattoo guy.

Axl tries to tap his nose sagely, but has such drunken imprecision that he settles for stroking his cheek instead.

"Where's Stax?" I ask.

"No-one's talking to you, forest girl," snaps the pockmarked guy.

These situations are always a margin call. Do you assert your dominance immediately, and risk sparking a bigger conflict you might lose? Or do you bide your time, and wait until the perfect moment to strike?

Oriana would fight immediately, and, knowing her, win. Me? I'm sitting on a giant stolen crystal that these guys don't know about. I decide to play it safe.

"Naw, she's all right," slurs Axl, throwing a drunken arm over my shoulder. "Where is the boss, though? He was 'sposed to meet us here a week ago."

"Half an hour," I mutter, shaking him off.

"The boss is indisposed. He's dealing with some

personal business, but he asked us to take delivery on his behalf," says robot guy.

"Personal business, hey? Has he got a guy back there?" chuckles Axl.

"Give us the drill," interjects pockmark.

He extends a demanding hand. Axl gives it a playful low-five, then creases up with laughter. The two cartellers' faces tighten.

"I'm gonna ask one more time, old man, before we take it from you. You get me?" says pockmark.

I'm glancing around the tavern. People have put their drinks down and are shifting to the edges of their seats. Hands are moving to holsters. Eyes are looking sideways.

"Yeah, I got it all right," mumbles Axl, reaching inside his pocket. "I got it right... *here!*"

Axl pistol whips the pockmarked guy square in the jaw. The big fella falls back, hitting the deck. In the same deft motion, Axl leaps back and is standing straight with his gun trained on the robot-tattoo guy, who has drawn his pistol.

The two men square up, each with a hovering trigger finger.

"Where's Stax?" demands Axl.

His slurred voice has disappeared, and he's suddenly stone-cold sober. The tattooed guy is shifting, nervously, clearly rattled at this underestimation of his opponent.

"I told you, Axl, he's busy. No need to get argumentative," soothes the man.

The pockmarked guy is coming to his senses. In the next few seconds, he's gonna draw his own pistol, and we'll be outgunned. I don't have a weapon of my own. My only hope is to attack while he's down. But if I do, all hell could break loose in here.

"Ain't no argument here, friend," says Axl. "Just

curiosity. Why is it, I ask myself, that our boss is messaging me to meet him in the bar all of a sudden? He ain't one for after-work drinks. Not in this shithole, anyway. No offence, Mira," he adds, nodding to the barkeep.

"Just gimme the drill and I'll let you walk away," says the tattooed guy, his voice darkening.

Other patrons are rising to their feet across the bar, hands on holsters. There's silence, save for the dazed groans of the pockmarked guy, who is now missing a tooth.

"See, the thing about Stax is he *never* sends messages in writing. He don't believe in it. With him, you always look him in the eye, no matter what the message. Straightforward, that way, ain't it? You know where you stand with everyone. You get a chance to read them," says Axl.

"Final warning, Axl. I'm not dicking around here," says robot guy.

"Steady, kid. I'd hate for you to overstep the mark. Look, I'm a reasonable soul. Tell me where the boss is and I'll let one of you live. Whichever one tells me first."

Robot-tattoo-guy glances at his fallen partner. In that split-second of distraction, Axl pulls the trigger. The bullet strikes the guy square in the chest. The guy pulls his own trigger in reflex, striking Axl's arm.

Both men fall backward, but Axl stays standing, clinging to the bar. A bottle comes crashing down on his hand, shattering everywhere. Still wielding the jagged end, the barkeep moves to stab Axl's bleeding hand properly, but he shoots her in the cheek.

She hits the deck, disappearing behind the bar, screaming in agony. A bullet from across the room hits Axl in the leg, this time fired by a patron.

Whatever ceasefire had held up until this point

evaporates in an instant. I throw myself to the ground as bullets fly across the room, as the two factions open fire on each other.

As I hit the dirt and sawdust, I lock eyes with the pockmarked guy, who is reaching for his pistol. If I don't leap now, I'm done for. I dive on him but the man kicks out a leg, whacking me mid-flight with his boot. I crumple to the side. I'm scrabbling around for a weapon. As he takes aim, my hand lands on a fallen ash tray, which I hurl at his head, scoring a direct hit on his eyebrow. Before he can recover, I am on him. I aim for his larynx but he blocks me with his arm. It becomes a struggle for the gun.

We roll and he is on top, using his weight against me. With a bang, his eyes roll back in his head. Blood seeps from his tear ducts and nostrils. He slumps onto me as a deadweight, pinning me to the ground. The back of his skull is caved in, and bits of brain are seeping out of the sides, turned to soup by whatever the hell kind of bullet that was. I do not know who shot him, but I owe them my life.

For a few moments I lay low, trapped beneath pockmark's stinking torso, before the gunfight in the rest of the bar comes to an end. A handful of losers make a swift exit through the main doors, while their less fortunate comrades leak into pools of their own blood.

A familiar boot kicks the pockmarked man's body off me, and a hand reaches down to help me up.

"I always hated this bar," grins Axl.

His wounded arm hangs by his side, bleeding into his shirt.

"I thought your leg got shot too?" I ask.

"Stun bullet. It wore off quickly cos I had a restoration patch handy. Never leave home without one."

"You need help," I say, eyeballing his arm.

"It can wait. Right now we need to find the boss. Come on – and take this."

He hands me pockmark's pistol. It's an old-fashioned revolver, without any of the standard biometric handle IDs most cartellers have. A perfect spoil of war.

"Which end do I put the arrow in?" I ask.

Axl stares at me in despair, then realizes I am kidding. He goes to slap me on the back, heartily, then curses as his wound reminds him that arm is out of action.

We make our way to the back of the bar, through the rear doorway, along a short, shabby corridor made of metal sheets at wonky angles, until we reach another doorway. Axl pauses and listens closely. Someone on the other side is groaning.

Axl gives a silent countdown with his fingers, then kicks the door open and leaps inside. For a middle-aged man on a greasy carteller diet, he is remarkably agile.

In the center of the room is Stax, tied to a chair. His eyes are swollen from beating, and his face is bruised and cut all over. Bloody saliva dribbles from his mouth.

"Sarge! What have they done to you? Those bastards!"

Axl rushes over, cutting his boss free. Stax slumps sideways, weak from the beating.

"Axl?" he says, feebly.

"It's me, boss. We got them, don't worry. Shit, let's get you out of here and cleaned up."

"The men-"

"They're gone. We killed most of them. A few of our boys are still loyal, don't you worry. They're keeping an eye on the bar in case those cowards come back."

"What happened to you?" I ask Stax.

"Mutiny," he croaks, spitting blood onto the floor.

"Bastards!" declares Axl. "After everything you did for

them. You were gonna share the pluridium spoils with them too! Well, screw them all. More for us now, hey boss? We did it – we got the other cartel's drill. Now we can extract the good stuff, and divvy up the riches."

Axl is beaming with pride. He earnestly searches his boss's bleeding face for approval. This guy was clearly the black sheep of his family. Somehow he has found a role model in Stax, a man ten years his junior, who gets himself strapped to chairs and beaten by his followers. Great choices, Axl.

"There isn't any," splutters Stax.

"Any what?"

"The pluridium seam... It was a mistake. There was only a speck and we found it by luck. The rest of the site is barren."

Axl's face falls.

"But... but there must be more? Did you look properly? We can go back with more men, *better* men, we'll find something boss, I'm sure of it!"

"We looked everywhere, believe me, there's nothing," says Stax. "When the men realized it was a fool's errand, they turned on me. Now the CEO will kill me for losing the township."

"It's not over yet, boss. Look what we found – show him, *chica*!" says Axl, eagerly.

I pull the quantum crystal from my pocket and Stax's eyes widen.

"Axl, we must hide that!" urges Stax. "If word gets out that we have a crystal, everyone will come for us. And right now, we're a soft target."

Stax tries to stand but cannot. Instead, he coughs up another fistful of blood, doubling over in pain.

"Let's get you cleaned up, boss."

"Are we taking him to a hospital?" I ask, a little too brightly.

"Why would we do that?" says Axl. "There's a medical station across town. Basic drone unit, it'll do the trick."

"But he is seriously hurt?"

"Yeah, that happens a lot here. Why else do you think we invested in a medical box? It's about the only thing that works in this town."

"You are saying a *box* can fix him?"

"Stop asking questions and start lifting."

Embarrassed at my naivety, I throw one of Stax's arms over my shoulder, and we heave him towards the bar.

"Hurry, Axl," mumbles Stax. "If word gets out that I'm down, there'll be a struggle for this town."

"No way! This town and this crystal are yours, boss. We got you."

As we haul Stax's broken body, Axl's words ring in my ears. *The crystal is yours, boss?* The hell it is. I risked my life to get that thing, and I'm damned if I hand it over to some ailing cartel boss who is about to get killed before he can pay me. I need to think carefully. The crystal is my ticket out of here, but Axl will not give up his half easily. He's too loyal to Stax for that. And as he showed in the bar, he is a lot more capable than I thought.

Axl and I carry Stax back through to the sawdust tavern, where the remaining men who are loyal to Stax are standing guard. One of them provides a hood and sunglasses to help cover the boss's face so he is not immediately recognizable in the street.

"The crystal," croaks Stax. "Gimme it."

Axl looks at me expectantly.

"We can talk about that later, surely the priority now is your medical needs?" I reply.

"I'd feel more comfortable about this whole miserable fucking situation if it was in my personal possession."

"To be blunt, Stax, you couldn't defend shit right now. A *child* could take it from you," I reply.

"Not for long. Besides, I got Axl now."

"You sure do, boss," chirps Axl.

"So gimme it."

"It's not yours," I say.

"I thought as much. All right let's say for a minute you do a runner on me and Axl here, cutting us both out of the deal. Where are you going to go with that big crystal, huh? And assuming you even make it there, who are you going to sell it to?"

I have answers to neither of these questions, and my mouth just hangs open, ignorantly.

"Exactly. You don't have a clue what you're doing, *chica*. Mark my words, anyone you take that crystal to, anywhere in this country, will simply kill you and take it for themselves. Right now, I may be crippled, and you may be the child that robs me in my time of weakness, but you should know, cities and cartels are bad places for children to be. It never ends well."

I'm chewing his words over. They have a distinctly bitter truth to them.

"How can I trust you to give me a cut of the profit?" I say.

Stax laughs, then grunts with pain. "You think Axl would be this loyal to me if I didn't look after my own?"

"I get the sense that Axl has daddy issues, so I am not sure he is the best litmus test."

Stax chuckles again. "That's what I love about you, Pabla. You use these fancy turns of phrase but really, when it comes to it, you don't know shit about the real world or how it works. By all means, beat your own path from here. See how far you get with that thing. And when the last breath leaves your penniless, broken body, remember this moment and know that it could have gone differently. That you could have been rich and retired if you had only accepted my kind offer."

"What the fuck is kind about your offer?" I snap.

"Pabla, *chava*, look around you. You're in a bar full of dead bodies of people who picked the wrong side. The people still standing are all on *my* side. Right now, you're standing because you're one of them. I could snap my fingers and any one of these folk would cut you down where you stand. We'd have one less person to split the crystal with. But I don't wanna do that. I want you to join my family. We can help each other to do more. You stole that hunk of rock, which proves everything I thought about you – that you've got something my men don't. The question is: are you stupid enough to throw this opportunity away? Or are you serious about wanting a better life than living in the mud and praying to the fucking wind in the trees?"

He holds out a bloodied hand, which is missing several fingernails.

"I got the crystal. *Me*. It was my idea, and my life on the line. You and Axl split your share with your other men how you like, but one third of that thing is mine alone. Are we clear?"

"It's a deal," says Stax.

I place the crystal in his palm, and he slips it into his jacket pocket.

"You're brighter than the rest of your village was, Pabla. All right Axl, let's go. I'm about to start pissing blood."

Axl nods for me to take up Stack's arm again, which I do. As we shuffle through the door and across the dusty street, I can't fathom whether that was the only sensible option on the table, or whether I just got verbally mugged. If so, then Stack's was right: I would have been screwed trying to sell that thing on my own. But that makes for circular logic, and I think that is exactly what he was banking on. Maybe Stack's is brighter than *I* thought.

The streets are quiet. A handful of people talk, sit, and drink, passing the time by the dusty roadside. A couple tend a cart selling some meat cooked in a single heated pot. It is unclear whether the severed dog tails pinned to the front of their cart are an advert or a warning.

As we round the corner, a man regards us closely. As we shuffle past, he peels off from the wall and disappears. This does not escape Stax or Axl's attention either.

"Axl?"

"I see him, boss. I'll go now."

"No – Pabla should go. She's the only one of us not injured. We can't risk failure."

"Go where?"

"Stop that man – hurry! He saw my face and he's gonna call another cartel. If they hear of weakness, they'll strike now and it'll be a bloodbath."

"Bullshit, you just took my crystal, now you're sending me after some stranger?" I retort.

"It's not like that. It's the same as what I told you in the bar. If another cartel comes, they will reward their own. They will take that crystal from you, or me, or whoever has it, and there'll be no splitting it among us. It will be theirs. You will lose *everything* you've just risked your life to earn.

You wanna get out of this miserable fucking country? Then stop that man before he gets us all killed!"

His words resonate and I break away, running back the way we came. I tear onto the main road where the man is marching toward the town boundary, presumably where the blackout zone ends. I am sprinting as he reaches for his phone. I have no idea where the signal boundary is, but I cannot risk him connecting. As I draw closer, I pull the pockmarked man's pistol from my jacket and take aim. I am about to fire when I remember the insanity of trying to shoot an arrow while running. I skid to a halt, drop to one knee, straighten both arms, and squeeze the trigger.

The bullet strikes the center of his back and the man falls forward in a heap. I run towards the body, to make sure he is dead. I am about to roll him over when he grabs my ankle, hauling me to the ground beside him. He is stronger than I had anticipated, and there is no indication that he was shot. Beneath his collar I glimpse a bullet-proof vest lining his skin. Exactly what I would wear if I lived in this snake pit of a town. If I live to see the end of this, I am stealing that thing.

He has me in a chokehold. I drive my thumbs into his eyes. He yells in pain and releases his grip, then elbows me in the face. I am dazed, trying to regroup as he grabs my pistol. I kick out, knocking the gun from his hands. It is out of both our reaches. With a growl, the man launches himself at me. He tries to put me in an arm lock but I twist out of it, reversing the move and pressing his wrist backward so that he screams. His knee smashes into my ribs, winding me. I take a swing but I am off-balance. He dodges easily, then kicks the crook of my hamstring, sending me crumpling to the ground.

Suddenly he is behind me and a wire appears around

my neck. He is pulling upwards and I am choking. My vision is turning red and there is a rushing in my ears as I suffocate.

Two bullets ring out and the tension vanishes. I collapse to the ground, gasping for air. The man crashes down beside me, his eyes fixed open as blood gushes from his head and neck.

"Twice in one day. I think I deserve some of your cut," grins Axl, helping me up.

He is beaming at me, looking fit as a fiddle. As I regain my breath, I notice the man standing next to him and do a double-take. Aside from a shadow of bruising and a few scabs here and there, Stax is looking entirely revived. He is standing tall and kicking the dead carteller's body over, inspecting the guy's phone to see who he was about to call.

"You... you are healed?" I say, astonished.

"I told you, *chica*, we got good shit here. You're not in the forest anymore."

"Whaddya reckon, boss? Can I patch her up?" says Axl.

Stax slouches over, thumbs tucked into his waist belt. He rocks on his heels with the cocky air of a man who once again owns the town.

"Well, we only reserve our fine medical kit for people on our side. But Pabla is one of us now, isn't that right, *chica*? You've proven yourself. I think you've earned a little patch-up."

He gives Axl a wink, and Axl taps a controller on his wrist. A medical drone emerges from the street behind us and lands beside me. Both men stand back and talk shit as the drone scans then delivers aid without any input from either of them.

It has tentacles like the one I saw in the forest yesterday, when it reattached the carteller's severed hands in moments. As the robot's limbs glide across my body, administering healing patches and injections, I feel a stinging sensation in my arm.

One of the tentacles has a laser appendage, and is burning my skin.

"Ouch! What the hell!" I cry.

I have detected foreign bodies in your epidermis. These may be parasitic or toxic, and should be removed as a precaution.

"Get the hell off me!"

Patient is refusing treatment. Treatment is suspended.

The tentacles retract into the drone's spherical body as I scramble to my feet, examining the invisible burn marks on my arm. It stings, painfully. The only relief is I bailed as soon as I did. If I ever see Oriana again, she had better still have that algal culture, because I am now a few hundred thousand cells short.

"What was that about?" frowns Stax.

"Your shitty machine just burned me!"

"Really? I'm pretty sure it was trying to help."

"Well that kind of help is not welcome."

"Could've fooled me. You seem to be moving pretty happily right now."

He is right. The rest of my body feels amazing. Not just patched up, but truly incredible. I have no idea how that box works, but I am swimming in endorphins right now.

"Pabla, I'll level with you. You're not gonna like what I'm about to say," begins Stax.

"If you are about to renege on our-"

"Cool your beans, nothing like that. On the contrary, it's a sign of my growing confidence in you that I've got a mission proposal."

"I am not interested. Axl said my share of that crystal is worth enough to get me out of the country right now."

"He's not wrong. The only problem is, with things like this, it takes time to find a buyer. It's not like I can just take this into a shop, we're in Mazonil for god's sake. There's the black market, or there's no market. But the big boss controls the black market, and we're trying to do this off-books so we can all go live the island dream you're talking about."

"How long will it take to sell?" I ask.

"We have to tread carefully, so probably a couple of weeks."

"Then I'll see you then."

"Not so fast. Because of the whole shit show with the pluridium seam that wasn't a seam, we're behind on the CEO's targets. We're supposed to be expanding his lands, and prospecting new sites weekly."

"I couldn't give less of a shit about your little cartel-company structure. Get me my cut of the crystal, and get it to me fast," I retort.

"I can't do that if the CEO's breathing down my neck, can I?" says Stax, tersely.

"And what are you expecting me to do about that?"

"The only thing you can do if you want to get your cut of the money. Help me get the CEO off my back."

"How?"

"That's the spirit! This way, kid, Axl's gonna fix you up with a backpack. I'm sending you back to the jungle."

CHAPTER FOURTEEN

We're clawing against the rusty bunker door, trapped between a wall of rubble and a Mazonilian military killing machine. The spider's eyes are glowing brighter and redder like it's powering up for something I *really* don't wanna be part of.

"Ramone, hurry up!" squeals Pietro.

"Push with me!" calls Ramone.

All three of us slam our shoulders against the thick door. It shifts but only a fraction.

"Again!" cries Ramone.

Blades are appearing on the tips of the spider's legs. We're about to be sliced and diced, and served up on a bed of dry leaves and orangutan fur.

With a screech, the door finally breaks open and the three of us tumble inside. Ramone's up in a flash, sealing the door behind us. No sooner has it closed than eight indentations appear in the metal, right at the level our backs would have been seconds before.

Ramone cracks a glow stick from his backpack, filling the small, windowless, concrete cell with green light.

"What the hell is that thing?" whimpers Pietro.

He's such a sap. I don't like spiders, least of all deathy robot ones, but at least I know how to hide it. It's important to act doubly cool when others panic.

"It is a civil war relic. Like a landmine, but more interactive," says Ramone.

"You make it sound like they got feedback on the old landmines. What is this, the new and improved customer experience?" I reply.

"Si. The spiders are much more effective at defending a territory. They are highly adaptive killers."

"Oh god," says Pietro.

"Dude, be cool. What's the one rule of spiders that everyone learns as a kid?"

"Their hairs are toxic?"

"Only forty percent of them have lethal venoms?" says Ramone.

"I was thinking more along the lines of 'it's more afraid of you than you are of it'?" I say.

"I think we grew up with different spiders," says Ramone.

There's a clang at the door. The spider's tapping a leg against the metal, probing it for weakness. Tap, tap, tap.

Pause.

With a piercing screech, the spider punches its leg through the door.

Pietro and I yelp in fear, though him much more so. Ramone pushes us back from the door.

"It is coming for us. We must move now," he says.

The only way is through a second door behind us, but it's sealed shut, this time locked by a padlock.

"This is hopeless! Do we even have enough air in here?"

cries Pietro. The scrawny researcher looks from me to Ramone in despair. "Well?"

"I think it's customary to infer a 'no' when people fail to respond to something like that," I advise.

"We're gonna suffocate down here!" cries Pietro.

"Hey, look on the upside, kid. We might find a small air crack we're not seeing? Then we can just slowly starve together instead."

Pietro wails with despair. I leave him too it; best he gets it all out of his system.

"We need to lure it away," says Ramone.

"I'd hate to sound like Pietro, big guy, but how can we lure anything anywhere when we're stuck down here?"

Ramone swivels off his backpack and pulls out three strips from the medical drone, plus a micro CPR unit he extracted from it earlier.

"Genius!" I cry. "You're thinking we let the spider kill one of us, then while it moves on to the next one, the third person revives the first. And we just do laps like that until someone rescues us?"

Ramone looks at me with serious loathing. I guess my elementary teachers lied: there *is* such a thing as a dumb question. Thanks for nothing, Ms Ratchet. Can I have a glass of milk and a cookie now? And maybe a cuddle? Ooh, Ms Ratchet, your perfume is intoxicating. Is that a designer brand? I know designer brands because I'm a classy gent. Maybe we should grab a drink sometime? Sure, I can help you take your jacket off. It *is* hot in here. Ooh, Ms Ratchet, you *are* naughty. Really? In here? Where everyone can see? What if the principal catches us? I know, there'd be so many legal repercussions, but ssshhh, don't think about that right now, Ms Ratchet, just listen to your body.

"Luke?"

"Huh?"

"I'm telling you to put the medical patch on! Where did you go?" snaps Ramone.

"Milk time. Uh, I mean, nothing. Nowhere. What? *You're* obsessed!"

"If we ever make it out of here, the record will show that you lost your mind first," whimpers Pietro.

"Hey, screw you, lizard boy. I was practicing an advanced form of mindfulness."

"Voyeurism, more like."

"Wait, there's a difference?"

"Meditation generally does not feature intercourse with one's elementary school teacher," says Pietro.

"I'm gonna have to agree to disagree on that, kiddo."

"Enough. Any more of your fantasies, gringo, and I will let the spider in myself," grunts Ramone.

My eyes dart to the door, where the spider is making two vertical incisions, cutting through it like a tin can.

"Put the patch on your neck," insists Ramone.

"What does it do?"

"God, do you listen to *anything*?" says Pietro.

"You know, Pietro, you're actually starting to *sound* like Ms Ratchet. In this light you even look a little like her," I muse.

"Both of you, patches on, now!" snaps Ramone.

Pietro and I apply them as instructed.

"Seriously though, what do these things do?" I ask.

"They lower your heart rate."

"How low?"

"Equivalent to a heart attack."

As Ramone speaks, I feel myself getting light-headed. There are shooting pains in my left arm, and a crushing sensation in my chest.

"Ramone, are you killing us?" gasps Pietro.

We're both trying to claw the patches off but they've dissolved into our skin. I'm feeling weak, and disoriented. Ramone's tapping on the CPR unit, punching in a program. The spider's cutting horizontally across the top and bottom of the vertical strips it's made, as it slices a patch out of the door. Its red eyes glimmer thorough the gaps.

Ramone hastens to the rear of the room and coats the padlock with a solution from the medical kit. It frosts over in seconds, emitting impossibly icy vapors in the otherwise sweltering bunker. He smashes it with the butt of his flashlight, shattering the lock.

"Ugh, Ramone?" whimpers Pietro."

"I know, I know, I'm working on it!" cries the ranger. He's tugging against the door but it's holding fast.

"We've got company... Lots of company!"

I follow Pietro's gaze to the wall behind me. Scattered across the floor, curled up on their backs, are a dozen war spiders. One by one, their red eyes light up. Their legs twitch into action.

"Freeze!" slurs Pietro.

"No use, boy," growls Ramone.

The spider outside punched through the door, revealing a large square hole in the center.

"But you said they're triggered by motion? We should stay still!" says Pietro.

"Too late. Our motion activated its attack mode. Now it's tracking our pulses," says Ramone. "The spiders conserve energy until they detect a threat. Now it is powering up to neutralize us. Just like its peers in here!"

The room is alive with twitching mechanical legs as more spiders wake from hibernation. Ramone slaps a medical patch against his neck. At the same moment, the first spider appears over the hole in the main door, dangling upside down and scanning for signs of us.

As its glowing red eyes lock onto Ramone, he throws himself at the CPR unit and initiates the program. The device bleeps then delivers an electrical shock to the ground. The spiders around us suddenly rise to their feet, alerted by the machine's presence.

"Get the door open, it's the only way!" cries Ramone.

We throw ourselves at the next door. All three of us are weaker now, and dizzy from the patches. We're pushing hard but it's refusing to budge. The most active spider pounces through the perforated front doorway and scurries toward the CPR unit. The device is ramping up, delivering pulse shocks at increasing frequency and voltage.

The spiders in the corners are coming online too, converging on the device. They swarm over it. Some get stunned by its discharges, while others slice into it with their razor blades.

"Push!" cries Ramone once more.

The three of us heave again, but it's wedged firm. A spider turns away from the main pack. Its eyes scan the three of us, then glow brighter as its body rotates to face us.

"Again!" yells Ramone.

The CPR unit delivers its final pulses before the spiders sever its circuitry. Battery acid spurts from its core, melting several of the spiders. The remaining robots turn their attention to us; the only pulses left in the room.

With a cry, we shunt the second door open and throw ourselves across the threshold into a corridor. Ramone rushes to seal us in but a spider's limb appears in the doorframe, wedging it open. More limbs follow, stacking vertically. The robots are pushing against him as a group.

"A hatch!" yells Pietro, pointing to an exit.

"Run for it!" cries Ramone.

We run for the far end of the tunnel but it feels like I'm wading through treacle with my pulse this low. Staggering, swaying, Pietro and I reach the hatch and prize the wooden slats apart. Ramone is sprinting towards us, having abandoned the door. Spiders tumble into the tunnel. Red eyes beaming, razor legs out, they immediately lock eyes on us.

In that same instant, the cartellers burst in through another door. Not seeing the spiders, their eyes fall on us.

"Now we have you, *mamaguevos!*" cries the lead main, raising his pistol.

But the spiders are now fully activated. Detecting stronger human pulses, they swarm towards the cartellers. Caught off-guard, the men are overwhelmed. They scream in agony as razor limbs butcher them.

Meanwhile our medical patches are wearing off. Ramone, Pietro and I are regaining our strength. Which means we're regaining our biometric signatures too, and will soon be magnets to these spiders once more.

We scramble up outta the hatch. Ramone is first out, immediately turning to pull me and Pietro up. One of the cartellers flings themselves after us, screaming for salvation as a spider slices into his hamstrings. Ramone intercepts the man, somehow stealing his pistol before kicking him back into the hatch.

We're all running for the canoe. Cartellers are following us; spilling out of the bunker. But with spiders clinging to their backs, they don't get far before the robots bring them to their knees, slicing through tendons and spinal nerves. The executions are messy and protracted, designed to traumatize any observers and create a perimeter of fear. Like we said, landmine 2.0.

We're about to climb into the canoe when Ramone switches direction for the cartellers' boat.

"Come on, it'll be quicker!"

Pietro and I dive in after him, clinging to the sides of the hull as Ramone hits full-speed reverse. We pull back from the shore as the spiders continue dismembering the screaming cartellers.

The machines are grotesquely methodical; first cutting ligaments in the legs, then the arms. With their victims immobilized, they attack the face; first removing the ears, then the nose, followed by the tongue, and one eye. With the victim quivering in pain, they slice off the skin from the bottom half of their face. Finally, they plunge a razor through each ear canal, ensuring that even the most advanced medics on the planet can never reverse their horrendous work.

With the cartellers mutilated, paralyzed, and bleeding out on the shore, the spiders' eyes shrink to a minimal red glow. Quietly, the machines scurry back inside the bunker, perhaps to hibernate, or to dig more tunnels at a glacial speed. Either way, I have no doubt they'll be ready for the next intruders.

Ramone spins our boat around and we power away, distancing ourselves from the dying cartellers in case they had time to put out a distress call.

A warm, metallic taste swirls in my mouth. Blood. I gingerly press a finger around my teeth; my gums are bleeding. Not like the gingivitis you get when you miss a tooth in your daily hygiene routine. This is like *all* my gums are bleeding out of the blue. The symptoms are getting worse.

As the speedboat bounces, my eyes fall on the bundled tarpaulin opposite me. It just moved of its own accord.

Pietro's thinking the same thing. I hold a finger to my lips and creep up to the sheet, then whip it off in a flash.

"Don't hurt me!" comes a cry.

"Woah, who the hell are you?"

A grubby man is curled in a ball, holding his hands up in surrender.

"I the driver, nothing more! Please do not killing me, señor!"

"You're a driver for the cartel?"

"I driver for anyone! When cartel ask me to drive, I saying yes. I not having choice."

"Sorry to break some bad news to you, pal, but you've not got any choice here either. Take us to whoever's running this part of the forest. We wanna meet your employer," I say.

"Are you crazy?" You wanna go *to* the cartels now?" says Pietro.

"This forest is a patchwork wasteland yet no one else knows about it. I want answers. We need to know who's behind the destruction on this scale, who their customers are, and what their endgame is."

"No way – that's journalism talking. I did not come to this country to hunt down cartels! I must find my ancestors' tribe. I have vowed to help them protect themselves and restore their habitats. But they can only do so with sustainable technology and expert guidance. I am the only person in Mazonil equipped with the breadth of knowledge required to achieve this."

"Jesus, kid, this is a conversation, not an academic funding pitch. Just admit you're too scared," I growl, dabbing a cloth inside my bleeding mouth.

"The *arrogance* of you Northerners! I am risking my life to be here. I will not allow you to ruin my plans for the sake of some article rich people in a developed country will read once then throw away forever, while you get some shiny accolade!"

"Contrary to popular belief, lizard boy, I ain't here for awards. You think you're the only one making tough choices? I should be in a hospital right now. My body's a ticking time-bomb but you don't hear me bleating about it because I'm focused on the bigger picture: saving this damned place."

"Do not paint me as selfish, you damned journalist. Everything I am trying to do is for the future of the people living in this forest. We *cannot* deviate from that cause. Ramone, back me up here?" pleads Pietro.

"Sorry, boy, but I am with Luke on this," says the ranger.

Pietro's face falls like he just got stabbed in the back. Ramone slows the boat and steps away from the helm to elaborate.

"The gringo journalist is right. We cannot keep fighting the cartels like this, racing from one skirmish to another. We must find the head of the snake." He turns to the cowering stowaway. "You, driver, take the controls. You're going to take us to the cartel behind all this. Not to the minions, not to the soldiers. Take us to the top."

CHAPTER FIFTEEN

PABLA

I am on my own, hundreds of miles from the township, deep in enemy territory. One of Stax's men dropped me here a few hours ago. He raced away immediately, not wanting to get further embroiled in the dangers of my mission.

This will be my first contact with the Hudara tribe. Older people from my village used to describe them as "our forest brothers and sisters", until relations cooled. Oriana once told me a rumor that the Hudara had found a way of mixing certain metals into fertilizer, magnetizing the forest so that drones cannot fly beneath the trees. To me this sounded genius – they had created a natural Faraday cage. To my elders, apparently, it was heresy.

Whatever the Hudara did seems to have worked. Stax's drones cannot penetrate the forest, leaving his men vulnerable. The two sides are locked in a grinding guerilla war, and Stax is under pressure to win it quickly. But the Hudara have spread across the land in small groups, stealthily repelling the cartel through lethal attacks on workers and equipment.

Which is where I come in. Stax's secret weapon. Or rather, his hostage of fortune. I have fallen victim to a sunk cost fallacy. If I do not do this mission, he will lose his position as a cartel leader, and I will lose my only way of recouping my share of the stolen quantum crystal. Paradise City glimmers in my mind, so tantalizingly close. If I just complete this mission, I can get out of this damned country.

Stax withdrew his men from this part of the forest ahead of my arrival. The tribe's annual sacred festival is coming, meaning the Hudara will convene in a hidden location for a short time. After that they will scatter again to defend their land for another year. This is our one chance to strike them down for good.

My task is simple: I must kill the Hudara chief. Under their sacred laws, this will force their tribe to surrender. At that point, Stax will send in his men to secure the land. They are waiting in a hover ship, hiding among the clouds, ready to swoop at any moment. All I need to do is find a clearing, where my tracker has signal to the skies, and say the trigger word twice: *falcon, falcon.* My phone will relay it to Stax, and his men will descend.

Of course, all of that hangs on me being able to find this elusive tribe in the first place. And more importantly, on them not killing me upon sight...

I have been trekking for two days now, searching for signs of the tribe. My arm is still tingling from where the cartel medical drone tried to laser off my algal tattoos back in the township. At least it healed the wire cuts to my neck. Overall the treatment left me feeling elevated for a short time, but that is wearing off as the fatigue of trekking sets in. I need a breakthrough.

Up ahead something red and white appears between the trees. I creep closer to inspect. It's a forest incantation; a ghoulish mask painted to invoke the spirits of the ancestors in times of need. It looks fresh. I scour the area and spot another in the distance. As I approach, I see a thin plume of smoke. Not the sort of thick, smothering cloud you get with a clearance fire. This is the tell-tale sign of a camp!

With a pang of excitement, I pick up my pace, trekking the mile or two it takes to reach the base. But when I arrive, it is deserted. The fire is a smoldering stack of embers. My eyes turn to the ground. By my estimation, three warriors were here. Based on the fur and bones around the fire, they hunted a monkey for food. The sight of the animal's remains sends a chill down my spine. Perhaps this is why we never fully allied with the Hudara. For the first time, I am grateful for the ink that was forced on me.

A creaking a branch makes me spin around. I am too slow on the draw; not that I have anything to draw. I raise my hands in surrender as a warrior faces me through their mask. Their bow is pulled taut and pointing at my chest. There are no medical drones out here, that is for sure. That arrow could spell my death. Everything hangs on these next words.

"May the bird nest proudly," I say.

The warrior says nothing, but makes a chirping sound. Two others emerge from the forest, drawing their bows as they see me.

"May... may the bird nest proudly, and your ancestors smile..."

"For the forest is theirs, and yours, and ours," replies the warrior.

The words are warm but their tone is not. I have said the greeting of their people, but the woman's arrow is still pointed at me. Have I missed something?

"What brings you to our land, stranger?"

"I am Pabla of the Centada. I come in peace, with a message for your chief."

"I can relay your message."

"I must deliver it in person."

"That will not be possible."

"It is important, it concerns the safety of your tribe."

"Our tribe is at war."

"I know. And I am bringing you a way to end it, so that you can return to your lives. Please, I understand that your festival is soon. Will you honor me by allowing me to join you, so that I may relay my offering? I am unarmed, and if your chief does not approve I will leave in whatever direction you choose."

The warrior keeps her bow trained on me and whistles again. The two others move through the trees on either side, holding my gaze. By the time I spot the fourth, to my side, it is too late. With a soft hiss, a dart flies through the air, striking my neck. As the sedative enters my blood, the forest falls black, and I crumple to the ground.

When I awaken, sometime later, I am in a canoe. The bump of the boat against the river bed is what has woken me, and the three warriors are climbing out. The leader extends a hand, pulling me up.

"Sorry we had to sedate you. We had to be sure you were unarmed before we took you in. And our location of the ritual must remain secret, I'm sure you understand," she says.

"Si," I reply, still a little dazed.

As I step from the canoe, I see the other boats camouflaged beneath mangroves. The excited chatter of an entire village wafts through the air. There is a celebratory spirit as people reunite for the first time in a year.

Lining the path from the river to the camp are totems; sticks adorned with decorative masks and headpieces, all evoking the spirits living among these trees, inviting their ancestors to gather too and be present with them for the festival.

The tribe must be several thousand strong at least; much greater than ours ever was. Some of the huts look semi-permanent, while the majority are temporary tents and hammocks pitched among the trees.

People sit in groups talking, drinking, and laughing together. Some are getting high on special plants, others are dancing. As we pass by they stop and mutter, pointing at me, staring. I am the only person here not bearing the Hudara people's distinctive red facial tattoo of three vertical lines on the forehead and the chin. The harpy eagle across my face and the dozens of animals and plants inked across my limbs all mark me out as different. Not a welcome thing in a time of war, especially not in their sacred camp. This is the one place the outside should never reach.

A villager glances at me then breaks away from their group and disappears up a path, entering a hut larger than all the others. The front is decorated by forest flowers and braided vines. Clearly it is the chief's hut. As the guards lead me towards it, I place a hand on my satchel, discretely feeling for my phone.

"Looking for this?" says the guard beside me.

He waves a metal cage at me, which is housing the device, and cutting it off from all external signals. The cage is crude, improvised out of discarded wire clothes hangers, presumably scavenged from the detritus that is dumped in our shared rivers by neighboring countries.

"Uh, yes, I was," I reply, blushing.

"The chief will decide when you can have it back."

"Of course... It is not tracking my location or anything, I just need it for the chief – to deliver my message."

The guard nods, fixing me with an unsettling, knowing smile, like she is happy for me to believe whatever makes *me* happy. It is the face people pull when they are in full control of a situation. It is not a face I like seeing on others.

The foremost guard opens the curtain to the chief's tent and disappears inside. After a moment, she reappears and beckons us in.

The interior of the hut is lit by candles and solar lamps, and smells strongly of incense. A woman is bathing in a tub fashioned from woven branches and waxy leaves.

"Chief Gayane, we have a prisoner from the outside," declares the guard beside me. "She requested to speak with you and was carrying this."

The guard hands over my phone to a maid, who approaches the bathtub and shows it to the chief. The woman in the bath is middle-aged and scarred. Her back bears the mottled skin of a burns victim, while her cheek is etched with the faded signs of a bullet wound.

"And who might you be?" she asks.

"My name is Pabla of the Centada tribe. My humble greetings, oh chief."

I bow respectfully, practically folding into a half pike. I have never greeted another village's chief formally before, so I am not entirely sure where to draw the line with the formalities. Best err on the side of groveling caution, I think.

"Stand up straight, and talk straight. I can't abide anything else. Understood?" snaps the chief.

Her face is stern but not unkind. She has the brisk, neutral pragmatism of a leader who has born the burden of responsibility for many years, and is used to cutting to the chase because of it.

"So, Pabla of the Centada, what brings you to my tribe?"

"I hear you are at war with the cartels, chief?"

"Not so."

"You are... *not*?"

"No. They are at war with *us*. We are not attacking, we are defending our home. Therefore the war is theirs; and the dishonor also.

Relief sweeps across me. Stax has not sold me a total red herring then. At least the war is real.

"That is why I am here, oh chief. I wish to offer a deal. A peace between your people and the cartel."

"Oh? And on whose authority would that be?"

"I am representing my tribe. We have struck a deal of our own with the cartel, to protect our land. We wish to broker a similar peace for you now, so that more of the forest may be protected."

The chief raises her arms and a maid sponges her down. I am not quite sure where to look. These people may have figured out Faraday cages, but apparently a bath curtain is a stretch too far? As the naked woman stares me out, I realize it is all part of her power play.

"A noble offer, Pabla of the Centada. Might I ask how you are able to represent both your tribe and the cartel?"

"I do not represent the cartel, oh chief. I am here on

behalf of my tribe only. It is our belief that negotiating with the cartels is essential for the protection of the forest. But we cannot do it alone, and fighting has cost us many lives over the years. You of course will know this too, chief?"

"You presume too much, Pabla. Why should we worry if defending the forest costs our lives? On the contrary, each death is but another soul liberated to drift between these trees."

"Of course, chief, but surely you can't hope to defend the forest if all your warriors end up as drifting spirits?"

"What makes you think that will happen?"

"You're losing fighters every month."

"The cartel are losing more."

"But they can replenish faster. They accept fighters from all over Mazonil and beyond; people who do not care for the forest or its people, but just want to earn a quick wage."

"Perhaps, but you're overlooking a key factor: the cartel are growing desperate. We have rendered their clearance drones useless, and we terrorize their soldiers with ambushes and superstitions. We are winning."

"With all due respect, Chief, I would not call hiding in the forest and seeing your people but once a year 'winning'."

"Stop thinking in terms of years and the lifetimes of humans, Pabla. It is the lifetime of trees we are interested in. For they hold our spirits, and the spirits of our ancestors, long after our bodies have decayed."

"You really think you can outlast the cartel in a guerilla war? You can't possibly raise families like this. How thinly will you have to spread yourselves as the months go on? Chief, I am here because there is a better way."

"Allying with the enemy, is that what you're saying?"

"The cartel were our enemy, it is true. But they have

enemies too. Namely, the other cartels. We have allied with our former enemy to protect our own community from encroachment."

"Are you really going to pretend to me that it is a partnership of equals?" snorts the chief.

"It is a partnership that works. Their weapons are superior, but our knowledge of the forest, the spirits in it, the way of nature, exceed anything they could dream of. Over time we will teach them our ways."

"You are naïve to think so. The cartels aren't interested in your ways or ours, they are mercenaries, united only by greed."

"You call me naïve but you will find I am pragmatic. There is a better future available to all of us, if we are willing to compromise."

"And there it is. The price."

"Of course there is a price, oh chief. The cartel must pay a price too; they must forgo their expansion ambitions and confine themselves to what land they have already stolen and cleared. We will lose those territories forever, but in return we get protection against incursions from other cartels, and we gain certainty that what forest remains will be respected as ours."

"So you propose we meet with the cartel and... what, Pabla? Give them half our land in exchange for a promise that they won't take more later? If your tribe has done that, then you are more stupid than we thought."

"We didn't give it away for free, chief. We were paid in credits."

"We have no use for money. The forest meets all our needs."

"Is that why you are relying on other people's waste for your security solutions? Nice Faraday cage by the way. We have reinvested the credits in equipment, sensors, and weapons. For the first time, we are able to monitor our entire territory, and meet aggressors with equal firepower. We have sold half our land to safeguard the rest for future generations."

The chief smirks like what I have said amuses her. She snaps her fingers and a maid drapes a shawl around her shoulders, pulling it tight at the front. The chief pauses as a healer takes her hands and rubs petals over them, muttering words of prayer, before the woman takes a seat on her ornately-carved wooden throne.

"It is funny you should mention future generations, Pabla. How long has this pact between the Centada and the cartel been in place?"

"A year now, and it is working well, chief."

"Interesting. Very interesting. So how do you explain reports from my scouts that your tribe is no more?"

"Your scouts are mistaken," I reply, curtly.

"These particular individuals are very reliable. One of them was uniquely well-informed. They told me the cartel destroyed your village, killed all of the warriors, and forced out the refugees. Which would make you not so much a negotiator as a survivor, would it not? Which is curious, because my scouts had a most disturbing report. One that I, as someone who loves their people above all, find nearly impossible to believe. That someone could sink so low. Apparently, the cartel were able to eradicate your tribe because one particular Centada betrayed all the others. Can you believe that?"

The chief folds her legs and rests her hands across her lap. She glares at me, coldly. My throat feels dry. I am glancing around, looking for an exit between the guards.

"Well?" she presses.

"Er... It is like I say, chief, your scouts must be mistaken. I assure you, my tribe is in fine health and prospering under the new arrangement. In fact, I strongly encourage you to meet with the cartel, so you too can understand what they have to offer your people. If I may have my phone, I can arrange the meeting?"

"Oh, that won't be necessary. My business with the Centada is done."

"But, chief, I have only just arrived. Surely you will consider-"

"I do not mean my business with you, Pabla. For you are not a Centada."

I blink, taken aback.

"But... you can see my tattoos plainly. I am as Centada as they come."

"No, Pabla, you're not. For a true Centada would never betray their people."

"I... I don't know what you mean."

"Oh, I think you do. Perhaps my scout could refresh your memory?"

The chief claps her hands and a curtain at the rear of the tent opens. A woman steps forwards with a quiver of arrows over her shoulder, and a vial of algae around her neck.

"Hello, sister," says Oriana.

CHAPTER SIXTEEN

LUKE

"Luke, wake up!"

Pietro's shaking me, he's right in my face, and he's looking concerned.

"Woah, what the hell dude?"

"You fell asleep!"

"Yeah, I figured that much. What's with the rude awakening, we're still on the river."

"You let your arm fall in the water!"

"So?"

I look at my arm and it's absolutely fine. Alas, the same can't be said for my hand, however, which is bleeding like an open bar at a wedding. Some river-dwelling bloodsucker has had a good chomp while I was out. It's chewed my middle finger down to the knuckle, peeling me like a god damned satsuma.

"Holy crap! How did I not feel this?" I cry.

"It's the merdows – they're descended from piranhas. Smaller, but in many ways more deadly. Their bite contains an anesthetic to stop their victims from resisting. Be glad your hand was only in there a short while. I've read of people having entire limbs stripped to the bone without realizing."

"How long does the anesthetic last? Oh fuck, I think I can answer that question! *Christ* that hurts!"

"It wears off when you leave the water."

"So water numbs the pain?"

"Yes, but that is how the fish evolved. They want you to return to the water so they can keep eating you. You must resist the urge."

"Easier said than done, brosef. You're not the one looking at your own knuckle bone!"

"You, carteller. Does the boat have medical supplies?" says Ramone.

"No, señor. They don't give us that stuff," replies the driver, failing to mask his delight at my injury.

"Will there be a medical kit at your base?"

"Maybe, who can say?"

Ramone nods, sagely, then grabs the carteller's arm. The boat swerves as he drags the man from the helm, leaving Pietro to leap up and stabilize it.

"No... no señor, please!" begs the carteller.

But Ramone's not in the mood for games. He slams the man against the hull and thrusts his right arm into the water.

"Please, señor!" yelps the carteller.

"Don't wriggle, you'll only attract more of them," grunts Ramone.

"*Pleeeease!*"

Ramone hauls the man's arm up. It's perfectly intact.

"Hmm. Maybe they need a little encouragement."

He grabs his hunting knife and pricks the carteller's middle fingertip deeply, then thrusts the man's hand back underwater. The guy writhes and squeals until eventually settling down with a whimper.

"Er, Ramone, that's probably enough," says Pietro.

"Huh? Oh, yeah," says Ramone, snapping out of whatever grim dream he was having.

He hauls the man upright again and seizes his wrist for inspection. The carteller wails in despair as we all see the damage. His middle and index fingers have been stripped from the nail down to the palm, leaving only sinewy strands of muscle and skin hanging off the pointy bones.

"What have you done to me!" cries the carteller.

"Given you some motivation. Now you will find a medical kit for the journalist, and help yourself in the process. It's a win-win," says Ramone, coldly.

Tucking his mutilated hand under his armpit, and groaning as the pain takes hold, the carteller barges Pietro from the wheel and takes the boat to maximum speed. Ramone was right: a little encouragement goes a long way.

As we progress through the river, the water darkens. An algal bloom covers the surface, interspersed by dead fish. The forest on both sides sickens, too, thinning out until only fields remain.

We pull up beside a wooden jetty. I can't tell if the sickness in my stomach is from my eviscerated finger, the bleeding in my mouth, or the gross monoculture surrounding us. As we step off the boat and onto the farm track, the scale of the plantation hits me. For as far as the eye can see, it's row upon row of perfectly aligned crops.

Tethered drones fly over the fields, spraying them with pungent chemicals.

"This farm is *huge*. Who owns it?" I ask.

The boat guy ignores me and races along the dirt path, his injured hand still tucked away. He's heading for a shed at the edge of the field. Pietro runs ahead, keeping pace with him, while Ramone stalks close behind, taking dignified but powerful strides to keep up.

I'm scurrying after them all, nursing my own injury. When I reach the shed, it's with huge relief that I see the carteller retrieving a medical drone from a cabinet. He flicks the device on and it quickly diagnoses the injury, applying healing bandages to his hand.

"Luke first," says Ramone, hauling the carteller away from the device mid-treatment.

I feel kinda bad for the guy, but also kinda not. The carteller backs away, cursing and wincing with pain. The healing drone attends to my injuries. The device is basic compared to what we get in the Northern Bloc, but it's a damned sight better than walking around with an exposed bone.

A clicking noise pricks my ears. I duck just in time as the boat guy returns, firing a pistol right at my head. Quick as a flash, Ramone's on him. He disarms the man with a series of blows.

"You little snake! Was that your plan all along? Bring us here, get your shitty little gun, and then kill us? Huh? Use us for fertilizer?" growls Ramone.

"Forest trash, all of you," spits the carteller.

He makes a desperate bid for the intercom hanging on the side of the shed but Ramone restrains him.

"I guess we can't trust you at all," says Ramone. "Any reason we should keep you alive?"

"Yes. So I can watch my comrades feed the three of you to my dogs!" he spits.

"Woah, dude, you've really taken a turn since the whole fish thing. I thought you were pretty mellow earlier, but now I'm like, 'who's this asshole?' It's like I barely even know you, man."

The carteller spits at me, prompting another gut punch from Ramone.

"Sorry to disappoint you, *comrade*, but your dogs will go hungry today," says the wily ranger. "If only I could say the same about the fish."

Smothering the man's cries, Ramone drags the carteller to the jetty. I pop my head out of the shed and watch as the burly silver-haired ranger hurls him into the water. He stands on the side, with his hands on his hips, looking disappointedly at the flapping carteller, who is yelping and splashing frantically as he tries to clamber out. But every time he places a hand on the side, Ramone kicks it away.

"Yo, Pietro, you're a scientist, riddle me this. Farm run-off causes algal blooms, right?"

"Correct."

"Which depletes the river's oxygen, causing dead fish, right?"

"Also correct."

"Reckon there's enough O_2 in there for those carnivorous merdow things? Or is Ramone just taking this guy for a swimming lesson?"

Pietro muses for a moment, while we watch the carteller yelp and splash around in the water.

"Interesting," he muses. "I would love to write a paper on this someday."

The carteller coughs several times, then stops struggling. He's face-down in the river, floating like a starfish. The water ripples all around him, buffeting his body like he's being pulverized on a paintball course.

"I guess that is a 'yes' to your question," nods Pietro.

Satisfied that the boat guy no longer poses a threat, Ramone rejoins us. My hand is fully bandaged, and the machine has injected me with something to stop my gums bleeding for a while, so that's a double-win. Although it printed out a little slip that says *SEEK URGENT HOSPITAL TREATMENT*. That makes me a little less confident in my prognosis.

We set off inland to find the people running this operation. I'm hoping my retina camera is capturing all of this, because it's hard to describe the scale of destruction around us. These people have torn up ancient ecosystems that took millennia to evolve, and for what?

"Look, a farmer!" says Pietro, ducking down.

We hide between the crops and peer out at the farmer, who is riding a harvest machine. Ramone raises the pistol he stole from the cartellers, but I stay his hand.

"You can't just shoot him!" I whisper.

"Why not? He is cartel!"

"So?"

"They are the enemy and we are at war!"

"Ramone, we're the good guys. We can't just pick off unarmed enemies whenever we like it. Boat dude aside. This is how wars self-perpetuate!"

Holy crap, am *I* the voice of reason here? That can't be good. Note to self: make new friends. If I'm the moral compass, things are going seriously wrong.

"A killing is justified," says Ramone. "The man is destroying the forest and its people. What I propose is not murder, it is revenge."

"Oh, so you're saying it would be a righteous kill?"

"Si."

"Nah, I can't get on board with that, brosef. It sounds like a real slippery slope."

"You truly believe the world will be a better place if we let him live, gringo?"

"I'm saying that's a serious and irreversible decision and we don't have all the facts yet."

"This is *so* typical of you Northerners. It is *exactly* what your governments said when Mazonil collapsed. You stood by, wringing your hands, and no one was brave enough to take a moral stance and accept that sometimes, bad people have to die in order to protect the good ones. Because of your cowardice, the good ones died, and the bad people now control this country. We are in this position because of you. So don't you *dare* judge me for wanting to take this shot!"

"Fine. Your call. Do whatever."

"What?" says Ramone, confused.

"I'm saying go for it, if that's what makes you happy."

"No, something has changed – your tone is off."

"My tone's fine. What you're hearing is probably that little thing called your *conscience*."

"Coño!" fumes Ramone. "*Fine*. I will sedate him with a dart. Are you happy now, white man?"

"Very!" I cheer. "Although it really triggers my guilt when you call me that. Can we agree on another nickname, like *legend*? Or *raptor*?"

Ramone grabs his dart gun and shoots at the farmer, hitting him perfectly in the neck. The man falls from the control seat into the soft mud. We scarper towards him to seize the vehicle, and bind him before he can call anyone.

"Er, is he supposed to be foaming at the mouth?" I ask, as we arrive.

"*Estas jodidamente bromeando!* He's having an allergic reaction to the dart," cries Ramone.

"For real? Damn. That is major bad luck," I sigh. "We

really tried, you know? Ah well. Let's hijack his truck and go find the base."

The three of us hop onboard the dead farmer's harvester. It's a tight fit, but it's an open casket, so Pietro and I are able to sit on the edges, while Ramone takes the controls.

"Let's see... That looks about right," he says, tapping a button with a home symbol on it.

Cartel HQ, here we come.

CHAPTER SEVENTEEN

PABLA

It is nighttime. I have been in shackles, tied to this post since Oriana knocked me out. Members of the Hudara tribe file by, ridiculing me, defecating at me, and pelting me with rotten food. Word has spread of my alleged betrayal of my people, and it would seem that such a thing is not taken lightly here. No wonder, these *malditos bastardos* have been fighting an unwinnable war for years now. The only power they have is the strength of their own delusion; the ludicrous idea that, armed with wooden arrows and make-believe spirits, they can control their future. If pissing on me is what it takes to sustain that delusion, then I truly pity them.

The guards drag me into the chief's tent and shove me down on my knees in the center of a congregation. Surrounding me are the Hudara elders, both old and upcoming. All regard me with a look of disgust, like I am vermin.

"All rise for the chief!" declares a guard.

The assembled elders rise to their feet, with a chorus of hacking coughs and clicking knees, as the chief enters. She is dressed in a ceremonial robe woven from forest vine, decorated with fresh flowers. She sweeps through the crowd then takes a seat on her wooden throne, prompting the assembly to return to their cross-legged positions. If I am still sitting in the mud when I am an elder, I hope someone shoots me.

That young carteller whose phone I stole days ago had that video which opened my eyes. Such a simple thing; a city with people of all ages sat at tables and chairs, eating in restaurants. How is it that those people have gotten themselves out of the mud, while this lot cling to the dirt, chanting and smiling as if there is dignity in their pitiful traditions? All I see around me is stagnation. I wonder if these elders have lied to their juniors, too? Let us find out.

"It is with a heavy heart that I must delay our ceremony of the ancestors," booms the chief. "We must first deal with an urgent matter of justice that has fallen at our feet."

Credit to her, the woman can project.

"Pabla of the Centada, you are hereby brought before this council of the Hudara elders to stand trial for crimes against your people. Do you have any questions before we begin?"

"Sure. Will you be getting into the bath again or is it shower time now?"

Ouch. Oriana just punched me hard in the jaw. I hope that was her inking hand. Maybe I can make her punch me enough times that she gets arthritis before they execute me.

"You will address this court with respect, and you will take seriously what is happening here," she growls.

Oriana's eyes are blazing as she takes her place beside the chief.

"Is it a Hudara custom for a defendant to be shackled and beaten by their accuser during a court session?" I ask.

"Only if they disrespect the court," replies the chief.

Across the floor is a kind of "evidence plinth". Sitting on it is my phone, still in the tribe's Faraday cage.

"Pabla of the Centada, you are accused of facilitating a genocide against your people. There is no more heinous crime. Do you wish to enter a plea at this stage?" says the chief.

"Not guilty. Also, I would like the record to state that the piss on my clothes is your people's, not mine."

Oriana moves to strike me again but the chief waves her away.

"She's got you trained like a dog, hasn't she, dear sister?" I call. "Then again, that is how we were raised, hey? Obedient, unquestioning dogs. Loyal to the end. I hope you are happy under your new master."

"Oriana of the Centada," interjects the chief. "The court invites you to give your testimony as accuser."

My sister steps into the center of the tent. As she speaks, she circles me, leaning into my ear, spitting her words, then stepping back and shouting to the assembled elders with righteous indignation.

"This woman," she begins, "I used to call sister. But she betrayed us. First, she brought prohibited technology into our village, against the rules of our elders. The phone she brought belonged to a carteller, and it led the enemy right to us. You will note how she has come here under the same auspices! She found your tribe and professed to be here to broker a peace deal, yet once again is carrying a cartel phone, and this time it's a *different* one. A *new* one. She is trying to betray you in the exact same way! Do not be fooled. She is a liar and a snake. When the cartel tracked her phone signal, they burned our entire village to the ground. Because of her actions, our father died in the blaze.

She was exiled from our tribe, but returned, pledging to fight alongside us and defeat the cartels in atonement for her sins. Yet this too was a lie! I watched as every warrior in our tribe died from a poison *she* brought into our village. The cartel followed her, ensuring not a single soul survived. They showed us no mercy. And that is exactly what I call on this court to do today. Show this vile wretch no mercy!"

Oriana's testimony is met with cries of outrage at my actions, and support for her proposed vengeance. She strides back to her place beside the chief and glares at me, arms folded, legs wide apart, eyes blazing. The chief raises a hand and the assembly falls silent.

"Pabla, you have been accused of grievous crimes. What is your defense?"

"It is simple, oh chief. I am the victim here," I reply.

This does not go down well with the crowd. Partly because of what I am saying, but also because my tone is not *exactly* conciliatory. It is kind of provocative. But the way I see it, if these regressive, backward-looking mud dwellers are going to kill me, then they might as well at least know exactly what I think of them and their traditions before I die.

"First up," I project, "on the charge of bringing illegal technology into our village, I want to clarify that that was a ridiculous and oppressive rule by our elders, which belied a broader technophobia and social coercion that enabled them to subdue and control our tribe. Let me put that simply, because I can see you are a simple people: they lied to us to keep us small. If my elders had embraced something greater than trees, mud, and fifty year-old technology, then my father would still be alive today. My *mother* would be alive. And countless others. It is the elders, not me, who have blood on their hands."

I feel like this might have landed better with the room if I had insulted them less. I will try to remember that next time I am being sentenced to death by a foreign tribe.

"As for the charge of treason," I continue, "Oriana knows that was never my intention. I consulted her when I first found the phone, seeking only to get my dying father to a hospital. So I will confess to only one thing today, chief. And that is what I said when we first spoke: I made a deal with the cartel to protect my people. Unfortunately for both sides, my people vowed to reject any deal and fight to the death, leaving the cartel no alternative but to 'cut to the chase', as they put it."

"For someone claiming innocence you sympathize a lot with the cartel," says the chief.

"Have you seen their technology? I saw a guy's hands get cut off, then reattached within moments, like it was nothing! In my community, that person would have been disabled for life. Which would not have been long, because they probably would have died of sepsis. So yes, when I look at the medical technology the cartels use compared to the useless relics our elders permit, I find it hard *not* to pick the side that *actually* looks after its own."

The chief rises to her feet and the room falls silent.

"Pabla of the Centada, you have shown no remorse for your crimes. You have expressed pride in your actions, and sympathy for those who slaughtered your people. These acts cannot go unpunished. For these crimes, the sentence can only be death. In your elders' absence, I solemnly call upon the elders of the Hudara to judge your fate."

The chief turns to the assembly.

"All those who believe the accused should be exonerated, speak now."

There is silence as the chief casts her fiery gaze over the crowd.

"Now those who believe the accused is guilty, and must face death, make yourselves known."

From all sides, the beating of chests fills the tent, as the elders vote overwhelmingly for my execution.

"Very well! It is unanimous. Pabla of the Centada, you have been found guilty on all counts. This court hereby sentences you to die. What say you?"

"According to my tribe's customs, a person sentenced to death has the right to face their accuser in final combat. I ask that you grant me this wish."

"Your dying request is to fight your own sister to the death?" says the chief, disgusted.

"It is not as selfish as it seems, chief. It will bring my sister the closure she needs, and a chance to avenge our father with honor, as she sees it."

"Oriana?" says the chief, turning to my sister.

"So be it," says Oriana, through gritted teeth. "It will not take long."

"Very well! Guards, provide each combatant with a knife. Elders in the front, you may move if you desire, though guards shall be on hand to contain the fight if needed," says the chief.

No one moves, save for two guards. One furnishes Oriana with a blade, while the other cuts my bindings, freeing me from the stakes and equipping me with a comparable dagger.

"Begin!" declares the chief.

Oriana squares up to me, feet planted wide, legs bent, ready to lunge or pivot nimbly. Her face is grim, entirely fixed on the task ahead. Whatever love there was between us died with the rest of our tribe. She is not just ready to do what is necessary, she is longing to do it. For her, this is redemption; avenging our father and her fellow warriors.

I have no desire to kill her. On the contrary, I still wish she would join me and the cartel, but this is no time for discussion. My aim right now is to avoid death. We both know she is the better warrior; stronger and more experienced. The only thing in my favor is that I have sparred with her since childhood. I know how she thinks.

As we circle each other, wielding our knives, I feel a sharp jab in my back. One of the guards has thrust me into the center. Oriana interprets this is a lunge, which it has to become mid-way. I clumsily shove my blade out as I stumble forwards. She dodges deftly, but I have to react super-fast because I know what is coming. As she steps to the side, she thrusts her knife out, aiming for my stumbling body. I throw myself to the ground and roll, narrowly ducking the blade.

Whatever dignity the Hudara elders purported to carry quickly evaporates in the face of some blood sport. The crowd are bating and heckling like we are bears in a pit. As I roll, the guards kick me, while elders jab me with their staffs.

As I stagger to my feet, Oriana advances. I have nowhere to retreat. With a cry, she lunges forward, feigning a stab with her right hand. But in the same move, she switches the blade to her left, and delivers a second thrust.

This is my only chance. I leap, twisting mid-air to dodge the stealth blade that I anticipated. Suddenly it is within reach, and un-guarded. I propel myself towards the evidence plinth. By the time the guards realize what is happening, I am upon it. I pry the faraday box open and seize the phone. I hurl the empty box at Oriana's head, forcing her back for a precious second, while wielding the knife around me to stop the guards closing in.

Stax is my only chance of survival. In the next few seconds, Oriana is going to deal me a fatal blow. My only hope is to broadcast our location, and hope the carteller was serious when he said he and his men were waiting in the clouds. I am banking *heavily* on them having a medical robot on board. Clutching the phone, I scream the precious trigger words.

"Falcon! Falcon!"

None of us are ready for what follows. The phone emits an impossibly loud, ear-splitting tone. The sound suddenly comes from every direction, like the cartel has hijacked the magnetized trees, using them to amplify the attack wave.

Everyone in the tent collapses in agony, clutching their ears. My head feels like it is going to burst. If there was a time to try and escape, it would be now. But I can barely stand. The sonic attack is disrupting my balance. I'm staggering from side-to-side with no control.

Someone barges into me and I hit the deck. Oriana lands nearby. She looks at me with popping veins across her forehead. Summoning every ounce of strength, she claws her way towards me as both our worlds spin.

Her discarded knife is lying in the mud, halfway between us. Our eyes meet and for a fraction of a second time stands still. Then we lunge for it. Oriana reaches first, but I grab her wrist. She's forcing the blade towards me. I bite down on her hand, drawing blood.

She drops the blade, screaming in pain, though I cannot hear her above the sonic weapon. She strikes my face repeatedly, dazing me further. I block her arm just in time as she goes for a larynx chop.

Suddenly the piercing sound vanishes. Someone has plunged a knife into the phone, destroying it and killing the signal. I seize upon Oriana's lapse in focus and throw her clear. I try to run but I find myself vomiting, my cochlea still spinning from the auditory attack.

Screams resonate beyond the tent walls. The sound of quadcopter blades and crunching branches fills the air. Flashes of light burst outside, reflecting off the tent's red fabric.

A guard stumbles into the tent moaning in pain, shuffling forwards with her hands outstretched. Her eyes are wide open but it is clear she has been blinded. Cries of "drone!" sweep towards us like a wave.

Oriana's hand seizes my shoulder and she spins me around. I intercept her hands but the knife is just inches from my stomach. She is so much stronger than me. There is little I can do to resist.

"It is not too late, big sister! Join my side and we can have a future together!" I implore.

Oriana's eyes narrow, full of hate.

"This is for father," she growls, before thrusting the blade into my stomach.

A drone flies into the room as Oriana and I collapse to the ground. My eyes clamp shut as the blinding light flashes through the tent, prompting more screams of pain. I peer out through milky vision as cartellers storm the tent in military uniforms. All have protective black goggles on. As my vision fades, I recognize Stax's figure strolling through the writhing masses, making a beeline for the wooden throne. The chief has fallen from the seat and is pawing the ground, blindly.

"Ah, you must be chief of the Hudara?" says Stax, cheerfully. "Goodbye."

He shoots her at point-blank range. The last thing I see is a calcified view of the bullet tearing through her skull, dashing the ground with her brains. As I land on my back, my hand moves to the gushing wound across my belly. Warm blood is seeping between my fingers. My vision is failing and Oriana is nowhere to be seen. I never thought my dying moments would be alone. With my final breath, I cry out Stax's name, then fall still.

CHAPTER EIGHTEEN

LUKE

We've been riding this harvester for three hours and my ass is numb. Ramone is content, sitting pretty in the operator's seat, while I alternate which butt cheek rests on the frame beside of him. I'm losing my mind as we ride this endless green treadmill of soya beans.

"Over there, look," says Pietro.

A series of warehouses appear on the horizon. As we cross the last few miles, the soil beneath the tractor becomes dry and brittle, crunching apart in pale lumps. The immaculate, identical crop rows are thinning out and shriveling. By the time we reach the warehouses, we're driving on sand.

We climb out and approach the door. To my delight, it's unlocked.

"Gotta love rural communities, so trusting," I remark.

"I will go first," says Ramon, drawing his pistol.

Fine. By. Me.

I love that he thought I was gonna go first. I *never* volunteer to go first. People who go first get shot. I volunteered to open the door, so that I could hold it open for someone *else* to go first.

I slip in behind Pietro, who is closely following Ramone. As we enter, the warehouse door closes behind us. Not in a creepy haunted-house way, just in a good draft-excluder kinda way.

This warehouse is huge. We're talking like ten stories high and many football fields long. It stinks, probably because it's rammed with cattle. Each row contains hundreds of animals, and the rows are stacked several dozen high. The whole place is like some giant cow vending machine.

Running along the side of the warehouse is a service path, which Ramone is exploring; cautiously peering into each aisle before proceeding. The row nearest us is full of calves. Pink-skinned and plump, they're lying down in their individual pens, separated by metal partitions. As we progress, the cows grow older. By the fifth aisle they're young adults, although their hides looks patchy and thin. Already, I've seen thousands of animals and not a single one is standing.

The cows' limbs are withered and deformed, seemingly bereft of bones or ligaments and too spindly to bear any weight. Most of the animals have only two or three legs, some have none at all.

As we continue onwards, the cows reach full maturity. Their limbs haven't grown, but their torsos are vast and swollen. The adults have outgrown their pens such that their heads are hanging off the edges, their necks pressed against the harsh metal and lined with abrasion scars.

The next row is making strange noises. Not the classic "moo" we're taught to sing as kids. These are pained squawks coming from malformed vocal chords. As we continue, the cause becomes clear. Rods have dropped down from the roof of each pen and are electrocuting the lame cows.

"Why the fuck would they do that?" I proclaim.

"The owners are compensating for the cows' immobility," says Pietro, grimly. "Electrocuting the muscles stimulates blood flow, allowing oxygen, nutrients, and artificial hormones to circulate."

"Why are the hormones artificial?"

"You think cows are this size normally? These poor creatures have been bred like this."

"It is barbaric," growls Ramone.

As the caged animals twitch and squawk, with bulging, pained eyes, I search for a way to stop the machine, but there are no switches or controls in sight. A mechanical noise rings out, and with it, a fresh chorus of distress that draws us to the next row.

Hosepipes are dangling from a monorail along the ceiling. There's one pipe for each column of cows in the aisle. The pipes are working their way down the rows from top to bottom, moving in unison. First, the lip of the pen tilts up, forcing the cow's neck up too. Then the hose covers the cow's face like an oxygen mask in an airline. Only, this isn't delivering air.

On the tip of each hose is a long funnel. It by-passes the cow's tongue and reaches through to their esophagus. The hose quivers and rattles as it force-feeds the animal, pumping it with a synthetic grain cocktail until the creature's stomach is full.

The funnel is then dragged out of the animal's mouth, cleaned by a mechanical appendage, then the whole pipe rack drops down to the next row of cows, and the process repeats with ruthless efficiency.

"Bastardos!" cries Ramone.

Pietro and I tear ourselves away from the grim feeding spectacle and hurry through the rows to find the silvery ranger. The cows grow larger and older with each aisle that passes, like we're watching a time-lapse video. The smell is getting worse, too. Something new is in the air. Chlorine? Yes, but it's masking something. What *is* that? My footsteps turn from dull concrete thuds to wet slaps as something liquid coats the floor of the aisles ahead.

Blood.

Unlike the battery of feeding hoses, this final machine is one of a kind. A dexterous, elite robotic butcher. Like all good headliners, this superstar waits for its warm up act to finish.

A basic assistant robot shoves a plastic bag over the cow's head and pulls it tight, suffocating the animal. The cow grunts and twitches but its bloated sides are hemmed against the cage, and its withered limbs are useless. The poor creature jerks its neck; the only muscle it can control. The inside of the plastic grows moist and clings to every contour of the cow's face; its flared nostrils, its screaming mouth, its straining jaw.

Finally, the animal drops dead against its cage.

The city can sleep safe for another night, thanks to the brave and heroic efforts of the suffocation bot.

With the cow asphyxiated and the crowd warmed up, octobot moves in for main show. That's what I'm calling the butcher robot, by the way, on account of it having eight limbs and a disturbing level of skill.

First, it deploys a circular bone saw to cut off the

cow's head, which it catches with one of its floating arms. Then it grabs the cow's body and hauls it from the crate, dangling it upside down. Blood gushes out through the severed neck onto the floor. I glimpse the cow's underbelly, which is covered in bed sores, and its udders have been crushed and necrotized by its own weight.

Suspending the carcass with one arm, and still clutching the severed head in another, the octobot uses its remaining limbs to skin the animal, then butcher it. A vacuum pipe sucks all the flesh away, while the skin is blasted with hot air then folded and stowed in a tray full of hides. Lastly, the bare skeleton is tossed, along with the head, into a trash chute on the wall. The sound of a bone grinder rings out from the metal hatch until octobot slams it shut.

With a job well-done, the robotic butcher and its heroic sidekick, plastic bag bot, move onto their next victim. The fresh cow is quivering with fear and covered in its neighbor's blood.

Pietro is hunched against the wall, vomiting. Ramone, however, is about to blow. With a cry of rage, he grabs the nearest cage and tries to force it open.

"Ramone, what are you doing!" I say.

"We cannot let this go on. We have to help them!" he cries.

"I'm with you dude but they're bred to be crippled. How would they escape? Where would we even take them?"

Ramone's hyperventilating. His shoulders are heaving and his fists are clenched as adrenaline courses through his veins.

"These are sentient, living beings," he growls.

"I know we have to shut this place down but we gotta be smart about it. Let's look for a control module," I urge.

As I try to pull Ramone away, there's movement in the ceiling high above us. A doorway in the warehouse wall has opened. It leads to a mesh walkway suspended above the rows of cattle. A pair of workers step onto it, chatting casually and seemingly oblivious to our presence. Both the man and woman are wearing overalls and rubber gloves, and are dragging a barrel towards the rear of the warehouse.

"We should get out of here before we're seen," whispers Pietro.

"Not yet! We have to know what they're doing here," I insist.

"I agree with gringo," says Ramone. "They may reveal the command module for us to hijack. Both of you, stay close to the ends of the aisles, those are the only places we can be sure they will not see us."

We follow Ramone, each spaced a row or two apart, moving from end to end in short bursts, while glancing up at the workers to check they're still oblivious. We follow them to the rear of the warehouse where we first entered, near the young adolescent cows.

With the barrel deposited, the workers split off. While one retraces her steps, we stay with the first man and the barrel. He descends to the bottom row of cows via a crane platform. We press ourselves flush to the ends of the aisles, peering carefully at the worker, who is now at eye level, albeit a hundred yards away in the center of the building.

The worker turns his back on the young cows and faces the row before them, which is obviously a wall of cows' rear ends. The man plunges his rubber glove into the barrel, coating it in a white sludge, then inserts it into the rear of the first cow, prompting a distressed squawk.

"Yeah, yeah," mutters the worker, as he moves onto the next.

I think the scientific term for this process is artificial insemination. I call it: fisting a cow without consent. Ramone and Pietro look queasy, watching the gloved man move from animal to animal with his liquid vat and mechanical platform.

As he reaches the halfway mark, a buzzer sounds from the front of the warehouse. He removes his glistening glove from the latest cow and hits a button on his crane. The platform shoots upwards, suspending him above the highest row, and forcing us to pin ourselves flat to stay hidden.

As the klaxon rings, orange lights flash across the warehouse. With a clunk and a shudder, the aisles creak forwards. Every vending-machine-style row in this vast warehouse is shifting forward to take its predecessor's place.

As the aisles stop moving, they click into their new positions. At the same time, the foremost aisle, where the resident cows were being decapitated and skinned by the octobot, is now empty. Through great cables and rails overhead, the whole aisle is being hauled upwards. It rotates onto its back and slides over the tops of all the other rows, dripping blood on them as it goes, until it reaches the vacant space at the rear of the warehouse. If you picture a garage door crowd-surfing, it's kinda like that. Just add blood and cages.

Now at the back, the stack of shelves is lowered into place, passing through a series of chlorine nozzles until it lands with a thud.The klaxon falls silent, the lights stop flashing, and the gloved worker descends with the crane to continue fisting cows. Pietro whispers, beckoning me to follow. Ramone's already leading the way, nipping between the ends of each aisle towards the middle of the warehouse, where the female worker is operating a control panel from the top of the walkway.

With the push of a button, two platforms descend either side of the central aisle, where the cows are swollen. The first is a pipe spanning the width of the warehouse. Face masks protrude from the front; one for each caged animal. The pipe stops a few rows from the floor and the masks latch onto the cows, covering their mouths and noses. The second platform pulls level behind the cows, holding a bucket to each cage.

Three robotic arms rise up from either side of the buckets; two forceps and one plunger. The woman flicks a switch and the status lights above the pipe rail switches from amber to red. The cows' heads jerk as they try to resist the gas.

The first animal's water breaks, quickly followed by another's. A cascade of amniotic fluid gushes forth as labor is induced across the entire row. A set of hooves emerge from the nearest cow's vulva, prompting the robotic midwife to spring into action. Latching onto the calf, it drags the infant out from the mother's womb and deposits it in the collection bucket.

Within a minute, the entire row of buckets has been filled. The gas pipe retracts and hovers mid-level, waiting to be deployed to the rows above. The traumatized cows groan, trying in vain to twist in their cages to see their young.

The row of buckets is raised to the ceiling, where it changes tracks on the overhead rails and moves to the back of the warehouse. From there it descends to the recently emptied, bleached shelves, and the quivering calves are tipped into the cages that will hold them for their entire lives. The cages are hosed once more, flushing the remnant birthing fluids off the calves, before a gray silicon teat drops down inside each pen, giving the calves pink fluid to suckle from.

Pietro tugs at my sleeve, too disgusted to speak. Ramone has found a doorway into the next part of the facility. As we pass beneath the giant *Warehouse 14* sign, a shiver runs down my spine. Right now I just want a warm bath, some soft jazz, a cuddle from Ms Ratchet, and to forget everything I just saw. But instead, I'm hurrying after Ramone and Pietro, and following signs towards a place I *really* don't wanna go: the processing plant.

CHAPTER NINETEEN

PABLA

I wake up with a gasp. My hands move straight to my stomach, where Oriana thrust the knife. A solid wall of skin greets my fingers. My brain is playing catchup with my surroundings. I am alive, and... on a boat? We are speeding across expansive blue waters, the likes of which I have never seen first-hand before.

"Boss, she's awake," says someone nearby.

I recognize the voice. Craning my neck, I see Axl sitting on the berth opposite me. I swivel my legs around and sit up, allowing my dizzy head to acclimatize as Stax joins us.

"How goes it, sleeping beauty?"

"The wound – the dagger – you healed me?" I stammer.

"That was a nasty scratch she gave you. But we took care of it, don't worry," chuckles Stax.

"My sister – the one who stabbed me – where is she?"

"Oriana?"

"You know her name?"

"She and I met one time, back when I was trying to buy the Centada land from your daddy. I thought she was grumpy that day. Now I know it's just her face."

"Is she-"

"She's been dealt with, along with the Hudara. That's all you need to know. Relax, Pabla, you did good."

My head is spinning as I recall the events before I passed out. I always knew Oriana was a fighter to the core, but I never thought she would *actually* try to kill me. Papai was right to ink the black caiman on her; cold and deadly, what better fit? I never would have dreamed that the cartellers who killed my father would be the ones to save me from my own sister days later.

"If Oriana and the Hudara tribe are all gone, why did you save me?" I ask.

"Because you delivered your end of the bargain."

"That has not stopped you from double-crossing me in the past?"

"True," chuckles Stax. "But like I said, you did good. You have proved you can be useful, and useful is worth keeping around. I think this partnership could work nicely, you know? Now have some food – I need you fresh for your next job."

Stax opens a picnic hamper and passes me a piping hot beef burger. The scent of burning cow flesh makes me gag, and I shove his hand away.

"Suit yourself," he shrugs, taking a bite.

The boat bounces and Stax freezes mid-chew. A look of horror grips his face. He is staring at the burger in dismay, pounding his chest as his face turns red. Axl leaps to his feet and pats Stax hard on the back, yelling at his boss to cough it out, which he fails to do. His veins are bulging, and his splutters are becoming weaker. Jumping up, I push Axl out of the way and grab Stax from behind, delivering a short, sharp abdominal thrust. The hunk of burger dislodges from his windpipe and disappears overboard.

"I guess that's karma," splutters Stax.

He tosses the rest of the burger overboard and slumps into a seat to recover. As the color returns to his cheeks, he chuckles with laughter. Axl passes him a beer and Stax toasts us both.

"Like I said, Pabla, I think this partnership could work!"

"Where are you taking me?" I ask.

"To a meeting. A *very* important meeting, with a very important person."

"Who?"

"The boss."

"The *big* boss," adds Axl.

"Which is why this is way above your level, rookie. But I need a face like yours for the meeting. Consider it a sign of trust that I chose you. Keep it up and you'll have your ticket out of Mazonil in no time," says Stax.

"I should already be getting out of Mazonil, that was our deal," I reply.

"Sure, but then you got stabbed, so now you owe us for medical bills. Don't worry, you can pay it off with this meeting."

"What must I do?"

"Speak only when spoken to, and back up anything the big boss and I say."

"What if I do not like what you are saying?"

"Then you'd better learn to like it quick, otherwise you'll be getting to know the ocean a whole lot better," says Stax, his charm vanishing.

The distant, gleaming white boat on the horizon is getting closer. Within a few minutes, we're pulling alongside it. Axl drops anchor while Stax smooths his appearance and pops another button on his shirt.

Freeship Tyrenel, reads the boat's inscription. As we float beside it, a ladder emerges from the hull.

"After you," says Stax, graciously.

I climb the rungs, passing two levels of tinted port windows before reaching the top deck. A servant welcomes me onboard with a bow, and offers me a cool, lemon-scented face towel.

In the middle of the deck are a series of elegant loungers. Three people are gathered across them in a horseshoe. A man and woman, both dressed in formal suits and sweating like pigs, sit opposite a man in a fluffy white dressing gown, who is telling a story and laughing heartily.

Stax joins me on deck, while Axl stays below, tending the speedboat. Stax mops himself down with the lemon cloth then whispers close to my ear.

"The man you are about to meet is more powerful and more dangerous than anyone you have ever known, myself included. Do not contradict him, do not insult him, and do not speak out of turn. Understood?"

I nod and follow him to the lounger area.

"Ah, boss, I see you've already got the party started!" chimes Stax.

I've never heard him sound so convivial, even with Axl.

"Stax, good to see you. And Pabla, of course, welcome to you both, do grab a sunbed. Come, sit, relax! We're all family here," beams the man in the fluffy robe. "What can I get you to drink?"

"Sparkling water would be wonderful, thank you Mr. K. That will do for both of us," Stax adds, cutting me off.

"Of course!"

The robed man claps his hands twice and a servant emerges from behind the cabin, placing two sparkling waters on the table before us. The servant is curvaceous in the extreme, with a tiny waist, and immaculate skin. Her skimpy uniform accentuates these features, and shows off more than enough of her cleavage to reassure me there will be a spare life raft there if this thing goes down. She moves with a gliding quality. As her eyes flicker, I realize the being I am looking at is an android. If the carteller's video of the restaurant with tables and chairs had impressed me, this fully automated humanoid robot is blowing my tiny forest mind. And I say that as someone who knows for a *fact* that I have exceptional IQ – I did a bunch of tests on our encyclopedia growing up. There was little else to do, plus it was something I could *just* about beat Oriana at.

"Gracious, Mr. K., How did she do that so fast?" says the suited man, marveling at the lightening arrival of our drinks.

Mr. K. claps his hands with delight. The man in the suit is ogling the servant with parted lips and an unpleasant breathlessness, while his female colleague is staring at the wall opposite with a tired, depressed look.

"Oh truly you two flatter me. Are you telling me this little gizmo hasn't hit your markets yet?" says Mr. K.

"No, I dare say she hasn't, otherwise I'd have had one long ago!" chimes the sweaty man.

"I'll see if I can pull a few strings, Ted. Perhaps I can rustle up an early release model for you both?"

"That would be truly splendid, Mr. K., goodness me yes," gushes the man.

"I'm fine," clips the woman, her lips pursed.

"I'm an investor in the Northern Bloc company which manufactures them," continues Mr. K., cheerfully. "*Comp-unions*, we call them. Wonderfully versatile machines, and highly customizable."

"But the drinks? How did she do the drinks? Your

colleague said sparkling water and she appeared with it poured within just a few seconds!"

"Prototype telepathics. She's the ultimate servant, anticipating your very needs before you even know you have them. When these two boarded the yacht, she scanned their impulses, and correctly anticipated that Stax would order two sparkling waters."

"Remarkable!" gushes the sweaty man.

"Quite," mutters the woman.

"One of my finest investments. Although perhaps we are about to surpass that today, Ted, Kate, hey? Let's talk business, now that my associates are here."

"Oh, must we?" laughs Ted. "Can't we squeeze in another tour of the aquarium?"

"All things are possible, my friend," crows Mr. K., warmly. "But I am anxious that I'm keeping Stax and Pabla here from their business back on the mainland. We have many clients, and we try to run things efficiently."

"Of course, yes, quite right," nods the man. "Ah – oooh..."

The servant robot is behind him now, giving him a shoulder rub. Kate, his suited colleague, equally clammy but not half as happy, opens a tablet and brings up several holographic displays of their project.

"As you know, our client is the second largest device manufacturer in the world," she begins.

"I thought they were first?" interrupts Mr. K.

"So did they, but it appears that their competitors in the Southern Bloc have made significant progress in the last two years. Largely on account of the outrageous tariffs their government has placed on our client's goods, but that's another matter. The point is, global demand continues to increase exponentially, and our client is preparing for a product launch next year twice the size of this year's. Our job is to scale up their supply chain to meet that demand in a way that aligns with the company's values."

"And what are those values, may I ask?" beams Mr. K.

"Innovation, inspiration, and impact."

"Beautiful, I love it. Some companies are all about profit and it is so vulgar, you know? It's refreshing to meet a client who dreams bigger than balance sheets. Olives?"

"No, thank you. We were certainly impressed by the samples you sent, and the work you've been doing for Sequestra. Indeed, they recommend you highly. But our current client is naturally worried about sustainability. It's a key concern for many of their shareholders."

"Or their wives, at least," snorts Ted.

"Absolutely, and such concerns are truly valid," says Mr. K., warmly. "I can assure you, Kate, sustainability is at the heart of our operations. That is why, in fact, I wanted you to meet Stax and Pabla today. Stax is regional director for the quadrant that would be serving your client's needs, so he knows all the ins and outs of our operations with a forensic boots-on-the-ground level of detail. While Pabla here is one of our rising stars, and our indigenous communities ambassador."

"Nice to meet you," says Kate, giving me a polite half-smile.

"You too," says Stax, jumping in.

"Pabla, please can you describe the company's commitment to running an ethical supply chain?" asks Kate. "What kinds of procedures do you have in place?"

"Oh, we have all the requisite measures in place, Ma'am," interjects Stax. "We pay fair wages to all our employees, many of whom are local people. We prohibit child labor, and even educate our workers' children for free, ensuring the whole family is looked after. In a sense, Ma'am, your client would be sending hundreds of Mazonilian children to school."

Kate nods and makes a note on her tablet, then scrolls to the next question. Her sweaty colleague is nodding sagely, with fluttering eyelids, as the robot servant moves to a scalp massage.

"What about biodiversity? That's another key concern for our client."

"All of our sites are net positive when it comes to environmental impact," smiles Stax. "You can see that from the satellite feed, no doubt. Thanks to us, and the generosity and integrity of our clients, we have been able to restore swathes of forest. By using Mr. K.'s patented mining technologies, we are able to ensure a minimal impact on the landscape. Whereas conventional mines have to clear a huge area to access rare earths, we operate more like keyhole surgery. Pin-pointing the precise location, making a single, non-obtrusive incision, and moving laterally from there, Ma'am. We've got a video of how it works, would you like to-"

"Mr. K. has already shown us the video, thank you," says the woman, crisply.

I am impressed. Stax's ability to bullshit on demand is second to none. The people in the suits seem to be swallowing it, too, and Mr. K. is surveying the whole exchange like a proud grandfather.

"Our client is also interested in exploring another project with you," continues Kate. "We have recently acquired a former state asset in western Mazonil."

Mr. K.'s smile falters. His eyes dart to Stax, who looks equally taken aback, and like his ass is going to get roasted later for not having furnished his boss with that intel. Mr. K. swiftly recovers and folds his hands across his knee, jovially.

"Congratulations on your new acquisition, I am delighted our brothers and sisters in the west country were able to assist," crows Mr. K. "What is the asset to which you're referring?"

"It's a former pluridium mine," explains Kate. "Our client's engineers believe there are significant untapped reserves beneath the site. However, all companies must now adhere to a carbon quota."

"New regulations from up high, you know how our government is," chips in Ted, waving his hand like he's wafting a fart.

"Our client wishes to move more of their operations to Mazonil, and consolidate their extraction and refining facilities."

"Of course, the relocation would entail a *degree* of impact on the forest," adds Ted, eyes closed and luxuriating in the massage.

"Not a problem," declares Stax. "We are perfectly equipped to help your client offset any impacts."

He glances at Mr. K. as he speaks. I get the impression that his very life hangs on how he performs in this next maneuver. Can he redeem himself for the intelligence failure?

"Our factories are clean by design," continues Stax. "We use carbon capture chimneys. The latest spec. Oh, we recycle materials from old government sites. Yes, uh, lots of good things."

"Splendid, splendid," mutters Ted, tilting his head forwards so the robot can massage the top of his neck.

"We would be looking to use the river for increased

exports," says Kate, "Is that something your company can facilitate at scale?"

"Absolutely," says Stax. "We're a multi-modal company, working in all manner of environments that Mazonil has to offer. We're experts at moving extracted and refined freight through natural waterways with minimal impact on the local environment. Indeed, Ma'am, just on the way here, my colleague Pabla and I were discussing the successes of our last waterway restoration. We even managed to reintroduce river dolphins to the area, isn't that right, Pabla?"

"Huh? Oh, uh, yes. Many dolphins," I nod, emphatically.

"Your client would do well to build this refinery soon, while other investors are dozing," says Mr. K. "The timing would give you the jump on their capacity for next year. I have it on good authority there may be some... *disturbance...* at your client's competitors' plants next year. But perhaps that is for another discussion."

"Our client is not entirely sold on your site just yet, Mr. K.," says Kate. "They're acutely aware of the history of landslips at the former state mine. What measures would your company take to mitigate against this risk?"

"Mmm. Mitigate," mutters Ted.

Mr. K. looks to Stax with a warm smile, but beneath it his eyes are blazing.

"Well, we, uh, plant lots of trees," stammers Stax.

"But you just acknowledged you would have to clear further forest to build the on-site refinery, how does that tally?"

"Well, uh, you see, Ma'am, the thing about refineries... is... uh..."

"Ours are immune from landslips," I blurt.

Stax and Mr. K. are staring at me with astonishment. Oh God, I am fully committed now.

"Uh, with sites like these," I continue, "we use the natural safe harbor of the water itself, by building a floating platform. It is basic Newtonian physics, but we use it to our advantage. The platform allows the refinery to rise out of harm's reach in the event of the landslip, while allowing us to reforest the land that would have been designated for the refinery site. By using a modular refinery design, to distribute the mass of the building across the floatillas, we are also able to harness both hydropower from the river itself, and piezo kinetic energy from the movement of the connectors between modules."

"Do you have a video of that?" says Kate, impressed.

"Not yet. Mr. K. has a patent pending on the design, so we're only sharing its details with our must trusted clients," I explain.

"Quite right, gotta protect the IP," mutters Ted.

Kate taps some more notes on her tablet, then banishes the hologram and stows it away in her satchel.

"Those are all of our questions, thank you all for your time. I know Ted and I appreciate it."

"Boy do we," chuckles Ted, as the robot massages his chest.

"Wonderful!" says Mr. K. "I'm so glad we could assist you both in this matter. Do reach out to me if you have any further questions regarding our sustainability. It is something we take very seriously."

He rises to his feet, claps both hands together, and humbly bows his head. Kate and Ted rise too, straightening their jackets and extending polite handshakes all round.

"We'll be recommending you to our client indeed," gushes Ted. "What a first rate organization this is. And wonderful to see a diverse hiring policy in action," he adds, gesturing to me.

The two suited visitors follow Mr. K. to a drone pad on the top deck, and depart in short order. Mr K. returns to the loungers and silently accepts a dark green beverage from the robot. There's an uncomfortable silence as Mr. K. drinks slowly, sipping and watching the quadcopter vanish into the distance. Stax is barely breathing, which gives me limited hope for my own survival chances.

"Thank you for coming, Stax. You may return to the mainland now. I trust you will keep me better informed in future?" says Mr. K.

His bright tone persists, but the smile is gone. Stax swallows nervously, and offers groveling assurances.

"Oh, and Stax, don't think I'm entirely out of the loop. I heard some disquieting rumors about a failed coup in your township. You wouldn't know anything about that, would you?"

Stax is squirming. "Aha, yes, ah, that... I'm not sure 'coup' is appropriate. It really was more of a minor disturbance, Mr. K. A few bad apples, swiftly dealt with. Your authority has been – *is* – stamped on the township. The entire region in fact. Just yesterday we took the Hudara territory."

Mr. K.'s eyes widen. I can feel Stax twitching with nervous energy as he capitalizes on this rare piece of good news, keen to sweep his failed usurpation of his boss under the rug.

"Good job, Stax. If that is true, then you must be exceptionally busy now. I will not keep you."

"Uh, no, very good, boss," says Stax, bowing. "We'll get going, then."

"Not 'we', just you," corrects Mr. K.

"Huh?"

"Your colleague is staying with me."

"She *is?*" says Stax.

"I am?" I interject.

"Goodbye, Stax," insists Mr. K., curtly.

"Uh, yes, goodbye, sir."

Stax throws a leg over the ladder then pauses, wistfully taking in the luxurious yacht, before glumly descending the rungs back towards Axl.

"As for you, Pabla," says Mr. K., placing a hand on my shoulder. "I have uses for you."

CHAPTER TWENTY

LUKE

The stink of this place is off the charts. I'm holding my nose as we pass through the automated processing plant. Output from all sixteen warehouses converges here, feeding a series of assembly lines where the meat is reconstituted into burger patties, steak slabs, and tins of mince. Beside me, a hose from warehouse fourteen is spitting cow flesh into a grinder, which produces patties, which get shrink-wrapped and sleeved.

I snatch a pack off the assembly line and inspect the cardboard overlay. *Crown Acre Farms*. Below the gilded, cursive title is a picture of a cow roaming freely in a luscious meadow. My eyes fall on a rosette on the bottom corner: *Responsible Farming Awards: Silver*. Christ, seriously? If these are real awards then I have major issues with the judging panel. And if they're fake awards, then why did the company give *themselves* second place? Besides, after everything we just saw, I'm wondering what the hell you'd have to do for bronze...

At least I've finally found a company we can pin this

place on. If I can get a photo of the label to my editor, maybe she can do some digging for me on her end. Dream scenario, she does a quick internet search and it reveals a series of smoking guns, a paper trail of corporate malpractice, and a boatload of evidence for the international courts to prosecute some big ugly multinational that's doing this.

How do I know it's a big ugly multinational? The fact that the label's printed in my language not Mazonilian is kinda a big hint. Hopefully they're registered in my bloc, so that our government can prosecute them. That's definitely preferable to it being a domestic outfit. I'm not sure I wanna try hand-delivering a subpoena to a cartel.

If my editor comes through then this product label is my ticket home. I've had my fill of Mazonil's horrors. Judging by the looks on Pietro and Ramone's faces, they're as eager to leave this place as I am. Ramone is scoping the corridor beyond and beckoning us through. Pietro and I catch him up, arriving in a deserted control room.

"Yo, Ramone, you've got a phone, right?" I ask.

"No, gringo."

"Sure you do – I saw you call Cynthia earlier to pick up those orangutans."

"I am saying 'no' to whatever you're about to request."

"I just need to send one *teensy* little picture message to my editor," I say, holding the meat pack up in front of my chest, trying my best to look cute.

"If I switch the phone on, we broadcast our location."

"We have to take that risk. If we don't, we could lose our chance altogether! Think about it, if armed workers come through that door right now, that's it, game over. I can't imagine for a minute they'd take well to me asking them to hold off the execution squad while I take a quick selfie with their snack packs of suffering and zip it off to my editor back home."

Ramone contemplates, chewing over the options with his fierce, uncompromising stare. Before he can respond, Pietro interrupts from across the room, hunched over a bank of monitors.

"Er, you guys might want to see this."

The monitors shows two different maps. One has lush forest, while the other is mainly crops and desert.

"Do you see?" says Pietro.

"See what? That it sucks to be the second map?" I reply.

"They're the same place! Look at the river."

"Is that the river we took here?" says Ramone.

"I think so," says Pietro.

"So what is this, some kinda before and after photo?" I ask. "Like when you sign up for a new diet, then realize the tablets are making your hair fall out and if anything, all that's happened is you've gained fat on your elbows?"

"It is not a before and after. It's a live versus a feed," says Pietro.

"Er, what?"

"The second map shows the real current state of the land. While the forest map is being used as a live feed projection of that same area."

"Like a video stream? Who the hell's tuning into this? Did the paint-drying channel go to a commercial break or something?"

"That's what I am showing you! All this time, you have been asking why the world does not see what is going on here, and now we have the answer."

"What, one video feed of a fake forest? That doesn't track. How the hell would this loop deceive thousands of international satellites peering down on Mazonil? Sure, I could see them hacking a couple of satellites, but military ones too? Private space companies? No way, they're too secure."

"What if they're not hacking them?" says Pietro.

"Whaddya mean?"

"What's easier than fighting the cryptography on every different satellite? Finding one way to dupe them all. All they need to do is broadcast a cloaking signal!"

"The video?"

"No – the video is a machine's translation for human eyes. The satellites themselves do not see like us. Which means the cloaking signal cannot just be the video. It has to produce the sort of electromagnetic readings satellites would expect to register over dense forest."

"I'm guessing that would have to be a hell of a strong signal?"

"Yes, and broadcast from multiple sites."

"Like this?" says Ramone, pointing to the far wall.

There's a bare-bones map of the entire country, showing terrain, roads, and the locations of old cities and townships. Plus one curious set of features: a series of pin-prick lights across the map. Most are white, others orange, and a handful red.

"That's it! It looks like a mesh network," cries Pietro. "Look, the white lights correspond exactly with the regions that have been heaviest hit by the loggers. Each light must denote a hub like this room. Maybe a smaller version of it, but something similar, controlling the satellite jammer."

"Wouldn't that require huge masts on the ground, to broadcast the signal?"

Ramone shunts a side door open and sticks his head outside into the daylight, then steps back in.

"Confirmed," he says. "There is a huge mast behind the last warehouse."

"Subtle," I mutter.

"This room must be controlling it!" says Pietro.

"So if we destroy this room, the jamming signal will vanish and the world's satellites will see the true state of the forest?" I ask, excitedly.

"The signal would only vanish over this region. The rest of the mesh network will still work," says Pietro.

"There must be some kinda center controlling *all* of it, surely?" I ask.

"There is – according to the schematic there's a command hub somewhere in the port city of Aquerba," says Pietro.

"Then we must go there," says Ramone. "I will destroy the hub, and we will bring the whole network down," he says, punching his palm.

"I'm with the big man," I agree. "If we do that, the rest of the world will see the scale of what's going on here and they'll have no choice but to intervene. I mean that seriously. This is gonna screw us all *really* badly. It's undone a *lot* of mediocre climate protection work."

"It's not that simple, guys," says Pietro. "There is something more urgent than the hub."

He points to the schematic.

"OK, so that dot is orange. What's the big deal?" I shrug.

"Did neither of you read the key?"

"There's a key? Ooh check it out, the yellow one's us! Woah, we are *not* where I thought."

"The orange one is the problem – it means the forest is earmarked for clearance," says Pietro.

"OK. We're all agreed that sucks, but I still think we need to prioritize getting the broader word out to as many people as possible."

"I agree we need to tell people what's happened, Luke, but this is different," urges Pietro. "This is *about* to happen – and we can stop it! Ramone?"

We both look to the silver-haired ranger for his verdict.

"You're both right," he sighs.

Ugh, honestly, *such* a dilf this guy. He'd make an amazing father. Unlike me. I'm an atrocious father. I should be back home raising my semi-estranged kids, but instead I'm in the middle of the rainforest trying to save the world from its own deeply flawed economic structures *again*. Oh, and my ear is bleeding by the way. Just thought you should know.

"Sorry, Pietro. I must side with Luke. We cannot guarantee to save those people in a meaningful way, Pietro."

"But that was our whole agreement! That's your thing, right? Defending the forest against the cartels?"

"In the most effective way possible," counters Ramone.

Pietro is pulling his hair out, getting really worked up.

"Woah, lizard boy, take a beat. We're all agreed that this decision sucks. But why do you care about this particular tribe so much more than all the others?"

"Because they're my family!" snaps Pietro.

Oh shit. It's really hard to argue with that. Before I can respond, a blade smashes down into the server stack beside me. Ramone has found a fire axe, and is attacking the mainframe.

"Woah, dude, what are you doing?"

"We should save Pietro's tribe, and we should take

down the command hub," he grunts, in between axe swings. "But right now, gringo, I am getting the ball rolling. I have let these bastardos win for too many years. If we die tonight, then at least we have destroyed one jammer!"

"Ramone, I think you've triggered an alarm," says Pietro, concerned.

"Of course I have triggered an alarm! I am hitting their computer with an axe! You two better help me before they come," snaps the ranger.

Pietro and I grab whatever implements we can find and help Ramone smash the room up until an electrical fire is in full swing.

"Ramone, let's go," I urge, "Under no circumstances do I wanna be acquainted with that gloved dude and his barrel!"

Ramone hurls the axe into one final computer then steps back, satisfied, as the maps fizzle out across the screens.

"Si, gringo. There is a truck parked outside by the mast. Now we run."

CHAPTER TWENTY-ONE

PABLA

We are preparing to disembark the yacht. I am wearing a tailored suit made of silk printed by Mr. K.'s ship, and fashioned by his drinks robot during the six hour cruise here. It feels tight and constricting, but they assure me it is a perfect fit.

I am giddy with excitement; we are about to enter Paradise City. My dream of escaping Mazonil is already becoming a reality. But I must be careful too. I am with dangerous people, and I am entering this city as their guest. If I step out of line, they could get me deported, and I could be back to square one with nothing. Assuming they do not just kill me outright. Until I have a sense of how this city works, I must keep Mr. K. sweet.

But as I enter the deck, I am perplexed. We are drifting towards an atoll with a few palms trees and not much else going on. An autonomous tug boat is pulling us into the shallows. It pauses alongside a floating buoy, which projects a holographic guard. The woman is smiling, and wearing a similar suit to me. Wait, am *I* a border guard now?

Welcome to Paradise City. Please provide your credentials.

Holy

Mr. K. conjures up a holographic briefcase and seems to swipe it from his wrist across to the buoy, where it reappears beside the customs guard. She places it on an invisible table and examines the papers inside, before stamping and returning them.

Thank you. Your credit is sufficient to enter. Welcome back, Mr. Kesquadora. Have a pleasant stay.

The hologram vanishes. As the tug boat drags us forwards, Mr. K. turns to me expectantly, like I was supposed to be blown away by that experience. Sure, the hologram was neat, but the island itself is desolate. Why are we even here?

As we pass beyond the buoy, my disappointment is flipped upside down. The scraggy desert island was a digital mirage – I am staring at a colossal, gleaming megacity!

"What the hell just happened?" I cry.

Mr. K. is laughing, delighting in my amazement as I drink in the spectacle. The scale is breathtaking; a real-life embodiment of the elite private cities I used to read about. It is a hive of activity, with drones and cars cruising among skyscrapers which interlink with walkways and twisting, gravity-defying architecture.

Welcome to Paradise City, says another woman as we disembark the boat.

At first I think she's a hologram too, until she places a gilded garland around my neck and a kiss on my cheek.

"See that building?" says Mr. K. He points to a gold-and-glass tower in the distance. It is shaped like an hourglass and covered in dangling green vines. "That's our hotel."

I think he expects me to be excited at this, too, but I

am becoming overwhelmed. Also, I have no idea what it is like to stay in a hotel. Apparently they are places of luxury, but anything that is not crawling with spiders and termites is already luxury in my mind. This *sidewalk* is luxury.

A square billboard pops up in front of my eyes, so close that I stagger backwards.

Welcome to Paradise City! Blue Skies Casino invites you to the VIP lounge, with three free spins on us.

The hologram features a small pale man with ginger hair and a green suit. He seems to have a pot of gold. Is he the manager of the casino? Why would he carry gold in a pot when everyone else uses crypto currencies?

I turn my head, trying to look past the advert, but it is following me, clinging to the center of my vision like a cataract.

As I try to wave it away with my hands, my eyes land on a puppy, which is tethered to the marina.

Have you tried Robo Pooch yet? Meet your new best friend! Cuddly and loyal. Yours for just eighty credits an hour.

Is that good? I have no idea what the standard rate is for hiring a luxury robotic dog. I shake my head harder, trying to dislodge the two adverts, but more are popping up in their place, bombarding my entire field of vision.

Try our new slimline formula and unlock your true beach body!

Tired of diet drinks? Step out in a synthetic-flesh avatar. Rent your dream body and score your dream date.

Experience the new Asrato Supercar for yourself. Because driving is a way of life.

Are you looking for a discrete, no-questions-asked legal team to take care of your personal estate? By moving your wealth to our Paradise City Trust Fund you could save billions each year. Call now for a free VIP assessment.

Mr. K. is laughing as I stumble around, barely able to see the sidewalk through all the pop-up holograms.

"First time with neural ads, hey? You'll get used to it, don't worry. They're only allowed to follow you for half a block, anyway. Then they have to quit."

I trip over the edge of the curb, falling into a perfectly trimmed hedgerow. I'm trying to claw the blinding ads and shouting voices out of my brain. People must be staring because I'm wailing uncontrollably.

"Woah, take it easy! OK, here, how's this?"

Mr. K. taps his wrist and the adverts vanish.

Ad blocker installed. Forty credits deducted.

"Better?"

"Much," I gasp.

Mr. K. raises a finger to the roadside and a driverless buggy pulls over. He ushers me inside, then climbs in too.

"So tacky. Who chooses a golf buggy?" he mutters, closing the door.

He swipes through options on the dashboard, selecting a holographic shell for the cart.

"Hmm... horse and carriage?" he muses.

A gleaming white horses appears, along with a black and golden wooden carriage, only to vanish as Mr. K. swipes his fingers again. A metallic green shell cloaks us instead.

"A tank? Come *on*, this isn't a stag party..."

The swiping continues at eye-watering speed until we find a design he is happy with.

"Campervan!" he cheers. "Absolute classic. It reminds me of my grandparents, you know? They used to tell us stories of their holidays in these things, before the government fell. I think part of me is still jealous of their childhood. Shall we go and freshen up before our first meeting? Onwards, to the hotel!"

This city is everything I have ever dreamed of and more. It surpasses anything the encyclopedia could have described. The atmosphere! The styles, the colors, the buildings, the people, the smells, the traffic, the billboards, it is all so much to take in, I dare not blink for fear of missing something incredible.

Of course, it feels bittersweet being surrounded by these riches. I am overjoyed to have made it here, and to finally be rubbing shoulders with the upper echelons of the global elite. But this way of life, this city, these possibilities were kept hidden from me for twenty years. As I drink it all in now, I cannot help but feel cheated.

We were brought up to believe that the great collapse in Mazonil was part of a global economic implosion. The elders said it brought every nation to its knees and forced the survivors to reconnect with nature. We reconnected so closely that both my parents died prematurely. Standing here, in the lobby of a hotel filled with wonders, the scale of the lie hurts.

Two waist-height robots twirl towards us, performing a synchronized welcome dance. They are miniaturized humanoids, dressed in grass skirts and coconut bras, which is weird given that neither of them have heads. Instead, their necks are topped off by gold trays. The dance culminates in the robots laying out rolls of red fabric for us to walk across as we approach the front desk. I am hesitating, marveling at the interior of the building, and unsure how to interact with robots, but Mr. K. walks on blithely, even seeming a little tired of the whole show.

Overhead, there is a domed ceiling above the reception playing sounds of the ocean. Suspended below it is a shimmering cloud. A *real* cloud. Somehow they have managed to replicate the atmospheric conditions for it in here. A child stands across the lobby from me, staring up in equal wonder at the melding patterns and colors they are projecting onto this floating marvel.

While Mr. K. talks to the receptionist, I feel a tug. One of the miniature greeting robots, with a tray for a head, is taking hold of my hand. It looks up at me like it has a face, but all I see is a flat gold disc and what looks like the remains of someone's cigar. The robot gently leads me away, beckoning me to follow. Its grip is soft, and its hands are coated with white velvet. It is taking me to a reclining chair with a bowl of water at the base, with fish swimming in it.

The robot stops and points from me to the chair. When I hesitate, it pats the seat encouragingly. I am about to oblige when Mr. K. grabs my arm.

"Trust me, you don't wanna do that," he says.

"What? Why not?"

"The laws in this city are... *relaxed*. Robots can do more here than in other countries. You should only engage with ones that will talk to you and explain their terms. Otherwise, you're playing someone else's game. Come on, our room's ready."

I look at him, warily.

"Not *that* kinda room, relax *chiquita*, you're not my type. It's a meeting room. Come, there are some people I want to introduce you too."

Mr. K. teases me for wanting to ride the elevator again as we emerge into a finely decorated corridor with striped wallpaper and old fashioned maps hanging in carved wooden frames. He opens the numbered door to our suite and ushers me inside.

The room is large, decorated in pristine white and cream, with touches of warm orange leaf patterns across the cushions and the walls. In the center are two large couches, one of which has a man sitting on it. He is wearing a robe, and his head is covered with some richly embroidered cloth and a jewel-encrusted ring. Is he a sultan?

"Ah, Mr. K., wonderful to see you," says the man, rising to his feet.

"You too my friend," replies Mr. K., as they shake hands warmly.

"I didn't realize you were bringing company?"

"Ah yes, this is Pabla, our indigenous communities ambassador. She's new to our team."

"I can see that," laughs the man.

The two men chuckle, and it takes me a moment to realize they are laughing at my open-mouthed processing of the room's splendor.

One of the tray-headed robots glides in bearing a platter of foods. Each item on the tray is entirely unique, but half the size and width of my little finger. Is food scarce in the city? I did not get that impression on Mr. K.'s yacht – he fed me well.

Each of the two men take a morsel from the robot's tray-head and pop it in their mouths, chewing nonchalantly. As the robot comes to me, I imitate the men's off-hand manner, tossing a tiny parcel of food into my mouth and crunching down.

My eyes pop as hundreds of flavors explode across my

tongue simultaneously; sensations I never knew were possible. Whatever cool visage I was aiming for has clearly slipped, because the two men are openly laughing at my reactions. But truly I don't care; this is not about them, it is about me and a whole new world of flavor.

"She's priceless, Mr. K. Where did you find this one?" laughs the man.

"To tell you the truth, Faizal, she found me, really."

"Really? Remarkable! Some of them are certainly becoming emboldened these days. I suppose with increased contact, it makes sense. Gosh, I can't help but watch her eat. It's *fascinating*. There's something so... *authentic* about the way she chews, don't you think?"

"I couldn't agree with you more. She's a real asset to my operations. As a matter of fact, I think she could be useful to your outfit too."

"Pray tell," says Faizal, popping another canape in his mouth.

"Last time we met, you spoke of some heat your company had been dealing with. From certain vocal factions in your bloc."

"Ugh, don't get me started on those petal-humping flannels."

"It sounded like Sequestra could use a hand in the PR department, and I thought who better than our very own Pabla here?"

"Mr. K., I *love* that idea. You're a genius, man! We could call her our... what did you call her again?"

"Indigenous ambassador."

"Right! It's perfect, we'll call her that. Then there can be no argument about Sequestra engaging sincerely and openly with local communities. With the petal-humpers quashed, maybe I'll finally have time to focus on our export markets," snorts Faizal.

"Of course, she would play equally well with your investors, I'm sure," adds Mr. K.

"Oh absolutely, they'll love her. She'll be the star of the next conference, I'm certain of it."

The businessman stops talking and whips a napkin off the robot's head. Turning to the side, he spits out the food he's been chewing, and dumps the soggy parcel on the tray. Mr. K. leans forward and does the exact same, before both men look at me with mild curiosity to see if I follow – but I cannot, having already swallowed my food almost as soon as it entered my mouth. Because that is how to eat, right?

"We'll need to manage her, of course," mutters Faizal, still staring at me. "We can't expose her to everything at once."

"Mmm, agreed. Mustn't let her become accustomed to such things; we'd hate for her to lose that raw innocence," mutters Mr. K.

"Pab-lah," says Faizal, leaning forwards and speaking up like I am deaf. "How would you describe the impact of Mr. K.'s work on your forest communities?"

"I do not know anyone who has made a greater impact," I reply, truthfully.

I am enjoying Faizal's tone less and less. His face scrunches up as he tries to figure out if my response was a compliment or insult to my boss.

"Let's talk international development. Tell us about the impact you think more investment from Sequestra and its international partners would have on your community's way of life."

The words tumble out before I can think.

"It would destroy what's left of our habitat, our way of life, probably kill off the last of my people," I say.

The businessman stares at me, open mouthed, then laughs heartily, assuming it is a joke. Mr. K. glares at me with the intense death-stare he gave Stax on the boat.

"Uh, or at least that is what I *used* to think of international development," I continue. "Until Mr. K.'s company arrived and did it right. Now thanks to him and his open-minded investors, we have schools, healthcare, and job security."

"Hmm. Better," replies Faizal. "And what would you say about Sequestra's products?"

"Oh, my apologies but I do not think I have ever used any of them."

"We used to hear that a lot!" chuckles Faizal. "But not anymore. Let me put it this way, how does the air in this city smell?"

"Uh... fresh?" I reply.

"Yes! Alpine fresh, to be precise. Not bad for a city running on shale gas. You can thank us for that. We take the city's air and make it breathable and pleasant. No-one else can do that at scale, you know?"

"Why would you need to clean the air? Air is clean already," I reply, baffled.

"Aha! Oh Mr. K., truly she is priceless. The shareholders will *love* her."

"I am serious."

The man's laughter falters.

"Why do you need to clean the air?" I insist.

"Er, because of pollution," frowns Faizal.

"Air pollution?"

"Well, yeah, it's kinda in the name," he snorts.

"But why is the air polluted?"

The man's eyes narrow.

"That's not our concern, or our problem. It's the city's problem, and they've turned to us to fix it," he replies.

"By making it smell like alpine mountains?"

"The scent is customizable. Next month the citizens have voted for freshly-cut grass. They could have selected all kinds of thing – winter spices, bubblegum, ocean blast-"

"But you're already by the ocean..."

"Yes, but not everyone can smell it."

"Because of the air pollution?"

"Where there is Sequestra, there *is* no air pollution. We scrub it, you breathe it, that's our motto. Ooh, forest fresh! That was another of ours. I think the city chose it a couple of months back. I'll have Mr. K. hook you up with a sample canister – maybe you can let me know if it's accurate or not," he chuckles.

"You could always visit the rainforest for yourself. I would be happy to show you around," I reply.

The man's smile slides away as he meets my unblinking stare.

"Ah, perhaps that's enough business talk for the moment," intervenes Mr. K. "Faizal, how is the family?"

"Bathroom?" I say, interrupting.

Faizal points me around the corner, beyond some sofa chairs with headsets and cables tethered to them. I hastily let myself into the toilet and lock the door behind me. I am alone with my reflection, and I see myself for the first time since we arrived on the island. With the dress and make-up on I almost look like I could live here; the city I thought I wanted. The place that makes its air too dirty to breathe, then pays someone to make it smell like another place.

My eyes fall on an ornament by the sink; a beautiful, curling, orangey sea shell. My mind is transported to my childhood, and mother showing Oriana and I how to listen to the sea by pressing it to our ears. Tears form in my eyes as I reach for the shell. My stomach churns as I turn it over, seeing the manufacturer's imprint in the base.

I need space. Somewhere to think, to breathe; a place that is not entirely made by people or their robots. I need *home*.

As I open the bathroom door, I overhear the men discussing business.

"She needs to be reined in a bit, obviously, but I trust you can do that?"

"You have my word," replies Mr. K. "I know how to break them in."

"Great, because once you've got her straightened out, she's gonna be dynamite with my investors. Heck, she might even shut the green lobby too. I can't get those people off my ass these days."

Silently, I back away and slip into the corridor. I have at most a couple of minutes before they realize I am gone, and in that time I need to get as far from this place as possible.

CHAPTER TWENTY-TWO

LUKE

I'm hot, clammy, and waking up to a blistering argument. It's a lot like my first marriage, except this time I didn't cause the fight. I'm in the back of a 4x4. Pietro's driving, Ramone's shouting, and we're swerving as they wrestle over the wheel.

"Woah! Boys, what the hell?" I yell.

"This scrawny bastardo has been driving us the wrong way!"

"Not... true!" grunts Pietro.

Ramone overpowers him, forcing us to the side of the road where Pietro slams on the brakes.

"Mind telling me what's going on?" I ask, nursing my forehead.

"We agreed we would go to Aquerba and shut down the anti-satellite command hub, but we are hundreds of miles off-course! This little rat took his turn at the wheel and let us both sleep while he drove us in the wrong direction," snarls Ramone.

"I am not a rat!" snips Pietro. "We agreed we would

save my tribe – the cartel could move on them any day. We have to warn them and help them prepare!"

"We agreed that they *should* be saved. We did not say they *would* be saved!" protests Ramone.

"OK, everyone be cool. It sounds like there were some serious crossed wires here. Ramone, Pietro's not a rat..." I begin.

"*Thank you!*" says Pietro.

"... He's a lizard with glasses," I finish.

"Coño."

"Pietro, be straight with me, did you trick us?" I ask.

"No! I am not a liar! While you were both sleeping we reached a fork in the road. I thought we had agreed my tribe was the urgent priority, so I took the turning for their territory."

"You should have checked with us!" growls Ramone.

"I didn't think I needed to check," protests Pietro. "When you were smashing the farm hub up with an axe you said 'we will save Pietro's tribe and we will destroy the hub'. What could be clearer?"

"It was the other way around, *cabrón*! I meant we will destroy the hub, *then* save your tribe. As in, we will save them *by* destroying the hub. We cannot be in two places at once!"

"OK boys, I've heard enough," I interject. "I think we've all learned a lesson about the importance of clear communication here."

"Si. I have learned that academics only hear what they want to hear," grumbles Ramone.

"And *I* have learned that cranky old rangers have major deficits when it comes to interpersonal skills," snarks Pietro.

"You want to take this outside, lizard human?" growls Ramone.

"Woah, big guy, take a beat," I interject. "He's lizard *boy*, and trust me, if you go outside with him you'll only find yourself in more conversation."

"I did a webinar in de-escalation methods-" begins Pietro.

"No one cares, kid. OK, this officially sucks. We're way off course and we need to decide how to fix this."

"I vote we continue on to my tribe. We're practically there now anyway," says Pietro.

"You were outvoted last time, kid, and now you're trying to force our hand. It's not gonna work!" snaps Ramone.

"Ugh, it *might* kinda work," I groan. "Look, Ramone, I hate to be 'that guy', but we gotta think of this in terms of net utility. We're here now, so the old plan is already wrecked. Sabotaging the new plan would benefit no one."

"It would teach this sniveling cheat a lesson!"

"For the last time, I am not a cheat. Would you really let a whole tribe die just to 'teach me a lesson'? Are you that selfish?" cries Pietro.

"You dare call *me* selfish? You fly into my country, barely with hairs on your chest, having spent a life reading books and eating food others have brought you, and now you lecture me about being selfish? I have spent decades patrolling this jungle, protecting the people, animals, and trees that depend on it. Saving them from the *truly* selfish bastardos who are destroying it. You think I want to live like a nomad? I do this because someone has to!"

"Yeah, well maybe if you did it *with* other people, instead of being a loner all these years, you would know how to communicate like a normal person!"

Ramone's face darkens. "I didn't choose to be alone. The cartel killed my wife five years into our fight against them."

"Ah crap," I sigh. "See, that's a rookie mistake, Pietro. Rule number one of journalism: always get the facts before you go to print. Rule number two is don't be afraid to massage them if times are hard, but that doesn't really apply here."

"Ramone, I'm so sorry, I had no idea," says Pietro, meekly.

"No, because you never thought to ask. Yet *I* am the selfish one?"

"In the poor kid's defense, Ramone, you're a very imposing and stand-offish figure. You don't really give off the vibe that you welcome personal questions."

"Don't I?" snarls Ramone.

"OK now I can't tell if you're being ironic or rhetorical."

"I'm being genuine!"

"Oh. Then we might need to work on your tone as well."

"Can we work on Ramone's elocution *after* we save my tribe?" says Pietro.

"Ugh, you two are so needy. Right, here's the plan: we go help Pietro's people now, ideally *before* the cartel arrives, then we go to Aquerba and find a way to destroy the main hub that's jamming all the satellites. Deal?"

"Deal," reply the other two.

"Yo, Pietro, quick question: how are you planning on tracking down this tribe of yours?"

"On the cartel's schematic this road cut right through the tribe's territory. Given that the pin was amber, I'm guessing the tribe has already been putting up some resistance. I say we drive until we meet it."

"Wait, your plan is to drive us into an ambush? Kid, I thought you were the smart one – that sucks!"

"We would surrender right away and explain we're not

cartel. I have been studying my ancestors' culture for many years and I am well-versed in their diplomatic customs."

"Your diplomacy won't count for shit if they take us out with a land mine. I know other tribes have been scavenging them from the civil war for self-defense," grunts Ramone.

"Ramone, I know you won't like this, but what if we use your GPS device to scan the area for life signs? We could pin-point the tribe and avoid land mines on the road. Of course, with the obvious risk of the cartel finding *us* once we turn the device on. Option two is Pietro's plan: we drive at full speed until we see or hit something, accepting that tribal medical facilities do leave a few things to be desired. Let's bear in mind that starting off our heroic intervention with a serious car crash might limit our ability to actually help the tribe at all. Which brings me to option three: we ditch the car, head into the forest, and trek on foot until one of the tribe's scouts finds us. OK, everyone hold up the finger of the option they support."

I support option one, Pietro two, and Ramone three. Crap.

"Oh boy. Looks like we're gonna have to do some kinda alternative vote system," I say.

"What's that?" asks Ramone.

"No wonder your country fell apart," snorts Pietro. "Were you still using first past the post?"

"It fell apart because bastardos from countries like yours *wanted* it to!" snarls Ramone.

"Woah, fellas, cool it! Ramone, here's how it works."

Just before I can explain the intricacies of the alternative vote system, a high-pitched motor sounds from the road. A hoverbike is racing towards us. Shots ring out, whizzing past our heads.

"Hold that thought, boys. I propose a fourth option on the ballot: run!"

Three days have passed since we were forced to abandon the road. Ramone's quick thinking and use of the carteller's old pistol saved our bacon back there. But it also involved blowing up our ride, to take out the enemy. Since then we've been on foot, trekking through the forest, and accepting that option three seems to have won the day.

Option three sucks. You know what else sucks? Being a white guy in the jungle. I'm being consumed by two things: mosquitos, and a profound sense of post-colonial guilt.

Smack. That's the sound of me slapping the billionth mosquito that's earmarked me as dinner.

"Don't slap them, it only makes it worse," says Pietro, again.

"Yeah, yeah, because blahdy-blah, increased circulation, they can smell my breath, whatever, man, I'm smacking them."

"Then you only have yourself to blame," he mutters.

"Oh, you wanna tug at that thread pal?"

"Be calm, gringo," interjects Ramone. "The jungle is making you irritable."

"Screw you, ranger man, don't pretend like *you're* the group's natural peace keeper. You're the impulsive brutish one, stay in your lane."

"OK. Here is Ramone 'staying in lane': be quiet or I will slit your throat and make a tent from your skin. Better?"

"No, that was obviously way too far."

"You did over-compensate," agrees Pietro.

"This conversation doesn't involve you, rat boy," snaps Ramone.

"Oh I think every conversation involves me, since you *blew up our ride!*"

"Gentleman, gentleman, cool it! We mustn't turn on each other!"

See? I'm totally the peace maker, and-

Oof. What the hell? Pietro's stopped walking and I've gone right into the back of him.

"Uh, little warning next time before you stop?"

Pietro doesn't respond directly. He merely points to the trees up ahead. Or rather, to the place where trees should be.

"We're too late," he croaks. "The cartel have already begun."

Machines made of clay and metal are ripping trees down. Animals screech as their homes are toppled. The machines fell, strip, slice, and pack the ancient trees with ruthless efficiency. Centuries of growth undone in mere seconds. The legacy of man, ladies and gentlemen.

There appear to be no humans on site, making it the first fully-automated cartel operation any of us have seen. The machines are skeletal, made of geometric mesh patterns and earthy colors.

The clearing is circular and over a mile in diameter. Within it lies a sunken level, where the ground has dropped away. In the crater is a huge mining drill, twisting like a giant egg beater in the mud.

The drill's powerhouse is a tower in the center of the mine, connected by a bridge on each side. The first bridge is carrying ore out of the pit. The second is still under construction, and is being built by a swarm of four-legged droids that remind me horribly of the spiders from the bunker.

The real wonder, however, lies on top of the central tower. A spiny, ultra-thin radio mast stretching high into the sky.

"You thinking what I'm thinking, gringo?"

"That Pietro needs a shower?"

"We must take down that mast. It will be jamming the satellites, and probably controlling the drones too."

"Exactly. What do you think, Pietro?"

"I think we should all stay very, very still," he whispers.

"Dude, why you going all funny on me now? Have you got jungle fever too?"

Lizard boy is standing frozen with his arms raised. As Ramone sees the same thing, we both raise our hands in surrender. Did I mention how much I hate option three earlier? It just found us, and it's got an arrow pointed at each of our faces.

Pietro falls to his knees. He spreads his hands wide and pushes them forwards and out like he's swimming breaststroke. He wriggles his body like a cobra, tilting his head up to the sky and sticking his tongue out with a deep hiss. Dipping his head back down, he closes his eyes and brings his hands together above his head in prayer, touching each shoulder then tucking his fingers under his knees and curling into a ball.

"Forest spirits, I am yours," he says, through the muffled folds of his legs.

The three tribal warriors stare at us in stunned silence,

then one of them lifts their mask and looks to me and Ramone. "Is he always like this?"

Pietro looks up, blushing furiously.

"I was doing our tribe's traditional greeting!" he protests.

"Our tribe?"

"I'm one of you," says Pietro, laying himself flat once again.

I'm sensing this is a very emotional and cathartic moment for lizard boy. I'm also getting the vibe that these three warriors aren't in the market for a scrawny, myopic, long-lost cousin.

"I think you have just demonstrated on *two* levels that that is not true," replies the central warrior, a squat man with *Delmo* tattooed across his chest. I'm guessing that's his name?

"I'm Delmo, by the way."

OK, so it's definitely his name.

"You can stop dancing now," he adds.

Pietro's the color of a tomato that just realized it bought the same dress as all the other tomatoes, before *they* all realized tomatoes don't wear dresses and they all got scammed.

"But... but my research was so thorough!" stammers Pietro. "You *are* the Namakaro tribe, yes? I recognize your headgear! And the stripes on your arms!"

"We are Namakaro, yes," replies Delmo. "But we don't do weird yoga or whatever that little dance was."

"It's the sacred Namakaro greeting!"

"No, you touched your left shoulder first."

"Because it goes left-right-under the knees...?"

"Ah, that is where you went wrong. It's right *then* left, then knees."

"Geez, and I thought *my* family was pedantic," I grunt. "Give the kid a break, he's travelled across the world to be reunited with you!"

"If he had studied properly, he would know that the order of movements he just did suggests he has a *very* different relationship with his mother than most Namakaro."

"Oh god, did I just...? Oh... No, no! Nothing like that!" cries Pietro.

The three warriors pack up laughing and help Pietro to his feet.

"Welcome home, brother. Who are your companions?" says Delmo.

"Oh, this is Ramone. He's a Mazonilian – but a good one. He protects the forest from the cartels. And this is Luke, he's... I don't really know why he's here. I think he's writing a book," says Pietro.

"Are you fucking *kidding* me, lizard boy? You scrawny Tai Chi piece of shit, you *know* I'm here to save the world!"

"How is that going for you?" quips Delmo.

"It's a work in progress, *thanks for asking*. It would be going a lot better if we were in Aquerba as planned, but lizard boy decided a family reunion was more important than destroying the cartel's mast network."

"You know how the masts work?" asks the warrior on the left.

He has the name *Ohalo* tattooed across his chest. Man, it is *so* useful that their tribe does this. You never have to worry about the awkwardness of forgetting. Like when you meet someone several times, but you forget their name on the third occasion, by which point you're way too familiar, so you can't ask them again because you know it would cause offence, meaning you spend the rest of your life calling them things like "champ", "pal", "friend", "buddy" – literally every synonym there is for a human being *other* than their own freaking name. And all because our society thought name badges were overkill! Well, not the Namakaro, these people have got it *down*.

Ohalo's got small eyes, a slender frame, and jet black hair shaped like a bowl, with an inverted "V" cut into the fringe.

"We think the masts are blocking the international satellites," replies Pietro, "stopping them from seeing what the cartels are doing to the forest. There's a network of them across Mazonil, though we're not certain how many or what their range is."

"There are seven cartel mines in our territory now, but this is the only one with a mast," says Ohalo.

"Seven?" says Ramone, disgusted.

"The cartel changed their strategy when we adopted guerilla war. They realized they would have to fight us one by one, across the entire jungle, as we spread ourselves out to cover as much territory as possible. It worked for a time, but now they are exploiting our thinness by dropping drones across the forest. The machines self-replicate, clearing the trees and building more parts until they grow big enough to scar the earth and begin the mining. If we do not reach them in time, the machines become too big to stop."

"What happens when you try shutting them down?" I ask.

"The machines fire projectiles at us. Lumps of rock, mechanical parts," says Delmo.

"No bullets or stun guns?"

"They don't seem to have that kind of tech – they are constructed purely from the earth. But they don't need those weapons when they can simply crush us. Sometimes they use whole trees as bludgeons. Some of our tribe have rifles, or EMPs, things they've scavenged over the years. The rest of us try to make do with the weapons of our ancestors," says Delmo, gesturing to their arrows.

Summoning all my maturity, I resist the urge to ask *how's that going for you?* and instead offer the warrior a sympathetic nod.

"Why's he looking at me like that? Is the white man having a stroke?" says Delmo.

"I hope so. Then maybe we'll get some peace," snorts Ramone.

"Ouch, dude! What's with the burn? I thought it was Pietro you didn't like?" I protest.

"I do not like either of you. This is a marriage of necessity."

"You three are married?" says Ohalo, eyebrows arched.

"Why, you interested?" I reply, with a wink, blowing his tiny conservative mind.

"No thank you, Latika here spoke for me moons ago," grins Ohalo, placing a hand on the third warrior's chest. "We Namakaro do not practice polygamy, it just causes rows."

"We do *not* row! We get along great – right, sweetie?" I say, putting an arm around Pietro.

"Ew, Luke get off me!"

"Bro, don't be so homophobic, it's rude!"

"I'm not being homophobic. I just want the record to be clear that we three are not married, and that you are not my type," says Pietro.

"That's ludicrous. I'm renowned for my universal appeal. Whatever, may the record officially show that you and I are *not* romantically involved. It's just you and Ramone," I grin.

The warriors look on with faint curiosity, while Ramone glares at me with murderous intent. Wait, did I hit a nerve?

"Ah shit. My bad, folks, I just remembered Ramone's a widow so that may have been insensitive. Jury's out. I was trying to do a subversive bit about sexual preferences and bigotry but I think somehow *I'm* coming across like the small-minded asshole. Can you believe that?"

"You are a white man in the jungle. Odds are *very* high that you're an insensitive asshole," shrugs Delmo.

"Pietro, you have made it to your family, so we shall part ways. Goodbye and good luck," says Ramone, straightening up. "Namakaro warriors, he's your problem now. Luke and I will go to Aquerba and destroy the mast network. Our vehicle was destroyed, so we are on foot. What is the best way from here?"

"The route is treacherous without the right knowledge. I propose a deal," says Delmo. "We will tell you how to reach Aquerba, if you help us stop this mine from destroying our land."

"Er, I don't wanna be rude bro, but I think that horse has bolted," I say, glancing at the desolate landscape.

"You are wrong, white man, this is a critical phase before the mine triples in size. In the next twenty-four hours, those machines will become too big and too numerous. This is our only chance to reach the processor in the central tower," says Delmo.

"Great. So you're saying if Ramone and I wanna get out of here, we have to help you get to the middle of that hulking great mine, dodge a bunch of machines that club people with trees, and shut down a server we've never seen before?" I ask.

"What a great summary! Let me know when your book is out, white man, that blurb has whet my appetite," says Ohalo.

"I'm not writing a book, I'm saving the-"

"No one cares," interrupts Delmo. "White man, you go with Latika for the raid. I will go with the big guy. Ohalo, you're with Pietro. Let's make this quick, and you guys will be on your way in no time."

Our respective squads take up position around the circular clearing, avoiding the gaze of the autonomous machines. As we prepare to attack, Latika shares a couple of facts with me about their little warrior troop:

1. This isn't their first rodeo.
2. There used to be four of them.

Ramone and Delmo are skirting the trees, getting as close as possible to the robot-building machine. That thing's churning out workers like an ant queen. The worker bots are clearing the forest so that the mine can grow, and anything or anyone in their way gets eliminated. Us included. Our hope is that if those two guys can kill the queen, it will shut down her entire hive.

Ohalo and Pietro have been tasked with the mast. They have to reach the tower in the center of the mine, find the controls for the satellite-blocking mast, and knock that fucker out of commission so the world can see this shit. We're counting on lizard boy's geekery to pull this off.

Latika and I drew the short straw: create a diversion. Pietro insists this is essential, because we'll be draining the drones' collective processing power, giving them less resource to detect the other security intrusions. But I think he just wants me dead so I can't tell anyone about that dumbass yoga ritual he did.

Fortunately, I feel confident Ramone's side of things will succeed. Mainly because he's got a portable EMP and a bunch of other gizmos he stole from the cartel's control room back on the farm. He spent a large chunk of the car ride tinkering with them, presumably modifying them to make improvised stun grenades or whatever the anti-drone version of that is.

OK fine, I'm the least tech-literate person here and I'm the only one from the Northern Bloc. There. I've said it. I'm a disgrace to my people.

"Let's go!" says Latika.

He's off, sprinting towards the nearest tree-cutting machine with a hunting axe in his hand. The others are holding position, waiting to see if our diversion works. God *dammit* I hate this plan. As I run out from the trees it feels like I'm stripping naked and showing my giblets to the drones.

Quick question: how does one disrupt the progress of a gigantic clay-graphene cutting machine four hundred times your size? I don't remember much about pottery classes, but the one thing I do remember is that clay can crack. I'm about to go full Greek wedding on this thing's ass.

Latika's way ahead of me by now. The guy looks about a zillion but his cardio is *incredible*. He dashes across the front of the tree cutter, halting the machine's spinning saw as it registers a human form.

The machine freezes. A graphene periscope rises from its head and swivels to follow Latika's progress. It seems to have decided he's hostile, because it's unfolding what I can only describe as a mechanical tail. The end is a large, thick digger shovel, but the 'tail' is made of some flexible polymer that looks part wood fiber and part metal. The tail swings at Latika, trying to swat him like a fly.

"Luke, now!" he yells.

That's my cue to do something heroic. OK, think, Luke, you got this! I dash towards the machine and leap onto its side, scrambling up the scaffold frame onto the roof. I'm passing over its semi-exposed intestinal tract, where logs are being stripped and sliced, then shat out as it ingests the next tree. The ground reverberates as the machine pummels Latika's shadow, missing him by decreasing margins each time. OK, this thing's a quick learner.

"Luke!"

"I'm on it!" I yell.

I'm about to smash the periscope with my hunting axe, when it spins around and looks right at me. God dammit, this thing's got ears too! The whole machine jerks sideways, throwing me off-balance. I land hard in the ground with the sorta thud that's gonna need so many chiropractor visits I might as well buy shares in the practice.

No time to book an appointment though – the machine's tail is swinging towards me. I roll to the side just in time as the digger tip smashes into the ground, showering me with dirt and wood shavings. I'm expecting it to recoil and swing again, but this time it tries a new tactic. It recoils the tail against its long body like a sideways whip, then unleashes it at me.

There's no way to run; my only hope is to jump over this thing. I have to time this absolutely perfectly or I'm history. Three... two... *one!*

I leap as high as I can, but it's not high enough. The tail clips my feet, throwing me head over heel. As I fall, my arms flail, instinctively, somehow grabbing hold of the tail. Now I'm dangling from this thing, as the machine tries to re-angle itself to be able to whack me into the ground.

But there's movement on the machine's back. Latika's made it up there and he's swinging at the periscope. Direct hit! The machine's eye crumples like a bent golf club, leaving it staring at its own back.

No time for celebration. The machine deploys its emergency evasive maneuvers and rolls over. As the tail lurches into the air, I let go, landing with an even greater thud. If I ever make it back alive I think I'll just cut to the chase and order a mobility scooter.

Latika's vanished. The machine is doing a full barrel roll. Its hollow, scaffold frame tumbles across the terrain, flattening the few saplings in its wake. I'm bracing myself for a Latika-shaped pancake to appear in the mud any second now, but he's vanished without a trace.

Holy crap, he's *inside* the machine, running like it's a hamster wheel! Under different circumstances, he would make an amazing ambassador for Zorbing. He's wielding his axe, swinging at some internal processor inside the machine, but it's somehow figured out he's inside. The machine stops rolling and starts writhing like a snake, trying to fling him out. Diced tree stumps are flying out of its rear end while Latika scrambles to keep hold.

Something shiny flies out of the machine's skeleton, landing in the mud by me. Latika's axe! Oh crap, he's *really* gonna need that. As I scramble towards it, a rumbling draws my attention across the clearing. Two more logging machines are headed right at us, periscopes raised, circular saws spinning.

Behind them I see the others dashing out from their hiding places among the trees and sprinting for their respective targets. I need to buy Ramone and Delmo enough time to take out the queen robot. I've got two axes, and zero plan.

"Luke, get inside the machine! It's the only way to stay safe!" yells Latika.

His voice is doing a sort of sonic zig-zag as the clay-fiber snake writhes, trying to expel him. He looks like hell; clinging to the inside of the frame, his voice wavering as he's flung around. I need to decide, fast; the wood choppers are steaming towards me like giant metal-mouthed caterpillars.

Scrambling from the ground, I sprint to the blinded one. I'm standing before its mouth, in front of a huge saw, and I'm acutely aware of the flashing red light above its sensors, which are trying to figure out what kind of tree I am.

The machine lurches towards me like an earthworm. I leap back just in time, while Latika yells a series of uncomplimentary opinions about my strategy.

"You gotta trust me!" I cry, darting sideways.

The wood chopper does another barrel roll to keep itself face-forward to me. Latika's yelling as he spins around like laundry, but it's for his own good, I swear. The rolling machine barrels into its wood-chopper peer, crunching its side against the other one's saw mouth.

Both machines come off badly in the impact, with the writhing one's hull fractured badly, and the other one's jaw hanging off in pieces. Neither seems to have much awareness of their injury, or of each other for that matter.

The injured newcomer spots Latika inside the other machine and lunges for him. Lifting itself off the ground, it tries to body-slam him, but crushes the frame of its peer in the process. Latika throws himself out of the way, landing between logs. The attacking machine wriggles but it's stuck; enmeshed in the other's skeleton.

Latika clambers out with a triumphant cheer, only to cut it short. Machine number three is ploughing towards us. But Latika's got a glint in his eye. He sprints towards the machine head-on. At the last second he leaps upwards, propelling himself over the spinning saw and using the momentum from the machine's reflex head-flick to acrobat up and over onto its neck. In the same slick movement, he decapitates its periscopic sensor, then drops through the skeletal frame to the creature's innards, embedding his axe right in its central processor.

The machine's power flickers out and it skids to halt yards from my feet, the spinning disc powering down with a soft whine. Latika hops out with a cheeky grin.

"Third time's a charm," he winks.

Those machines learn fast, but God damn, Latika learns faster.

His smile vanishes. I turn around, following his gaze over my shoulder. A swarm of four-legged reconnaissance drones is scarpering towards us, pouring out of a nearby prospecting hole. There's no way we can fight this many of them; fleeing is the only option now.

We're running right for the mine shaft. Ramone and Delmo are on the far side, hacking their way into the static queen machine's controls. Pietro and Ohalo are half a mile from them, nearing the center of the mine shaft as they hurry across the bridge.

The pit is our only hope. If we can get onto the far side of the bridge, we can create a bottleneck, taking away the bugs' swarm advantage so we can tackle them one by one. Though the way they're scarpering makes me doubt I can swing an axe as fast as they move.

We're crossing the walkway but it's narrow and only half-constructed. The two sides of the bridge haven't been fully connected yet. The platform thins out to a single beam which stops short of the other side, which connects to the central tower.

Latika lies down and presses the beam, testing its strength. Satisfied it can hold his weight, he backs up. With a run and a leap, he launches himself off the tip of the beam, flying through the air. My heart's in my mouth as I watch him fall short. His toes dust the opposite ledge and he plummets, catching the far beam with his fingers.

"Help!" I yell.

I'm waving frantically to Pietro and Ohalo, who are at the far end of the bridge, attacking the mast unit. I point downwards. Pietro peers over the edge and sees Latika's dangling legs and rushes towards us.

"Not you!" I yell. "Send the other guy! Ohalo!"

Pietro backs up and swaps places with the warrior, returning to the interface panel, while Ohalo sprints towards us.

I glance back over my shoulder. The robot bugs have reached my side of the bridge, but the mesh walkway is slowing them down; their pincer legs keep falling between the gaps, stranding many of them.

But the others have figured out an alternative route. They're tip-toeing along the edge rails, which are solid; they're steadily progressing towards me. I've got thirty seconds tops to get Latika rescued and get my own, much fatter ass over that gap.

Ohalo arrives on the other half of the bridge, panting from the quarter mile run. He kneels down and grabs Latika's hand, hauling his husband up from the edge. They fall back onto the walkway and cling to each with relief.

If I don't move now, those bugs are gonna dice me up like sushi. But Latika barely cleared the gap to the other side, and he's a slim guy. I'm gonna have to take even more of a run-up. OK Luke, deep breath. You got this. Don't. Look. Down.

"Make way, one more coming through!" I yell.

I'm building up steam, I'm leaving the platform, I'm running on the beam now and there's no turning back or slowing down. I'm ready to leap when

What the hell? The platform is moving!

A klaxon is barking and the entire central column is rotating. Pietro's lying on his back opposite a smoking control panel, looking like he just got fried. God damn lizard boy, he just *activated* the whole freakin' mining pit!

I'm skidding to a halt, which is impossible to do on a tight rope, especially one that's moving downwards. Both my platform and the half with Ohalo and Latika opposite are descending. As my balance fails entirely, my brain makes a split-second decision. A decision I'm gonna be questioning for years to come. I'm falling. My body throws out every limb, in every direction, trying to grab something to save my sorry life.

My legs splay either side of the pole and I land on my nuts with an agonizing impact. The momentum throws me to the side and I'm rolling off. I throw my arms up, catching the top of the beam just in time. Now I'm hanging upside down like an impotent monkey, as the bugs scratch and clatter their way towards me.

"Luke, you gotta jump!" calls Latika.

I'm craning my head backwards, looking at them inverted. Their platform is dropping lower than mine. If I swing, I might be able to make it. But not if I'm facing backwards, first I have to turn around.

Cursing the day I ever decided to become a journalist, I release my legs from the pole. Dangling only by my hands,

I'm face to face with the underside of the half-bridge. One of the bugs is crawling right at me, clinging to the pole!

With a wail, I swing my leg up and boot it off the side. I cheer with disbelieving laughter as it falls to the bottom, smashing across the rocks deep below.

"Luke, hurry!" yells Latika.

Above me the other bugs are reaching the edge of the walkway and are testing out the beam. My armpits are screaming under the strain of keeping my pudgy middle-aged body from falling into the pit. With great effort, I twist myself around.

"Rock your legs!" calls Ohalo.

I'm swinging them and it looks like we're playing a torture version of charades. Perhaps this is me doing a movie about dolphins on a heist. If that movie doesn't exist yet, it should, and if I make it out of here alive, I'm pitching that thing.

I'm about to propel myself to the platform below when the tower column judders again. Ohalo and Latika stumble sideways, grabbing the railing for support as their half of the bridge rotates away.

"Hey! Come back!" I yell, dangling helplessly.

They're looking at each other in despair. Behind them, in the central column, Pietro's clutching a multi-tool, and looking deeply confused as he prods and thumps the control box. Above us, the other bridge is rotating in the opposite direction but at its original height, making me nauseous. I can feel a bug's pincers scratching along the pole I'm hanging from; it's barely a yard from my fingers now.

"Guys! A little help!" I scream.

As Ohalo's bridge swings back into view, my screaming intensifies. Two arrows fly towards me as both warriors unleash their quivers.

"Hold still!" yells Ohalo.

I can't see what's happening to the bugs behind me, but I'm squealing and wriggling like a greased piglet as the barrage continues until their bridge is swept out of range again. Glancing down at the quarry, I see the last few bugs smashing into the ground beside their stricken peers.

"Luke, get ready to jump!" yells Latika, as they rotate back towards me.

"We'll catch you!" insists Ohalo.

I'm staring down at the approaching half-bridge, knowing I've got precious few seconds to make the jump and land on a platform barely wider than my love handles. As I get ready to swing my body, a searing pain cuts through my little finger.

A stray bug has reached me and is sawing my pinkie off!

"Luke, you gotta jump now" yells Ohalo.

"I'm a little tied up! Mother *fucker* that hurts!" I yell.

With a cry of anger, I release the afflicted hand and try to shake the bug off. But the little bastard's clinging on! It's dangling like a piece of sticky tape, except instead of glue, the thing keeping us together is a serrated pincer skewering my finger.

Something latches around my ankles. I glance down at Ohalo's level and see a cord trailing from me down to them. What little slack it has is fast disappearing as the bridge rotates away.

"Luke, hold on! We got you!" yells Ohalo.

He's *holding* the other end of the rope, while Latika frantically ties it to the bridge. Before I can yell "let go!" the rope tightens and I'm wrenched off the beam.

Time stretches as I fall, only to rebound as the cord re-tightens. I'm trailing from the rotating bridge like an inverted kite. I swear I should have blacked out, but the pain from this little bloodsucker's keeping me horrifically aware of every terrifying detail, as the entire mine spins around me.

I'm being reeled in like a whale; painfully and without dignity. Two sets of hands grab hold of my waist and haul me onto the bridge. Ohalo grabs the robotic bug and rips it away, smashing it with an axe. I yell in agony as the tip of my pinkie gets sawn off in the process, disappearing over the edge of the bridge.

"We've got company," says Latika.

He and Ohalo are out of arrows and our bridge is fast approaching its elevated other half, where half a dozen bugs are crowded onto the beam with crouched legs, poised to leap at us.

"Get ready to repel!" yells Latika.

"With what?" I cry, nursing my bleeding pinkie.

Ohalo drags me back and takes my place. As the bridges become aligned, the two warriors swing their axes like bats, smashing the bugs out of the air as they leap towards us, pincers raised like daggers.

We pull clear of the bridge again but three bugs made it. The two men scream as the pincers carve through their flesh. I leap forwards and rip the nearest one from Ohalo's leg, hurling it over the side. Ahead of us, Latika tears a bug from his torso and smashes it against the side of the bridge, crying with anger until it's just a pile of twitching shards.

"Guys, we need to get away from the edge *now*," I say, as the beam comes back into view. More bugs are lining up, ready to pounce.

But as we scramble to our feet, something remarkable happens. They fall limp like someone's pulled the plug on the whole swarm! All three of us cheer with joy as the bugs slide off the pole into the mine below.

"They did it!" I cheer.

From our sunken position, I can't see the upper lip of the mine, but clearly Ramone and Delmo have succeeded in disabling the queen unit for the site's machines. As if all my prayers are being answered at once, the bridge stops rotating too. A whoop of delight emanates from Pietro at the central tower.

Latika and I help Ohalo to his feet and hobble towards the central column, where Pietro's working fast. As it stands, there's no way for us to get back up to ground level, other than the rungs on the side of the tower. From there, we can reach the main, intact bridge like Pietro and Ohalo originally did. But first, we gotta make sure this huge mast tower is well and truly offline.

"Pietro, tell me we can get the hell out of here?" I gasp, as we catch up with him.

"I'm nearly there. The mast has barely any security on it; I don't think they expected anyone to ever find it."

"So what's taking so long?"

"They've not labelled any of the protocols in the system. It's all pure code so I'm flying blind. It's like ripping out cables randomly to see what works."

"That's what set the bridges moving?"

"Exactly."

"Can't we just cut all the power and have done with it?"

"It's risky. I don't know what that might do."

"On behalf of my severed pinkie, your half-baked 'precision strike' method sucks. Kill it all, and kill it fast. I'm reckoning the cartel's already got people on their way here, given that we just sent every machine in this place haywire."

"OK. Here goes," says Pietro.

He punches a series of commands into the computer

interface, prompting reams of code to reel off the screen. It delivers a series of asterisks then goes blank.

"Mission accomplished!" I cheer.

A creaking from deep below us signals the opening of a series of shafts in the base of the mine. Yellow vapors gush up through the openings.

"What the hell is that?" cries Ohalo.

"Oh crap, we've triggered the ventilation protocol," says Pietro. "They're flushing the noxious gases out of the mining pits underground. We need to get out of here before it chokes us!"

Latika's way ahead of us, and is crowbarring the tower's door open. Blood trickles from the wounds on his bare chest as he works through the pain. Ohalo joins him and together they fling the door open, revealing a spiral staircase inside.

"What if there's gas in there too?" I hesitate.

"Then we're cooked," says Ohalo. "But at least it will be quick. Out here, the exposure could take an hour to reach lethal levels. Strong chance the cartel would find us in that time, and they would only make our deaths last longer. I am taking my chances in here. Sorry about your pinkie."

Ohalo sets off with Latika, followed by Pietro. Cursing, I rush after them, closing the door behind me and sealing our fate.

Several hundred steps later we emerge onto the upper bridge. We're alive but there's still a half mile bridge to cross. As we run, I can only hope Pietro's one-hour estimate was right. I can already feel my throat and lungs tingling.

The unmistakable chopping of a quadcopter rings out above us.

"We've got incoming!" yells Ramone, as we near the far side of the bridge. "Get to the forest, we'll hold them off!"

As we sprint for the trees, the quadcopter dips down

towards us. Bullets ping off the walkway as we run. Ramone shoves us towards the tree line, while Delmo takes up a shooting position behind the control panel, knowing it's one thing the cartel will be reluctant to fire at.

"Use the last resort!" yells Ramone.

Delmo takes aim and fires. I whoop with delight as his modified arrow embeds into the hull of the quadcopter, sending electrical sparks across its frame. The craft drops out of the sky like a lead balloon, with the crew crunching into the ground with it. A crumpled door bursts open and two cartellers spill out. Swaying dizzily, they open fire at us, spraying bullets across the field clumsily. As they fire, the sound of a second quadcopter approaching fills the air.

This one's hovering overhead, too high for an arrow to reach – not that Delmo has any EMP ones left. A door slides open and a package is tossed out. As a parachute deploys, the crate drifts down gracefully, and the second quadcopter pulls away, retreating the way it came.

"Razor drones!" yells Latika.

I have *zero* desire to find out the specifics of what the hell a razor drone is. Sprinting with every fiber of my being, I race towards the forest, crossing the tree line well after the others. Remind me to hit the gym later – once I've seen my chiropractor. And a pinkie surgeon.

"Get down!" cries Ohalo.

Crackling like fireworks, the crate explodes upon touchdown. As I hit the deck, my ears are filled with the splintering of wood and the scratching of metal. Peering between my fingers, I glimpse the nightmare around us. I didn't think anything so insane could exist.

Rocket-propelled razor boomerangs.

"Get to the big tree!" yells Pietro.

I have no idea what makes lizard boy the boomerang

expert here, but I'm damned if I stay still and get crushed by a tree. Trunks are falling like blades of grass beneath some screeching invisible lawnmower.

The six of us tumble into the hollow of a vast, ancient tree. The one with tons of roots that grow vertically downwards from its branches. I don't have time to explain, look it up if you don't believe me.

We cower and watch in horror as everything around us is reduced to kindling. Within the space of a few minutes, our tree is the only thing left standing for acres. A screeching sound grows louder as the three boomerangs take a hell of a final run-up. With a shuddering thwack, they smash into the ultra-thick trunk above us.

Red lights are flashing on the tips of the boomerangs, with a faint digital beep, both of which are getting faster.

"Everybody out!" yells Latika.

The boomerangs detonate as we run, exploding the tree and sending shards of burning shrapnel through the air. The fire ignites the piles of sawdust surrounding the mine, where trees were recently logged. By the time we reach the far side of the clearing, the forest behind us is ablaze. The two crash survivors from the cartel take pot shots at us as we run, but between the mine gas and the blaze, they've got problems of their own. As the final bullets peter out, the six of us disappear into what's left of the forest.

CHAPTER TWENTY-THREE

PABLA

I burst through the elevator doors and into the lobby. I am pacing for the exit, trying to look casual. A woman watches me from a gilded couch. She mutters into her wrist then stands up and straightens her suit. Her black shoes are polished, with a flat heel and sturdy grip. As she turns towards me, I sense she is not one of the hotel's guests.

I pivot and head the opposite way across the lobby. A robot with a bowtie and horn-rimmed glasses is standing behind a plinth, clutching an old-fashioned book and ink pen.

"Excuse me, Ma'am, do you have a reservation?"

I ignore him and hurry through into the restaurant, where diners are sat around huge pristine plates with miniscule portions of foamy, spiralized dishes on them.

"Ma'am, please stop. Uh, you too, Madam!"

The door-robot freezes and retreats, bowing to the other guests, for fear of spoiling their ambiance as the black-shoed woman marches after me. Up ahead I can see an exit onto a street. But the robotic waiting-staff have all stopped serving and are staring at me, their heads rotating in synch as I move past them. Are they about to intercept me?

I speed up. There is a meal cart up ahead, bearing silver platters of squid tentacles and shark fins. They are arranged in a wreath. In the center is a flower sculpted from the tongues of assorted mammals.

Seizing the trolley, I throw it sideways, splattering the guests in entrails. Dragging it behind me I leap into the revolving door as a cacophony of outrage erupts from the trillionaire patrons. I time the release perfectly; snatching my arm away just in time to escape into a vanishing segment of the door, and leaving the trolley with enough momentum to get it inside the segment behind me.

The door shudders to a halt; wedged by the trolley. There is a wafer-thin opening ahead of me, but it is dwindling; the woman pursuing me is forcing the door the other way with all her strength. The trolley holds firm just long enough for me to squeeze through the gap and escape outside.

Or at least what I thought was outside. This street is actually the inside avenue of a huge shopping mall. Tropical rain lashes down on the glass arches soaring high above us. The ceiling echoes with ethereal tones like they have synchronized a choir to sing with each raindrop.

Up ahead there is a painted green cross protruding from the side of a mahogany-fronted store. The brand name holds no meaning to me, but I know that green crosses are used for medical facilities. From what our elders used to tell of the old world, the emergency services were interconnected. If I get inside, the people at this hospital might be able to call the police. A city like this *must* have police.

"I need help!" I cry, as I sprint up to the android behind the service desk.

Certainly. I am here to help. Please, come this way.

The robot guides me to a partially screened-off area on the same level.

What are the problem areas you're dealing with?

"I am under attack! A woman is chasing me, I think she works for the cartel who destroyed my village and I need you to get help!"

That sounds very stressful. I can detect elevated cortisol levels in your bloodstream, which is a contributing factor to the ageing lines emerging on your face. I suggest we start with a small botox to tidy things up, then perhaps we should discuss breast augmentation?

A floating graphic appears above me, mirroring my body, but it is a modified version of me. The robot beside me opens a drawer and retrieves an adhesive skin patch, then reaches for my neck.

"What the hell are you doing?"

I am applying localized anesthetic to make the surgery comfortable.

"Surgery? I want the police!"

I hear you, girl. It is a crime you're still single. Don't be glum, it's nothing a quick nip and tuck won't fix.

As the robot leans towards me with the patch, I throw myself from the chair and stumble out from the screened area. But the carteller is standing in the mall's entrance, scanning the thoroughfare. As she locks eyes with me, I make a dash for it; sprinting through the main concourse, dodging shoppers and drones as I run. The woman gets caught in a tour group and I seize the opportunity to disappear, throwing myself into the nearest space.

People all around me are hovering at different levels in the air. They are wearing headsets that cover their eyes with a black screen, while giant fans keep them floating. The room is laid out like a pinball machine, cluttered further by groups of friends watching each other take turns on the *Zero Gravity Experience.*

I weave between the big circular fans in the floor until I reach a dead end. Quick, I must double back. Too late! The carteller has cut me off. She is running for me with a murderous look. There is only one way out.

I leap onto the rim of the nearest fan. Cranking the dial up to maximum, I throw myself out flat. Instantly, I am blasted up into the rafters, along with the screaming rich child whose birthday I am ruining.

The carteller glares up at me then follows, diving into the airstream. As she soars upwards I claw my way along the ceiling tiles. The escape route is terrifying; I plunge several feet each time I cross between jet streams.

Something brushes my ankle. The woman is swiping at me; she is almost in range. Down is the only way out of this! I tuck my arms in by my sides and make myself vertical, plunging like a stone. I am inches from the bottom when the fan ceases and an emergency protective air cushion deploys. A siren rings out to alert the attendants as I roll onto the floor and run away.

The carteller drops with a yelp, landing in a crumpled heap between a bewildered honeymoon couple. As I race onwards, a chill greets me. Something white and powdery crunches underfoot. What the hell? This is *snow!*

"Watch out!" comes a yell.

Freezing white powder sprays over me. I shake off the deluge to find a skier in full winter gear standing beside me.

"This is the end zone, you shouldn't linger here!" they yell.

Seeing past the irked woman, my mouth drops. There is a snowy hillside stretching off for hundreds of yards into the distance. The ceiling rises in step with it, projecting images of blue skies and fluffy white clouds, with the occasional animation of flying reindeer.

More skiers are speeding towards me, with warning cries as they try to brake. I dive out of the way, leaping onto a ski-lift, and find myself hitching a mechanical ride up the fake mountain. Dammit, the carteller is climbing onboard too, a few rows back. Oh crap, and she is loading some kind of a gun!

I duck down just in time as something flies overhead. A person in the row before me grunts, then drops face first into the snow below us with a dart sticking out of their neck. Three security drones appear in a flash and surround the carteller as she tries to leap to the row nearest me.

Unauthorized weapon detected. Commencing emergency arrest.

The carteller curses as the drones restrain her limbs then knock her out with a stun charge and drag her from the elevator. With a sigh of relief, I relax into my seat and stare at the mountain top ahead.

But as my eyes settle on the summit, my heart freezes. There is a suited man staring at me, speaking into his wrist. Of *course* Mr. K. was not going to let me go that easily. I scan the hillside for an escape route. If I stay on this thing they will catch me for sure. If I try to get back down the hill, it will take me forever because I have no idea how to ski, and they will simply intercept me. Wait, over there, a service level!

Without a second thought, I throw myself from the seat, landing in the powdery snow below. The cold is piercing against my bare feet and legs. Skiers curse me as I stumble and wade across the hillside to the emergency door at the side of the slope.

As I rush into the corridor, sweet warmth embraces me. In fact, warming up has never felt so good. *Nothing* has ever felt this good. It is like there is something sweet in the air that is wrapping my whole brain up in a fluffy blanket.

Don't be shy, whispers a soft voice.

I do not know who is speaking, but I trust them implicitly. My mood is changing too; all my stress is fading away. My guilt and worries go with them. The only thing I can feel is pleasure. Something soft is stroking my arms; velvety hands are soothing me and drawing me in.

I am standing inside an open-plan shop that reminds me of old-fashioned hair salons from the mid-twentieth century. The velvety hands are guiding me towards an empty seat. All around me, men and women are seated in luxurious recliners with satisfied expressions. Some of their lips are parted, others appear to be nibbling. Some are even strapped into their seats, salivating. All of the customers have huge shiny chrome cylinders over their heads which come down to their lips.

The male carteller bursts into the shop, knocking over a bunch of seats and shattering the illusion. Suddenly I become aware of the velvety hands stroking me. They are emanating from a tall, thin, black robot, built like an arching streetlamp. Tentacle arms wriggle from its stick-thin body, caressing my arms, while electrodes dangle from its stooped mouth, connecting to my temples.

I rip them off and sprint through the shop floor as the carteller gives chase.

Thank you for visiting the Pleasure Palace, reads the inscription above the threshold. *Welcome to the Den of Champions* reads another, flashing up in front of my eyes as I burst into a massive new complex. Darkened lighting, lush red carpet, glitzy machines and tables covering the entire floor, all with immaculately-dressed people glued to them.

First visit to the casino? Have a spin on us!

The animation of the red-haired casino manager in the green suit appears before me again. He flips me a holographic coin with a wink, then puffs on his pipe and disappears in a shower of gold.

I hear the clattering of spindly mind-sex robots being flung over behind me and I sprint into the casino, knowing I have seconds to shake off the carteller. I throw myself into an aisle between two rows of gambling machines. The lights are dazzling, as unicorns and fairies leap between devices, giggling, frolicking, and chasing rainbows.

As each machine bombards me with neural ads I grow dizzier; the blocker Mr. K. paid for does not seem to work in here. Everything is becoming a swirling mess of chiming cash registers and chuckling munchkins. I reach the end of the row and slump against the wall, hiding in a crevice between two machines and burying my head between my knees.

"There you are!"

My head snaps up to see the owner of the voice. It is a rotund man with a satin cummerbund and jewel-studded turban.

"You're late. Don't protest, this is the third time in a row! You need to get your act together. *Literally.*"

He grabs me by the wrist and leads me to a doorway, pulling out a lanyard from around his neck. I am about to break free when I see the carteller standing among the card tables, scanning the casino. I guess I have to take my chances with turban man.

We are marching through a dark, narrow corridor. I can hear muffled laughter through the wall, and someone speaking through a microphone. We are approaching a doorway lit by a purple light. Beside it is a woman with a headset and a clipboard.

"I found her!" cries turban man.

He shoves me forward before the woman, who looks at me, perplexed.

"What? But she's already here."

The woman points to a young lady of similar height and complexion to me, who is waiting in the purple-lit area beside a curtain. She is dressed in full tribal headgear, with a mixture of tattoos and body paint that I have never seen before, almost like she is wearing every tribe's customs at once. Beyond her is a stage with a woman telling jokes under a spotlight.

"Gods above! Who the hell are you, then?" cries the turban man, accosting me.

"I am Pabla of the Centada tribe!" I cry. "I need your help – please, someone call the police. A cartel has destroyed my entire village! They burned everything and they are killing the last of my people. I am *begging* you to help!"

"Hey, shut your mouth and go steal someone else's act!" snaps the young lady by the curtain.

Behind her the comedian is leaving the stage to much applause. The young lady straightens her headgear and decorative feathers then waddles onto the empty stage imitating our sacred dance. The audience go wild with delight.

"Nice try, sweetheart, but like she said, we already got the forest act tied down," says the woman with the headset. "Try the casino across town. Unless you wanna come back and try out as an Indac? Different make up, similar gig though, right? The audience ain't gonna know the difference."

"I am not acting here, I am serious. I need your help!"

The turban man scowls at me.

"OK, kid, if you can't take constructive criticism you're never gonna make it in this town. Security!"

<hr>

The security guards throw me out of the casino and into the mall without further discussion. Panic sweeps over me as I recognize the man scouring the bar opposite.

I dart into the nearest store, praying the carteller has not seen me in those precious seconds. A smartly-dressed robot approaches with a sympathetic expression.

Are you OK, Madam? My database says you are: concerned.

"I am being persecuted and I need some place to hide. Please, for the love of my ancestors, *help me!*"

Of course, Madam, step this way.

"Thank you. Can you call someone?"

Absolutely. You can call whoever you like on the Transverse 9000. Name anyone, living or dead, and we'll connect you with an authentic synthesized avatar. For a small upgrade fee, you can add visual synthesis to the call.

"I... I can call the dead?"

Anything is possible with the Transverse 9000.

"I... I want to call my mother."

Processing. Please hold.

The robot places its hands against my temples. A tingling sensation spreads across my scalp as the screen in its chest flickers. Its belly slides open, revealing an old-style telephone. I snatch it up, breathlessly.

"Mother?"

Pabla, bambina, it is me. How are you, mi querida? Is everything OK? You sound worried! Talk to me darling, it is OK, we can work it out together. I miss you so-

The phone line disconnects with a click, and a plain dial tone takes place where my mother's voice once was.

"Mother? Mother, come back!" I cry.

Thank you for trialing the Transverse 9000. To resume your call, please purchase credits from this instore agent.

"But... But my mother's voice... she was just there! How? Is she... Is she alive?"

Transverse uses the latest in neural interfacing technology to synthesize authentic conversations based on user memory data. Do you wish to continue with your purchase?

"Yes but I... I don't have any money," I stammer, my mind reeling.

The robot's smiling face vanishes, giving way to a cold, neutral expression and a harsh tone of voice.

Confirmed: insufficient credit. Please exit the store. Good day.

"What? No, I cannot go back out there – I am being followed, remember?"

Exit the store. Good day.

"You said you would help me!"

Exit the store. Exiting.

With a jolt, the ground shifts beneath me. The entire floor is rotating like a treadmill, conveying me to the exit, while the robot and furniture hover in place on motorized wheels, fighting the flow of the room.

I bump over the lip of the shop and stumble into the main concourse. There is no time to stop; the carteller is just yards away and about to turn around! I keep moving and plunge into the store ahead, passing through layers of rippling silk and incense.

I emerge into a meadow. There is a trickling stream, and a short bearded man playing a harp. It all looks so lifelike. I prod the man in amazement.

"Oi!" he yells, briefly stopping his harping.

Can I assist you?

A robot has appeared at my side. It is wearing a toga, a green laurel wreath, and has golden feathered wings on its back.

"Uh, yes please," I say, deciding to try and keep it vague this time.

One moment please: performing preliminary credit scan. Good news: you are eligible for an in-store line of credit, with only eighteen percent compound interest. Terms apply. Would you like to proceed to the fitting room?

The folds of silk curtain billow behind me. There is a man's shadow moving closer.

"Uh, yes, hurry!" I urge.

The robot leads me into a dressing room.

Optimizing fabric and pattern to your complexion.

The robot reaches up and pulls down a sheet of fabric from the ceiling. Four extra arms unfold from its back and wrap the sheet around me, pinning it in place, snipping away the excess, and sealing the sides with a resin of sorts. Within a minute, I am staring at myself in the mirror, in a brand new tailored dress, surrounded by sixty percent of the offcut source material.

Do you like it?

"It's... uh..."

This dress is only a preview, of course. Let's try a few more patterns shall we? Then we'll strip you off for a more accurate fitting of the chosen design.

As the robot undoes all of its handiwork in the blink of an eye, the dressing room curtain sweeps open. Mr. K. is standing in the threshold, flanked by both of his security guards.

"Did you really think you could hide? That's what I love about you people. So naïve. I hope you enjoyed your little adventure. It's the last one you'll be having for some time. I can't say I'm not disappointed. Sequestra were genuinely impressed by you, Pabla. We could have made a lot of money together. No matter; other opportunities await. They always do."

He turns on his heel and leans into the woman carteller.

"Put plenty of straw in the crate, she's gonna be in it a while. Oh, and tell Stax he's got a delivery coming."

CHAPTER TWENTY-FOUR

LUKE

I finally catch up with the others down by the river. We've been running for like a gazillion years and I am *not* in good enough shape for this shit. It feel like we're in dense forest again but there's a huge cable cart running overhead, a little way off in the distance. It's laden with rocks and stretches as far as I can see.

The others are looking at me with curiosity as I crease over my knees, wheezing from the run. They arrived some time ago and have been standing for a few minutes, collecting their breath and setting up Ramone's canoe-printing machine.

Save for Delmo and Ramone, all of us have pretty nasty injuries. Ohalo and Latika are tending to their bleeding wounds with moss from the forest. I'm still missing the end of my finger, which hurts like balls. While Pietro for some reason has turned gray.

Something churns up from my stomach and I barf on the mud. It's dark red. That can't be good.

"You OK, gringo?" says Ramone.

"Never better. What's up with lizard boy?"

"Nothing, I'm fine," mumbles Pietro. "What's the plan?"

"I think we've shaken the cartel off," says Delmo. "You helped us destroy their mine and shut down their mast for the time being. For that you have our eternal thanks. But the cartel will be back with more drones. We must share what we have learned so that others in our tribe can defeat them also."

"We still need to take down the rest of the mast network," says Ramone.

"That's two masts we've hit in twenty-four hours. The cartel will be on high alert now," I note. "We need to move fast if we're gonna knock out the whole grid. Pietro, what did you see in the mainframe? Did you get any more intel we can use to infiltrate Crown Acre Farms, or their HQ in Aquerba?"

Pietro dismisses the question with a wave of his hand and dribbles on the floor. No, wait, he's beckoning for something. Pen and paper? Ramone furnishes him with both, and Pietro sketches two triangles side-by-side, intersected by a thick wavy line.

"Wait, I know that logo! That's not Crown Acre at all..." I say.

"Who is it?" slurs Pietro.

"Gah... I'm trying to remember. I've seen it before... they were on TV! Big company. Huge! Sequa? Sequoti?"

"Sequestra," says Ramone, darkly.

"Yes! That's the one! You know them too?"

"From my days in government. They lobbied hard to get access to the forest. Our department pushed back. We used to call them the cartel. Of course, that was before the actual cartels took over. Crown Acre Farms must be a subsidiary or even a client of their subsidiaries because Sequestra are giants."

"Their logo was on the mast," says Pietro.

"Seriously dude, what's up with you?" I ask.

"I said I'm fine," he snaps.

"OK so either the cartel have stolen some of Sequestra's equipment, or that company is living up to its original nickname. If the giants of Sequestra are truly behind this, then those two masts we just shut down might not have made the slightest difference to the international satellites watching Mazonil. Sequestra are risk averse, secretive, and they don't dick around. Shit, I think I underestimated the scale of this whole thing. They'll have fail-safes in place for sure. Pietro, you're the tech nerd, what do you think?"

"Hypothetically, if the cartel boosted the signal from the other masts we saw on the schematic, they do have enough of them across the network to compensate for the two we knocked out," he muses. "It... it is possible you are correct: we have not yet sufficiently disrupted their satellite jammers for the world to see the damage on the ground."

"*Fuck*, then we're basically still at square one!" I cry. "So long as the heart of the network is active, they can do whatever they want and no one outside of Mazonil will know. All we've done is let them know the masts are a target now. We have to take down central hub *stat*."

"Namakaro warriors, we held up our end of the bargain and destroyed their mining machine. Time to keep your word and get us to Aquerba," says Ramone.

The three warrior place their fists over their hearts and nod in solemn gratitude.

"Of course," replies Delmo. "There are three options for reaching the port from here. River, road, or rail. Each has its own dangers, but this is where we must choose."

"Wait, did you say rail? There's a *train* network running through here?" I ask.

"Where did you think that cable cart leads?"

"I guess I didn't give it much thought, on account of being attacked by robotic bugs and *exploding rocket boomerangs*!"

"The rail road is four hours' walk that way," says Delmo, pointing across the river. "Trek in this direction, keeping the sun at your back, and you'll reach the cable cart after thirty minutes. You can follow it to the rail road."

"Is a train the quickest route?"

"Yes, but it is the most dangerous. Lots of cartel work on the railway. The river is much slower, but much safer."

"Does the river option sound good to everyone?" I say.

"We will take the train," says Ramone, firmly.

"OK, it is vote time," I sigh. "Pietro, what do you think? Yo, Pietro?"

Lizard boy is swaying precariously. He's muttering something incoherent and dribbling. As I reach to pat his back, he collapses to the ground.

"Pietro? What's going on? Speak to me!" I yell.

"His leg," says Ohalo, grimly.

All eyes are on Pietro's calf muscle, which has a deep gash across it that looks swollen and infected, and is swelling his circle of freckles down there.

"What the hell is that?" I ask.

"He must have stepped on a viper," says Latika. "They are traps the cartel lay in our territory. It is like being licked by a komodo dragon; you only realize it is fatal as your strength slowly fades away. Pietro probably didn't even notice when it happened."

"But... I've got the same thing on my leg," I say, confused. "How come I'm fine?"

"You don't have our blood. There's nothing for the viper to poison in your veins," says Delmo.

"What's so special about your blood?"

"He didn't tell you?" says Ohalo.

"Pietro, what are these guys on about? What's so special about your blood? Is this a Namakaro thing?"

"It proves his ancestors were of the forest, like us," says Ohalo. "We are each born with repeated patterns of freckles across our bodies, which we incorporate into tattoos as we age. But Pietro has no tattoos, just the marks he was born with."

"And the viper targets these marks?" presses Ramone.

"Yes. It kills the algae in our skin."

"Wait, you have algae in your skin? Like, the stuff that grows on ponds? It's *in* you?" I ask.

"True synthesis with nature. We use the algae to help us live in full harmony with the forest," says Delmo.

"But the algae itself remains secret, or so we believe," adds Latika. "The cartel do not yet know *why* the viper is poisonous to us, they are just delighted that it is, and that it is ineffective on them. They discovered our intolerance only recently by luck, and are happy to exploit it."

"I don't get how that's possible? Are we genetically separate species now?" I ask.

"No. It is simpler than that. The viper kills the algae, and the algae kills us. You see, when the algae dies, it becomes toxic. Our body has no way to deal with that, so we die. It is the perfect weapon. It means their men can work in our forest unthreatened, protected by these new bio-mines that only threaten us."

"Unless your friend gets a transfusion soon, he will die," says Ohalo.

"You're all from his tribe – can't one of you three give him blood?" says Ramone.

"Not without contaminating ourselves. We need proper equipment. I know a place that will have some, but he will be very ill by then. We must leave at once, using the river," says Delmo.

"The canoe is yours," says Ramone, gathering up his machine, which has completed the clay build. "Luke and I will go by foot to the rail line."

"We will?" I say.

"Yes. Unless you have given up on saving the world?"

It's taken a few days, but Ramone's finally figured out how to use my ego against me. I'm not gonna rise to the bait like some egotist. No siree. Luke Remini is bigger than that. True heroes take adversity quietly in their stride.

"So long, gentlemen. Look after lizard boy, and stay safe," I say, with a deep voice and a gracious bow. I don't need to tell them I'm going to save the world. Deep down, they already know.

"Good luck, Pietro," says Ramone.

Pietro mutters something vague and waves feebly as the warriors load him into the canoe. With a solemn nod, they cast off. Head held high, like a true hero, I set off for the rail road beside Ramone.

"Stop walking like that," mutters Ramone, brushing past me.

"Walking like what?"

"You are *such* a loser, gringo," he sighs.

Pff. Yeah. A *hero* loser. He can walk like a regular conscript all he likes, but *I'm* gonna stride like a badass who just chose to risk his life once again for the greater good. I'm a man of the people. A limping legend. A swaggering sensation.

Dammit, I think I pulled my hip flexor.

The warriors made a critical error when they said it was a four hour hike to the railway. They didn't factor in my fitness. Thanks to years of finely-tuned neglect, a recently induced hip injury, and a healthy dose of radiation poisoning which I've been handling stoically, my walking pace is on the modest side. I'm also not accustomed to hiking through an overgrown sauna with a missing fingertip.

Dusk falls as we reach the terminus of the cable cart and I have mixed feelings. Obviously I'm thrilled that the hike is over. This is good news for legs belonging to Luke Remini. What sucks is the huge factory ahead of us that's burning off plumes of gas.

The refinery is weird. The factory has dammed the nearby river, tapping into the free source of pressurized water. The cable cart dumps its rubble into holding tanks, which get flushed out by the dam water. The water splits the earth into smaller chunks and separates out the clusters of the minerals they want.

This process is repeated several times, with various chemical agents being added to each tank, and the byproducts being either extracted into either a dry container for solid minerals, or flushed into the outbound river channel.

The extracted material seems to fit into three categories. Mainly iron ore, tin, and coal. But the real headline acts are the precious, ultra-rare flakes of pluridium-B. A non-explosive variant of the highly-sought after metal, according to Ramone.

Speaking of the rugged ranger, where *is* that dude? I get

jumpy when he disappears without saying anything. It usually means he's up to something I'm not gonna like.

"You're gonna wanna run!" he yells, bursting around the corner.

"What? Why?"

"Because I'm teaching this place a lesson!"

Oh crap. That's his way of saying: *I'm blowing the place up.* I'm racing after him through the warehouse. Workers are on an assembly line. They look totally different to the militant cartellers who attacked us at the mine. This lot are wearing uniforms; cargo trousers and polo shirts with some logo I can't make out. I think it's a leaf? It's immaterial, because we're all about to get blown up, and I have it on good authority that everyone's naked in the afterlife anyway.

A fire alarm rings out and the workers look up. They see Ramone's figure and scream like *he's* a carteller. It's pandemonium in here. They're running from us, we're running from the impending explosion, and I'm wondering whose crib we're actually about to blow up.

As we pour out among the workers, we stumble into the rail yard, where a train is being loaded. Workers are shouting, while a signal master frantically gestures at the driver to depart and get the cargo clear of danger.

The hulking great wheels creak into motion.

"Ramone! The logo, look!"

The freight carriages are covered in graffiti, old government logos, and rusty brands I've never heard of. Save for one, pristine cart. It's hermetically sealed, and features an unmistakable logo on the side. Two twin triangles and the smooth wavy line, symbolizing billowing wind or fresh air or whatever the hell they claim it is they do.

It also says *SEQUESTRA* in capital letters.

"Hurry up, Remini!" yells Ramone, sprinting ahead.

The train's picking up speed.

"Stand back!" yells a rail worker.

He's waving his arms but he's not firing a gun, or even reaching for one.

"Ramone, I don't think these people are cartel!"

"Think less, run more, gringo!" he yells.

He leaps onto the side of a carriage with a sliding door that's fractionally open. Clinging to the side, he extends an arm for me to grab.

"Come on!" he yells.

"I'm trying!"

The train's picking up speed. It's now or never.

I throw myself at him, clasping his arm desperately. My legs are dragging across the ground as the train accelerates. With a groan, Ramone hauls me into the darkened carriage.

"You... are a fat bastard," he pants.

"It's taken years to hone this physique," I wheeze. "Thanks though, I owe you one."

"Move, and your friend gets it," comes a growl from the shadows.

Ramone raises his hands in surrender. A blade glistens against his jugular vein.

"Take it easy, friend, we have no quarrel with you," says Ramone.

"I couldn't agree more," replies the voice. "I rarely have a quarrel with the dead."

CHAPTER TWENTY-FIVE

PABLA

My crate hits the ground with a thud. There is a creaking of wood and a loud crack as someone crowbars the lid off.

"Hola extraña, did you miss me?"

Stax is peering down, grinning at me with his painted red lips and bristly handlebar moustache. Beside him, Axl is holding the crowbar.

"Ugh, she stinks!" yells Axl, covering his nose.

"That, she does," chuckles Stax.

I would insult him but my throat is like ash. The water dispenser ran dry two days ago and my head is pounding. I am nauseous from days of travel stuck in this wretched cage, trapped in the darkness while my muscles cramp horribly.

My body and mind are sluggish, weakened by the transit, but there is something more. My skin feels brittle and prickly like I am covered in burns. The black tattoos adorning my body have turned gray; those precious pockets of algae living in my epidermis have been deprived of sunlight and appear to be dying. I cannot believe it took the destruction of my village for the elders to tell us what they had put in our skin. But now I know I need more than food and water to recover. Without sunlight, the colonies in my skin will collapse, perhaps taking me with them.

"I warned you not to speak out of turn on Mr. K.'s yacht, but did you listen? Did you *hell*," says Stax. "You thought you were special, didn't you? You figured you could *usurp* me. After everything I have done for you! But here's the rub, *jungle blood*. Your little dream of escaping to the city was always a fantasy. Your kind cannot handle modern civilization, it drives you all loco. You quickly end up running through the streets like squealing piglets, begging us to put you back where you belong."

Stax gestures to the water dispenser, which Axl duly tops up. I drink thirstily, desperately hydrating my parched throat. The more I swallow, the more my groggy brain protests until suddenly a tidal wave of nausea takes control.

I'm spewing across the filthy straw lining of my cage while Stax and Axl laugh.

"You bastardos would watch another human drink your piss?" I splutter.

"It ain't *our* piss, sweetheart. It's the dog's," laughs Axl.

This forces more vomiting, but my stomach is empty now. As putrid bile and saliva hit the straw, my world tumbles. My crate is being up-ended, tipping me sideways. I land hard on the floor amid a deluge of soiled straw.

"See this?" says Stax.

I am in a cage and Stax is kneeling beside me, tapping the metal bars from the outside. His gloating smile has gone, and he's staring at me with true disgust.

"*This* is where you belong, forester. This is you now."

"Why don't you just kill me?" I rasp. "It's what you did to the rest of my people."

"After the disrespect you showed me on the yacht,

chica, I would *love* to do that. But unlike you, I respect my superiors. I am *loyal* to Mr. K."

"Only when your own schemes fail."

"Shut your mouth, girl. Speak like that again and I will cut your tongue out, do you hear me? The only reason you are still alive is because of Mr. K.'s orders. He is making an example of you as a warning to those who might cross him."

Stax straightens up and walks to the wall, where he turns on a fan heater and cranks up the dial to maximum. Hot air wafts towards me, sending a heat-shiver through my body.

"Sweet dreams, Pabla. If you struggle to sleep, just remind yourself that you deserve this. Oh, and rest assured, *chica*, this is just the beginning."

Stax and Axl leave, slamming the office door behind them, and flicking off the lone ceiling light as they go. I am alone in the darkness, sweltering in a cage full of my own mess, with nothing to drink but dog piss, while Stax's parting words echo through my mind.

You. Deserve. This.

Three days have passed in Stax's office. I have not spoken since our first reunion. Every night he ramps up the thermostat and leaves me to bake in the darkness, only to offer some vile hydration in the morning. Today was vinegar, and it was a step too far. My body could take no more.

I am slumped against the side of my cage, barely conscious and too weak to move. Stax is standing over me, muttering to Axl about my deterioration, finally noticing something is wrong with my skin. I catch fragments of their words, and concerned mentions of Mr. K.

I black out again, and when I come around, one half of the cage is open. Axl is attaching sensors from a medical drone to my body.

Diagnosis complete. Patient is suffering from sepsis, acute dehydration, malnutrition, muscular atrophy-

"Yeah, yeah, just get on with the treatment," interrupts Stax.

Patient should be horizontal to aid recovery. Intravenous saline fluid is required. Please supply this unit with purified water sources or administer to patient directly. Preparing targeted laser treatment to detoxify contaminated blood.

"No!" I groan.

"What do you mean 'no'? You are dying, *cabrona*. This machine is going to fix you! And keep Mr. K. off my back..."

"No... laser."

The drone thinks I am contaminated and wants to cleanse the algae from my system. But I could be the last of my kind, the last true forest person. My people's legacy must not be eradicated because of my failures. I have to resist.

"Sunlight..."

"What are you rambling about, *puta?*"

"Need... sunlight."

Axl holds a cup of water up to my lips and I drink, clumsily. Most of it goes down the front of my filthy dress, but even that mild cooling sensation brings fleeting relief to my prickling skin.

"I need sunlight," I say.

"You're in no position to make requests."

"My biology is different to yours, my people need sunlight."

"What part of being a prisoner do you not get, jungle blood?" spits Stax.

"The machine does not know my people, it is making a mistake. The laser will not cure the sepsis, it will kill part of me. My skin needs sunlight – it is the only cure."

"What if she's telling the truth, boss? If the machine kills her by accident, Mr. K.'s gonna kill us on purpose," Axl mumbles to Stax.

"OK, mud girl, here's how this is gonna play out," says Stax. "We're gonna give you water, and nutrients, whatever that machine decides is the bare minimum to keep your miserable heart beating. And I'll give you sunlight too... *If* you apologize for the disrespect you showed me on the yacht."

"You burned my village to the ground! You *tricked* me so you could poison my people! You stole our land and cleared our sacred ancestral trees! Now you are holding me in a cage and asking *me* to apologize?"

Stax crosses the dusty office to the far window. He peers outward, basking in a ray of sun as it warms his face.

"The choice is yours," shrugs Stax.

"Boss, if she refuses she'll die and our asses are on the line!" says Axl.

"Fine. I am willing to wait for my apology. In the meantime, she may have a maximum of one hour of sunlight per day. We are not aiming to have her fighting fit, Axl. Don't forget, she's a living piece of memorabilia. A collector's item; a souvenir from that time someone foolishly tried to exploit Mr. K.'s goodwill. She can earn more sunlight hours as and when she apologizes."

Stax crosses to the adjacent window and tweaks the blinds, angling the light rays onto the floor. Axl removes the medical drone from me and, with much grunting and scraping, shunts my cage along the floor into the illuminated spot.

"There," says Stax. "Clock's ticking for the day, so make the most of it."

He slams my cage door shut and tucks the key in his breast pocket.

"It doesn't have to all be bad, Pabla. Maybe in time you'll earn walking privileges again? You know, in a year or so. But we've got a long way to go before that. And remember, it all starts with an apology."

The grinning carteller stares at me for a moment, expectantly. Summoning what little strength I have left, I part my lips and lean to the edge of the cage.

"It's like you said, Stax. I deserve this."

My hour of sunlight is over in the blink of an eye. I have tried to rotate my body so that every patch of tattoo gets some direct light, but it is hard to maneuver in the cage, and doubly-so when the slightest movement feels like climbing a mountain. There is a bowl of cooked rice by my cage but I have not touched it. I will keep the algae alive to preserve my people's legacy, but that is all. After everything I have done to my tribe, I am not worthy of being fed. I should be another dead body in the mud.

Footsteps are climbing the stairs. Stax enters the office leading a group of militia men in rag-tag uniforms.

"Ah, this is our resident pet. Say hello to Pabla."

"Hellooo Pabla," chuckles one of the men, waggling his fingers between the bars.

If I had the strength, I would bite them off. Which I think is the reaction he is hoping for. But I am focused on conserving energy, and soaking up every last second of sunlight.

"That's enough sunbathing for one day, don't you think?" says Stax, drawing the blind. "Truly, we spoil her."

The men chuckle and follow him into a side room, closing the door behind them. As I slump against my cage in the gloomy darkness, I hear muffled fragments of their conversation. Something about a final tribal stronghold. They have finally located it and are planning a major offensive to clear the land. There is talk of a forest assassin who has been spreading terror among the cartel camps, striking as they sleep. The visitors are asking for extra drone resources to fight back when the warrior's name makes me sit up like a bolt.

Oriana of the Centada.

My sister is alive! And she is giving these bastardos hell. This changes everything. If she still has the algal vial, then our people's legacy may yet live on. I have to save her; to find her before their drones do – and to warn the other tribes that the cartel has discovered their final "stronghold", wherever it is.

Reaching feebly through the bars, I grab a handful of rice and press it to my chapped lips. Hearing my sister's name has given me renewed purpose. I need to recover my strength, because it is time that I, too, fight back once more.

Eight days have passed since I arrived in Stax office. It is night time, and the room is dark, save for slivers of ambient light from the bar across the street. My eyes are shut, as I mentally rehearse my route for the hundredth time. Hours of constant observation, silently paying attention to every detail of every visitor's movements in this festering building, has allowed me to build up a mental picture of its layout.

It all hangs on tonight. The night guard is drunk – he is always drunk. Stax does not know, because the guy uses a hipflask, and only starts drinking once everyone else has left. He uses a metric ton of mouthwash each morning, and chain smokes cigarettes to cover his tracks.

But tonight, he is going to be doubly drunk because it is his birthday. I cannot decide if it is cute or pitiful to think of a washed up, middle-aged carteller celebrating his birthday like this.

Clip-clop, clip-clop, turn, clop-clop-clop, clip-clop.

He is coming up the stairs, which I know for a fact have a twist eight steps down from here. Wait, scratch that, he is going back down because he has forgotten something. His steps are uneven, and he stumbles into the wall as he turns. So far, so promising.

Ah, I recognize that familiar tinkling sound. One of the guard's many visits to his pissing pot in the corridor downstairs. Again, something I doubt Stax knows about. I have learned to gauge the level of his intoxication with the tone of the pitter-pattering piss, as he sloshes around and dashes it across the floor tiles. Conditions are perfect: the guard is wasted and humming to himself.

A chair slides downstairs and a TV flicks on. Ugh, the drunken idiot has forgotten all about my food. It is probably cooling on some ledge halfway down the stairs.

"Hey! Gonsalo!" I yell. "Gonsaaaaalllooooo!"

The TV flicks to mute.

"What?" he yells.

"I need you!"

"I'm a guard not a maid!" he bellows, flicking the TV back on.

"Gonsaaaallloooooo!"

I am putting on a voice, obviously. Gonsalo is a sad, lonely man, and he responds favorably to soft, teenage tones from women in cages. It is a wonder he is still single. What a catch.

The TV is still on, but he is stomping up the stairs, making a show of his macho displeasure, when really, we both know he loves having an audience. I am the best thing that has ever happened to his miserable night watch. I always wondered where cartellers go to retire when they are too clapped out to be of use in the field. And now I know; night duty. Assuming they live long enough to see retirement. If my sister has anything to say about the matter, that number will be dwindling by the day.

The door opens with a bang and Gonsalo staggers in, bringing with him a waft of hops so pungent it is detectable even over the squalor of my cage.

"What you want?" he grunts.

"It is my dinner time."

"Dinner? You already ate!"

"No, you plated it up, got halfway up the stairs, then abandoned it, went for a piss and watched TV."

Gonsalo thinks for a moment, then a smile spreads across his doughy features. He crackles up with laughter like a naughty schoolboy.

"Si! I did to that," he whispers, like teacher might hear.

"If I starve to death on your shift, who do you think Stax is going to blame?"

"Me!" he whispers, giggling even harder.

"Best go fetch that food then, hadn't you?"

The food is critical to my escape plan. It is the only thing I can think of that might actually work, and it has to be today, when Gonsalo's judgement is fully compromised.

He returns a moment later, clutching a bowl of rice with grains and muck down one side.

"I may have dropped it. Don't tell Pabla, she hates bits in her food," he whispers.

I take the bowl from him and prod around the bowl for a patch of rice that is not covered in dirt.

"You know, jungle blood, I reckon outside of that cage you'd be alright-looking," muses Gonsalo.

He's got his hands on his hips, and is swaying as he sizes me up, chuckling.

"Always wanted me a wife."

"Never gonna happen, Gonsalo."

"Aw c'mon, it's my birthday!"

"You heard Mr. K.'s orders. I am not to be touched. I am an example," I say, pretending to chew.

"It could be our little secret?" whispers Gonsalo, with genuine optimism.

Game time. I throw my back against the cage with a clang. Spluttering grains of rice for maximum effect, I rasp like I am choking.

"Hey... hey what is this?" says Gonsalo, nervously.

I thump my back against the cage repeatedly, like I am trying to dislodge the blockage.

"Hey, I'm serious! Don't be goofing around!"

With a final splutter, I slump sideways onto the floor and lay still.

"Hey! Hey, wake up! Jungle blood! Pabla? Pab- Oh shit. Oh Christ. Fuck, fuck, *fuck!*"

Gonsalo is panicking. He is rattling the cage door. He knows if I die, *he* dies. He is juuust functional enough to remember that. Now I need him to remember that the key to my cage is in his pocket.

The lock jangles and turns. He is doing it! The door

squeaks open and he stumbles down onto his hands and knees to reach me. This is my chance to strike. I have spent eight days discretely stretching and moving all my muscles so that I am ready for this moment. If I get this wrong, they will tighten everything for sure. My one chance to save Oriana and the last tribe will be gone forever. I *have* to get this right.

"Pabla? Hey!" he slurs, reaching into the cage.

My ears are pricked to every nuance of his motion. His knee hits the frame. As I feel his boozy breath against my cheeks, I know he is overreaching. Now!

I spring from my position and grab him by the neck, rolling on top of him. In the same motion, I shunt his hands outwards so his torso falls to the ground. Before his dizzy brain knows what is happening, I am out of the cage, and shoving the rest of his sorry ass in there.

The door clangs as I slam it shut, locking him inside. I know the code to Stax's safe, having seen him punch it in all week when he thought I was asleep. In a flash, I have punched in the combination and got his keys. Gonsalo's drunken whining fades behind me as I speed down the staircase and through the deserted house, letting the burbling TV drown out his voice. Within seconds, I am in the garage, on Stax's bike, and tearing onto the open road. I am a prisoner no more. I am a warrior, and my revenge is just beginning.

CHAPTER TWENTY-SIX

LUKE

As the train accelerates, the stranger presses the blade closer to Ramone's neck. Her skin is darker than his, and her accent thicker. Her body is covered in ornate tribal tattoos, culminating in a striking black caiman across her forehead. The creature's uncompromising jaws match the fearsome glint in her eye. I have no doubt that she will slit Ramone's throat in a heartbeat. This woman is a killer.

"Let's all just take a moment," I say, hands raised. "Would you mind telling us your name, Ma'am?"

"My name is go to hell, white man. You have to the count of three to get off this train or your friend dies," she replies.

"He's not my friend," grunts Ramone.

"Really, dude? *That's* the battle you wanna pick right now?" I say, more than a little hurt.

"She should know you have no significant emotional ties to me. This negotiation will only be constructive if we have a common understanding of leverage. Otherwise she's just committing herself to counting down, then slitting my throat, and still having to deal with you, That's a bad outcome for everybody, I'm sure she would agree," says Ramone.

"Stop saying 'she'," snaps the woman. "Talking about someone in the third person when they're in the same room as you is rude."

"You haven't told us your name!" I protest.

"Her name is go to hell," growls Ramone.

"Your friend's cute," she snorts. "It's a shame I'm gonna have to kill him. Unless, of course, you get off the train. Three..."

"Are you insane? It's moving!" I protest.

"Two..."

"I'd be jumping into the cartel's arms!"

"O-"

Before she can finish the word, Ramone elbows her in the ribs and breaks free of the chokehold. She screams in anger and lunges forward, swinging the knife. Ramone parries, knocking her hand against the hull until she drops it, but she counter moves, kicking his knee in. As Ramone falls to the ground she leaps upward, grabbing hold of the overhead railing and spinning around mid-flight. In the same move she clamps her legs around his neck and falls backward. He's choking and can't reach her. His legs flail helplessly while he tries to punch her torso, but with her arms free she's blocking him easily.

My eyes fall to the corner of the carriage, where she came from. Glistening in the shadows is a glowing vial. Snatching it up, I hold it out by the gap in the train door.

"Let him go or I throw whatever the hell this is under the wheels!" I yell.

The attacker freezes, staring at me. Ramone's tugging at her legs while his face turns purple.

"You have no idea what you're doing!" she cries.

"Then let him go, and I won't have to do it!"

"Ignore... what... she... says..." rasps Ramone.

"It's *rude* to say 'she'!" yells the assailant, tightening her legs.

"Hey – *hey*! Let him go or I toss this! *I'm* counting down this time! Three-"

"God *dammit*!" yells the woman.

She releases Ramone and kicks him away, snatching up her knife while he scrambles to the side to gather breath.

"Give me the container," she growls, pointing the blade at me.

"Put the knife down and promise we'll talk," I insist.

"Container first."

"Don't do that," rasps Ramone.

"Obviously I'm not gonna do that! I'm not a total idiot!"

The train jolts between tracks and the vial slips from my hand. I frantically slap it between my butter fingers but it's like a wild salmon, evading my frantic attempts to keep it aloft. I'm gasping in panic while the woman cries in fear.

I catch the vial mid-air and clamp it to my chest, slumping back against the carriage wall in relief. With genuine fear on her face, the woman slides her knife across the floor, then holds out her hand for the vial. I oblige. Ramone and I have the knife now, although technically Ramone already had a knife of his own. Which is a good point, actually.

"Dude, how come you didn't use your knife?" I whisper.

"It's in my bag," he mutters.

"You keep your knife in a bag? That's not very practical."

"I don't normally. I was trying out a new system."

"Why? You have a holster!"

"I wanted the holster for snacks."

"OK well your new system sucks worse than your ability to make friends. Fortunately, I am exemplary at making new acquaintances," I say, turning to our attacker. "So, knife lady, who are you, and why do you hate award-winning journalism?"

She looks to Ramone with confusion. "What is white man talking about?"

"Ignore it. He tells everyone we meet."

"Not everyone," I correct. "Just most people."

"It sounds like your friend is very insecure," says the woman.

"He is not my friend," grunts Ramone.

"Stop saying that! Bro, I do have feelings, you know? Besides, I just saved your life *again*, so how's about a 'well done Luke'?"

"What are you two doing on this train? You do not sound like cartel," frowns the woman.

"Cartel? We're the *anti*-cartel! We're the goodies! The heroes! The dream team!" I say.

"Ah, now I see why big guy does not want you as a friend. You are a dork."

"You're taking *his* side?"

The woman shrugs. "You seem annoying."

"*Thank* you," sighs Ramone.

"She just tried to kill you!" I protest.

"I was letting her win," he mutters.

"Really? Wanna go another round?" snorts the woman.

"Go to hell, 'go to hell'," says Ramone.

The woman chuckles.

"That's a point," I say. "Tell us your proper name, otherwise in my head you'll just be 'knife lady' forever."

"My name is Oriana, and I am the last surviving member of the Centada tribe."

She takes a deep breath and straightens up majestically.

"Sweet. OK none of that means anything to me, but then again I don't really know much about your culture. Ramone, is that ringing any bells?"

"I am familiar with the tribe but only by name. I am sorry to hear of your plight, Oriana. What happened to the rest of your people?" says Ramone.

"We were betrayed by one of our own."

Her voice cracks as she says this. I sense it's a raw nerve.

"Raw nerve, huh?"

They both look at me incredulously. I think this is one of those 'sensitivity' moments my therapist was talking about.

"Yes, asshole. It is a raw nerve when your entire community is murdered."

"Oof. OK, I'm sensing some emotional baggage here, so I suggest we keep it light for now and wait until we know each other a little better before we get too bogged down in our personal lives."

"See what I mean?" says Ramone.

"El es un coñazo," nods the woman nods, wearily.

"Cut it out, you two! I didn't secure a peaceful resolution to your little mud wrestling contest there just so you can make me feel like a gooseberry. I used to be in the three musketeers, dammit! In fact, our third member just fell sick, so we *are* looking for a replacement, if you're available?"

"You are asking me to join you?" says Oriana. "I don't even know who you two are, or what you are doing here."

"Oh, right. I'm Luke, I like ginger kombucha, bebop

jazz, and meeting new people. That's Ramone, he likes the rainforest, animals, and being left alone."

Ramone nods, pleasantly surprised by this summary.

"None of that explains why you are on this train," says Oriana.

"We're travelling to Aquerba to destroy a network of satellite-blocking radio masts that the cartels are using to cover up the most aggressive deforestation operation in history," says Ramone.

"Dude, stay in your lane. Synopses are *my* gig!" I protest. "You can't just leap in and give one. You need the skills! I recently got praised by the Namakaro people for that very attribute."

Ramone shrugs, giving me the floor to elaborate.

"I mean... in this instance I guess you covered most of the salient points..." I mutter.

"So you two are fighting the cartel too," muses Oriana. "I have been searching for the remaining forest tribes to seek refuge. Our lands have been destroyed, and I must deliver this vial to them so that my people's genetic legacy is not lost with them. This black algae keeps us alive and in harmony with the forest.

"I have been attacked and thwarted by cartels at every stage of my journey. I killed as many as I could, but the last escape was a close one and I nearly lost the vial. So I have been forced to abandon my goal of finding the Northern stronghold of tribes, and I am instead heading to the coast – to Aquerba, like you. My father, may his spirit rest, said that before the great collapse of Mazonil there were charities there. He said those people came from abroad to help us. Maybe some of them are still there, and can get this vial to another country. At least, until the forest is safe again."

She chokes up at the last words, like she doesn't fully believe such a prospect is possible.

"I might know someone in Aquerba," says Ramone. "We went to school together before her family moved to the coast. I think her parents worked for an NGO. She might have some contacts who can help," says Ramone.

"You would do that?" says Oriana.

"We forest people must help each other. No one else will."

"*Ahem,*" I say, loudly.

"Yes? Oh, right. Apart from him."

"He doesn't seem that helpful," whispers Oriana.

"Hey! Third person, much!" I protest.

The two laugh at me like they're star-crossed lovers and I'm a juggler on their first date. Ew. I preferred Ramone when he was the stoic single type. I'm not sure I wanna see silver fox Ramone doing his thing.

"What do you two want in return?" says Oriana.

"I think *somebody* wants to get laid," I mutter.

"Ignore gringo," frowns Ramone. "We could use a warrior, if you will join us, Oriana. You are a better fighter than either of us, and we will need someone with your skills if we are going to take down the hub server."

"Hub server? What's that?"

"We believe a company called Sequestra is running the satellite jamming network via a central hub in Aquerba. When we get there, we will find them and destroy it," says Ramone.

A clang rings out through the hull, followed by another. Multiple clangs. It's like the sound of rain on a tin roof, but with more ding. Like someone tipping a bucket of magnetic letters onto a fridge.

"You mean *if* we get there," says Oriana, reaching to retrieve her knife.

The clattering intensifies. It's wrapping around us from all angles like someone's popping metal bubble wrap against our half of the carriage.

"You know what that is?" asks Ramone.

Oriana holds a finger to her lips and edges towards the open carriage door, clutching the dagger. Ramone rises to his feet, quietly retrieving his own knife from his backpack. I'm feeling really left out of the knife club, and make a note to discuss inclusive group dynamics with the others later.

A small metal cube latches onto the upper lip of the doorframe with a ding. Oriana's frozen, holding out a hand to keep me and Ramone at bay. The sound of the train clattering over the tracks accompanies our silence as we wait for another metallic 'pop'.

The cube hangs there like it's glued to the doorframe, apparently doing nothing. Then it starts to pulsate, swelling at the sides like it's *breathing*. A soft yellow glow is growing brighter from its core.

"Shit, it has us!" gasps Oriana.

She smashes the butt of her knife against it, shunting the magnetic cube out into the dusk air. In the same breath she grabs the carriage door and hauls it shut, sealing us in darkness.

"Tell me that's not what I think it was?" I ask.

"You've also seen those before, gringo?" says Ramone, flicking on a flashlight.

"Not first-hand, thank fuck. But a bunch of military papers were leaked last year, and those little bastards were among some of the experimental technologies they were testing. Wait, Oriana, you knew it was scanning us, which means you've seen them before, too? How the hell did you escape?"

"Blind luck. We passed through an area where their signal seemed to break down. They went into some kind of standby mode and I was able to escape."

"Maybe the train passed one of the satellite masts?" suggests Ramone.

"Or it could be a defect? I've not heard anything about these things making it out of beta testing. The ones on this train could be stolen prototypes." I counter.

"You mean there are more of them onboard?" says Ramone.

A metallic clang rings out against the sealed doorway. Then another. A small square patch of door starts to glow red. It doubles in size, becoming a rectangle. Then again. The metal's hissing, bubbling. Suddenly, the glowing patch falls inward, landing on the floor with a thud. A cluster of cubes are clinging to the back of it, glowing white-hot. One by one their swollen backs burst and they deflate, losing their color and shape, leaving behind a molten residue on the still-glowing metal.

There's no time to question what just happened, because we've got incoming. Dozens of fresh cubes tumble off the roof and in through the perforation. As each one lands on the floor, a faint yellow spark appears within it, growing brighter by the second.

"Run!" yells Oriana.

She darts to the far end of the carriage, opens the loading hatch and crawls through onto the roof.

"Is she insane?" I cry.

But Ramone's not hanging around either – he's straight

after her, leaving me alone in the carriage. But it's not dark anymore. The fallen cubes are glowing bright yellow, and tumbling towards me like someone smashed a bunch of Rubik's cubes across the floor and told them all to go kill Luke Remini.

I scramble for the hatch, dragging myself halfway through. The others made it look so much easier than this!

"Idiota! You're supposed to go legs first!" yells Ramone.

I'm bent over this loading hatch like a screaming clam, with my face dangling towards the blurry track racing beneath us, while the killer cubes roll towards my rear end. I feel two sets of hands drag me upwards and next thing I know I'm on the roof, wailing.

More cubes are rolling up from the sides of the carriage, studding the top with glowing yellow lights. It looks weirdly beautiful, and part of me wants to take a mental picture of this for my scrapbook of bedroom refurbishment ideas, but when you're being pursued by experimental military technology it's *really* important to stay focused. The scrapbook will have to wait.

"You two go on – I'll hold them off!" yells Ramone.

He's rummaging in his backpack for some kind of disrupter. Oriana's already clambering along the next roof. There's an empty flat-bed carriage with a release lever on the end. If we can reach it, we can cut the cube-infested carriages loose!

I scramble after Oriana, turning at the last moment to check on Ramone's progress. He's been overrun! Something's gone wrong with his device and the cubes are latching onto his legs. I'm watching in horror. I've seen the test videos for these bastards and I know what happens next.

More cubes are tumbling towards him with speed, rolling up from all sides of the carriage. As they get within a yard of the other cubes on his leg, they stop rolling and fly through the air, like they've been snatched in magnetically. They're clamping together, weighing Ramone down and forming a perfect seal around his leg, interlocking and spreading up his body. It's like watching someone get mummified alive by fairy lights.

He's crying in pain. The latched cubes are swelling and glowing brighter, creating a shimmer as they vibrate. If they reach his vital organs, he's doomed; they'll raise his core temperature so fast he'll be boiled alive in his own liquids. It's possibly the most awful, and most versatile technology my country's military has ever devised.

"Luke, take the bag!" yells Ramone.

As he drags his anchored leg across the roof, he hurls his backpack at me. It's arcing high – I have to leap backwards to catch it. But as I land, my leg hits something soft. I'm falling through a canvas roof!

I land hard on top of something that feels like another human. It sounds like one too, and they're cursing me to hell. I'm flailing around on my back, being buffeted by the train and the people under the canvas. Oriana's in the middle, being punched and grabbed by people fighting her through the sheet.

As I stagger to my feet, someone pops up beside me like an olive-green ghost. My reflexes kick in and I punch them square in the chops, sending the poor sucker down. But their comrades are more savvy. The sound of ripping canvas erupts either side of me as two cartellers cut their way out of the sunken roof. One is facing the wrong way, and I get a clean sucker punch in before he can turn around. He slumps before me and I snatch his gun. The other carteller lunges at me with a knife, but the stun gun fells them in their tracks.

I trip over a hidden body, landing on something soft. I think this is a sleeper carriage? I wonder if that comes out of their wages, or if room and board is a taxable perk? I'm about to stun whoever's grabbed my leg, but I realize I can't see Oriana. She's been dragged under!

I lift the nearest tear and step under the sheet. Huge mistake, I'm immediately pounced on. Someone's smothering me with the fabric. I'm trying to fight back but I can't see shit and someone else's legs are tangled in mine. It's carnage down here. People are yelling, kicking, punching, and stabbing blindly in the chaos.

A flash of bright yellow flies past my eyes and the carriage jolts as something heavy lands with a thud. I'm feeling around in Ramone's bag, desperately pressing every button and pulling every pin my fingers touch as I suffocate under the sheet.

A blinding burst of light shoots out from the bag. Everyone in the carriage hits the deck, yelping with pain. I can only assume their ears are ringing too. Seizing my chance, I break free from the smother-hold and fight my way back to the surface. Oriana's clambering out too, kicking a dazed carteller off her leg.

The device worked! The yellow cubes have fizzled out and are falling off Ramone's body as he scrambles to his feet. Christ, they'd nearly reached his ribcage. But now they're coming away in chunks like he's ripping off a suit of armor.

"Get to the next carriage!" yells Ramone.

Oriana and I clamber up the exposed frame and leap to the flat, empty platform ahead. Ramone lands soon after, shaking the last cubes off his person.

"The lever!" he cries.

But Oriana's already on it. She heaves it to the opposite side, severing our link to the sleeper carriage. As the cartellers scramble through their fabric roof, taking dazed potshots at us, cries of panic ring out. The cubes are glowing again.

We watch in exhaustion as our half of the train accelerates away from the cartellers and the tumbling yellow blocks. Oriana howls with triumph, raising the vial above her head like a trophy.

"That was a hell of a close thing," pants Ramone, relieved.

"You guys reckon there are more of those cubes on board?" I ask, nervously.

"No idea, but we can't take any more risks," says Ramone. "It's a long way to Aquerba. We need to get inside a carriage, stay hidden, and take turns to be on watch duty. I vote gringo gets first shift."

"What? How's that fair? I'm spent! Do you have *any* idea what it's like being middle-aged? I'm old, dude! But everyone still expects me to keep working!"

"I'm older than you, gringo. Quit whining," snorts Ramone.

"For real? Woah, your skin looks amazing. What's your secret?"

"All in favor of white man taking the first watch, say aye," interjects Oriana, raising her hand.

Ramone copies, and she nods as if the motion's passed.

"Wait, that's only a simple majority! I think we should discuss alternative voting methods."

"Good night, gringo. Enjoy first watch," chuckles Ramone.

Ugh. I hate this train. This is *exactly* why people prefer

flying. It's got nothing to do with price. It's about the ratio of assholes to hours onboard. As the two members of the knife-owning club pick their respective sleeping spots, I take my pew on a crate in the center. I'm clutching Ramone's dim night light, and wondering why there's a warm trickle passing down my cheek. Oh great, it's blood. Yup. I'm literally crying blood now. God dammit. It would be *really* great if my body could just keep its shit together for a couple more days. I seriously hope this Sequestra hub is next to a hospital, or I'm screwed.

CHAPTER TWENTY-SEVEN

PABLA

I have been driving for hours, racing through the night on the hoverbike I stole from Stax. Have I ever ridden one of these before? No. Have I seen cartellers riding them, and explored them through the encyclopedia? Yes. Is passive training enough?

Absolutely not.

Fortunately, the road I am on is straight like an arrow. The only things I have to worry about are being hit at an intersection or caught up by the cartel. Dawn has broken, which means right about now someone will be discovering the drunken night guard slobbering in my cage. I don't think today's gonna go well for Gonsalo. But let's be clear, he works for a cartel and thought he was entitled to my body because it was his birthday. Excuse me if my heart doesn't bleed for that old drunk.

There's almost certainly a tracker in this bike, which means Stax's men will be after me. The only advantage I have is being a few hours ahead of them on the road, but I cannot stay on this thing forever. At some point the road will run out – in fact, I am banking on it. For hours I have been speeding through endless hectares of farmland and smoldering clearances. A forest is the only place I can hide, and it is not compatible with the existence of this road.

If you want to know how I am feeling right now, I suggest you go and betray everyone you know, regret it deeply, get imprisoned in a cage, then escape knowing that if you are caught your one chance to save your sister's life, and the last of your kind, will be lost forever.

It is not a great feeling.

Further complicated by the fact I do not know precisely where my sister and her tribe of survivors are, I am just heading along the open road on which they were last sighted in the north. Stax is preparing to move on the community at any moment. I *have* to get there first. The only thing giving me hope is the patchy return of trees around me.

Wait, what is this? A truck parked at the roadside. It is the first working-condition vehicle I have seen since leaving. Which tells me cartellers are somewhere ahead. But which cartel?

I ease off the accelerator for the first time in hours. I know first-hand that cartellers are not above stealing from each other. On the contrary, it is an essential part of their strategy. So either I am about to get hijacked by a new cartel, or this is one of Stax's crews and they have been put on alert to intercept me. I have seen cartels use tripwires in the past – "gravity rugs" they call them. Invisible cables laid across the road that deliver an upward charge when a vehicle crosses over, turning the people on board into human throwing darts.

Time to make a decision. If I slow down further, it will be easy for them to shoot me. If I go fast and I hit a gravity rug, then it will mean paralysis and a slow death asphyxiating on the roadside. Both of which I have seen happen. If those are my only choices, then it is simple. I will take a clean death by my own hand over an enemy bullet any day.

Redoubling my grip, I hunch over the handlebars and crank up the power again. But as I speed forwards, someone staggers out from the trees. They are injured, clutching their ribs like they have been shot. Their skin is like mine, and their body painted and decorated with tattoos. It is a warrior from the Namakaro tribe!

They have seen me coming. First they raise their hand in despair, then they turn to run; they think I am cartel too. I hit the brakes and the bike shudders to a stop. I am still some way from the staggering tribesman, who is trailing blood as he limps across the road. A gunshot rings out from the trees. The bullet strikes the fleeing man in the back. He drops to ground, dead. Cries of despair ring out from the forest, mingled with shouts of abuse.

If I want to make it out of here alive, I need to make a break for it at full speed before the cartellers emerge from the woods. But I would be abandoning whatever other foresters are trapped with them. In these past weeks I have turned my back on my people many times just to save my own skin. I am damned if I do it again.

I leap from the bike and tow it off the roadside, hiding it between some trees before hurrying through the overgrowth on foot. There is a slope leading down to a riverbank. On the side is a canoe, and five people. Two of them are cartellers, armed heavily. Opposite them are the captives; two tribesman and a paler-skinned foreigner. The cartellers are making the foreigner place zip-ties around the tribespeople's wrists. He is swaying as he does it, like he has been hit in the head, or is drugged or something.

With the warriors restrained, the cartellers cuff the foreigner. A third carteller returns from the roadside execution and orders them all to march up the riverbank towards the truck. I am outnumbered and outgunned, and I need a plan, fast. The only way I stand a chance is to pick the cartellers off individually, but for that I need to separate them somehow.

Their vehicle! I dart out of the forest, across the road, into the opposite line of trees. Under cover, I sprint towards the cartel's truck, while they march their prisoners up the steep, slippery bank.

A stroke of luck – this is an ancient Mazonilian truck. It was never equipped with finger print scanners, it just uses an old fashioned metal key. I yank it from the ignition then sprint back among the trees. It is not long before the group emerges from the forest, with the cartellers prodding the drowsy foreigner forwards at gunpoint. All I need to do is watch and wait. The timing will be critical.

"What do you mean they're not there! Coño!" yells the lead carteller.

A row erupts between the three gunmen over who had responsibility for the keys. One of them is sent back into the forest to search for them, while another searches the vehicle. The other simply berates the prisoners.

I seize my moment and dart across the road, into the opposite line of trees. As I run, one of the captive tribesmen sees me, but gives nothing away. I can only hope they are more loyal than I was.

The carteller is cursing his luck as he stomps through the mud, retracing his steps, searching for the key. I stalk him halfway down towards the river, then get as close to him as I dare. Silently, I lay the keys down in the mud, near the group's footprints opposite a dense cluster of ferns. I am holding my breath as the carteller huffs and puffs, stomping around the mud. Finally, he turns around and spots the glistening set. Half cheering, half-cursing his idiot colleague, he marches towards them.

As the hapless carteller stoops down, I spring from the ferns. Flying silently through the air, I land on his back and drive Gonsalo's hunting knife deep into his neck.

The man crumples beneath me, gurgling in a pool of blood. I wipe the blade clean on his sleeve, then steal his gun and take the keys from his hand.

A carteller calls from the roadside, demanding an update. I am sprinting up the bank, parallel to the dead man's trail. The carteller shouts again, first growing impatient, then becoming concerned.

I crouch in wait by the roadside verge. Sure enough, the second carteller approaches, calling out to his comrade. I throw the knife, striking him square in the chest. He sinks to his knees, gasping. In the same motion I break cover and open fire on the carteller searching the car. His blood splatters the windshields and he disappears from view. But I know that is not enough – if people in the township had bullet proof clothing, I bet cartellers in the field do too. I need a headshot.

The sickly foreign captive is on his knees, hands raised in surrender. The warriors, however, have seized the moment. One of them rushes to the verge and throws his hands over the stabbed carteller's neck. He drags the man backwards, using the zip ties around his wrists to strangle him. The other warrior has grabbed the man's gun, and is circling around to the truck with me, moving in a pincer motion. The bleeding carteller is out of sight, having dropped below the window line.

The warrior nods to me, signaling he is ready to move on my mark. I leap up and smash the passenger window, then hit the deck. As a hail of bullets fly out through the empty frame, the warrior appears at the opposite window and fires into the truck, striking a fatal blow.

He pulls the door open and drags the carteller out. Blood trickles from the bullet hole in the side of the man's head. The second tribesperson appears clutching the strangled carteller's knife and cuts his comrade free.

Liberated, my helper rushes to his fallen kinsman; the first man I saw getting shot in the back. The free man is shaking him, calling his name, while the other guy helps the drowsy foreigner to his feet.

The grieving man wails, rocking over the body of his peer, while the others approach me, wearily.

"Thank you for saving us. I am Latika of the Namakaro."

"Pabla of the Centada," I reply. "Who is the outsider?"

"This is Pietro. He is one of us. Well, half us, half foreign," says Latika.

Latika has his name tattooed across his chest, as per the Namakaro custom. He glances at my swirling range of tattoos and sees their gray hue. We lock eyes, both knowing it means my algae is in poor condition. His knowing gaze tells me his tribe did not live under the same shroud of secrecy as ours. Perhaps that is why we drifted apart.

Pietro has a young face, with thick, wiry eyebrows, green eyes, and a circle of dark freckles on his cheek. He is about to speak but then turns away to vomit. He is leaning against the truck, steadying himself and groaning. My eyes fall on his calf, which has a gash on it. The skin is swelling and looks red raw. As I look closer, something around the inflammation catches my eye. Another circle of freckles. These ones look gray, but the shape is unmistakable – it's a direct match to those on his cheek! freckles.

"I know that pattern of freckles on his skin – he has inherited our algal blood! How is that possible for a foreigner?"

"You would have to ask him," replies Latika. "Assuming he ever recovers the strength to speak. He has been poisoned by a cartel viper trap. We need to get him to the northern stronghold urgently. Only an algal transfusion can save him now."

"The stronghold! You know it? I am searching for my sister – she was heading there! Oriana of the Centada?"

"We only know the stronghold by reputation. My people's territory is far from here, much like yours. And like you, I suspect we are fleeing for the same reason. I'm sorry, I do not know of your sister."

I try to recover from the crushing disappointment. It was foolish to let my hopes get raised like that.

"We all need to keep moving," I say. "The cartel will be tracking the bike I stole, and these guys too, I am sure of it."

"We must lay our leader to rest first. He was the bravest of all of us."

"But... he was running away?" I say, instantly regretting my clumsiness.

"He knew it would bring almost certain death. We were outnumbered and at the mercy of their weapons, yet he took the one chance he could to overcome the cartellers. He made for the road, calling to our ancestors for a miracle. And here you came. Through his sacrifice, you saved the three of us."

"No one else would call me a miracle. I know my people

see me as a curse. I am just sorry I did not arrive sooner," I reply.

"Delmo died with honor but his spirit must be returned to the forest before we flee this place. Please, will you help us ensure his passage?"

I am scanning the road, anxiously. There are no signs of other vehicles, but they could appear at any moment. Traditional mourning is often slow. We will have to cut some corners. I pop the trunk of the cartel's truck and grab a coil of rope.

We bind it to the dead warrior's ankles, then throw the other end over the branch of a tall, thick tree. Latika and I haul the body up until Delmo's body suspended above us, among the lower forest canopy. The other grieving warrior, Ohalo, has crossed the dead man's hands across his chest and bound them in place, giving the body a sleeping quality as it dangles.

Latika ties the rope off securely around the trunk, and says some hushed words with his arm around Ohalo, before the pair follow me and Pietro back to the truck. The hoverbike would be faster for sure, but it could never hold all four of us, especially with Pietro too weak to hold on.

"You must think I am mad," croaks the foreigner, as we pull away from the carnage. "Mad to have left a safe country to come to the forests of old Mazonil."

I can't help but smile. "A few weeks ago I would have shouted you down for making such a stupid decision. But since then I have seen the outside world. I get why you wanted to leave it well behind."

This seems to bring Pietro some comfort as he passes out with a worried look. Latika confirms the young man still has a pulse, but he is unresponsive. We drive for several hours before the road comes to an end. It is a weird patch of rubble, where the forest has been cleared and the ground dug up, but the surface was never smoothed or completed. Instead, abandoned machinery sits all around, some with missing parts. I seriously hope Pietro has regained some strength, because from here on out thick forest awaits, and we can only continue on foot.

We have been trekking for several hours and Pietro's exhaustion is forcing us to take another break. Ohalo and Latika are arguing about who is navigating, and which is the best way to the tribe. Everyone, it seems, is relying on third-hand rumors of where this northern stronghold is.

I step away from the group to clear my head. The cartel could still find us; we are within a few hours' walk of where we abandoned their old truck. If they trace the signal there, they could launch drones to find us in hours. We have to keep moving.

Ahead of me is a valley that has been cleared of all greenery. The ground is so dry it is cracked, and the dusty orange expanse is filled only with jagged rock and occasional dead branches.

Something shimmers on the cliff opposite, catching my eye. It is miles away, so almost impossible to make out clearly, but instinctively I step forwards to peer closer. The shimmering intensifies as I lean over the edge.

Suddenly the ground crumbles beneath my feet. I am plummeting, tumbling down the rocky cliff face. But the ground feels soft and cushioned. Moments later I land in a soft, earthy pile, among leaves and twigs. As I shake the dirt from my face, getting my bearings, I recoil with a cry.

The pit is full of skeletons. Many have cracked skulls

bearing the puncture marks of arrows. Where there are bodies, there are snakes. I am on my feet, knife-in-hand, searching the pit for signs of movement.

"Pabla? Are you OK?" calls Latika.

"I am down here! Over the cliff!"

Before I can say "be careful", Latika is tumbling towards me. I leap out of the way just in time as he lands among the leaves.

"It's a trap!" cries Latika.

"But who set it? Not a cartel – they do not work like this."

"A dead tribe? By the looks of these skeletons, whoever set this thing hasn't visited it in some time," he ponders.

"Which means we could be trapped here forever, unless we can find a way out."

"But how did it look so different from the top? There was none of this soil or leaves, the whole valley looked barren – and so much higher?"

"Are you two OK?" calls Ohalo.

He appears at the edge of the pit, peering down at us.

"Woah!"

He stands up again, then crouches to confirm his hypothesis.

"It is a mirage!" he declares.

"You're sure?" calls Latika.

"Positive!"

Ohalo and Latika whoop with joy.

"Er, can someone explain what is going on?" I ask.

"Latika, I can see the beacon – it is in the pit beside you," calls Ohalo.

Before I can ask what the beacon is, Latika throws himself at an empty bird's nest in the corner of the pit. He presses it four times in a distinct pattern.

"It's working!" cries Ohalo, from above.

To my astonishment, a ladder appears at the side of the pit. Latika wastes no time in scaling it and vanishing from view. I follow after him, emerging on the opposite side of the pit to Ohalo and Pietro. Latika is searching for something with great excitement.

"Try the boulders?" calls Ohalo.

"What are we looking for?" I ask.

"The token," cries Ohalo.

"What does it look like?"

"This!" declares Latika.

He grabs a bird's egg from between two rocks and clutches it between his palms. It dissolves in his hands, coating them in a blue goo that trickles off his fingers like yolk. As the liquid hits the ground, it drains away into a metal grill that appears through the earth.

Genome confirmed. Welcome, forester. Opening gateway.

With a bleep, a bridge extends out from our side of the pit towards Ohalo and Pietro. No sooner are they across and by our side than it retracts and disappears once more. Pietro's drowsy eyes widen as he looks over my shoulder. As I follow his gaze, my jaw drops.

The barren valley has disappeared. In its place is a lush, broad island brimming with forest. It is miles wide, and surrounded by a wide, flowing river.

"The northern stronghold," declares Latika, proudly.

"How do we make it across?" I ask.

As if reading my mind, a rope bridge rises out of the water and hovers at the surface, where the river laps across the wooden planks. When I say "rope bridge", it is really more of a "rope tunnel". The bridge has a wooden plank base, but its sides and ceiling are made of a rope mesh.

"Is it safe?" mumbles Pietro.

"It is the only way, we can get you across, amigue," says Latika.

With trepidation, Ohalo and I set off onto the bridge, with Latika and Pietro following. The wooden slats are slippery underfoot, and the rope mesh at the sides wobbles too, making it hard to stay balanced. Now I understand the rope ceiling – the overhead structure is taut and offers the best option for stability as you carefully place each foot forwards.

My stomach is churning as we cross the vast river. I cannot believe how close I am to seeing Oriana again. I am anxious, too. I must warn these people of the impending cartel attack, but they may not listen to me. If word of my betrayal of the Hudara tribe or my own people has preceded me, then I would be safer going back to that snake pit.

We are several hundred yards into the crossing when Ohalo stops abruptly.

"What is it?"

He points silently to a small bird that has come to rest on the ropes above us. It is cocking its head, staring at each of us in turn. Its head twitches three times and it takes off with a flutter, beating its wings back to the island. The bridge shudders.

"What was that?" calls Latika.

Another jolt. This time a creaking resonates across the bridge as the sides shift. The water level suddenly rises above my feet and up to my shins. The rope tunnel is sinking!

"Something has triggered the security protocol! Everybody swim for it!" yells Ohalo.

"You must go without me, you'll never make it," gasps

Pietro.

Latika looks from him to Ohalo, knowing the distance to cover is immense, and the bridge is dragging us down by the second.

"I said go!" he cries, shoving Latika forwards. "You already risked your lives to save me, and it cost you your leader. I won't let you two die for my sake!"

"You heard him, go!" I yell, pushing Latika and Ohalo forwards. "I will help him, you two must get to the other side and tell them to raise the bridge!"

Latika and Ohalo take a deep breath and dive forwards into the water, racing for the far end of the tunnel.

"You must leave me, go with them," insists Pietro.

"No. You are of the forest, and I do not leave my people behind. Not anymore. Come on!"

I throw his arm over my shoulder. Using the overhead mesh to steady the pair of us, I hurry forwards, wading through the waist-high water. Latika and Ohalo are far from the end and this rope is too thick to cut through.

As the water climbs to my chest, it becomes too hard to walk.

"Pietro, I am going to tow you. I need you to stay relaxed OK?"

Pietro is too feeble to protest to anything I suggest. I lay him flat on the water and grab him by the chin, then kick backwards, pulling the pair of us along the rope. I am forcing myself to swim faster, dragging and kicking with all my might, but the shore is too far away and the tunnel is still sinking. We are never going to make it.

"Pietro, start oxygen packing!" I cry.

I hope to god he knows what that means, because our air is fast running out. The tunnel is just inches above the surface of the water. I grab my last desperate breath before the cage forces us under the surface for good.

I open my eyes in the blurry river water. It is brown and foggy, the others have disappeared from view. I am praying they are near the shore. I am dragging Pietro's body, kicking and hauling our way through this watery cage but the end is nowhere in sight. The air is ebbing from my body. I can feel the pain stabbing at my chest as I fight the reflex to breathe in. My movements are growing slower, my muscles are failing. I can no longer grip the rope to pull us ahead. With feeble final kicks, my body falls still, suspended in the submerged tunnel, clutching Pietro's chin in my hand as the last bubbles escape my lips.

Something firm swells upward, striking my chest. The wooden slats are digging into me. There is a rushing of water. Suddenly we breach the surface. I gasp and splutter for air, my eyes bulging as I try to process what is happening.

People are running down the bridge towards us. Latika and Ohalo are soaking wet, but they are alive. They made it to the other side! They haul me and Pietro through the dripping tunnel onto the shore, where we collapse onto the sand, groaning in despair and relief.

"We made it!" splutters Pietro.

"What... what happened?" I stammer.

"They must have had a sensor glitch because they classified us as hostile," says Ohalo.

"No glitch!" booms a voice from the trees.

A party of warriors emerge from the trees, escorting some slower, stooped figures. Two people I am overjoyed to see alive, and who are disgusted to see me walking among them. Latika and Ohalo step aside with their arms raised as

Elder Tanok approaches, pointing a bony finger directly at me.

"Arrest that woman!"

Two warriors seize my arms and force me to kneel as Tanok's lips tremble with anger.

"By the authority of last elders of the Centada, I seek justice for the crimes this traitor has committed. Pabla, formerly of our tribe, you have betrayed your people and broken the order of exile. You have left no alternative, and shown no remorse, and you are hereby sentenced to die."

Villagers are carrying Pietro to the infirmary for urgent treatment, but they are uncertain whether they have enough pure algae left to neutralize the viper toxins. Apparently access to the culture has become contentious as only one of the three vials in existence has thus far made it to the stronghold. But as I hear Latika and Ohalo talking to the healers, I realize the vial is not from my tribe. Meaning Oriana is still somewhere out there, fighting the cartels, and trying to find this place. They cannot put me to death like this, I *must* have the chance to atone before my sister. If I die without setting things right between us my soul will never be at rest.

While Pietro disappears from sight, I am being taken elsewhere. They are dragging me across the island like a common criminal. As I am hauled along, I realize the scale of this bustling community. I have never seen so many indigenous people in one place before; this is like the truly ancient civilizations of Mazonil. Of course, those legendary citadels fell centuries ago when foreign traders brought diseases and violence. Yet here, thousands upon thousands of foresters are living side-by-side, seemingly rebuilding that great civilization before my very eyes. Is this what we could have achieved, or inherited, if the colonists had never come?

The island is a hive of activity as thousands work all around me; tending trees, cultivating fruits and root vegetables, building freshwater captures, repairing drones and other scavenged devices, whittling arrows, distilling poisons, hewing ropes and mending fabrics, building huts and weaving roofs, training young warriors in combat, and, of course, bathing in sunlight to recharge their skin. I never thought such a thing was possible for our people – not on this scale.

We arrive at an assembly of elders and the guards throw me to my knees. I only recognize a handful of Centada. The others all bear a range of headgears and body paint from other tribes. Elder Tanok, that crinkly, duplicitous founder; chief proponent of our village's old creation myth, and technophobic zealot, addresses his peers.

"Coalition of elders, I come before you as a formality only, and I shall make this brief. This is a matter of justice unique to the Centada tribe, and thus a matter for our own tribal courts. I await your acknowledgement so that we may proceed to dispense justice to this most vile of traitors," he declares.

"What do you plan to do with the accused?" asks another elder.

"She shall face execution for her crimes. She has been found guilty and been banished once already. Her return to tribal territory uninvited can mean only one thing: she seeks to betray us again, and must be treated as if she were an enemy combatant in the field."

"Wait, we wish to speak in her defense!" calls Latika.

He and Ohalo push their way forwards, their scarred-chests bared.

"You are not Centada, thus you have no legal standing here," says Tanok.

"On the contrary, this is a matter of Namakaro law. Your prisoner has intervened to save our lives from the cartel. By our customs, she is entitled to our protection as an honorary member of our tribe," says Latika.

BEST. DAY. EVER.

An adjudicator bangs their staff on the ground.

"The council acknowledges the Namakaro claim," says the adjudicator. "The accused will face a coalition jury, as per the laws of the northern stronghold."

"So be it!" spits Tanok. "Elder Shanarani will avail you all of this traitor's crimes, and you will soon agree with us that death is the only answer fit for this criminal."

Tanok sits down, simmering with rage, while Shanarani steps forward to prosecute me before the hundred or so other elders present.

"Pabla, formerly of the Centada tribe, you have been found guilty of the following crimes by a previous jury of the elders. Bringing prohibited technology into our tribal boundaries and in doing so leading the enemy to our doors. Your actions facilitated the destruction of our village and the death of your own father and our Inkmaster. You were exiled by the tribe, and your return is a breach of sacred Centada law, the punishment for which, as well you know, is death."

"Surely you can't mean that her presence on this island is a breach of her exile? This is not Centada territory," protests Ohalo.

"She destroyed our home, forcing us to move here.

Where our people go, so do our laws and traditions," replies Shanarani.

"We have already heard a defense from the Namakaro, is there another who will speak in the accused's defense?" calls the adjudicator.

"There is one who cannot be here to testify, as he is receiving urgent medical treatment," says Ohalo. "May I speak on his behalf?"

"You may," says the adjudicator.

"Our companion, Pietro, came to this country to help his ancestors. He may only be half-Namakaro, but his soul is truly of the forest. Pabla rescued Pietro along with my husband and I. She killed three cartellers in the process. Not only that, but when you deemed her to be an enemy, and lowered the rope bridge to drown us, she refused to abandon Pietro. She stood by him, fighting with her last breath and risking her life to try and save him as a fellow forest person. Whatever her sins of the past, she has surely atoned for them with our three lives."

Ohalo bows and steps back as the elders murmur among themselves, considering his words.

"Pabla, why did you save these strangers?" asks the adjudicator.

"It is as Ohalo said: because, like me, they are of the forest," I reply.

"You are of the cartel!" spits Tanok.

"Thank you, elder Tanok, we are aware of the prosecution's views. The accused is entitled to defend herself. Speak, Pabla," says the adjudicator.

"Elders, I confess that I broke my tribe's rules. I brought technology into our village. Not to harm my people, but to broaden our minds. Something our elders had worked for years to prevent. And now, like hypocrites, I find them seeking refuge among you, their more enlightened peers. They are happily benefiting from defensive technology that masks their presence on this island, and drones that can protect the boundaries. Yet they decried these same virtues as sins for our whole lives. I may have broken their rules, but they broke our trust long before that.

"To the charge of murdering my own father, I say this: my *elders* are the true murderers. They denied us modern medical technology, preferring to prop up their own lies rather than admit the truth and save those who needed it. My father would have survived his cartel injuries were it not for them. My mother would have survived her cancer were it not for them. So to the last elders of the Centada I say this: I am not the traitor you have painted me to be. You bred us in the light of the laboratory, filling our skin with genetically engineered solutions, only to raise us in the darkness of ignorance, deliberately shrouding our treatment behind ritual and myth. Your fear is what made our tribe weak. The blood of our kin is on your hands."

I am panting, breathless, as anger and grief pour out my mouth in a tirade. I glare around the crowd as I finish, ready to confront anyone who dares to challenge my testimony. As the crowd deliberates, elder Shanarani rises to her feet, apoplectic with rage.

"You call us hypocrites for risking our lives eighty years ago so that you could have a future. The landscape we were navigating then was more complex than your generation can possibly imagine. Against all odds we succeeded in leaving the destructive, collapsing cities. We returned to nature and took our place as custodians of the forest. We built our villages from *nothing*. All that we have taken from the land we have given back ten times over. To do that, we had to cut ties with all that corrupted *our* elders. We knew abandoning technology would shorten the lives of some of our tribe. But that was a price worth paying to ensure those lives had *meaning*. And yet here you stand, Pabla, having single-handedly undone all we set out to achieve. You have the audacity to call us hypocrites when you yourself are fleeing into the forest, as we did all those years ago. Like we did, you are seeking refuge from the forces of the cartels, their cities, and their destructive technologies!" cries Shanarani.

This is met with murmurs of sympathy from the assorted elders, many of whom clearly remember the old Mazonil. I wait for their consternation to die down before I reply, fighting to control the anger in my voice.

"I have not come here to seek asylum, elder Shanarani. I am here with a warning."

"Speak, Pabla. What is this 'warning'?" calls the adjudicator.

"Elders, the cartel know you are here. They know of the stronghold and they are coming to destroy it."

"She has betrayed us again!" cries Tanok.

Outrage and fear flutters through the crowd, while the adjudicator bangs her staff, demanding quiet.

"We have modified the cartel's own masking technology to hide this island and its inhabitants from them. We have gone undetected for years under this system. On what basis do you issue such a 'warning'?" asks the adjudicator.

"Yesterday I was trapped in cartel captivity, as I had been for many days, being held in a cage. I heard them discussing the northern stronghold. They have triangulated your position and are planning a major offensive to permanently clear our kind from the forest."

This is met with consternation.

"Do you have any proof of this claim?"

"No. Only my word."

Tanok spits on the ground in disgust, while Shanarani laughs cynically.

"We must weigh the credibility of this testimony against the gravity of the threat. If we lose the stronghold, there will be no hope for our people," says the arbitrator.

"That is the whole reason I came here, elders. I know how urgent this is, you *have* to prepare for their attack," I insist.

"There is nowhere further for us to flee. Preparing for a siege would be our only hope of defense," says an elder.

"Indeed. This is no trivial suggestion, Pabla. To prepare for a siege, we would have to forgo all other activities, from building homes to tending the forest around us. We've not yet finished cultivating new crop beds for the increased population, but you're asking us to cease this and turn all hands to war? We would be eating our reserves within days," says the adjudicator.

They're teetering. They still don't believe me, and it's going to cost the lives of every last soul on this island. I *have* to make them understand I am genuine. But it may be the last decision I make.

"Allow me to speak plainly, elders. Just as my elders did not share with me the whole truth growing up, I am withholding some truth from you now. After my initial exile, I returned to my tribe the same night. The elders and others had already left to seek refuge with you here, but the Centada warriors had remained behind and were preparing to defend our lands to the death. I attempted to strike a bargain with the cartel, to secure my people's lives in exchange for a peaceful surrender. They reneged on their side of the deal, and poisoned the warriors. The only one to escape was my sister, Oriana. I helped her to kill a carteller, to ensure she escaped with the algal vial. But not before she tried to shoot me dead in revenge for our father's death.

"Returning to our camp alone, I saw a carteller get horribly injured, losing both hands in an explosion. In our tribe, that man would have died from blood loss or infection, or at the least been maimed for life. And yet they brought out a device that healed him before my eyes. That same equipment could have saved my father, my mother, and *countless* more of my people over the years if only the elders hadn't prohibited all discussion of the technology.

"I became disillusioned by the lies I had been fed as a child. I wanted to see the rest of the world, to feel like the one in control for once. I wanted the power and the technology of the cartels, and, with nowhere else to turn, became embraced by our enemy.

"My first mission for them was actually against another cartel. We stole equipment, so that the group I was with could extract pluridium from my ancestors' forest. I ended up in the township where a carteller slit my throat. They healed me instantly, and offered me a way to escape Mazonil forever.

"To earn my passage, I led the cartel against other tribes, resulting in the capture of the Hudara people. From there, I was taken abroad. They used me to recruit foreign investors for their projects plundering our lands, and I helped them. But when I finally arrived in Paradise City, I saw what my elders had known all along. In gaining what we do not have, they have lost everything we do.

"I resolved to undo my wrongs. I sought to escape the cartel but I was captured and imprisoned. It is in captivity that I heard of my sister's survival. I was told she was active in the north, assassinating cartellers and spreading fear in the enemy. When I learned of their plan to attack her, and you all, I resolved to escape so that I could warn you. That is why I am here, and *that* is the whole truth."

There is a stunned silence while the elders process all that I have said. Leaning shakily on his stick, Tanok rises to his feet and points a trembling finger at me.

"Death!" he declares.

This is met with discord among the assembly, and conflicting calls for justice. The adjudicator bangs her staff once more, restoring order.

"Pabla. We have heard your testimony. The elders of your former tribe are seeking the death penalty for your crimes. How do you plead?"

"I make no plea with regards to my innocence or guilt, because it is of no consequence to my goal here. As your prisoner, I cannot find my missing sister, Oriana, and I will carry that pain into the next world. But I have delivered my warning, and that is what will determine the future of our kind.

"You may kill me if you decide that is what I deserve. All I ask is that you heed my message with the utmost gravity. The cartel are coming for all of you. If you do not prepare to fight them now, you will lose, and they will show you no mercy. I pray that you make the right decision, and learn from the mistakes of my tribe."

I kneel humbly before the assembled elders. I am drenched with the shame of my recent actions. If I die here, it will be a coward's fate. To atone for my treachery and the lives I have cost will take a lifetime of work, and I do not think that will be an option for me.

"Assembled elders of the stronghold council, it is time to vote," declares the adjudicator. "You have heard the testimonies on both sides. You must weigh them with an even heart, taking into account the prosecution, the accused's own confessions, and the statements in her defense. All those in favor of execution, stand now."

Tanok and Shanarani rise to their feet, ashen-faced. Almost half of the assembly rises too. The adjudicator's scribes on either side count the numbers, then she beckons all to be seated before asking those in favor of leniency to stand.

The scribes finishing counting and whisper a verdict into the adjudicator's ear.

"We have a deadlock! Thus it falls to me to decide the accused's fate. On behalf of the assembled elders, I sentence you to fifteen years' imprisonment."

There is consternation from all sides at this compromise, but the adjudicator bangs her staff once more, with a raised hand.

"*However*, in light of the disquieting intelligence we have received, we do not have the time nor the resources to be imprisoning people. The cartel are coming for us, and we need every fighting hand we can get. Therefore, I move to suspend the accused's sentence, pending battle. I require a sponsor for this act."

As the adjudicator casts her eyes across the assembly, Latika steps forward.

"I will sponsor the accused."

"You are aware of the consequences of this, warrior?"

"I am, your honor."

"So be it. She is hereby your ward. She shall fight with honor to protect us. Should she break any further laws or betray us in any way, you will both face the immediate death penalty. Furthermore, should we overcome the grave threat facing us all, you both shall serve two-thirds of the accused's sentenced time. The motion is passed."

The adjudicator bangs her staff, and the guards loosen the ties binding my wrists.

"I hope you're happy, judge, you have doomed us all!" spits Tanok.

"We shall find out, elder. But doom may be coming to us whether we seek it or not. Assembly, go to your people now and spread the news. War is coming. As of this moment, the stronghold must prepare for siege."

CHAPTER TWENTY-EIGHT

LUKE

"**W**ake up."

Two words you only ever wanna be the one saying. Much like "your round", or "your kid". Oriana's kicking me awake with the sort of firmness and callous disregard I usually have to pay for.

"We're there," says Ramone, peering out of the carriage door.

Ugh. Golden boy's already up, I see.

The train is slowing to a trundle as we squeak our way into a terminal. Robotic cranes are unloading the cargo and depositing carts onto conveyor belts.

"When do we get out?"

Before anyone can answer, there's a loud clang overhead. We're all thrown sideways as our cart is plucked from the train and swept through the air. Ramone scrambles back to the door as we touch down onto one of the many processing rows.

"Now!" he hisses, leaping from the cart.

Oriana and I follow suit. He lets me fall into the dirt, while graciously helping Oriana. She lands, then wipes out his legs for being patronizing. I'm trying *real* hard not to laugh in Ramone's face as our eyes meet in the dirt.

The strapping ranger is back on his feet in a flash, brushing it off with a scowl as he and Oriana stride forwards among rows of sorting bots.

"The plant looks automated, we should be able to get through without problem," he says, his voice gruffer than usual.

"Wait, who appointed Ramone as tour guide?" I ask, catching up with them. "As a celebrated orator, I feel I'm a more natural choice for the role. I once received a standing ovation from multiple audience members for my starring role in *Pirates of Penzance*."

"OK, 'great orator', do you know how we can find my friend in this city?" says Ramone.

"Er, not off the bat... I'm still processing the idea that you *have* a friend."

Oriana chuckles at this, prompting a grumpy snort from the ranger as he presses ahead.

"You are full of shit, gringo. I will find the way," snaps Ramone.

We follow him into the assembly room, which is a thrumming cacophony of machines grinding and hammering raw materials into finished parts.

"What is all this stuff?" says Oriana, peering down at the assembly lines.

Wood shavings are being fed into a machine, pulped, then spat out the other end as paper coffee cups.

"Disposable cups," I explain.

"Who would throw away a cup? Cups are useful," says Oriana.

"Not these cups. They only last a few drinks, then they get kinda gammy and full of bacteria, you know?"

"We use wood cups over and over with no problem," she frowns.

"Yeah but they're heavy."

"Not really."

"Yeah, but these cups are for city people. You know, on the move, morning commute, cuppa hot Joe?"

"So they *do* reuse the cups?"

"No they chuck them away."

"Every day?"

"Sometimes multiple times a day. Who wants to carry around loads of used cups? Think how dumb that would look!"

"But if the cup was made of thin wood you could reuse it, then you only need one?"

"Look, Oriana, it all comes down to clothing. Maybe one day scientists will invent jeans with pockets big enough for a single reusable cup, but technology just isn't there yet."

"How about a small bag?"

"Yeah that would work."

"But you don't use them?"

"Not for cups. More like... Actually I don't know what we use small bags for."

"At least these cups are recyclable, I guess. They won't have to keep cutting down trees to make them, they can just reuse the paper from this," muses Oriana.

"Ahh... sure. Let's go with that."

"What? Is it not recycled?"

"Well... you see that nozzle at the end down there? It's spraying them all with a teeny tiny coating of plastic. Makes the cup nice and waterproof. And also, uh, kinda non-recyclable."

Oriana hurries down a spiral staircase to the factory

floor and marches to the end of the cup processor, snatching a stack out of the end box.

"I can't see the plastic?"

"No, it's misleading, I'll grant you."

"And this symbol – I have seen it in our encyclopedia. It means recyclable, no?"

"Er, OK. So *technically*, one *could* separate the two materials out again, but the byproducts are too low quality to upcycle again, so they're kind of only good for incineration. Coffee-scented kindling. Cute, huh?"

"So why print the symbol on the side?"

"Think of it more as an emoji. It makes customers feel good about their choices. Plus it's a reason to take it back to the café that sold it to you. They have these special bins you can put them in while you order your next coffee. It's basically the circle of life, through the lens of a coffee bean."

"So the dirty cup goes in a special bin in the coffee shop because of a symbol that says recycling when it cannot be recycled but people get to feel good anyway?"

"*And* they get more coffee. Now you're getting it!"

"But where does the cup actually go?"

"Dunno, some developing country? The materials are so crappy no one in my country bothers to process them domestically. A recycled coffee cup ain't gonna cover the pension scheme for a human workforce in the Northern Bloc, plus all the machinery costs, is it? Better to ship it all abroad. Let some out-of-school orphans sift through our shit. It's not a trade policy per se, it's more of an unspoken rule."

"You give your trash to poor nations? How generous," says Oriana, flatly.

"Er, actually we sell it to them."

"But you said the materials are useless?"

"OK so there's *just* enough useful stuff in there for them

to turn a profit. Well, obviously not what companies in *my* country would consider a profit. But in a poor country they're desperate enough to slave over the ten percent that's useable. Once they've got the remnants of my skinny mocha chai latte off it, am I right? Just kidding – I always go full fat."

"Wait, but if the orphans only recycle ten percent, what happens to the other ninety percent?"

"They burn it. Or dump it in rivers. Come on, they've gotta get rid of it somehow – that stuff's an eyesore. The orphan thing isn't gospel, by the way. Sometimes they use really old people too. Though technically I guess all old people are orphans, in a sense. Huh. That sucks. No wonder we all crave hot milk. Though word to the wise – you gotta add something to it. Otherwise people think you're a pervert. Hence: coffee."

"I'm still confused. You are saying ninety percent of these coffee cups cannot be recycled, and you said they put it in rivers? But it's got plastic in it. That's toxic, surely?"

"Oh, yeah, it causes all kinds of problems. Tumors, birth defects, brain degeneration. You wouldn't want it in your sandwich, that's for sure! Although it's almost certainly somewhere in there. You know they found it in carrots a few decades back, can you believe that? Plastic *inside* the carrots. And on the top of our highest mountains. And the bottom of the ocean. And at the poles. Man, that stuff gets *around*. It's actually kinda weird we order hot drinks in it. Maybe that's *not* healthy..."

"So everything we are looking at right now is a machine that turns trees into pollution?"

"Hmm. You raise an interesting point. To which I riddle you this: do we ever turn trees into anything else? Furniture and coffins excluded."

Oriana looks physically sick clutching the disposable coffee cup, as her eyes take in the thousands being reeled off the production line in front of us.

"White man, why do your people do this?" she spits.

"Great question. I guess I haven't really pondered it much. But just thinking off the top of my head here, I reckon the jeans and emojis are at the heart of the matter. Either that or we're just a whole nation of unspeakably selfish assholes!" I chuckle.

"Your people suck," says Oriana.

"Yeah, hearing it aloud now I'm actually inclined to agree... OK, I'm making a note to sign an online petition when I'm back home. Thanks Oriana – you've really turned me around on this whole issue. Next round's on me, whaddya say?"

"I would rather be boiled alive."

"Great! I'll pencil you in as a 'maybe'."

"Guys we need to keep moving," calls Ramone.

We follow him through to the next warehouse, where a separate feed of cargo is coming in from the train. Yuck, this lot stinks of metal. I'm pretty sure the fumes in here are shaving days off my life with every breath I take.

This plant is doing smelting, laser cutting, and heavy packing. But it's a slick, fully autonomous operation, with cutting-edge robots in a glistening, ultra-modern facility. Something's not right. This is *way* too upscale for a cartel operation.

"What are the machines making?" asks Oriana.

"Batteries, I think. Although the other half looks like a filter of some kind."

As we reach the end of the line, the two rows come together to form a central output line, where an overhead robot twists, turns, and packs them together. The logo on the side draws a collective sense of unease. Two equilateral triangles side-by-side, with a thick wavy line crossing both. It's the unmistakable trademark of Sequestra.

"I think these might be air filters?" I say.

"Get down!" hisses Ramone.

A security drone floats in through the ceiling duct, passing in from the warehouse beyond ours. It's scanning the room, about to exit through the other side when it stops and freezes overhead. It's descending, coming to inspect our hiding place beneath the conveyor belt.

"On my mark, everyone get to the exit!" whispers Ramone. "Go!"

He rolls out and fires a stun blast at the drone, knocking it from the air. An alarm sounds across the factory. Metal shutters are rolling down the outside walls as we rush for the exit. Oriana draws an arrow and fires it into the control panel by the door, freezing its shutter mid-drop. She throws herself under the gap, and leaps up on the other side, continuing to run.

I throw myself down at the gap, roll to the side, and grind to a halt.

"Little help!" I cry.

Oriana turns and stares at me in disbelief as my fat midriff keeps me wedged in the gap. With an unnecessarily brutal kick, I feel both of Ramone's boots land squarely in my buttocks, shunting me through like a champagne cork being popped. As rail workers look up in bewilderment, I scramble to my feet and race after the two foresters, as they sprint towards the sprawling shanty town ahead.

Aquerba is a contradiction. By size of population it would qualify as a city, but in terms of infrastructure it's a giant favela. The only exception is the old citadel in the middle. Its majestic walls were built by colonists from the Northern and Southern blocs centuries ago when they first "discovered" Mazonil. If you ignore the fact that the citadel was all constructed by enslaved locals, then the architecture has a certain romance to it.

Of course, people in developed countries don't like to think of themselves as global aristocrats with a fetish for subjugating others. It really puts them off their coffee. So we've learned to make our imperialism more subtle. We dress it up behind trade tariffs and development loans, but it's all designed to maintain the status quo.

"You don't like it here?" says Oriana.

"You read minds, hey?"

"No, but I'm pretty good at faces."

"This place gives me the chills. It's like I'm visiting the sins of my forefathers. Ugh, white guilt is *draining*, you know? I'm gonna have to book a whole other session with my therapist after this. Say, you ever been to a city like this before?"

"Only once, and it was much smaller. A township. My father and I met with a cartel to strike a peace deal but it didn't work out. You?"

"Only on the news. I'm not used to seeing shanty towns up close. They're... scary. I know these people are just trying to get on with their lives, but I'm kinda terrified I might get dragged into a hut and eaten at any moment. Is that racist? Maybe I'm being too specific. I think non-specific fear of the unknown is acceptable, because it's just the human condition, right? But it gets sketchy when you try to articulate that fear, because then you accidentally accuse entire communities of being cannibals just because you're out of your comfort zone and just wanna feel safe and familiar and surrounded by what you know and holy crap I'm sounding like one of them, aren't I?"

"Who?"

"The colonists who built that fucking wall! Oh god. Do I feel guilty enough? Am I overlooking some of my privilege? Does being afraid of the huts make me racist? Oh God, it's like this place is giving me a personality disorder."

"I don't think that is a disorder, gringo. I think that is just how white people are meant to feel these days," says Ramone.

"It's overwhelming, dude! Can't I just socially hibernate for a few more decades then check back in when everyone else has worked through this stuff? Once all this is done I swear I'm gonna move back in with my ex-wife and the kids and just have a quiet life in a mathematically diverse suburb where all of us are balanced minorities and my choice of neighborhood acts like a permanent get-out-of-jail card for accusations of cultural appropriation because I can just say I'm going to a barbeque."

"Sure, and after this I will just return to my ancestral forest because the modern world scares me too. Oh no wait, I cannot do that because these people destroyed it," snaps Oriana.

"Sorry, that was insensitive. I'm working on my sensitivity. I was recommended a self-help book actually – even added it to my wish list. So, you know, that's a step forward."

"Keep it down," hisses Ramone.

He throws out a hand and we linger behind a wonky hut made of rusty metal sheets. A pair of cartellers are patrolling the street, enjoying a wide berth from the locals.

They approach a trader and hassle the husband and wife for a bribe. When it's not forthcoming, they throw the couple's table top over, scattering their fruit stock among the muck. When the man protests, they give him a good kicking for his insolence, before continuing their rounds.

"Ramone, tell me you know where we're going?" I whisper. "I don't wanna get killed in a shanty town. Wait, that came out wrong... I mean I don't wanna die *period*! But, er, if I *do* die here, it would be an honor, and I would be following local customs in a respectful and non-appropriating way. Not that I'm saying the local culture is defined by gang violence and street executions... Wait, but if I'm denying that that's their culture then me dying here *wouldn't* be an act of appropriation at all. It would just be an act of senseless violence, right? Huzzah! In your *face* cancel culture. Remini for the win!"

"I'm going to find us a route in, you two wait here. Forester, if the gringo keeps talking shit, feel free to appropriate his tongue with your knife."

"Gladly," snorts Oriana.

OK, I do *not* think it's illiberal of me to say that it makes me uncomfortable when those two flirt over ways to hurt me. Last time I checked, cupid was supposed to be the one firing arrows, not getting his danglies cut off by some intergenerational newly-weds.

Ramone disappears, leaving Oriana and me crouching behind the hut.

"He seemed mad at me. You think he's pissed?"

"Yes," grunts Oriana.

"Did I do something to offend him?"

"You talk too much. It is painful for everyone."

"Sorry, I know... My mouth just kinda runs away from me when I'm anxious. I usually take a number of medicines for it, but my doctor recommended I dial it back. Apparently the pills were giving me a dangerously inflated sense of confidence. My therapist informs that when you're being tortured in a dark lab by a pair of scientists, the 'normal' response is apparently *not* to goad them like it's a sex game. You live and learn, hey? In hindsight, that medication is responsible for a number of spinal issues I have. Though on the theme of medication, I should actually be on a whole load of other stuff right now..."

"White man, shut your mouth."

"OK pleeeeeease don't read into this too much but... *make me?*"

Oriana elbows me hard in the jaw. I fall on my ass with a grunt, nursing my split lip.

"You're supposed to be laying low! What happened" hisses Ramone, returning.

"White guilt over here just got a hard-on thinking about his own mortality."

"Jesus Luke, how does *anyone* manage to make people long to kill them, while also making it such a repulsive goal?" says Ramone.

"You used my name! We *are* friends!"

Ramone grabs me by the collar and drags me to my feet.

"You know you can judge a person by the friends they keep?"

"I've heard it once or twice."

"*That* is why we will never be friends, gringo."

"*Dayummm,* Ramone, you're really doubling down on the macho lone wolf act, huh? If I didn't know better I'd say you *genuinely* don't like me!"

"I do not like you at all."

"Good thing I know better."

"I am telling you straight."

"Sure. Same page."

"Are you even listening to me?"

"I sure am, *buddy*."

"God dammit, I *am* gonna kill you!"

"Oh yeah, do it baby, come for me, I'm ready!"

My unintended slip into "bedroom voice" throws Ramone off his gait.

Abandoning his assault with disgust, he shoves me away and briefs Oriana directly.

"It is as I thought: the old gate is the only way in, and it is protected by guards. So I've found us a smuggler," says Ramone.

"No way," I protest, "I used a smuggler to get into this damned country and I ended up being mugged on a donkey over an eight hundred foot drop."

"No donkeys, I promise," says Ramone.

"OK, then you have my full support."

"I am glad to hear it, gringo, because we are going through the sewers."

I know what you're expecting. You're thinking we're gonna crawl through some winding underground labyrinth of shit and emerge caked in an entire citadel's worth of the brown stuff? In fact, you're not just thinking it, you're kinda hoping it. You're curious, aren't you? How much *literal* shit can this guy take? And how would he even do that? It's not like they put on diving suits or anything. What if it goes in his eye? Doesn't that make you go blind? Or worse, what if he swallows some?

See, *that's* what makes you and I different. I don't need to see someone crawl through tunnels of human excrement just to know it would do ruinous things to their digestive system. Not to mention their love life. And their sense of self-worth. But you're champing at the bit, just *longing* to see how I pull off a daring heist against a powerful cartel now, when I emerge literally wearing their freshest turds.

Well, put this in your pipe and vape it. I emerge from the sewer not only *uncovered* in excrement, but actually smelling better than I have done all trip. We found an abandoned crate of cologne down there and availed ourselves of the various fragrances on offer. Ramone went for guava, Oriana for tea tree, and I went for popping candy. What? I miss home.

When the government of Mazonil started to fall apart eighty years ago, the citadel's already-crumbling utilities fell into disuse. The sewers eventually got sealed off by the cartels that took over the town – to stop people trying to flush into a huge stagnant pit beneath all their houses. *Then* they sent a bunch of captive workers – aka slaves – down into the crusty ex-sewers to clear them out with shovels. This was a different cartel, by the way. One stuck *outside* the citadel, trying to get themselves inside its hallowed walls by using the existing network of colonial sewage tunnels running through it. They succeeded, and ran a successful smuggling business for many years. It was, in fact, a genius business model. They would trade goods and weapons with their cartel rivals via third party vendors and collect the monetary proceeds. After that, they would sneak into the citadel through the tunnels, smuggle half of the stuff they sold back *out* of the city, and sell it to the cartel again a few weeks later when their stocks had mysteriously run out early.

Apparently it worked extremely well until a new crime boss took over the citadel. She smelled a rat and had her gang coat all purchased goods with a time-stamped UV marker. When the vendors tried to re-sell them stuff they had previously bought, they were caught and tortured until the whole scam was exposed. The remaining cartel smugglers fled the citadel, abandoning the tunnels and whatever goods were in them at the time. It seems the citadel has changed hands a number of times since then, and the locals have learned to keep the town's secrets to themselves.

Which is why, decades later, the three of us are able to crawl through these pristine stone tunnels without concern, and arrive in the heart of the citadel, led by our child smuggling guide. To be clear, I'm not in favor of child labor under any circumstances, including recycling, which is why I'm insisting we don't pay the kid. Ramone calls me a colonialist asshole again, which gets my back up, so I explain to him that I'm actually *breaking* the cycle of exploitation by not endorsing illegal employment of minors. If anything this kid should be in school. And besides, I lost all my money when I got mugged on that donkey.

To our mutual surprise, Oriana pays the kid. It turns out she's been pickpocketing her latest cartel conquests as she goes, and it's payday for this little street urchin. Fortunately, I'm a father, so I know how to handle this.

"Don't go spending it all on sweets, ya hear me?" I say, kneeling down.

The kid looks at me, baffled.

"I'm going to spend it on school."

"Uh, yeah, that's what I meant. Get yourself an education, kid, you deserve it. No more scraping around disused poop chutes for you."

"Hey, kid, speaking of school, do you know where the citadel's elementary is?" says Ramone.

"Si, señor."

"I need you to take us there. Keep to the quiet streets, out of sight of the guards, OK?

"Understood, señor. No guards. Follow me."

As much as I enjoyed our torch-lit tour of the underworld and the flickering cave paintings of a curry someone ate one time, it's great to be above ground again. The citadel is a bustling maze of winding streets and quirky alleyways; the product of centuries of tinkering, revolution, and semi-stringent planning restrictions. It's like a world heritage site that someone dragged out of a lost and found box. Beautiful, battered, and definitely pre-loved. It's the citadel version of me.

The child leads us through a tour between tall stone buildings with ramshackle terracotta tiles and faded wooden shutters. The paint is peeling from every surface, and chunks of plaster are missing from the walls, replaced by plants growing through every nook and cranny available.

There, ahead of us, is the citadel's elementary school. Although some of the kids look like they're pushing high school age. I'm getting the sense this is its *only* school. What kind of kids go here? Is this the developing world version of being a rich yuppie brat? Does even thinking that make me a total asshole? Probably yes on both counts. But I'm just trying to assess this place objectively: there's clearly no functioning welfare state here, so education must by default be private, which would make it the domain of a relative social elite, and thus a vehicle for perpetuating inequality within this microcosm. Jesus, when you put it like that, *all* schooling should be banned. I think I need to stop thinking for a bit – I'm starting to sound logical and that's generally cause for concern.

The citadel has an upmarket feel compared to the shanty town encircling it. From above, it must look like a flower; a stamen of stone surrounded by petals of steel. Am I laying it on too thick with the nature analogies? I usually get more opportunity to show off my wafer-thin scientific background.

The school's situated in a central square, across from restaurants and market stalls. The children don't *look* like the offspring of ultra-violent thugs, they look pretty damned regular.

Plastered across the school wall is a mural of a tanned man in a white-and-cream pinstripe suit. He has a beaming smile, dimples, and open arms. Children of all creeds are painted below him, reaching up adoringly.

"What's with the creepy sugar daddy painting?" I ask the kid.

"He owns the citadel, señor. He rebuild the school when last cartel go."

"Huh. A real man of the community. Does he have a name?"

"Mr. K."

"Weird name. But then again, he commissioned the graffiti equivalent of his own stained glass window, so that'd figure."

"That's her," interrupts Ramone.

He points across the market to a figure by the school. She's standing watch over the kids playing in the yard.

"What are we waiting for? Go ask her! Every second we're here risks the cartel taking this vial from me!" urges Oriana.

She's gotten a lot tetchier since we emerged from the

sewer. I'm guessing she's not a fan of being inside man-made walls, least of all those constructed by enemies of her past, which are now inhabited by enemies of her present.

We follow Ramone closely as he approaches the woman.

"Hey stranger," says Ramone.

OK, he's *definitely* putting on the moves here. This is a whole new level of sultry smolder for the lone ranger. These two have got *history*. The woman looks up at him and her mouth drops a fraction. She recovers in a flash, settling on a look of polite indifference. It's a weird way to flirt back.

"Do I know you, señor?" she replies.

"Asha, it's me. Ramone," he says, his sultry voice cracking.

"Sorry, señor, you must have me confused with someone. I am Dirrin. Perhaps you knew my sister? I regret to inform you she passed away many years ago."

Ramone's jaw tightens. Is it just me or are his eyes misting?

"May I ask what she died of?"

"It is not known, but the speculation was that it was water borne; something that came from the south, most likely by night."

"The work of mosquitos?"

"Perhaps she was lucky. They were not nearly so dangerous as the hawks."

"I am sorry, for your loss, Madam Dirrin, and sorry to bother you. We will leave you in peace."

The child coughs beside us.

"Oh, and if your school has room, you have a new pupil. I believe the amount he is carrying should cover his passage through the grades?"

Ramone steps aside and ushers our child-guide-who-definitely-wasn't-a-slave-but-was-clearly-an-underage-worker-but-might-in-some-ways-be-considered-a-very-young-intern forwards.

"Can we leave him in your ward?"

The child hands over a pouch for the woman to inspect. She takes a quick glance at the stack of credits inside and looks at Ramone in astonishment.

"Yes, this will more than suffice, señor."

She kneels down to the child and returns the pouch to him.

"Take this to the office inside, young man, they will register you."

The child's older-than-his-years façade vanishes and he skips through the playground with excitement, disappearing inside the school.

"Forgive me, señor, I must ask you and your friends to leave now. The school is private property."

"Of course. Thank you for your time."

Ramone bows his head and turns on his heel, leaving a flabbergasted Oriana and I to hurry after him.

"Dude, what just happened?" I whisper.

"We just set up a meeting, gringo, that's what happened."

***

Four hours later and we're laying low in a dusty old tavern in the backstreets of the citadel. When we arrived, the locals were *not* welcoming to us, until Ramone said Asha had sent us. Which makes no sense, because that Dirrin lady already told us Asha was dead.

"Hey stranger," says a familiar voice.

The woman from the school lowers her hood and grabs

Ramone in a tight embrace. She's switched out of her work clothes and somehow knew to meet us in this dusty tavern at this time, even though those two only exchanged a handful of words and Ramone's never been here before. Like I said, they got *history*.

"Asha!" he sighs, burying his face in her shoulder.

OK, so clearly she's dropped the whole "Madam Dirrin" act. She's one hundred percent Asha. I knew it all along, I'm very perceptive.

"Luke, Oriana, meet Asha. This is my-"

"Ex?"

"*Sister*," snaps Ramone.

"My bad. Does that mean she's available?"

"Does he always talk about people in the third person?" says Asha.

"I *know* right? I told him it's rude but he won't listen," chimes Oriana.

"Hey, enough of this 'he' business! Wait, OK I see what you two are doing, very clever," I mutter.

"He's smart," says Asha.

"Yes, looks can be deceiving, can't they?" chuckles Oriana.

"Well, Madam Asha, it's an honor to finally meet you, and there's no deception from what I'm seeing – you clearly inherited all the looks in your family. Am I right, Ramone?"

I pat his chest, laughing, but he deadpans me.

"Dude, you are the worst wingman ever?"

"Estúpido coño. This is my *sister*," says Ramone.

"Exactly! You should be giving me the inside scoop!" I whisper.

"I am sorry we had to meet like this, brother," says Asha, cutting across me. "The cartel have eyes and ears everywhere in this town. Everywhere but here. It is one of the few old family-run places left in the citadel, and the only place people like us can still talk openly, without fear of Mr. K.'s goons cracking down."

"If you need a goon of your own, I'd be happy to apply for the role?" I offer, graciously.

"I am Oriana," interrupts the forester, shoving me aside. "I am from the Centada tribe. Ramone said you can help me. Apologies for cutting to the chase but my mission is urgent, and if I let Luke speak again you will probably leave in disgust."

"Don't worry. I will cut out his tongue if he disrespects me again."

"That is what *I* said! Oh my god, we are going to get on great!" cheers Oriana.

"You're supposed to be a school teacher!" I protest.

"Madam Dirrin is a school teacher. But school's out, bambino, and Madam *Asha* is an underground resistance fighter," says Ramone.

"Thank god we're above ground," I chuckle, lightening the mood.

"Is he always like that?" says Asha, wincing at me like I'm a giant talking verruca.

"He is," mutters Oriana.

"Hey, again, I'm *right here*!"

"And who's a good boy?" says Asha, ruffling my wispy hair.

Holy crap, I think this is the first non-violent contact I've had since landing in this country. I know she's being sarcastic but joke's on her because I will TAKE it. Mmm. Ruffle that hair, lady. God damn, she really is mesmerizingly beautiful. Not that it should matter. My therapist tells me inner beauty is what counts. I've definitely subscribed to that notion since I started resembling a spud with man breasts. That's what two divorces and fatherhood does to a guy. But it's cool, Asha may be out of my league but I've still got a way in: I'm best buds with her brother.

"Ramone, your friend's dribbling," says Asha, retracting her hand in disgust.

"Pull it together, gringo, or I will cut your balls off," growls Ramone.

"What is it with your family and cutting bits off of people?" I ask.

"It works," shrugs Ramone.

"Asha, can you help me?" continues Oriana. "This vial contains an algal strain that is unique to my tribe. It has been cultivated by our elders for generations, but now that our homeland has been lost to the cartels, it is under threat of permanent destruction."

"I mean no disrespect, Oriana, but why is your tribe asking you to risk your like for some algae?" says Asha, puzzled.

"Oh, right. It is in our blood. I mean that literally. See these freckles on my skin, see these tattoos? My people live in symbiosis with the strain. We give it an oxygen and water-rich habitat. It gives us energy directly from the sun."

"You're telling me your tribe has found a way to photosynthesize?" gasps Asha.

"In a sense. The algae does the actual chemistry, we just reap the benefits. But it means we can live in harmony with the forest around us, and protect the creatures we share the space with rather than hunt them for meat we no longer need."

"This is incredible!" says Asha, turning the vial over in her hands.

"Sister, are you still connected to the overseas network?" says Ramone.

"What's the network?" I interject.

"Under Mr. K.'s rule there's been a partial return of foreign aid to Mazonil, administered through his cartel, of course. Most of it's in the form of business deals, but occasionally our school will get a new classroom or computer. The network is a small group of NGOs who are still willing to risk delivering aid to our country. We're due to receive a shipment in two weeks' time. Presumably you want me to get them to take it back to a safe country, Oriana?"

"Yes! More than anything."

"I have to warn you, I've never tried smuggling anything out through the network. If it's discovered, it could jeopardize our only inbound source of aid. But for your people's sake, I will take this risk."

"Maybe you should ship it in two stages?" I suggest. "You know, keep one half hidden here until you know the first batch arrives safely?"

"That's not a bad idea, chico," says Asha. She ruffles my hair again. I pretend to scowl, but can't help but lean into her caressing fingertips.

"Is that... popping candy?" she asks.

"Yes, Ma'am, yes it is. A classic young scent on a mature body," I reply, leaning in.

"Were you aware of how creepy that sounds before or after you said it?" she frowns.

"Definitely after. Ramone, did you pack any of that lemon stuff in your bag?"

"No."

"Are you saying that because you didn't? Or because

you don't want me smelling nice. Or because you don't want me smelling nice while I hit on your sister?"

"You're *not* hitting on her," growls Ramone.

"Hey, little brother, relax. I can handle myself, thank you very much."

"When was the last time you two saw each other?" says Oriana.

"Twenty years ago, maybe longer?" muses Asha.

"So, roughly around the last time Ramone smiled?" I mutter

"You don't need to smile when you're on your own," growls Ramone.

"Arguably the most tragic thing anyone has ever said in the history of words. Thanks for that. You are truly the least sociable being I have ever met."

Oriana gets up from the table where she's been working and holds up half a vial. Well, not the vial exactly, but half the liquid contents inside it. It's being kept in one of those super malleable smart-skins; like a water balloon that can be molded like putty – or in this case, twisted in two without spilling everywhere.

"You'll need something firm to protect it in," says Oriana.

Ramone retrieves a solar cell casing from his backpack and hands it over. Oriana carefully presses the algal putty into the container, then gives both portions over to Asha.

"Thank you for doing this for my people," says Oriana, sincerely.

"Let's just pray that it doesn't get detected on board. The ships here keep things loose for obvious reasons, but you never know when they might decide to do a spot-check to keep the shareholders happy."

"The cartel have shareholders?" I ask.

"The cartel's *bosses* have shareholders," replies Asha.

"What do you mean?"

"Look around you. Does anyone here look like they have the kind of money you'd need to run an international shipping operation? Our city is entirely dependent on the 'goodwill' of a private overseas company. It's the only multinational willing to risk trading with what's left of Mazonil."

"Trading? But how would anyone here pay for imports?"

"They don't. The corporation uses Mazonil as a PR exercise, presenting themselves as social champions bringing aid and investment to the developing world. In reality, their ship delivers a meagre amount of aid. Most of it's munitions for the cartels, and equipment for their factories. They dump the cargo, then fill up the empty ships with loot from our forests."

"So it's a white-collar smash-and-grab?" I ask.

"That's Sequestra for you."

"*Sequestra* run the aid shipments?"

"You know them?" says Asha.

"We've been chasing their trail for hundreds of miles. They're what's brought us from the forest mines to this crumbling shitho-... I mean, *characterful* seaside town."

"You discovered they're behind the mining operations, then? Of course, officially the cartels are running the mines, but Sequestra pay the cartels for the produce," says Asha. "Mr. K. is the bridge between the two. A man with two passports, a bunch of shell companies in his name to funnel the paperwork through, and an aptitude for violence. He's the perfect conduit between their world and ours.

"Brother, when we grew up we thought our country was imploding because the government was too weak and corrupt to stand up to the cartels. But our government wasn't weak, they were brave; growing out of the ashes of a country once-addicted to oil. The last governments tried in vain to protect our rainforests and their people, but they were fighting an invisible enemy with deep pockets. They sponsored the cartels' activities, triggering the civil war, and bringing Mazonil down to its knees. We've never recovered, and it's because of Sequestra."

"This Mr. K. must die," growls Ramone. "For years I've been searching for the head of the snake. Now, we have it."

"Dude, can you stop saying 'head of the snake'? It's kinda tacky."

"You'll never get close enough to him," says Asha. "He's too well protected. And even if you did kill him, Sequestra would find another stooge in days. He's not the first, and he won't be the last."

"We're not trying to kill Mr. K.-"

"Speak for yourself," mutters Ramone.

"Our *goal* is to expose Sequestra's illegal activities to the world. Their paperwork trail is the thing that will hang them. That and incontrovertible satellite evidence. My point is, the international courts will be able to stop them. Make them pay to restore the damage they've caused. But for that to happen, we need to take down the servers. *That* is our primary objective," I insist.

"What are these servers for?" asks Asha.

"Across Mazonil, Sequestra and their cartels have installed satellite-jammers. The masts broadcast a false signal into space."

"You mean no one outside of Mazonil even *knows* what's happening here?"

"Not yet, but we're going to change that," I insist. "We

need to locate the server hub and destroy it. Do you have any idea where it could be?"

"I've never seen such a thing in this city, so they must be hiding it," muses Asha. "The safest place to hide anything would be the old Port Authority Building. No-one calls it that anymore, though. These days it's Mr K.'s building."

"How do we get in?"

Asha looks uncomfortable for a moment, avoiding our gaze.

"It's tricky," she mutters.

"Asha?" presses Ramone.

"I can tell you how to get in, brother, but I dare not for fear that I will lose you forever."

"Please, Asha, this is important. I am but one soul. The forest is all souls."

Asha sighs.

"Fine. I'll tell you, but you have to promise not to die."

"Deal," I say.

"Not *you*," snaps Asha.

"I promise," says Ramone.

"Very well. One of my pupil's parents works as a cleaner at Mr. K.'s building. She was late collecting her child yesterday because of a back injury. Apparently she and the other house staff had been made to install a bunch of new furniture. Word on the street is Mr. K.'s throwing a huge engagement party, it's going to truly extravagant."

"OK, I'm gonna jump in here real quick," I say. "We just got off the jungle train and climbed through a disused sewer - we're not dressed for a fancy party."

"Don't worry, white man, we will find you some fancy clothes - I know your people get anxious without them. Besides, we have time on our side - the party's not until next month."

"A *month*?" splutters Oriana. "My people don't have that long!"

"Our situation is urgent," I add, mindful of my deteriorating body.

"Beside, staying here is dangerous," says Ramone.

"Do any of you have a better plan? If so, by all means, do it. But last I checked, you three rocked up here because you've been chased to the edge of Mazonil and are desperate. Yes, it's dangerous here, but so is the rest of the country, and this is your only chance at taking down Mr. K. Trust me, I've lived here for years and this is the first time there's been talk of hundreds of people coming to his mansion. If you want to strike the heart of the cartel, then you must be patient. I know a place you three can stay undetected and regain some strength. You can use the time to study Mr. K's security and plan the attack."

"Somewhere to *rest* - sweet Jesus now we're talking! Asha, I can't thank you enough," I gush.

"Don't thank me just yet - you've not seen where you're staying," she chuckles.

CHAPTER TWENTY-NINE

PABLA

No one on the island was expecting more refugees to arrive, least of all now. Their timing could not be worse. Just as the Centada, Namakaro, and many other tribes did, these people have left their warriors behind. Meaning the newcomers crossing the rope bridge are those who are too young or infirm to fight. We are about to face down an enemy that has forced us all here. We need warriors more than ever, not hopeless mouths to feed.

As the last pair of elders shuffle across the final planks, a tree-top scout cries out from the riverbank.

"Enemy sighted!"

Refugees hurry inland, spreading word of the cartel's arrival, while warriors like myself and Latika run to the shore, knowing we must get eyes on the opposition at once. This will not be a war fought on an open battlefield. Both sides are preparing for a siege. Strategy is our only weapon now, and we must conserve our energy.

"Chief, should we close the bridge?" calls a warrior.

Chief Sukil, the woman voted leader of the resistance

by the assembly of elders, stands on the shore, surveying the enemy with us.

"No. Leave it up. We must bait them onto it. Bring our defenses forward, blockade the beach!"

The order echoes down the chain of command and rigs are dragged onto the sand. They are sharpened logs, tied together with vine. They look like they are there to stop invading vehicles from crossing the beach, but in reality they are decoys, designed to funnel the invaders towards pits that have been dug and masked.

Across the flowing brown river, the cartel are setting up camp on their shore. Mechanical robots are constructing pulleys and ladders from the cliff edge down to the pit, paving the way for foot soldiers to follow. Within minutes, the shore opposite has been transformed into a crawling hive of robots, all of which are rapidly building more machines, and unloading cargo from the roadside above.

"I don't understand," says a warrior near me, "There are only thirty of them? We easily outnumber them a hundred to one!"

The man is right, there are only thirty human cartellers present. But they are not planning on fighting us one-on-one. Among the cartellers, a man swaggers onto the beach, prompting a flurry of pampering and the urgent lowering of a luxury deck chair. The man takes a seat and accepts a decorated cocktail, while a servant cools him with a huge feather fan. I know Stax is an asshole, but he's really kicked it up a gear in the days since I escaped.

He claps his hands and six giant boxes are hauled onto the sand, where they are nested on top of sturdy tripods. Seconds later, a wave of something loud, rhythmic, and angry-sounding hits our side of the river.

"Oh god, is that their idea of music? Maybe we should surrender now," says Latika.

"We've got incoming!" yells the scout.

Along from the booming speakers, a fleet of drones is rising from the ground and coming at us at full tilt.

"Archers ready!" cries chief Sukil.

A hundred archers take position on the shore. As the drones get closer, I recognize their shape, and the glowing orange spark at their tips. Latika knows them too.

"Pyro drones," she growls.

"They're gonna burn us all, that's their plan! *Cowards!*" spits Ohalo.

"Archers, draw!" cries Sukil.

The creaking of a hundred bows spreads either side of me as the drones near the halfway point across the river.

"Hold... Hooold!" calls the chief.

The two outer drones suddenly veer inwards, smashing into the others in the middle. All four drones fall from the air in a cloud of fire and smoke, as their splintered parts rain down into the muddy waters.

"Archers, stand down!" calls Sukil.

There is much cheering and celebration as the cartel drones fail to penetrate the stronghold's cyber shield. On the shore opposite, Stax is out of his chair and barking with rage at his men, who are scrambling around to find a solution.

A second wave of drones takes off from the shore, but this time they are flying *away* from us.

"What are they doing?" says Latika.

"Running scared!" cheers Ohalo.

I am squinting to see them as they fly away like an old airplane taking off, climbing diagonally into the horizon until they vanish among the clouds. For a few moments there is a fresh cheer of celebration, as visiting warriors assume this is down to another triumph of our cyber shield, but their voices swiftly peter out. Four black dots are emerging through the gray, growing larger by the second.

"They are coming right at us," I cry.

"Have faith. The shield will protect us," says a fellow warrior.

"Archers, draw!" calls the chief.

The drones are clearly visible now. They are rocketing towards us at incredible speed, red pilot lights fixed on our position like hawk eyes. They are fast approaching the mid-way point of the river, where the shield kicks in. But something strange happens.

The pilot lights go out. The drones' humming rotors fall quiet. They speed across the threshold without a glitch.

"They are still coming!" cries a warrior.

"Why isn't the shield stopping them?" gasps another.

"Oh crap – they know the shield only works against active devices. They have shut the drones down completely. They are using them as projectiles!" I gasp.

"Archers, loose!" cries the chief.

Hundreds of arrows soar into the sky, only to be brushed aside like matchsticks by the oncoming drones.

"Brace for impact!" cries the chief.

But the drones are still too high. As the four defunct machines hurtle towards us, I realize what is happening.

"They are not aiming for the beach... they are aiming for the forest! Chief, it is a kamikaze mission. They are using them as napalm!" I yell.

The drones soar over our heads and disappear behind the wall of trees. Booms ring out from the forest as great balls of fire and smoke rise from the canopy.

The chief barks into her radio urgently, "Fire teams, go!"

"Chief, the cartel is launching a boarding party!" cries a scout.

Across the river, the robots have printed their first fleet of gun boats, and have fitted them with outboard motors. Three pairs of cartellers leap in and take to the water. As they speed towards us, a fresh wave of drones takes off from the shore, speeding away into the clouds.

The three gunboats spread out wide across the river. On each boat, one carteller is steering from the back, while the other is poised at the gun turret, ready to unleash hell on us bare-skinned warriors.

"Defensive positions!" cries the chief.

Across the beach, dense clay panels rise up from the sand. The assembled warriors take refuge in groups of ten behind the nearest ones, with the archers braced against them ready to spring up and fire.

As the cartel see us taking cover, they unleash the guns, firing thousands of rounds at us from three angles.

"Engineers, now!" cries the chief.

Explosions ring out across the river. The stronghold have floating mines! Two of the gun boats are destroyed by direct hits, while the third is upturned, throwing the cartellers into the water.

"Archers, loose!" yells Sukil.

Archers spring up from behind their shelters and open fire, killing the two bobbing men. No time for celebration. Four drones soar overhead and blasting into the forest with a thundering crash.

Scouts cry out from the treetops, bringing our attention urgently back to the beach. Dozens of amphibious hunter drones are emerging from the river and driving onto the shore. With armored exteriors, they are impervious to our arrows. Their roofs are fitted with spinning sprinklers, which are spurting out thin jets of liquid. Screams ring out from the front line as droplets rain down on the warriors. This is a chemical attack.

"Fall back!" cries the chief. "To the trees, hurry! Send in the enforcer!"

Cries for the enforcer echo through the chains of command as the thousands of warriors fall back from the beaches. Dozens lie face-down in the sand, smoldering where the acid has burned through their flesh.

A series of thundering footsteps grow louder. With a crash, the enforcer bursts through the tree line and onto the beach. The broad metal exoskeleton increases her size tenfold, and her strength orders above that. Somehow the tribes have managed to cobble this thing together out of scavenged cartel parts and civil war relics. It does not look pretty, but it looks mean as hell, like the woman piloting it.

With a cry, the enforcer leaps over the barriers and smashes her mechanical fist down on the first amphibian, crushing it immediately. Other landers swarm towards her, trying to overwhelm the lone fighter. A mechanical staff extends from her hands and she bats the attackers away. But new machines are appearing faster than she can destroy them. The landers are forming a circle around her, keeping her pinned while others crawl ashore.

The enforcer screams in pain as the machines change tactic. They are no longer targeting the fleeing warriors with their acid sprinklers. Unifying their jets, they are aiming for the same patch of her armor. The metal is smoldering and burning apart as the jets of liquid eat through it. The woman screams as the acid reaches her flesh. With a last act of defiance, she rips her power core open and ignites the cells. A ball of fire consumes them all. When it retreats, all that remains is the burned out shell of the empty battle suit, and the charred, broken shells of the landers.

But other amphibious robots are still progressing up the beach. They seem to be converging on a single direction like they are honing in on a signal.

"They're going for the stronghold's server!" cries Latika.

"Deploy the EMP!" calls Sukil.

"But chief, that will knock out our mirage!" says a warrior.

"If we don't do it, those machines will wipe out the server *and* every living thing on this island. Do it now!" she yells.

As the commanders turn their keys, an invisible pulse bursts across the island, detectable only by the slight shimmer in the sky as our shield, fails, and the landers power down.

"Chief, the cartel are launching a new drone!" cries a scout.

Across the shore a white drone is speeding towards the half-way line. It pauses and scans the perimeter, then crosses the invisible threshold, realizing the shield wall has fallen. As it reaches the beach, a vast holographic projection of Stax's pissed-off face appears above us all.

"Hola folks, I'll make this quick. You outnumber us. Well done. But that counts for shit 'cos we outgun you. I *will* win. The sooner you realize it's inevitable, the sooner we can get this over with. Much as I enjoy hurtling fire drones at you, it's not a very cost-effective way of doing business. So how about you all just surrender now and I let you live? Or you can keep fighting me and waste everyone's time until you finally realize there's no way you can possibly win. Rest assured, if needed, I will gladly burn your shitty island to the ground, along with every last one of you. But that will be the last thing I do. First, and most importantly, I will make you all suffer for disobeying me. So I strongly advise you to take my generous offer. What do you say?"

The thousands of warriors scattered among the trees and at the edge of the beach wait in silence for the chief's response. She steps out from behind her shield, plucks a spear from the ground, and hurls it at the white drone.

The warriors cheer and beat their chests as Stax's image vanishes, while the frazzled drone drops from the air, disappearing beneath the waves. From across the water, Stax's voice resonates through the loudspeakers.

"All right then, have it your way. But for the record, it didn't have to be like this."

Across the waves, caterpillar drones are dragging something with ropes. It is a mast of sorts and they are raising it into an upright position. There is a spinning turbine behind the tip, like a windmill, but with a tub attached. So maybe it is more like a gigantic hairdryer? As it comes online, a faint breeze fills the air. A powdery cloud is spewing out of its tip and drifting towards us, spreading across the sky like a drop of blood diffusing in water.

"What are they doing?" asks a warrior.

"The sky is changing color!" calls another.

I watch in horror as the sky overhead turns from dappled blue to a vibrant, dazzling green. But it goes further than that – it is not just the sky that is green, it is *everything*. It is like they have put a filter over the entire island. The sand, the water, my own arms. All are now reduced to shades of this smothering green.

Stax retakes his deckchair throne across the waves and toasts us with a fresh cocktail. Chief Sukil straightens up beside us, staring across the ocean, her expression grim.

"Why are they shining green light on us?" asks Latika.

"They're not actively shining green light on us. They're *removing* all the other frequencies, stopping the rest of the light spectrum from reaching us," I say, my mind racing.

"Why the hell would they do that?" says Ohalo.

"Isn't it obvious? Green is the only light plants cannot absorb."

"So?"

"So they do not need to watch the island burn. They are going to watch us starve instead. The siege is truly beginning."

One Month Later

It is my turn to fetch the water for Latika and Ohalo. I sit up and pause for a moment, knowing to wait for my head to stop spinning before trying to stand. Using a tree as a crutch, I rise to my feet and survey the green world around me.

Through a month of unending green light, only one color has grown more dominant across the island. Black is spreading further each day as the plants die, losing their one reflective pigment. It is becoming harder to navigate between spaces and feel like I am dreaming, where half the world is shrouded in night time, and the other half drowned in a chemical filter.

I pass the sentries standing guard, looking out across the water. They are asleep on their feet and I can hardly blame them. Our island's rations were already stretched to breaking point *before* the siege began, but we knew we could survive thanks to the algae in our skin. Because it was engineered to be black, it can absorb this green light that plants cannot. But we are still suffering, because that algae has been robbed of the rest of the light spectrum it relies on. Plus its human hosts are exhausted and often dehydrated, further straining the symbiosis. The gray blotches of dead algae are hard to detect in the monochrome lighting, but if you know where to look, you start seeing them on the skin of everyone here. With each day that passes, we are crawling closer to death.

I place a tender arm on the sleeping sentry's shoulder and pass across a flask of fresh water.

"Stay hydrated, friend. It will help your skin."

They drink it, gratefully, and I return to the purifier to refill the flask for the others.

We managed to put out the fires caused by Stax's drones on the first day of the siege, but it took the efforts of the entire island. Fortunately the elders had anticipated this sort of move – after Latika and I lobbied them to listen – and we dug a series of fire trenches across the island, which helped slow the spread long enough for us to get each blaze under control.

The only thing that has kept us alive so far is the fact that Stax does not want to waste money on more pyro drones, or risk losing boats to river mines. Plus, he is enjoying it. He tells us every day through his loudspeakers.

It turns out Stax is a master of psychological warfare. Something I should have known from being caged by him. Every hour, he gives us an update on the luxuries on the other side of the river, regaling us in great detail of the resplendent meals, snacks, and drinks he is enjoying. He goes a step further, interviewing each of his men in turn throughout the day as they eat a meal "live on-air", as he calls it.

But this morning, his gloating voice is quiet. I am squinting across the water, bringing my foggy brain into focus. His throne is empty. Where is he? There – several feet away, under the dining tent, he is having a meeting. Is it a meeting? It is hard to tell from here. Stax and two cartellers are sitting before a row of screens, all seemingly deep in concentration. What are they waiting for?

A cloud of sand bursts up through the shore before me, like a land mine just exploded. But there is nothing on the surface to have triggered it. The explosion came from underground!

Cries of "attack!" echo across the shore.

Sand is bursting upwards across the beach like it is on the wrong side of a firing squad. My jaw drops as I see what surges through the blast holes. Drilling machines are bursting up onto the beach. Their drill heads detach, falling sideways into the sand, revealing quivering barrels.

I realize what is happening and dive aside as the first barrel rockets forwards, flying into the tree line and exploding with a shower of fire. More drills burst through the sand and detach, launching their payloads until half of the island's green wall is ablaze.

A chilling war cry echoes from the sand holes and I cannot believe my eyes. Hundreds of warriors are pouring up through the tunnels. But these are not cartellers, these are painted, tattooed, mask-wearing warriors like us. They are people of forest, yet they are charging towards us with axes and arrows raised, screaming their cries of attack.

Our malnourished watch guards are already falling to the enemy's arrows. I have to get back to the others and warn them. I have to get my weapons!

As I race through the trees, my body burns reserves of energy I did not know I had. I am about to scream the most feared and taboo word known to any refugee. One word that transcends every culture and every dialect in the forest because of the depth of its meaning. It is reserved for the most heinous of betrayals; when a whole tribe betrays all others and preys on them like parasites to prolong their own survival in the face of the cartels. We have one word for these traitors, and when it is uttered, it means a fight to the death. As I run, I scream at the top of my lungs, rousing warriors in all quarters. The cry spreads faster than the fires burning through our forest.

Take cover.

They are here.

The scourge has arrived.

Three days have passed since the scourge invaded our island. The people of the stronghold have vanished into the shadows of the island's burning, dying trees. We lie in wait, covering ourselves under dead ferns and leaves, hiding in ditches and pits, picking them off when we can, but knowing they are stronger and better equipped than all of us.

This is not like fighting the cartellers who used to invade our forests. These people are *of* the forest. They know how to track us, how to discern our mock bird calls to each other, how to spot our hiding places, and they are closing the net; sweeping through the island in packs, hunting us down like dogs.

To fight them in the open would only bring death. Each scourger is armed with cartel weapons. Rifles, stun guns, and grenades. Our only hope is to pick them off like snipers, with precision arrow shots. But that requires getting close.

One slip or misfire and your cover is blown. They will gun you down, or sometimes let you run until you collapse with exhaustion, knowing they can keep pace with your beleaguered body easily.

The only slender advantage we have is that our eyes are more adjusted to the eerie green lighting. We have learned to discern shadows and depths with nuance, among the monochrome vision. They are still adapting. Every now and they, they trip, or fall, and one of us gets away. But it is the exception, and it is blind luck. After a month of starvation and days of being hunted, it is beyond question. We are losing this war.

"It is the only option," I insist.

Tanok shakes his head, bitterly. "We will not negotiate with these vandals. I would sooner die!"

"That wish will come true today unless we sue for peace," I say. "You are old, Tanok. You have seen five generations of forest people live and fall under your cloak of secrecy. If you are welcoming death now it is only because it will bring respite from your failures as an elder."

"Enough!" interjects chief Sukil.

"I am with Elder Tanok in saying that surrender is unpalatable. However, it is a better option than the total eradication of our people and our customs. As Pabla is saying, we must sue for peace."

"How?" protests Latika. "They have us pinned down across the island. Your dampener is the only thing stopping them locating us with drones. If they disable it, it's game over even sooner."

"I will go to Stax and speak with him," I say. "I was his prisoner once and I know his vanity. He will relish the chance to humiliate us further. He knows how bitter surrender will feel to us, especially after we have held out for so long."

"What will be our terms?" asks Ohalo.

"That they withdraw their forces and allow us to perform proper rituals for our dead. Then they must allow us to leave without further conflict. We will head for the border and seek refuge with Mazonil's neighbors."

"But where would they put us? There's no rainforest left in any of our neighbors' lands," says Ohalo.

"Soon there will be none here either," says Sukil. "If our culture survives, then there will be hope that one day we may revive the forest. But if we die with it, then both hopes are lost forever."

"What if Stax refuses our offer?" says Latika.

"Or kills Pabla on the spot?" adds Ohalo.

"Then she will die with some semblance of honor! As will the rest of us," spits Tanok.

"For once, elder Tanok, we are in agreement," I reply. "We must accept that we cannot protect the island against them. They have sentenced the forest to die, because they wish to extract minerals from under its skin, to sell overseas, to power indoor ski slopes and casinos. That is the price of our homeland. I say our final act should be scorched earth. If they deny us life, and habitat, then we will deny their material desires. If I do not return, or send word of a peace deal, you must ignite the pluridium reserves beneath the ground."

"That will destroy the whole island!" says Latika.

"And it will ensure our enemies bear no fruits from their attack on us," nods Tanok, starting to understand. "A final act of protest may deter them from attacking whatever tribes there may be left elsewhere in Mazonil. Much as it pains me to say this, and I want to be clear that this is *not* any kind of exoneration for her past transgressions, but in this motion, I second Pabla's proposal."

"Then it is decided," says Zukil. "Pabla will go to the cartel and sue for peace. If she fails, we will ignite the pluridium chambers. Our homes, our bones, and their profits, will return to ash. Go, Pabla. You are our last hope."

Latika and Ohalo embrace me in turn. I pause before Tanok, but he stares at me with bitterness. There is no forgiveness to be found from that man's cold heart. As far as he is concerned, I brought this on all our heads. That was always his problem. He was so blinded by his own shortcomings, he cannot comprehend the notion he might have failed long before I did.

Leaving the secret bunker, I stealthily make my way through the forest until I am confident I am nowhere near the entrance, and have not been seen by the scourgers. I pick two ferns from the ground and hold them crossed above my head; the universal tribal symbol for peaceful surrender.

As I walk to the shore, I whistle a bird song, drawing attention to myself so that the scourgers see my stance. Soon enough, I am being escorted by enemy warriors across the beach and down into one of the sand tunnels. A guard loads me onto a quad bike, and the journey begins.

When we emerge on the other side, several minutes later, I am overwhelmed by the brightness of the daylight. The colors bombard my senses as I escape the green light filter they have pumped over our island for so long.

"Pabla? Is that really you?" comes a laugh.

Stax waves to me from his throne, beckoning me over

like a long lost friend. His men jostle me from the bike and throw me onto my knees before him.

"Woah, *chica*, you need to *eat*. You look thin, girl. Does everyone look like this on your island? God damn, I didn't realize it was inhabited by skeletons."

"It soon will be unless you agree to our terms," I reply.

"You're here to negotiate? Bold move amigue! You seem to be laboring under the misapprehension that you have some kinda leverage here?"

Stax laughs, and his men join in heartily.

"You underestimate us again, Stax. We have leverage all right. The one thing you need from that island – we know you are after the pluridium reserves. I am here to tell you that either you allow us to evacuate peacefully, or we will blow your precious minerals up, and it will all have been for nothing."

"The minerals?" laughs Stax. "You mean these things?"

He brings up a holographic map of the island's topography, revealing the chambers of pluridium beneath the surface.

"We've already mapped all the ins and outs of the pluridium, *chava*. Why do you think we wanted this island in the first place? My warriors on the ground already know what they're doing. They've had thirty days. They've sealed those chambers with anti-inflammatories. You people couldn't blow it up if your lives depended on it. Which... they do!" he chuckles.

"If you knew this all along, then why the hell did you let your men bring me here?" I growl.

"I wanted you to have a front row seat. Now you get to enjoy the view alongside me, while we watch the last of your people burn. Axl, prepare the pyro drones."

"Uh, you sure boss? Our allied tribe is still on the island. If we napalm what's left, we'll be burning them too."

"Uh, *duh*. Then we won't have to pay them a single credit. More pluridium for the rest of us, boys!"

"Good point, boss," nods Axl. "Launching the fleet now."

CHAPTER THIRTY

LUKE

"Sshh, keep it down, white man!" hisses Oriana.

In my defense, it's *really* hard to crawl through a ventilator hatch that's built for thin people. Or air. Especially after spending a month cooped up in a chicken shed, living off bread, beans, and water. Plus some very dubious medication Asha scavenged for me, which is definitely wearing off.

I land on the floor in a crumpled heap and Oriana chastises me again. How am I supposed to keep it down when I'm dropping out of a ceiling? It would be *real* nice if one of my accomplices had thought to help me down, but apparently they're too busy securing the perimeter or whatever.

I dust myself off and replace the metal grill. As a kid I was always taught to leave things as you found them. I always like the double-edge vibe to that mantra, because it meant if you went somewhere nice, it usually took minimal effort to leave it nice. On the other hand, if you're at a friend's house and you step into their skid-mark-covered crapper, well then it's bombs away...

We're dressed like we're about to pull off a gallery heist. Or perform an improv troop sketch. Black chinos, black shirts, surly faces.

"Is this not art!" I cry, dramatically.

Ramone and Oriana glare at me.

"Sorry, I thought we were about to do a bit about modern theater. You know, cos there's no set, we're dressed in black, and all about to assume alter egos – *aka doubling roles*. Hey? Cos we're a small cast?"

"We live in the forest, *cabrón*. We have no idea what your country's modern theater scene is like," snaps Oriana.

"It's a lot like this to be honest. Low budget, immersive, and irritatingly meta. You're basically experiencing it right now. 'Is this not ar-"

"Stop saying that!" snaps Ramone.

"Sorry, I've just realized how insensitive I'm being. We're in the basement of an old colonial building, and here I am *assuming* you two would be interested in my culture's post-modern theater scene. God, I'm truly making *all* the same mistakes as my ancestors!"

"Did you turn up with a bunch of non-native diseases and wittingly spread them to cripple the native resistance before launching a slave trading empire?"

"Uh, no...?"

"OK good. Then you've not made *all* the same mistakes," says Oriana, coldly.

"Still, I feel awful. This is your country, and this building is built on stolen ground. I think we should all take a minute to acknowledge that."

"Gringo, we do not have time for your white guilt!"

"I just want to show you I respect the validity and equal stature of your culture! Not that you *need* my validation, of course. Perhaps we could do something appropriate to your cultures, instead? Do you guys have a pre-heist version of a rain dance we could tap into? I think it would be a really good warm-up exercise. It's important to be bonded as a team before undertaking group activities. I learned that at theater camp. God, not that I'm here to force my cultural learnings on you. Aha. Er, I'm here to learn *from* you. But not in a dated ethnographic 'othering' way. Just think of me as a fly on the wall. Not that there should be any kind of wall between us. Ah shit, this is all coming out wrong. I swear I'm not Hitler!"

"Boy, white guilt sure is a *lot* to deal with. I can see why so few of you bother with it," says Oriana.

"*Thank you!*"

"Not where I was going with that."

"Gotcha."

"Are you two ready?" grunts Ramone.

"Yeah, just gimme one sec."

OK guys lemme bring you up to speed – but I gotta be quick cos the others are hassling me. Asha put us in touch with the woman who cleans at Mr. K.'s business address – aka the old colonial port authority building which is secretly owned by Sequestra and leased to a bullshit shell company operated by Mr. K.

The cleaner confirmed there's an underground basement carpark, which has unguarded air vents. Asha rigged us up with a gizmo that tricked the building's external sensors long enough for us to get inside and through the vents. Now we're in the basement, surrounded by the insanely lavish cars of Mr. K.'s guests, who are continuing to arrive, as they pass through the cartel security checks above ground.

We've got ourselves some wristbands, courtesy of Asha's woman on the inside, so we're all set to get in unchallenged.

It kinda feels like I'm going to a weird music festival, but I gotta remember we're actually here to locate and disable the cartel's mega satellite-blocking hub server that they're running on behalf of Sequestra. I have every confidence all of this is making perfect sense to you right now, because I know you pay close attention to my words.

For example: Teal.

There'll be a test on that later.

"Luke!" hisses Oriana.

"Sorry, I'm back. Let's rock and roll. Are we all clear on everybody's roles?"

"Obviously yes, we discussed them before climbing into the vent."

"Yeah but just for everyone's benefit, I think we should recap. Make sure we're all on the same page."

"For who's benefit?"

"Everyone's!"

I am *so* good to you.

"Ugh. He wasn't paying attention," groans Oriana.

Look, and now the others think bad of me because of it. I hope you appreciate this because I take these bullets to my fine reputation so *you* don't have to. Shh – listen up, Ramone's about to explain it all again.

"Luke, you're pretending to be a wealthy foreign investor who is looking to expand into Mazonil via Sequestra's network. I am your bodyguard and Oriana is the maid."

"*Event planner*," snaps Oriana.

"Sorry, Oriana is the 'event planner'."

"I think the air quotes are a little harsh, Ramone, that's a real job people do," I reply.

"I am not demeaning the job. I am saying it is a bad cover for her."

"Because I'm a woman?" says Oriana.

"No! Because you have never set foot in this building, and anyone hearing your job title is going to expect you to know where everything is. You might as well paint a sign on you saying 'come ask me questions!' It is the *worst* choice for trying to blend in."

"I'm inclined to agree with Ramone," I add.

"What? So now you *both* think I should play the maid?" fumes Oriana.

"I didn't say anything before because I didn't want you to think I was being sexist!" I protest.

"Because you thought that as a woman I wouldn't be robust enough to handle the notion that you might be suggesting I play a maid for legitimate non-gendered reasons?"

"Ummmm... yes?"

"*That's* sexist."

"And patronizing," agrees Ramone.

"Shut your mouth, 'body guard'. You couldn't have picked a more stereotypically macho role if you tried."

"I did try. And you're right, I couldn't," shrugs Ramone.

Oriana rolls her eyes.

"What, you're just gonna let that lie?" I protest. "You busted my balls for me *not* saying you should be maid, but when he openly says he's shotgunning the macho role, it's fine?"

"It is not 'fine', white man, I am just not going to bother changing him. He has been living alone in the jungle for twenty years. That requires a whole new level of fixing. Better not to even start."

"So by that logic you see *me* as having enough potential for change that you would bother to correct my deeply rooted behavioral flaws?" I reply. "We should get a drink when all this is done."

"Wouldn't you rather I *served* you a drink? I can wear my maid costume if you like," she says with a foxy wink.

I'm grinning like a Cheshire cat that's hung like a horse and goes like a rabbit; an abomination to nature, but *surely* worth trying at least once.

"She's being sarcastic, coño," mutters Ramone.

My smile falls. Though curiously the hard-on sticks around. Wait, am I so broken and accustomed to rejection these days that it's how I get my rocks off? Crap. My therapist warned me about this. Get dumped enough times during a state of extreme arousal and you'll develop a Pavlovian response to the situation. Thinking about it, this isn't the first time this has been a problem for me. I tried to apply for a mortgage a few months back and the bank turned me down cold. I stepped out of the manager's office with a flagpole you could see from space.

Oh shit, my tear ducts are leaking blood again. Ramone and Oriana are looking at me in alarm like I'm causing a scene, which is insensitive more than anything, because a scene is precisely what I wanted to create before they vetoed my theater dreams. I dab away the crimson discharge and make a mental note to never ignore my doctors again, then quickly shift the attention away from me before they drop me from the heist.

"OK, so to be clear, you're *not* gonna be the maid?" I check.

"Not for you," scowls Oriana.

"But for the mission?" presses Ramone.

"Why can't *you* be the maid?" snaps Oriana.

"Because I have to be the security guard!"

"You brought me into this mission because you needed a warrior," she fumes.

"Yes, and you *are* a warrior! No-one's saying you are *actually* a maid!"

"Not that there's anything wrong with being a maid," I interject.

"Why can't I be the guard?" says Oriana.

"Because we have to blend in, and people will get suspicious."

"Of a female bodyguard?"

"Yes. I'm afraid the mercenary gunslinger industry isn't as progressive as other businesses. So we need you to play the housemaid, even though Luke and I both know deep down that you are the warrior here."

"Ugh, society is full of *idiotas estúpidos*. I will do it, but only if you acknowledge that although you are pretending to be the bodyguard, you are in fact the housemaid here."

"There is no shame in that," shrugs Ramone.

"If anything, it's actually kinda sexist that you would try to use that as a slur," I add.

"Don't even get me started on you, 'international investor'. Ugh, enough of this, I will play the maid and school you both after. Let's go," says Oriana.

We tailgate some other guests and climb the stairs into the sprawling mansion complex, where music is playing, and a couple of hundred guests are chatting over drinks and canapes. I gotta hand it to Mr. K., the guy has a classy pad. *Very* sensitively decorated. New-money types can often have vulgar taste, but he's struck a wonderful balance with the selection of art on the walls. Nothing worse than someone who's culturally out of their depth and just tries that bit too hard, you know what I mean?

The three of us split up immediately. Which is baffling,

because Ramone's supposed to be my bodyguard. I guess if anyone asks, I'll have to tell them he's getting fired shortly. Ah, he's at the bar getting us both drinks. Legend. Oh crap, someone's engaged him in conversation. They're both looking at me. Ramone's whispering something to the guy. The guy looks at me again then bursts out laughing and pats Ramone on the back. Ramone toasts the dude then comes back over with our drinks.

"What were you two talking about?"

"Nothing. We were just sharing a private joke."

"About me?"

"Here's your drink."

"Wait, you refuse my very sincere offer of friendship for days on end, then in the space of two seconds you become best buds with some random carteller, using *my* appearance as the thing you bond over?"

"Relax. I knew you would forgive me."

"Oh? And what makes you so sure?"

"Because that is what friends do," grins Ramone.

He pats me on the shoulder, then breezes away with his drink. I don't know whether to laugh, or cry, but my arm feels like it's glowing.

More guests are coming up the staircase, forcing me further into the room. I strike the aloof air of a rich client inspecting an art gallery. Nose held high, eyelids half shut, and downturned sagging lips like the weight of my own money is *such* a drag.

"Psst!" comes a whisper.

Oriana's in a doorway, and is signaling for me to go through it. There aren't any other guests that way; it's clearly an off-limits area. Damn, she works fast. But cartel security are stationed around the huge open plan floor, up against all the walls. One of them's even dressed like a lifeguard, keeping an eye on the drunk guests in the pool, on-hand in case any of them start drowning and need to be put out of their misery with a bullet or two.

Oriana moves away from the doorway carrying a tray of glasses, then barges into another waiter. As the tray falls to the floor and the contents shatter spectacularly, she goes on the verbal offensive, castigating the hapless waiter with such force that even *he* thinks the collision was his fault. While all eyes are on the diversion, I slip into the corridor.

It's quieter through here, and I'm hella exposed. I need to be quick. I follow the winding passage, taking a number of turnings, and generally adhering to the principle that the quieter the party gets, the closer I am to finding the secret stuff.

"Freeze!" comes a voice behind me.

I raise my hands in surrender then turn around slowly, following the guard's instructions. The woman's got a gun trained right at me, and a jaw set like concrete.

"What are you doing back here?" she growls.

"Uh, looking for the bathroom?"

"It's nowhere here. Get moving."

"Can I ask a personal question? Are you a professional female bodyguard?"

"You sound surprised?

"I guess I am. Women are underrepresented in criminal activities in my culture."

"I am glad to be doing my bit. Now move."

"Oh, I'm moving. No arguments here."

"What the hell's up with your eye – are you crying *blood*?" she says, disgusted.

"For the record, that tone is hurtful. Don't worry about it – it's nothing major. Just an allergy I have."

"To what?"

"Radiation."

She frowns at me, trying to figure out if I'm being serious or sarcastic. I *wish* it were the latter. Shit, she's growing more suspicious of me by the second.

"Show me your wristband again, mister... Where did you get this? Hey, it's a staff wristband!"

Oh crap. That's my cover blown. I'm closing my eyes, waiting for the bullet to blast my brains out, when there's a grunt and the sound of a body hitting the floor.

"Ramone! How did you know where to find me?"

"I followed the scent of incompetence."

"Hurtful, but I'll allow it. Is she gonna be OK?" I ask, gesturing to the guard.

"She's stunned, but it was enough of a dose to knock her out for several hours."

"OK good. I didn't want her to die."

"She's cartel, Remini. Don't get attached just because she's a woman."

"Not like that – I just mean she could be a positive role model for young girls considering a life of crime. It's important she's given visibility in society."

Voices from the corridor force us to halt our conversation. We grab the unconscious guard and drag her into the nearest room.

"Holy crap, this is the server room!" I gasp.

Ramone's glaring at me with a finger over his lips.

"Sorry," I whisper.

The approaching voices continue past our turn and further down the main corridor. We peer out to see who it is. Credit to the mural artist, they captured Mr. K.'s likeness *perfectly*. I've never before seen him in the flesh, and yet there's not a doubt in my mind the handsome, grinning man ahead of us i the boss of the cartel. As for the extremely attractive younger man leading him by the tie, I'm not sure, but I don't see an engagement ring on his finger. Oh Mr. K., you are such a disappointment! One day I truly hope I find a monogamous gang leader. I guess today isn't that day.

Ramone darts back to the server room and grabs the guard's gun; one capable of delivering fatal shots.

"Where are you going?" I hiss.

"Stay here!" he whispers.

"Ramone, we need to take down the hub server!"

"You do the server. I will deal with Mr. K. It is time to cut off the head of the snake!"

He's gone before I can ask him never to say that again. Now I'm staring at a room full of servers that I have *no* idea how to take down, wishing Pietro was here, and sensing that Ramone's years of pent up rage are about to upend our entire plan.

"You need a hand?" comes a voice.

Oriana's standing in the threshold, dripping in spilled drinks.

"Yes! Oh my god you're a sight for sore eyes. Do you know how to disable a hub server?"

"What part of growing up in the forest in a technophobic society makes you think that is something I would know?"

"I didn't want to make assumptions, but OK, fine, great, we're both useless!"

"If either of us should know how to destroy this thing, it is you – you are from the Northern Bloc!"

"Hey, that's a massive stereotype. Not *all* Northern Blocers are useful."

"Figure something out quickly, white man, because I told my supervisor I was coming down here to change. They will be expecting me back in a few minutes."

"Wait, you *actually* work here now?"

"Of course not! I'm just saying, they know I am down here and a delay will look suspicious! Ugh. Where is Ramone?"

"Cutting off a snake's head."

"*Now* is the moment you choose to be racist?"

"What? No, I- Forget it. OK. We need a way into these servers. Think, Luke, *think*."

"Fine. You better 'think' fast. I will keep watch."

She takes up position in the corridor, gun in hand, while I pace among the blinking servers, trying to think of a way to take them down permanently. It's not as simple as smashing them up – much as I enjoyed that last time – there'll be backups in other locations, no doubt. To do this properly we need to *infect* the whole network, and that means hacking our way in. There's only one guy I know with those kinds of skills, and the ability to do it at speed. I can't believe I'm about to do this. I've gotta call Chang.

Something in my guts is hurting like hell but there's no time for antacids – Chang just picked up. Ugh, like I wasn't regretting my life choices enough already. There he is, leaning back in his damned reclining chair, puffing on a preposterous cigar, with that infuriating pubescent excuse for a moustache clinging to his smirking face.

"Well, well, well. Look who *not* dead," crows Chang.

"Save it, kid, we can do this some other time. I'm in a tight spot and I need your help."

"The famous Luke Remini needing help from Chang? Let me think. I running business. You previous customer.

You *not* paying as agreed. You *bad* previous customer. Hmm... I gonna saying: no."

"Let's be fair, kiddo, I paid *most* of the money, then you tried to have me killed!"

"Don't act surprise. Beheading was very clear in service contract."

"I never signed a contract!"

"You didn't? Huh. Gimme you email address, I get my secretary send you one."

"Chang, I've been to your office. I *know* you don't have a secretary."

"Half right. You been to *my* office. You *not* been to Chang secretary's office. Aren't you supposed to be award winning journalist?"

"Quit the horseplay, Chang, I seriously need your help! I'll pay any price you name, so long as it's not licking your toes or something weird."

"Interesting. You phoning me, revealing you still alive, so mission must be important enough you willing to risk death for it. But *not* so important you would sucking Chang toe for it? Curious. What is mission?"

"Ugh. Chang, don't make me say it, please."

"Chang cannot helping if Chang not know mission."

"*Fine.* I'm trying to disable a conglomerate-cartel server hub that's running a network of powerful satellite jammers across the Mazonillian rainforest and masking the greatest acts of deforestation in human history, which is being sponsored wittingly by the world's second largest tech company, and *unwittingly* by millions of its zombie-ethic customers."

"That was good blurb, Lukey."

"Thank you!"

"Mission sounds serious."

"It *is*! The fate of the last rainforests rests on us taking this network down. If we don't do this, they could be lost forever before anyone finds out. It's already disrupting the global water cycle, and carbon cycle. Species are going extinct by the hour and indigenous populations are being purged!"

"Yes. Very bad. But to be clear... you *won't* sucking Chang's toe to save it all?"

"What? Why are you so obsessed with the toe thing! It was a throwaway example!"

"But now is a test. You asking me take great risk with poor credit history customer. I must knowing you serious about mission."

"Chang. Even the thought of your feet makes me queasy, let alone the idea of putting one of those mustachioed little cheesers in my mouth. Oh Christ I'm gonna barf!"

"Pity. I guess world will lose rainforest because you selfish."

"What? That is *such* hypocrisy! Now that you know the situation, if you *don't* help, you're being *more* selfish!"

"Chang don't care if customer call him selfish. But customer care if Chang call *customer* selfish."

"Chang, quit the riddles and be straight with me. If I get you 'shit ton money' as you put it last time, will you help me?"

"No. Chang require toe sucking."

"Let history reflect that *you're* being the asshole here."

"Choice is yours, Lukey."

"Dammit Chang, I do *not* wanna suck your toe!"

"Shame. Guess you won't be journalist of the year again, then," he shrugs.

"Son of a bitch you take that back."

"Suck my toe."

"You suck *my* toe!"

"What the hell's going on in here?" yells Oriana, bursting into the room.

Chang and I stare at her in mutual embarrassment. Wafting through the corridors beyond us is a chorus of *Happy Birthday Mr. K.*

"Who the hell is this guy? He looks about twelve," says Oriana.

"Fourteen!" snaps Chang.

"This is Chang. He's the most talented hacker in the Northern Bloc, but he's refusing to help save the *planet* unless I agree to suck his-"

"OK! Haha thank you Lukey, yes big joke. We all laugh now. Haha. OK no more joke from Lukey in front of nice lady please thank you."

Holy crap. This is amazing. Chang wants to impress Oriana.

"Ugh, Chang, I was just telling Oriana earlier that you could hack this server hub in under five minutes if you put your mind to it."

"But I told Luke here that I once met a guy who did it in four," she adds, cottoning-on.

"Four? Is child's play!" scoffs Chang. "Wait there."

There's an awkward minute while we listen to a number of echoing engagement party speeches reverberating through the corridors. Curious that Mr. K. would have an engagement party on the same day as his birthday. And also choose to duck all the speeches and hook up with a greased-up escort. But like I said, I've yet to find that solid parent-figure in the criminal underworld.

"Ha!" declares Chang, moments later.

"You're in?" I gasp, staring at the open control screens.

"Like I say: child's play."

"We need him to disable the network permanently," I whisper.

"Not bad, *chico*," says Oriana, addressing Chang's hologram. "Reckon you can take this little server down for good?"

He's like putty in her hands. What a chump.

"Luke, I've got a crick in my neck, would you be a *cariño*?" she adds.

"It would be my honor."

I'm in there in a flash, rubbing her tense shoulders and latching onto every *mmm* and *ooo* she utters as my thumbs work their magic. But just as I'm about to deploy my patented, award-winning elbow technique, an alarm sounds. A flashing light pops up across the hacked servers.

"Uh-oh..." groans Chang.

"Uh-oh? No, no 'uh-oh', Chang! What's going on?" I exclaim.

"Is not me! Something else. Alarm trigger in master bedroom."

"Shut it off!"

"I can't, it needing master password!"

"Then hack it! Isn't that what you do?"

"It not cryptographic, it physical pass key. You must finding key! Oh no, full alarm state engaging."

"What does that mean?"

We don't need Chang's reply to find the answer. A full-building siren sounds and the overhead lights turn red. Gas vents from the ceiling ducts. A steel shutter descends across the doorway.

"Get the door!" I cry.

Oriana dives for it, ramming a fire extinguisher under

the falling shutter. The lid creaks then snaps off under the pressure. Now it's just metal crushing metal.

"Chang, shut the gas off!"

"I can't, I locked out of system. You must getting key!"

"We can't get the key if we choke to death!"

"I looking, be patient!"

"Patient? Mother fucker there's *poison* coming in from the *ceiling*!"

"Don't shout! It very triggering for Chang anxiety."

"You're a criminal boss! Like *hell* you have anxiety!"

"It very stressful job. You try doing it alongside high school!"

"Chang!" I rasp.

"OK, third panel to your right! Code is 44907, it holding oxygen masks!"

Oriana's up in a flash, punching in the code. She rips the compartment open and tosses me a mask. We each yank the straps over our heads and gasp with relief as filtered air flows into our lungs.

"Thank god for that," I wheeze.

"Thank *Chang*," mutters Chang.

"Dude, focus. Where's this key?"

"It says contact system administrator. Who is Mr. K.?" replies Chang.

"The master bedroom, quick!" I cry.

Oriana and I stumble out into the gas-filled, red-lit corridor. Kitchen staff and waiters are stumbling out of their rooms choking and sliding to the ground. A figure approaches through the mist, standing upright, with a gun raised. Oriana darts to the side then takes out the guard's legs and pounces on them. She rips off the guy's breathing mask then seizes his gun, knocking him out as he struggles.

"Sorry... terribly sorry!" I mutter, stepping over the foaming kitchen staff.

I'm always conflicted when the secondary staff in a baddy's house bear the brunt of retaliations like this. Are they truly bad people? Or just caught in a bad system?

"Help me!" wheezes a waiter, grabbing my arms as he sinks to the floor.

"Hang on buddy, I'm gonna get you that guard's breathing mask. Hang tight! Wait, is that an 88 tattoo?"

OK, question answered. I shall be submitting a complaint to Mr. K.'s HR department once this is all over. Their vetting procedure *clearly* leaves much to be desired. I kick off the white supremacist waiter and hurry after Oriana. She boots open the master bedroom door and bursts inside, gun drawn.

"Freeze!" she yells.

Ramone's on the floor, bleeding from his shoulder. Mr. K.'s butt naked and clutching a pillow in front his junk, while pointing a gun at Oriana. His naked, oiled-up escort is on the bed, looking terrified. Ah, probably because he's choking from the gas exposure.

I need to get a mask to Ramone ASAP but if I break the standoff, it could get us all killed.

"My men are on their way. There's nowhere for you to go. You might as well kill yourselves now," spits Mr. K.

"You look a *lot* friendlier in that school picture, can I just say?" I point out.

"Drop your gun, carteller. It is over," growls Oriana.

"You will die like the rest of your vermin tribe, girl. Drones, purge protocol, now!" he yells.

The two ornate gold ornaments either side of the bed unfold a set of wings and take to the air. Hovering at chest level, they scan the room and lock targets on me and Oriana. Their laser canons are charging up.

With rings on his fingers and bells on his toes...

"What the hell?" snaps Mr. K.

The drones are rotating on the spot, as the synthesized voice rings out again.

... He shall have Chang, wherever he goes.

"Chang! You did it!" I cheer.

"Ramone needs air!" yells Oriana.

Chang fires a stun charge at Mr. K., freezing the carteller rigid. I drop to my knees and hastily revive the ailing Ranger, cradling his head in my arms like a true friend, while Oriana keeps Mr. K. at gun point.

Drop your guns, naked man, says Chang, speaking through the killer drones.

"You just froze me, *imbécil,* I can't drop anything. But I can tell you that right now you're making the biggest mistake of your life," growls Mr. K.

I could saying same about your cartel.

"What you talking about, Chang?" I probe.

You wanna tell them what your men in the forest are up to right now?

"I have no idea what you're talking about," spits Mr. K.

It rhyme with glapalm glombing the glorthern glonghold.

"You're doing what?" screams Oriana.

Before I can say anything, she's leaped over the bed, disarming Mr. K. and pistol whipping him to the ground. She grabs his hair and drags him to his knees.

"Call them off or I will end you *right* now!" she screams.

"How do you expect me to call them when you've got me at gunpoint?" says Mr. K.

Chang dialing your man now. Stax, yes? It ringing. Here, I put his voice through.

A man answers the phone.

[- Yo, boss! Great timing, we're just about to light these jungle bloods up! You want to watch? -]

"Stand down the attack," says Mr. K.

[- Ha! Good one, boss. For real, lemme get you up on video cam. You're going to *love* my new pet, by the way. Look who I got back! It's your favorite 'head of indigenous partnerships,' Pablaaaaa! -]

A holographic screen appears above Chang's floating ornaments, depicting Stax, the cowboy carteller, and some indigenous woman who's being held at gunpoint beside him.

"You son of a bitch!" screams Oriana.

The indigenous prisoner's head snaps up at the sound of Oriana's voice. As does Stax's.

[- You OK there boss? Wait, are you naked? Is there someone with you? -]

"Tell him to release the prisoner and stand down or I will make you die *slowly*," growls Oriana, leaning close into Mr. K.'s ear.

"Listen to me, Stax," grunts Mr. K. "I need you to stand the attack down."

[- Are you fucking kidding me? Boss, I been camped out here for a *month* watching these mud-dwelling *pendejos*! -]

"And now I'm telling you to pack your bags and get the *fuck* back to your township, before I come over there and rip your god damned balls off! You really wanna test me again?" yells Mr. K.

[- You know, boss, I must respectfully decline that order. You're not thinking straight. -]

"Dammit Stax, do as I say or I'm a dead man!"

[- Sounds to me like you're in a bind there, boss. I'd love to help, but if you're a dead man, then that's one less person for me to split this pluridium island with. Sorry, boss, I appreciate all the opportunities you've given me but at this juncture in my career, your death is just good business sense. Also, I'm not sorry. I've wanted to do this for years, *coño.* -]

"Pabla! Stay strong, I will come for you!" yells Oriana.

[- Fight them to the end, sister! -] yells the woman beside Stax.

He punches her in the jaw for her insubordination, prompting Oriana to pistol whip Mr. K. again in retaliation. But Stax is laughing.

[- Oh chiquita, if you think you beating that old bastard is gonna stop me, you're sorely mistaken. You would be doing me a favor. Don't worry, your sister here won't die just yet. She gets to watch me napalm your little 'stronghold' first. And there's nothing you mud dwellers can do about it neither. -]

Actually, that not true. Chang find way to being very helpful.

[- Wait, what the.... Turn them off! I said *off!* Everybody get down! -] cries Stax.

As a hail of bullets rings out, the cowboy's line goes dead.

"Pabla? Pabla!" cries Oriana, aghast. "Chang, what is happening out there?"

I giving Stax some encouragement to surrender. Chang turn all drones against cartel. Is every effective. They all running now.

"Is Pabla safe? Chang, tell me!"

Checking... Wait, I can't seeing. Someone throwing me out of system. Security fighting back. Oh shit... Lukey, I losing control of mansion doors. *Security are venting basement. They coming for you all.*

"I warned you," growls Mr. K.

"We need to get back to the hub room!" I cry. "Chang, we *gotta* shut it down before they reach us!"

You needing physical key, Lukey!

"I'm on it!" yells Oriana.

She grabs Mr. K. by the dog collar around his neck and shoves him from the room, using him as a human shield to force the advancing cartel security back. Chang flies overhead and attacks them with the ornamental kill drones, providing us cover as we sidestep into the hub server room.

"Insert the key," growls Oriana.

"You don't know what you're doing," splutters Mr. K.

"On the contrary, we know *exactly* what we are doing. We are showing the world what your cartel and its partners have done."

"Sequestra will come for you," snarls Mr. K. "They are more powerful than you can imagine."

"Let us see if that is still true this time tomorrow," says Oriana.

According to system, to get full access you need him right hand on scanner, left eye to scanner, and some sort of key.

"This thing?" I ask.

I'm lifting a delicate gold chain off Mr. K.'s sweaty neck. The small pendant fits perfectly in the security scanner, while Oriana manhandles Mr. K.'s other assets into the various scanners.

We in! cheers Chang. *Releasing virus... now!*

Oriana and I step back and watch in awe as the racks of blinking servers fall dead one after another. A wall schematic of the cartel's entire Mazonilian jammer network is going dark like a spider's web being swept away.

"Chang, are you getting a clear satellite feed now?" I ask.

Holy crap! Where the forest go?

"I need you to call my editor right away, Chang. She recently shipped you a biological clone of my severed head so I'm sure you got her details. Tell her I say hi, you two will get along great. Get this data to her urgently!"

Roger that, Lukey. But before I calling her, we should discussing my fee.

I'm about to tell that cigar-chomping brat to get his priorities in order, when an excruciating pain grips my entire middle. It's like my entire gut is contracting, folding me over like a clamshell.

"You OK, gringo?" says Ramone, catching up late to the party, and looking irritatingly alluring in his air mask.

"My... insides...."

As I try to speak, blood spurts from my mouth, ruining Mr. K.'s carpet. Wait, why do I care about that dude's carpet? He's a carteller! *And* a terrible host – he's not spent *any* time with his guests. Oh crap, the pain is getting worse.

I fall to the ground in a heap.

Lukey, you trying get out of paying?

Someone presses their fingers to my neck.

"His pulse is all over the place. I think he's dying," says Oriana.

Someone scoops me up off the floor. There's something bushy and white brushing against my face. Is that – Mmm, Ramone's chest hairs. OK sugar daddy, I would've preferred Oriana's fiery embrace but I guess I can die in your arms instead.

I scanning him with drone. Oh boy, Lukey, your organs not good. You dying.

"Then do something, Chang!" yells Oriana.

Hey, I hacker, not doctor.

"Then hack a medical drone!"

Lukey, you cannot dying before you pay Chang back. Is very important for business that customer staying alive to make payment.

The three of them are arguing, trying to locate a medical kit within the city, but I know it's no use. You don't come to Mazonil knowing you need a whole new set of vital organs and expect to make it out alive. I take one final glimpse at Ramone's bristling chest hairs and contoured pecs and sigh, wishing I had spent more time in the gym. Goodbye, cruel world. In the immortal words of my ex-wife's divorce lawyer, I took more than I gave.

CHAPTER THIRTY-ONE

PABLA

tax steps away to take a phone call, leaving me to wallow on the shore while I watch the stronghold island burn beneath a cloak of green light. Stax's tone is obsequious – suggesting he's speaking to his boss, Mr. K., the bastardo who had me put in a cage.

Beside us Axl is overseeing the cartel's technicians. They are preparing the fleet of pyro drones to fire bomb the entire island, killing the last of the refugee population and the cartel's tribal allies. Not to mention all the forest creatures and plants that will perish with them.

They are planning two sets of strikes; the first will dump mounds of fire suppressant above the pluridium chambers. The second is the total opposite; a fire raid to torch the remaining patches of forest and people out of existence.

Stax grabs a fistful of my hair and drags me into the camera frame. My jaw drops as I see my *sister* beside Mr. K. Has she capitulated after everything we have been through? Wait, Stax and Mr. K. are arguing. The boss wants him to stand the attack down – holy crap, Oriana is saving us!

"Boss, something's wrong! We've lost control of the fleet!" cries Axl.

The drones are taking off from their hangars, while the cartel's chief technician is tapping desperately against the control interface, which is not responding.

"What the hell's going on? Fix it!" yells Stax.

"I can't, boss, someone's locked us out and they're modifying the registry," stammers Axl.

"Speak plainly, man!"

"They're... oh god... They're overwriting the safe list. No, they're *inverting* it!"

The nearby drones power up their forward lasers.

"The safe list?" says Stax, his face suddenly falling. "You mean-"

"The drones no longer recognize us as allies!" wails the techie. "The hacker is switching the profiles. Now the machines think we're the-"

The techie falls silent as a laser beam cuts through his torso, splitting him in half. Stax yells in alarm, rallying his men to shoot down the drones. But he is too late, the machines are already cutting them down in their tracks.

"Hold them off!" cries Stax.

He thrusts Axl forwards into the line of fire and sprints towards the ladder on the side of the cliff.

"Get here, jungle blood!" yells Axl.

Axl grabs my neck and pulls me tight to his body, wielding me like a shield as he tries to keep the drones in front of us. With a gasp, his grip falters. As I prize his fingers off my body, his head falls clean off his neck.

A scream rings out from the side of the cliff. Stax is on the ladder, trying to shoot back at the drones while climbing urgently. He wails in agony as they slice off his firing hand, leaving him scrambling upwards, clutching the bloodied stump to his chest. But as he reaches the top, a familiar, four-legged armored bot peers over the edge. The carteller's agonized screams fade into a putrid gargle as the lander squirts acid onto his wretched body. His slimy remains streak down the ladder and splat into the pit below.

Throughout this I stay rooted to the spot, not daring to move lest a drone decide I am cartel. In under a minute, all twenty of Stax' remaining men are dead. A handful have made it into boats and are motoring across the river, only to fall victim to the tribal water mines.

Oh god, I have to warn the elders what is happening! If they think this is an attack on them, they will ignite the pluridium and destroy the whole island. I have only seconds to act. With the last of my strength, I throw myself at Stax's liquid remains and grab his fallen gun. Changing the stun charge to 'signal', I power the gun up to maximum, then fire a glowing tracer blast clear over the island. I try to fire another but my body is so depleted I cannot squeeze the trigger any more. This is it. They have one chance to see the signal, or all is lost.

Six Days Later

"Pabla, can you hear me?"

The voice is distant, muffled. I try to sit up but my body feels like lead.

"Take it easy. Here, drink this."

A cup finds my lips and water trickles into my mouth. My foggy brain clears as the cool liquid awakens my senses.

"They tell me you have been out for several days. Most people have, actually."

The stranger's fingers press against my temples and remove the wet headband that is wrapped around my eyes and ears.

"We had to cool your body to give it a chance to detoxify while the algae regrow. The sudden return of full daylight seems to have overwhelmed people's bodies."

As the headband peels away, the stranger tenderly dabs my eyes dry. As I blink them open, my heart skips a beat.

"*Oriana!*" I gasp.

Without hesitation I throw my arms around my sister, briefly forgetting the deathly feud between us. She hugs me back, until I break off the embrace to touch her face and arms, checking she is really there. We giggle with joy, like two childhood best friends reuniting.

"What is this place?" I ask, taking in the rows of beds beside me.

"It is a field hospital," replies Oriana. "You are back on the island."

"But the stronghold was burned – there were no buildings standing when I left. How is this place here now?"

"If you feel strong enough to walk, let me show you," smiles Oriana.

I take my big sister's hand and follow her past the hundreds of other patients being monitored by their loved ones, foreign-looking medics, and hovering medical drones. We step out of the huge field tent into the remains of the island.

My hopes falter as I take in the scale of destruction; the charred land, the smoldering stacks. But somehow, because of us, some forest remains.

"Who are these people?" I ask, looking around.

"Volunteers from our neighboring countries."

"But how did they get here? No one considers Mazonil safe enough for outsiders."

"The international council sent peace keeping troops. They are banishing the cartels from all forest lands and dispatching volunteers to help us replant everything they destroyed."

"Pabla!" comes a cry.

Two sets of arms throw themselves around me, cheering with joy. Through their excited proclamations I realize it is Latika and Ohalo.

"You survived!" I chime.

"Thanks to you!" says Latika.

"No, thanks to my big sister," I correct him. "This is Oriana. *She* is the one who saved us. She took down Mr. K."

"I had help from some good people," she shrugs.

"Are they here too?" I ask.

"No, we parted ways. They have other work to do. But my place was always back with the forest, and with my people. *You* people."

"Room for one more?" comes a shy voice.

"Pietro!"

I throw my arms around him. There is something about being reunited with a life that you saved. It really cuts through the fact we have only properly met once before.

"You are alive," I say, delightedly.

"Thanks to you and the Namakaro tribe's finest," he grins.

Latika and Ohalo take grand bows and strike exaggerated warrior poses, making us all laugh.

"So what now? Do we form, like, one big super tribe?" asks Ohalo.

"How many of the elders survived?" I ask.

"A few. None from our tribe," says Oriana.

"Does that make *us* the new elders?"

"You are in a power vacuum. *Anyone* can claim to be a leader," says Pietro.

"Huh. Now I understand how someone as useless as Tanok came to be in charge."

"Hey, he wasn't all bad. He just wanted the best for our tribe," says Oriana.

There is an awkward silence, as the cracks in our relationship resurface. I guess there's still work to be done there after all.

"So... speaking of power vacuums, I overheard some of the NGO seniors talking," says Pietro. "They're looking for people to lead a mission to find the remaining tribes in Mazonil's eastern regions. I volunteered, though I don't think they'll want me. I'm not much use in the field. But I think you four might be perfect for it."

"What are they proposing?"

"Aid."

"The tribes will refuse it. They do not want to be treated as dependents. The whole point of tribal living is that we are self-sufficient, and can live sustainably off our own land," says Oriana.

"Not that kind of aid. I am talking logistical and legal aid. They want to start with a census, then a history, and use those as the starting points to help re-establish tribal territories that will come under international protection. The only other aid on offer is in reforesting. And... er... one other thing... They want to offer the black forest algae to all the tribes."

"Of course. The algae was always intended to benefit all forest people. But only two out of three vials survived. How will there be enough?" says Oriana.

"Perhaps with this offer of aid, our new allies could help

us to synthesize more of it?" I suggest, tentatively. "We would oversee the distribution, of course, and make sure each tribe's wishes are respected. But we can't do it without an Inkmaster," I add.

Oriana glares at me, nostrils flared, as she processes this blasphemous suggestion of a technological intervention.

"As Inkmaster, I only have one condition," she says, sternly.

"Yes?"

"That my little sister comes with me," she chokes. "I am never letting you go again."

"Ditto that," I grin. "OK team. Let's do it."

CHAPTER THIRTY-TWO

LUKE

The ocean breeze is dancing across my skin while the sun sets, filling the sky with a multitude of blues and pinks, stirring my senses with the sort of boundless optimism you usually only get after a truly cathartic dump. Somehow, my heart is still beating. Oh no wait, I know *exactly* how. I've got a ton of wires sticking out of me, a bunch of temporary organs plugged into my body, and a stolen cartel medical drone following me wherever I go. Fortunately, it's administering a pitch-perfect dose of pain relief meds right into my brain, so I feel like a mother fucking *cloud* right now.

"Ew, Luke, why would you send me this!" cries my editor, down the phone.

"I told you, Lanelle, I didn't have time to edit the camera feed."

"You should *always* edit retina footage, Luke, otherwise people end up getting first-person camera work of your wrinkly junk in the shower. *Gross!*"

"Skip forward."

"I *am* skipping forward. You take *really* long showers!"

"In my defense, I was about to enter a failed state. Who knew how long it was gonna be before my next hot shower?"

"Oh god, is that a hooker?"

"OK maybe I should've edited the pre-trip footage. Skip to the bit with the donkey."

"You got a *donkey* involved?"

"Not with the hooker, Jesus! I mean on the bridge – when I was being smuggled."

"OK, I've skipped way ahead. I'm looking at the jungle. You're running and... did you just jump into that river? Luke, you know Mazonil has some of the highest waterfalls in the world?"

"I know that *now*, yeah. Look, just skip through using the blink marker. I bookmarked all the key Sequestra footage as it happened."

"Woah, that's a Sequestra logo... On..."

"On one of the satellite blocking masts. I know, crazy, right?"

"This is the smoking gun! Wait, they put their logo on the *trains*?"

"I think they thought no one would ever trace the two together. The trains were part of their PR campaign about inward investment into the 'developing' country. Aka the failed state that *they* helped topple just so they could properly steal its resources. Have you got to the pluridium mines yet?"

"I'm watching it now. God, cartel just loves to burn trees – it's like the forest has no value to them at all."

"That is *exactly* the problem. Don't worry, boss, it's all in my write up."

"I know that, Remini, I edited it. It goes live in an hour from now, by the way. We'll drop the first video with it, then release the rest across tomorrow. I can't wait to see the Sequestra board try to squirm their way out of this one. They can evade all the taxes in the world, but *this* is one bullet they can't dodge."

"Mmm, trying out the slugline? I'm not sure. Try 'Sequestra: Plundering In Your Name'."

"Too much, we don't want to alienate the readers."

"Those fuckers *deserve* to be alienated! This whole thing's their fault! If they bothered to ask even the slightest questions about *where* Sequestra was getting all its materials from, maybe the forest wouldn't be the way it is!"

"That's a harsh reductionist view of your readership, Luke. People have a lot going on in their lives. It's our job to make this kind of stuff accessible so they can make informed choices and vote well."

"Who is the floating woman?" says Ramone, emerging from below deck.

"Ah, Ramone, meet Lanelle, the editor of my people-pleasing paper."

"Oh grow up, Luke. I'm running the story, aren't I?" she snaps. "Who is your friend?"

"I am not his friend," grumbles Ramone.

"No-one's buying that anymore dude. We're *definitely* friends now."

"Is that true?" asks Lanelle. "If so, I am genuinely happy. Luke won't admit this but he actually struggles to make friends. He presents as very confident but really he's trying to fill the emotional cavern left by two divorces and a nomadic career."

"Woah, boss, mind easing up on the over sharing?" I

protest. "Although now you mention it, Ramone and I do have a *lot* in common there. He's a forest ranger, by the way. Self-appointed. Though right now he's our prison warden. How is our guest down below?"

"Still sleeping," grunts Ramone.

"Please tell me you're using the term 'prisoner' metaphorically," groans Lanelle.

"Don't worry about it, boss. It's all in hand."

"Last time you said that you were illegally entering a prohibited country. So I *do* worry, Luke. Tell me *exactly* what you're up to."

"We're sailing Mr. K. to the International Criminal Court to stand trial."

"Mr. K.? As in-"

"The cartel boss sponsored by Sequestra, yes."

"Why the hell is he in *your* custody? Neither of you are cops!"

"It's not like there was a police force we could call back in Mazonil. And if we'd hung around, the cartel might have rescued him before the international peace keepers arrived. It's best for everyone that he sails to justice off-grid."

"Since when do you 'sail' anywhere, Remini?" says Lanelle, her eyes narrowing.

"Er, since I took down a crime boss who owns a superyacht."

"I trust you're planning on delivering this yacht to the prosecution too, as one of the accused's assets?"

"Don't get weighed down in the specifics, boss."

"Luke?"

"Gotta go, boss, got another call coming in!"

I cut her off mid-protestation. In fairness, I wasn't lying – I *do* have another call coming in. I'm just not planning on answering it.

"I know his face," says Ramone, pointing to the next caller's floating hologram.

"Yup. And you'll understand why it's best we check in with him later," I say, tapping the 'reject' button.

Luke? I know you there Lukey, I seeing you.

Dammit. I forgot he could do that.

"Oh, hey Chang! Great to see you. We were just talking about you!"

Who that?

"This? Oh, this is Ramone. You helped save his life, actually."

Hello Ramone. I Chang. You owe me colossal money.

"Chang, Ramone is from the forest. He doesn't deal in currency. Besides, he never made a deal with you, so don't try pulling that move now."

You make deal though, yes Lukey? You owing Chang colossal money. Again.

"And this time, there's no need to send assassins after me. I've got your payment right here."

I not seeing it. Move camera. What you show me?

"Welcome to your new floating palace! This superyacht is *yours* to enjoy. Or sell. Whatever you want. I'm gonna give you the coordinates when we get into harbor, and you send someone to pick it up for you, OK?"

What make you think I have someone in International Quarter who can simply collecting yacht for Chang at drop of hat?

"Er, because I know for a fact that you maintain a web of debtors who you can pressure into anything?"

Oh yeah. Good point. But is not enough.

"Hey, we agreed I paid the rest forward, all right? I brought you into the mission, and gave you the inside scoop. You're one of a handful of people who know Sequestra's stocks are about to take a nose dive. Did you bet against them like I said?"

Big time. You?

"If I had any money to my name, I would. But I did this job on spec. The paper's gonna sort me out but their finance team seems to work about one day a year. Plus there's some stuff with a donkey that I need to clarify. So are we all clear, Chang? You get the yacht, plus the stock market profits. We're even, yeah?"

Only if shares clear. If it not working, I coming for you, Lukey. You can't using Chang like charity service. Chang is businessman. He taking debt seriously.

"Shouldn't you be finishing your homework about now?"

Chang's eyes narrow and he clicks off the call.

"Looks like it's just you and me buddy," I say, patting Ramone on the back.

"You saved my country. I was wrong about you, gringo. Thank you."

He places out a hand for me to shake. I slap it away and grab the man in a huge squishy bear hug.

"What will you do once we deliver the prisoner?" continues Ramone, stoically pretending the physical contact isn't happening.

"You mean what's my next challenge? Great question. I think it might be my biggest yet. I'm gonna try to save my marriage."

Ramone looks at me blankly.

"OK buddy, quick tip, where *I'm* from, that usually gets some kinda 'knowing laugh'."

"I see. What is it we 'know'?"

"Oh boy. This is gonna be a long voyage."

Get the bonus chapter
See how Luke's ex-wife reacted to cupid's return.
Exclusive for mail list subscribers.
marcusmartinauthor.com/ps

It's Marcus here. Thanks so much for reading this copy of *People of Forest*, I truly hope it resonated with you. I'm an independent author, which means I publish all my work myself, and bear all the associated costs. The traditional publishing industry is incredibly tough for new authors to break into. After my first series *Convulsive* was rejected by fifty different agents, I realized that to achieve my dream of becoming a writer, I would have to strike out by myself. So I did.

It's terrifying, but I know I can do it; I have wonderful readers like you, who send me encouraging emails out of the blue which always brighten my day. It's my sincere hope that you may be kind enough to sponsor my next book by donating at marcusmartinauthor.com/support. On the next page you'll find out why, and what a massive impact your support will have.

It took five years to write and self-publish the *Convulsive* series alongside stressful day jobs, often working seven days a week. But within six months of completion, the series hit number one in the international Amazon bestseller charts for its genre. That was the single greatest moment of affirmation I could've wished for. I quite literally danced around the room with joy. It didn't come with a windfall of cash like you might think - book margins aren't big - but it was enough for me to finish recouping the editing costs and fund an audiobook version. In fact, since starting out, I've reinvested every cent I've ever earned from my books straight back into my writing - because I know it's the only way I'll grow.

It's still early days for me as a writer, which makes each new book a white knuckle ride. In 2020 I took a leap of faith and left my job to become a full-time author, knowing I would be living off savings and reinvesting any profits to make it work. In that year I gave it my all, and wrote four new books, one of which you've just finished.

I want to continue. My aim is to write four books a year, and keep bringing bold sci-fi ideas to readers like you. I know I can do it, but I'll be honest: there's still no guarantee it'll work out. Mainly because I don't get advances on book deals like conventional authors do.

I love creating new worlds, and I'm a damned hard worker. If you believe my writing deserves a future, and would like to see more books from me each year, I would be so hugely grateful if you would support me with a donation of your choosing. It only takes a moment, just visit **marcusmartinauthor.com/support**

With the support of readers like you, I can produce more groundbreaking sci-fi. I would be humbled to offer you an acknowledgement in one of my future books, and you will have my heartfelt thanks forever.

In gratitude - Marcus.

Cambridge, England, 2021

Finality

Eerie. Familiar. Radical.

A heartbreaking and poignant metaphysical sci-fi novel. Standalone.

Available now in ebook, paperback, hardcover, and audiobook.

Don't miss Marcus Martin's next book.

Join the email list:

marcusmartinauthor.com/email

subscribers also get free advanced copies

and exclusive content.

ACKNOWLEDGMENTS

My sincere thanks to these wonderful people for helping me get *People of Forest* over the line: Chris Hutchings, Marie Thorpe, Rick Hannegan, Martin White, Sue Jackson, and Gopel Kotecha. Thank you for your support, encouragement, and advice along the way.

Mum and Dad, thank you for instilling in me such a love of trees. Tania and Lottie, thank you for opening my eyes to a kinder way of living on our fragile and remarkable planet.

To the legends at Thrive Cambridge, Karina, James, Brad, Gemma, and the whole team, thank you for making that journey accessible to everyone through love and determination. Likewise to Emma, Johanna, Paul, and Jay at Full Circle Cambridge, I know you all work tirelessly to make our planet a better and kinder place. You are succeeding, and I am so grateful for everything you do.

Finally, to the tens of thousands of people worldwide working behind the scenes in government departments, NGOs, charities, and start-ups, striving to make our global community greener and fairer, thank you. You give me courage in our future.

*To all the brave souls committed to reversing climate change.
To those on the front line through no fault of their own. To
those taking a stand, to demand the change we need.
Together, we can do this.*

Marcus Martin is a British author based in Cambridge, UK. He originally trained as a composer and classical pianist at King's College London & the Royal Academy of Music, before taking a meandering route into a Master's degree in the psychology of music at the University of Cambridge, followed by a postgraduate diploma in religion and politics.

Marcus has performed at the Edinburgh Fringe Festival a number of times as both a stand-up comedian and actor. After living and working in the US and Germany for six months he returned to Cambridge where he wrote and staged his first three plays, before embarking on a career in authorship.

He's worked as a barista, a decorator, a builder's assistant, a teaching assistant, a data entry clerk, a marketing executive, a compliance officer, a pianist, a choral assistant, a musical director, a script editor for BBC Radio 4, a voice actor, and a jingle writer, to name but a few.

Alongside books and voice acting, he's host of the cult sci-fi podcast *Make It Soon*, which brings scientists and comedians together to discuss iconic sci-fi inventions that are becoming a reality. Listen for free at makeitsoon.com

Marcus is currently working on a new book series, as well as several standalone novels. He loves receiving emails from readers, and replies to each one. You can reach him at: marcus@marcusmartinauthor.com

For a sneak peak of Marcus's upcoming releases, join the email list at: marcusmartinauthor.com/email

You can also follow him on social:
facebook.com/MarcusMartinAuthor
goodreads.com/author/show/17601586
bookbub.com/authors/marcus-martin